I WAS NOT THRILLED (AT ALL) THAT I'D BLOWN THIS DATE THE WAY I HAD.

But one could not say I wasn't thrilled I'd blown this date and now had a real excuse to get out of it.

Mag's eyes narrowed and he stopped bending over me, holding the ice to my head, and bent *into* me, pulling the ice away and staring into my eyes.

He held three fingers up to my face. "How many fingers do you see?"

"Three, Mag, stop it. I'm okay. I just…"

"What, Evan?"

God, really, was he actually that handsome?

And right there, hovering over me, looking concerned, which made him even *more* handsome?

"Evan?" he called.

"Your eyelashes are very curly," I whispered.

That was when he did it.

His gaze changed, it was an amazing change I felt in amazing places, it shifted to my mouth, and I felt that too, it was also amazing, and last, he murmured, "Baby."

"I'm not your baby," I breathed.

His gaze shifted back to my eyes, and he rumbled, all sexy, hot and sweet, "Oh yeah, you are."

Praise for Kristen Ashley

Dream *Maker*

KRISTEN ASHLEY

A Dream Team Novel

FOREVER
NEW YORK   BOSTON

Copyright © 2020 by Kristen Ashley
Excerpt from *Dream Chaser* copyright © 2020 by Kristen Ashley

Cover design by Cormar Covers. Cover copyright © 2020 by Hachette Book Group, Inc.

Forever
Hachette Book Group
1290 Avenue of the Americas, New York, NY 10104
read-forever.com
twitter.com/readforeverpub

First mass market edition: May 2020

Forever is an imprint of Grand Central Publishing. The Forever name and logo are trademarks of Hachette Book Group, Inc.

The publisher is not responsible for websites (or their content) that are not owned by the publisher.

The Hachette Speakers Bureau provides a wide range of authors for speaking events. To find out more, go to www.hachettespeakersbureau.com or call (866) 376-6591.

ISBN: 978-1-5387-3386-8 (mass market), 978-1-5387-3387-5 (ebook)

Printed in the United States of America

OPM

10 9 8 7 6 5 4 3 2 1

CHAPTER ONE

I Can't Even

EVIE

I...can't...*even*," I snapped at my windshield as I slammed on the brakes when the car started to pull out in front of me, and I knew it wouldn't stop because they couldn't care less I was only three car lengths away and going five miles (okay, maybe ten) over the speed limit.

"Stupid millennial!" I shouted when I noted the age of the clueless person driving.

Of course, I was a millennial.

Which meant, obviously, I could call my own people stupid and clueless.

Some Gen Xer said something like that, it'd tick me off.

But right then, I had visions in my head of ramming him from behind just to make a point à la Evelyn Couch in *Fried Green Tomatoes.*

Sadly, Evelyn's insurance was great, but mine wouldn't take another bust-up, of which I'd had many (and this might have a *wee* bit to do with me going five, more like ten miles over the speed limit on more than the regular occasion—then again, I was always in a hurry and it was no lie that wasn't hardly ever my fault).

Another reason my insurance agent was going to blackball me to all insurance companies happened right then.

My phone rang.

And I looked to it instantly.

What could I say?

I'm a millennial.

The call was from my mother.

Normally, it was a very good possibility, to the point of it being a probability, I would avoid my mother's call.

Today, I could not.

So I snatched up my phone and engaged, hopeful to the last (in other words, delusional) that maybe for once, I might have backup in the current situation I was going to have to handle. A situation, like all of them, that was not mine.

"Hey, Mom," I greeted eagerly.

"Evan, darlin', please tell me you're going to see your brother."

Oh, I was going to see my brother all right.

In lockup.

Again.

I was Norm from *Cheers* at Denver County Jail.

"Of course I'm going to see him," I replied.

"Okay," she said, sounding relieved.

I understood her relief.

And my heart sunk.

Because it was not about the proud mother of a good little sister looking after her big brother.

It was a good little daughter doing what a mother should

be doing and thus the mother didn't have to do it, which was good, since she wouldn't do it anyway.

Again.

"Tell him his momma sends her love and if he needs anything..." She trailed off.

Call your sister, Evan, I finished for her in my head.

"Mom, I gotta say, this is the last time—"

"Okay, honey, good chat. I gotta go. I gotta get to work."

She did not.

She was unemployed.

Again.

"Talk to you later," she went on. "Come over for dinner. Your stepdad and I miss you."

With that, she hung up, not setting a dinner date, not staying on the line long enough for me to share with her I was D...O...N...E *done* with sorting Mick's crap and not ending the conversation saying such as, "I love you, you can't know how much. You're so responsible, I've no idea how you got that way, but we're so lucky you did because I don't know what we'd all do without you."

No, she did not say that.

I tossed my phone to the seat, drove to the jail, and as I was pulling in the parking lot, I heard it buzz with a text.

I glanced at it, looked back out the windshield, and muttered, "Oh boy."

I found a parking spot, shut down my car and snatched up my phone again.

I went to texts.

I read the latest and then, because I was clearly in the mood for self-flagellation, I scrolled up and read it from the top.

The tippy-top stating the text string was with DANIEL MAGNUSSON.

Hey, this Evan?

   Yes, is this Daniel?

Mag. And yeah.

Mag.
   Who called themselves *Mag*?

   Hi.

Hey, we doing this?

"This" being going on a blind date because our mutual friend Lottie (who'd set us up, like she'd set up all my girl-friends at the club where we worked with friends of her fiancé, Mo) would not let it go even though I got the impression both of us consistently, and for some time, tried to put her off.

For my part, I knew I did just that.

And his "we doing this?" solidified the impression he did too.

   Sure.

You climb?

   Climb?

Indoor climbing. Rock walls.

Rock walls?
   Was he insane?
   No.
   I did not climb.

I owned eight pairs of Chucks in eight different colors.

But I did not own a single item that might be construed as anything that had anything to do with physical activity.

This was partly because I stripped for a living, which was physical enough.

This was also partly because, when I wasn't stripping, I was so busy doing everything else, I didn't need to work out.

How about we go for ice cream?

That got me about two full minutes of continual dot, dot, dots, which did not turn out to be a textual opus.

It turned out to be three words.

Right. Sounds good.

Such a lie.

I knew he thought it didn't sound good.

He probably had protein shakes for breakfast and lunch and an unseasoned chicken breast for dinner.

What could I say?

He was Mo, Lottie's fiancé's former roommate, and Mo was a commando.

And so was *Mag*.

That was what I'd guess commandos ate.

That and rations.

You open Tuesday?

Yeah.

How about 6:00?
Liks. In Capitol Hill.

I know it.

See you there.

    Great. Yes.
    See you there.

This had all happened last Thursday.

    It was now Tuesday and my hope was that his latest text would be about canceling.

    It wasn't.

    It was,

Hey, we still on for tonight?
Because Mac won a gift card to a restaurant.
It expires tomorrow and if someone doesn't use it,
it'll be wasted.
She's offered it to us.

Mac, by the by, was what some people called Lottie, seeing as her last name, for the time being, was McAlister.

    And considering she wasn't close with her dad, she was totally going old school and taking Mo's name when they got married.

    "Yes," I said out loud to my phone. "We're still on, after I go in, see my brother, listen to him beg me to post bail while I try to find the courage to tell him this will be *the* last time *ever* I post bail for him or get his ass out of whatever jam he's gotten himself into. Then I'll fail to find that courage. I'll then go to my second most often visited hotspot in Denver. Saul Edelstein, bail bondsman. But I actually do not want to have dinner with you, alpha male, probably toxic male. Though Mo isn't toxic, he's very sweet, but Lottie warned me you had 'issues' and needed someone to settle you down, and apparently, she thinks I'm that person."

I stopped talking to *Mag*, who Lottie told me was actually called Danny, who wasn't there.

And I stared at the phone thinking that the issues Lottie didn't share with me, but the girls at the club did, were that some woman had broken Daniel Magnusson's heart, and like a definitely toxic dude, his strategy for curing it was sleeping with everything that moved.

However, to be honest, although this appeared to be one more project I didn't need, even if Lottie hadn't been entirely forthcoming, my sense was that mostly Lottie seemed like she wanted to fix us up because she liked us both a lot, thought we'd be good together, look out for each other, and in the end, be happy.

I could not imagine what she was thinking.

A commando was *so* not my style.

A manwhore?

Totally not.

My last boyfriend was shorter than me by two inches, weighed twenty-five pounds less than me and his skin had not seen the sun for probably five years and not because he was a vampire.

Because he was a gamer.

I liked him.

We shared a lot of the same interests. He was funny, he could be gentle, he listened, he wasn't all that great in bed, but he gave it his best shot, and he felt safe.

Of course, his eventual utter lack of interest in anything but gaming led to the demise of our relationship.

So now, I missed him.

Or the him I'd had before I lost him to gaming.

My thumbs flew over the bottom of my phone screen.

Sounds good.
When and where?

I was folding out of my car when I got back,

I'll pick you up.
At six.

Pick me up?
　　For a date?
　　What was this?
　　1987?

　　　　I'll meet you there. Where is it?
　　　　And 6:00 is good.

I was nearing the door when I received,

Picking you up, Evan.
Six.
I don't think it's fancy.
But I don't think it's T and jeans either.

Then,

Mac gave me your address.
See you at 6:00.

Of course she did and of course he was old school too.
　　No one got picked up for dates anymore.
　　And now I was stuck for a whole dinner.
　　It was easier to feign a headache or, better yet, period cramps and duck out if I had my own ride.
　　"Damn," I whispered, standing outside the doors to the jail.

I texted,

> **See you then.**
> **Looking forward to it.**

I got back an unconvincing,

> **Yeah.**
> **Me too.**

Now I had to spend at least a couple of hours with this guy rather than snarfing down a quick cone while we mutually agreed we didn't suit, shaking hands, then I'd go home and give myself a facial or watch some Japanese anime or repeat a binge watch of *Fleabag* or something.

Ugh.

I entered the jail, did the rigmarole check-in, and while doing it, caught up with Officer Bobbie behind the desk (bad news for Bobbie: her kid had the flu so bad, they had to hospitalize him, good news: he was okay now, and mental note: stop by the jail and give Officer Bobbie something fun to give to her recently very sick kid).

Then, I was sat in front of a video screen and I waited for Mick to appear before I grabbed the handset.

But when he appeared, I didn't grab the handset.

My heart started beating in a strange way I'd never felt before.

It was like there was nothing in my chest cavity, it was hollow, save my heart, and my heart was thumping in there, all alone.

I snatched the handset so fast, my hand was a blur.

And I nearly came out of my skin listening to the warnings about how the police were recording our visit.

When it was done, his name jumped out of my throat.

"Mick?"

"Hey, Evie," he said, his voice wrong, wrong, *wrong*.

Tentative.

Trembling.

Scared.

My cocky, criminal, wastrel, good-time, bad-decisions big brother didn't get scared.

I leaned forward. "Mick—"

"You're gonna get a text, honey. Take it, and ... you know. Just take it and do right by your brother."

Oh God.

"What?" I asked.

He leaned toward his screen too.

"You ... are gonna ... get a *text*, Evie. *Take it.* And ... do *right*."

What did that mean?

Before I could find some words to ask him to share in ways that wouldn't get him into trouble, or later be used to incriminate him, he kept talking.

"I'm counting on you."

"Mick."

And then he did not ask me to go to Saul.

He did not say the reasons for his current accommodations were all a mistake.

Or he'd been in the wrong place at the wrong time.

Or they'd brought him in on nonsense to lean on him to rat on someone else.

Or one of the hundred other excuses he used.

He did something that sent ice splinters tearing through my veins.

He pressed his middle three fingers to his lips, then pressed them to the screen, hung up his handset, stood and walked away.

CHAPTER TWO
Urban Outfitters

EVIE

W hat am I doing?" I asked my reflection as I leaned away from my bathroom mirror and stared at myself.

I was holding a mascara wand in one hand, the tube in the other, and I'd just finished putting on some powder, a little blush, minimal highlights on my cheekbones, under-eye-shadow base over my lids up to my brows to even the skin tone and now mascara.

I didn't wear makeup unless I was stripping, first, because I had two pounds of makeup on when I danced and that not only felt ick, I figured I was already over my quota, and second, I just didn't wear makeup.

Okay, lip gloss that was actually lip *treatment* disguised as lip gloss, of which I had varying colors, but only because this was Denver, Denver was arid, and if I didn't my lips would be chapped all the time.

So might as well throw a wave at something girlie while I was keeping my skin healthy.

Now, I was going on a date with Lottie's commando friend and suddenly I was a traditionalist.

Or, probably more accurate, I was going on a blind date with Lottie's commando friend after my brother freaked me out about some text I'd be getting where I'd have to "do right," whatever that meant.

And since Mick Gardiner hadn't done right since he was around the age of two, his version of doing right did not bode well for me.

I'd pushed the wand into the tube and was about to grab a wipe and take all the makeup off, add some moisturizer (again: Denver) and maybe some powder so I wasn't all shiny, and that was it, when someone knocked on my door.

I looked down at my phone on the basin, touching it to activate the screen.

6:04.

"Hell," I whispered, tossed the tube in the basket that contained my measly collection of cosmetics, grabbed my lip treatment that was a shade called "buff" and dashed out of the bathroom.

I slicked on the gloss as I shoved my feet in chili-red Rothy's points, grabbed my blazer that was on the bed and rushed out of my bedroom.

I tossed the blazer on the kitchen counter, the lip gloss on the blazer, at the same time I hesitated because I realized I hadn't put on any jewelry and considered running back to my room in order to do that really quick.

This was when another knock sounded at the door (apparently Daniel Magnusson was not patient).

This possibility led my mind to race to the hope that, regardless of his apparent impatience, Mag was like Mo.

Maybe not as humongous as Mo (though, that wouldn't be bad, Mo didn't seem cuddly as such, more like terrifying and able to tear you limb from limb with his bare hands, but he looked sweet and openly happy anytime Lottie cuddled him).

But definitely as soft-spoken and gentle and loving as Mo was with Lottie.

I mean, it would not suck having a man in my life, that man being like Mo.

I could pay my own bills (and sometimes my mother's, and a lot of the times, my father's, this being the reason why it was taking forever to earn my degree—I kept having to sit out semesters because of lack of funds, the sole reason why I stripped, because I didn't make Lottie-style tips, but strippers at Smithie's made a bucketload).

I could take out my own trash.

But it'd be nice to have someone around.

Okay, so maybe it would be nice to have someone around to listen to me bitch about my delinquent brother or my user mother and the many times they inveigled (or out-and-out connived) me into getting involved in their messy lives.

But it also would be fun to cook with someone again.

Or have someone to go see movies with, then dissect them after.

Or go out and enjoy some really good food together, good food that came with good conversation.

Or take a vacation and not think of anything but whatever excursion we'd planned that day.

So, all right.

Maybe I should give this a real shot.

Lottie was good people, a good friend, a good woman.

She wouldn't steer me wrong.

I went to the door, looked out the peephole and froze stiff.

Mo was six five, bald, with unique but handsome features (when you got past the terrifying) and was the aforementioned humongous.

The man outside was not any of that.

He was...

He was...

I watched as he lifted his hand again to knock, I unfroze, unlocked and threw open the door, blurting, "I forgot to put on jewelry."

His chin jerked into his throat, his torso swayed back, and his electric-blue eyes did a slow sweep of me, from hair to Rothy's. Those eyes grew alert, then they grew appreciative, and after that, his mouth curled ever so slowly into a sexy smile.

Ohmigod.

Oh man.

Oh hell.

Damn.

He was...

He was...

All that dark hair, longish, flipping and curling and falling into his eyes.

Tall, maybe not as tall as Mo, but not too far off.

Way taller than me, and I was five nine.

Fit.

Oh God.

So fit.

Not humongous, but lean, broad of shoulder and chest, trim of waist, and bulky of thighs.

Dark gray trousers, light-blue button-up, and he'd done a French tuck.

The *Queer Eye* boys would give him an A++++.

"Evan?" he asked.

"Danny?" I mumbled.

"Mag," he stated.

"Uh . . ." I kept mumbling. "Lottie said—"

"Lottie's bustin' my chops," he told me then softened his next with a grin. "No one calls me Danny but Mo's sisters and that isn't at my request."

"Oh," I whispered.

"You forgot your jewelry?" he prompted.

My hands flew to my earlobes as I said, "Right. Um, come in. I won't be a second."

I stepped back, opening the door wide for him to enter.

He walked in and looked around.

I closed the door.

"Let me guess," he said as he stopped looking around and turned to me. "You drive a Prius."

"Well, yeah," I replied.

He busted out laughing.

My nipples tingled.

Ohmigod.

What was happening?

He was *so* not my thing.

I was a freak.

I was a geek.

And as such, I was into freaks and geeks.

Stick with what you know.

But the sound of his laughter . . .

The look of it on his face . . .

Okay.

I changed my mind.

I was not giving this a shot.

No.

Absolutely not.

My brother was in jail (again).

My mother was unemployed (again).

My stepfather (this one number two) was undoubtedly stepping out on her (again) so she'd dump him (again) only to take him back (again).

My father was a professional pothead disguised as a guitar teacher, and underlying all of this, for decades, he'd been a grower and dealer. But now, since marijuana was legal, he worked part-time at a dispensary, and he'd started that because he thought he'd get an employee discount but stayed because he enjoyed communing with his brethren.

Last, my little sister spent all her time attempting to garner followers on social media as well as get on reality programs, therefore how she paid her bills, I had no idea, but if my mind went there, it grew troubled.

Oh, and I was going to get some text from someone, and my brother needed me to do right by him, which undoubtedly would not be right by me.

I did not have the time, or the inclination (that last was a bit of a lie) to be charmed by, become besotted with and put the effort into taming a brokenhearted manwhore who was so pretty, my heart wept just watching him laugh.

But in the end, that heart would just be broken.

Because he'd break it.

"What's funny?" I asked.

"You might have wanted to leave some of the stock of Urban Outfitters for the other nostalgics," he answered on a grin.

Did he...

Actually...

Say that?

"Some of it's from Anthropologie," I sniffed.

He busted out laughing again.

"And some of it is vintage," I snapped over his hilarity.

Now, he looked like he was fighting bending double with his amusement.

"What do you drive?" I queried.

"F-250," he answered, still chucking.

"Sorry?"

"Ford F-250. A truck. A big one. And no, it's not diesel and it absolutely does not plug into anything."

I felt my lips thin.

He grinned again.

"I see we're gonna discuss global warming over dinner," he noted.

"There's nothing to discuss. The globe is warming. Thus, we *all* should take some responsibility for turning that around. End of topic," I retorted.

He was *still* grinning when he said, "Chill, Evan. I'm teasing you. Your pad is tight. I like it. And cross my heart," and he did just this with a very long, well-shaped forefinger, "I put all my leftovers in those reusable ziplocks Mac bought all the guys, and as often as I can, I refuse a straw."

"The end of the world as we know it isn't funny," I informed him.

"I'm not kidding."

I studied his face in an attempt to ascertain if that was a lie.

He was apparently being honest.

Or he was a good liar.

He smiled at me again and said softly, "Your jewelry."

"Right," I muttered, turned and walked back to my bedroom.

My mind ran amok (mostly with thoughts about how soft his hair might be, then trying to stop thoughts of how soft his hair might be) as I put my little gold ball studs in my ears and one midi-ring on my left forefinger that had a line of tiny emeralds across the front.

This completed my outfit of army-green crop pants, gray scoop-necked, relax-fit tee (which I'd also given the French tuck), and the sand-colored blazer I was going to don when I got back to the kitchen.

I walked out and I did so carefully because Mag was still standing in my living room, he was watching me, and I was known to be a klutz and I did not want to date this guy, but I also did not want to make a fool of myself in front of him.

I went to the kitchen to shove my phone and lip gloss in my little bag and put on my blazer.

As my kitchen had a huge opening to the living room over a counter delineated by a column at one end, Mag asked through it, "Did you put on your jewelry?"

"Yes."

There was a pause then, "Did good, babe. As gorgeous as you are, you don't need much."

My fingers stilled.

I wanted to be offended he'd called me "babe" and thought I needed his approval of my accessorizing.

All I could hear was the word "gorgeous."

And this was the charm I needed to guard against.

The problem with that was it felt too nice aimed my way.

I didn't know what to do, or say, so I looked down to my bag, fumbled my lip gloss, it fell off the counter, I bent to retrieve it...

And then, typical, within minutes of meeting him, I gave him a massive dose of the real Evan Gardiner.

This being, I slammed my forehead into the edge of the counter.

And that hurt.

A lot.

"Shit. Evan," Mag called.

But I did not reply because I was in the midst of over-compensating the recovery. Staggering back, I slammed into the counter behind me, the edge of it digging painfully into the small of my back, and between the crack on my head making me dizzy and the sting in my back, I went down, flat on my ass.

Fabulous.

Mag was there in what seemed like half a second, crouching beside me, his long, strapping thighs splayed wide, his trousers molded to the curves and dips of his clearly muscular knees, his hand coming toward me.

I started to rear away from it, and he murmured, "Whoa," and again moved fast so I banged the back of my head into his palm, which cracked against the cupboard.

I heard Nancy Kerrigan's plaintive cry in my head, but mine had to do with why I'd given in to this date.

"Oh God, sorry," I muttered, totally mortified.

"Just...don't move," he ordered, taking control of my chin and lifting it slowly.

I forced my eyes to his face to see him examining my forehead, but that close, I could see how curly his eyelashes were.

Not good.

Because they were *awesome*.

"Smacked yourself a good one," he murmured.

Man.

This was just...

Humiliating.

"I think you need ice," he went on.

"I—"

I stopped speaking because he moved fast again, doing this to pick me up.

Pick me up.

One arm under my knees, one at my upper back.

I was so stunned by this maneuver, not only him doing it, but his being *able* to do it, I said not a word as he walked me to my couch, laid me down on it, then strode back to the kitchen.

I heard the ice machine grinding and then he returned with a bundled dishtowel.

"Lay back," he demanded.

I reclined against my fringed toss pillows and Mag gently set the bundle on my forehead.

"You need at least fifteen, twenty minutes of that, which means we're gonna miss our reservation. I'll order a pizza," he declared. "Let me guess. Your half, veggie."

I was not thrilled (at all) that I'd blown this date the way I had.

But one could not say I wasn't thrilled I'd blown this date and now had a real excuse to get out of it.

In an effort to do that, I peered out from under the towel and started, "Danny—"

"Mag."

"Sorry."

"What?"

"What?" I parroted, because he wasn't close, but he was not far, and I could see how curly his eyelashes were again.

"You said my name."

"I did?"

His eyes narrowed and he stopped bending over me, holding the ice to my head, and bent *into* me, pulling the ice away and staring into my eyes.

"What day is it?" he asked.

"Tuesday."

"Who set us up?"

"Lottie."

He held three fingers up to my face. "How many fingers do you see?"

"Three, Mag, stop it. I'm okay. I just…"

I didn't finish.

"What?" he asked.

"Just…"

I again didn't finish.

"What, Evan?"

God, really, was he actually that handsome?

And right there, hovering over me, looking concerned, which made him even *more* handsome?

"Evan?" he called.

"Your eyelashes are very curly," I whispered.

That was when he did it.

His gaze changed, it was an amazing change I felt in amazing places, it shifted to my mouth, and I felt that too, it was also amazing, and last, he murmured, "Baby."

"I'm not your baby," I breathed.

His gaze shifted back to my eyes, and he rumbled, all sexy, hot and sweet, "Oh yeah, you are."

My toes curled.

"Danny—"

"Mag."

"Mag, I—"

My phone buzzed with a text.

He looked to the kitchen counter, to me, put the ice back on and ordered, "Hold that."

I did as told, and he straightened and took the single step it took him with his long-ass legs to get to the counter.

"What the fuck?" he asked.

I kept the ice where it should be but tipped my head to look at him only to see him reading my screen.

Yes.

Reading my screen.

"What are you doing?"

His eyes dropped down to me. "Who you gonna meet at Storage and Such on East Colfax at eleven fuckin' thirty, Evan?"

Uh-oh.

"*Why* you gonna meet someone at Storage and Such on East fuckin' Colfax at eleven fuckin' thirty?" he continued.

I pushed up and reached out a hand. "Give me my phone."

"Answer me," he demanded testily.

I twisted in the couch to put my feet on the floor, saying, "I've known you all of ten minutes. You can't read my texts and it's none of your business who I meet where."

"You got a situation?" he asked.

I didn't.

My brother obviously did.

"No," I semi-lied.

"You keep bad company?" he asked.

I didn't.

But my brother totally did.

"No," I did not lie, though I had a feeling, if I went to Storage and Such on East Colfax, I would be.

My phone chimed again with another text and his eyes went direct to it.

Now . . .

Really.

I stood, pulling the ice off my head and snapping, "Danny!"

He looked to me and growled, "It says meet outside unit six and come alone."

I slowly closed my eyes and let my head fall back.

"Evan."

He was still growling.

I said nothing.

Come alone.

Mick, what mess are you in now? I thought.

"*Evie,*" Mag clipped.

I opened my eyes and righted my head.

"There's a favor I need to do for my brother."

"At eleven thirty on East Colfax?"

I tipped my head to the side and shrugged, but that was a sham seeing as a chill was racing up my spine.

"Lie down. Ice on," he bit out.

"Danny—"

"Lie your ass down and get that ice back to that bump, Evie, then we'll talk."

"We won't talk, you'll just go. Obviously, the date's off for this evening. We'll reschedule."

Or we would *not.*

"Mac says you're a genius," he announced, apropos of nothing.

I blinked and asked, "What?"

"Lottie. She says you're a genius."

Wow.

That was nice.

"She says you told her that you took apart a radio, and put it back together," he carried on. "When you were six."

I did do that.

My mother thought I was a freak.

My father bought every broken radio he could find at thrift shops, brought them home, made me fix them, then sold them at triple what he bought them for.

I didn't, incidentally, see a dime of those earnings.

I was six, but, you know, *allowance*.

Maybe?

Mag continued talking.

"So, genius, look at my face and tell me if I'm leaving."

I looked at his face.

I then became suddenly exhausted as the weight of my visit with my brother and all that might mean settled hard on my shoulders, and I decided to stretch out on my couch and put the ice on my head.

"Good call," he muttered.

One could say I was correct in my concerns about Daniel Magnusson.

I didn't know if he was toxic.

But he was a bossy damned alpha.

And meddling.

"I don't like you," I told the ceiling.

"You like my eyelashes," he said as I heard him settle in my armchair.

I made no reply.

"Talk to me," he demanded.

I sighed.

Then I stated, "I think my brother is in a bit of a bind."

"And this requires *you* to go to Storage and Such in the dead of night?"

Hmm.

The crack to my head was wearing off (though the humiliation lingered), and as it was, I was belatedly sensing this might be a boon.

I got the impression he liked me.

Even if I was a freak and a geek.

Even if I got snippy about global warming (as one *should*).

Even if I cracked my head on the counter and landed on my ass in my kitchen.

Even if I was not at one with some guy I barely knew helping himself to my texts.

But first date already ruined, it would be annihilated if he knew about my family.

He'd never want to see me again.

I slid my eyes his way. "My brother can't go as he's incarcerated."

Mag just stared at me.

"And my father can't go because my brother and my father haven't talked to each other in five years due to the fact they're the same person in two different bodies and evidence suggests they don't like themselves all that well, seeing as they carry on doing stupid, risky, escapist stuff. So, onward from that, they hate each other's guts."

Mag said not a word.

"And my mother can't go because she's probably stalking my stepfather, who's probably out with a woman who is not his wife, and she's desperate to catch him so she can do what she enjoys the most. Screeching, throwing dishes, acting like the wronged woman when he's cheated on her countless times before, and she took him back, and generally causing a scene that may, or may not, end in the cops breaking it up."

Mag remained quiet.

"And my sister can't go because she's likely deep in the throes of strategizing an epic selfie that she'll post to her over twenty thousand followers, of whom she personally knows maybe fifty. This in her drive to become an online personality to A, garner her own reality program or B, get her cast in a current or future reality program or C, garner sponsors that will allow her to make taking selfies her profession."

He spoke then.

But not to share his hasty goodnight before he beat his retreat.

He asked a question and proved he had a one-track mind; it just wasn't the usual track.

"And what favor does your brother need you to do, meetin' someone at Storage and Such on East Colfax?"

I closed my eyes and answered, "I don't know."

"You're not going."

My chest jolted at this implacable statement, and I opened my eyes and slid them back to him before I shared, "I'm not a massive fan of bossy dudes."

"And I'm not a massive fan of women doing stupid shit out of the kindness of their hearts that ends with them getting their asses in slings."

Well then.

There wasn't much response to that.

Except...

"Danny, I barely know you, you can't tell me what to do." I lifted my free hand his way when it appeared he was going to speak. "And even if I knew you for years and we were the best of friends, you still couldn't tell me what to do."

"Evie, nothing good can happen at a Storage and Such at eleven thirty at night."

He was undoubtedly not wrong.

But as gorgeous as he was, I suddenly did not see him.

I saw my brother, his manner, heard his voice.

And I knew, even though I really, really (*really*) did not want to, my brother was a fuckup, but he was my brother.

Which meant I was going to Storage and Such that night.

"Evie," he whispered.

I focused on him and saw clear as day written on his face that he'd somehow read my mind.

"I'm going with you," he declared.

Oh no he wasn't.

"You can't. They said come alone," I pointed out.

"Do you know what I do?" he asked.

"You're a commando."

His lips quirked.

And.

Dayum.

How had I not yet noticed his lips?

Also, why did God want to punish me so much that I was now, when I'd decided he and I weren't happening, noticing his lips?

Lips that were better than his eyelashes.

Better than his hair!

"I'm not a commando," he told me.

I was oddly disappointed in receiving this knowledge.

"As such," he finished.

I perked up.

"What I do . . ." He moved his head on his neck in a strange way that had me captivated, before he shared, "This is like, sixth or seventh date stuff. Maybe ninth or tenth."

Oh boy.

I sensed a girl could be highly addicted to Daniel "Mag" Magnusson by the sixth or seventh date.

Definitely the ninth or tenth.

By that time, she'd put up with *anything*.

"Anyway," he said. "I can't tell you what it is, exactly, that I do."

Oh boy.

"Seriously?" I asked.

"Missions are confidential. All of them."

"Missions?"

He nodded.

Missions.

"Oh boy," I whispered.

"It's rarely dangerous," he stated.

"All right," I mumbled.

"Well, more accurately, *occasionally* it's dangerous."

I stared at him with my mouth open.

"I might be able to say it's a bodyguard gig or...other, but not with any detail."

I continued to stare at him.

He cleared his throat. "Getting to the point, I can go with you and they won't know I went with you."

"How would you do that?"

He grinned. "We like to use words like 'covert,' but mostly, I'd hide from a vantage that I could keep an eye on you."

As I was still staring at him, somehow, I read that he was feeding me a line, being cute in order to get his way.

"Forgive me for saying this, but that doesn't sound like the most comprehensive of plans."

"I'm really good at hiding."

I bet he was.

He wasn't finished.

"And I have a gun in my truck."

Oh *boy*.

"I'm also not a big fan of guns," I shared.

"I'm not surprised," he muttered.

"My brother has a particular skill with messing up his life, but I can't believe he'd put me in any real danger."

"How about you go in with backup anyway."

"Danny—"

"Mag."

"Mag—"

He leaned toward me and cut me off.

"This is the deal, Evan. No matter what, I'm gonna be at Storage and Such at eleven thirty. You kick me out of your place now, I'm also gonna put in a call that will mean I can read your texts and listen into any phone conversations so I can see or hear if you try to change plans, and then I'll be there. So let's just order pizza, eat it, get to know each other a little bit, then hit my place so I can bulk up on ammo and get a secondary weapon before we go out to Colfax and do this shit."

I could not believe what I just heard.

And shockingly, what I couldn't believe was not the part about ammo and secondary weapons.

"You would invade my privacy like that?"

"Yup," he said without delay.

"That's . . . that's . . ." I turned to my side and got up on an elbow, keeping the ice to my head, "indescribably uncool."

"From my perspective, I'm tryin' to be a good guy. I'm offering to look out for you, help you out, make it so you don't have to go it alone, so I think it'd be 'indescribably uncool' if you put me in a position to have to invade your privacy."

"That's a convenient twist," I bit out.

His rather attractive brows shot up. "You have no qualms with goin' to some storage place at eleven thirty at night?"

I was trying not to think about doing that.

In fact, I was focusing on this insane conversation in order *not* to think about doing that.

He read that in my face too, I knew it when he muttered, "Right."

I glared at him.

Then I plopped to my back and closed my eyes, declaring, "I'm done talking to you. Like . . . *for forever*."

"So, veggie for your side of the pizza?"

I hated veggie pizza.

Soggy onions?

Yuck.

"Sausage and pepperoni," I mumbled.

He sounded amused when he noted, "Your silent treatment doesn't last long."

"I'm talking to the ceiling," I told the ceiling.

"Is sixty bucks gonna fall outta the ceiling to pay for the pizza?"

Say what?

I opened my eyes and tipped my head to look at him again.

"What pizza costs sixty bucks?" I asked.

Grinning at me, he lifted his long, attractive forefinger upward and said, "The ceiling's that way."

I rolled my eyes and plopped again to my back.

"And we're also getting boneless wings, cheesy bread and cannoli," he informed me.

It was good we weren't ever going to go on an actual date, or anything beyond that, because it was obvious if we did, I'd probably have to buy workout clothes.

One thing was certain, he didn't simply consume protein shakes and unseasoned lean meats.

I heard a rustling, which I assumed was him getting out his phone.

"Evie," he called.

When being forced to eat veggie pizza was not on the table, I was back to the silent treatment.

"Evie," he called again.

Great eyelashes.

Great hair.

Great lips.

Great fingers.

And he had a great voice, especially when he said my name.

I let out an exasperated breath.

Fingers curled around my wrist, the ice was pulled away, and I had another close-up of his eyelashes because he was bent to my face.

Ugh.

"I know what she told you," he said.

I forgot my silent treatment and asked, "Who?"

"Mac."

I remembered my silent treatment.

"She told you that you needed to sort my shit."

I stared into his eyes.

Was that blue even natural?

It was impossible!

"But all that shit you spewed about your family," he went on, and I tensed, but he smiled. Wide and white. "Mac is no fool. This isn't about you sorting my shit. It's her setting me up to sort yours."

This, I did not put past Lottie.

And thus, I decided, when I saw her again, Lottie would be getting my silent treatment.

Though, hopefully I'd be better at it by that time.

I wanted to be wrong, but I was pretty sure I growled.

That only made him grin even wider before he touched my nose with his finger (touched my nose!), put the ice back and disappeared from view.

I heard nothing until I heard his phone clatter on my coffee table.

He then said, "I got us cheesecake too."

Gluh.

I had, until then, prided myself that I never, not ever, put on a pair of yoga pants.

But Athleta, here I come.

"Now, babe," he continued, his voice fading in the direction of my kitchen, "you got any beer?"

CHAPTER THREE

Storage and Such

EVIE

I'd fallen asleep.

Not good.

But before that happened, Mag had done an about-face after he found I had beer (though I didn't like to think of it as beer, as such, considering it was only *technically* beer seeing as it was ale) and brought us both opened bottles.

It was then, proving he could be a decent guy, or at least he could pretend to be one, he'd shared that on any normal first date that was going to last at least six hours, for some of it, we'd be engaged in activities that didn't require us carrying on a conversation to get to know each other better.

I ignored his double entendre after he suggested we eat pizza while we watched a movie.

I could use a reprieve from his attention, so I'd jumped on that with barely veiled enthusiasm.

Something he found amusing, and didn't hide, so I hid how I liked that I amused him.

After I agreed, I ignored the squishy, warm feeling I felt when he asked if I'd seen any of the *John Wick* movies, saying he'd seen them all, but wouldn't mind watching them again.

I'd seen them all.

And wouldn't mind watching them again.

This indicating we might have the same taste in films, which, for me, was *huge*.

I then was forced to converse with him while icing my forehead and alternately sipping the beer he'd brought me.

During this, I learned his parents were still together, he had a younger sister, they all still lived back in Minnesota where he'd grown up, and his younger sister was imminently marrying a guy Mag was not altogether fond of.

He did not dive deep into that.

He also shared, not surprisingly, he was a high school football star who a couple of colleges had wanted to give a scholarship.

But as he had not been "super hyped to spend another minute in a classroom," he'd gone against his parents' wishes and enlisted in the Marines.

However, parlaying this information changed his affect so much, seeing it manifest itself in pretty much every inch of his frame, specifically his expression, I felt my stomach twist.

He did not delve deeply into that either.

This instead led him to ending the conversation, rising from his chair, checking my bump, muttering, "I think we kicked the swelling," and thus, he took away the ice.

All the way.

Meaning, he took it to the kitchen and dealt with it.

I didn't have to move.

Shortly after, the pizza arrived.

Totally 1987, Mag refused to allow me to give him any money to pitch in for the food.

Though mostly sweet, he only argued for a couple minutes about me renting the movie.

I did not keep a normal, healthy schedule. My stripper work started at seven at night, ended at two thirty in the morning, and the various other jobs, both paid and unpaid, that I had besides kept me on the go.

So, in the end, it was fortunate that Mag decided not to invade my space on the couch and instead eat his pizza and watch the movie in my armchair, because I fell asleep on my couch.

Mag woke me by calling my name, and when I opened my eyes, I saw his eyelashes because he was again bent close to me.

Thus ensued another squishy feeling.

"Sorry, babe, we gotta get going," he said quietly. "It's ten and we need to swing by my place, get my gear, get you kitted, and I gotta have time to recon that facility. I've never been there before."

I didn't get a chance to ask what getting me "kitted" meant or apologize for falling asleep on him.

That said, he didn't seem upset I had.

He seemed mellow and relaxed, and I didn't want to, but I liked that he seemed that way with me in my space after only knowing me a couple of hours, some of that time I'd been sparring with him, some of it making an idiot of myself, some of it asleep.

He continued speaking.

"You'll have to be seen going in alone, so we need to take two cars. You can follow me to my place."

With that, he took my hand and tugged me out of the couch.

I then drowsily went about the business of putting on my shoes that I'd obviously kicked off in my sleep, donning my blazer, grabbing my phone, bag and keys, and mindlessly swiping on another coat of lip gloss.

Though I became mindful of this when I noticed Mag watching me do it, and he was watching appreciatively.

I tucked my lip gloss in my bag, followed him out, locked my door and then we got in our respective vehicles and I followed him to his place.

He guided me to guest parking, parked somewhere else, then joined me at my car and took me up to his condo in LoHi.

I was coming back to myself, digging out from under all the shit that was clouding my brain, and during the drive, I'd realized my mistake in sharing with him all the things I'd shared, primarily about my family.

I should have been niceish, but aloof in a way that could be construed as borderline impolite, which no man would want, instead of mysterious, which I figured a man like Mag might take as a challenge.

However, I did not do this.

So, I decided to start.

ASAP.

What did not occur to me during the drive from my oldish apartment complex in Platt Park—which was a two-story rectangle with entries to the units on exposed walkways on the inside of the structure, these surrounded a pool that someone had jazzed up and included a communal grilling-and-hanging-out area and a lot of tall, shady trees—was that I didn't have to follow him.

It was hours after receiving those texts.

I didn't know how long it would take Mag to set up hacking my phone, but with less time to do it, maybe I could have gotten away with getting away from him.

Something I could easily do in my car by simply *driving away from him*.

Instead, I followed him to his newish, sleek, modern, hip condo complex in one of the trendiest neighborhoods in Denver.

And there I stood by his massive kitchen island, staring at his living room that was filled with sleek, modern, hip furniture.

He was in his bedroom, out of which, right then, he emerged.

I ignored the gun in a shoulder holster that was now marring his awesome light-blue button-up, as well as what looked like two extra gun clips hooked to his belt.

Instead, I watched him throw a jacket on the island out of which he pulled a tangle of wire.

"You have exceptional taste in home décor," I shared.

His head came up from his detangling duties and he grinned at me.

Evie, stop making the man smile, I chastised myself as my breasts swelled in response to that smile. *Making him smile is not borderline impolite. It's FLIRTING.*

"It's all Mo's," he informed me. "My shit, after the breakup, I put in storage. When Mo moved in with Mac, he didn't need this stuff anymore, so I sold my crap, because it was crap, bought his, and before you get any ideas, Mo didn't pick it either. He engineered a personal shopper, some lady who worked at some furniture store, and she did it."

"I cannot imagine how it would reflect poorly on Mo that he's able to select a couch," I noted.

He looked down to his wires, stating, "Yeah, well, you don't have a dick."

"I know many men who come with that equipment who have opinions on couches," I retorted.

His head came up and he grinned at me again.

Stupid Evie!

I decided it was time to get into his shoulder holster and ammo clips.

"Just to say," I dipped my head to his chest, "we're not facing a zombie apocalypse."

Okay.

What was with me?

It seemed I just couldn't help myself.

Because he started chuckling, I started reacting to his chuckles in a variety of warm ways in a variety of places in my body, all precisely as I'd intended.

He began to round the island to come to me.

"In my life, I've learned you can't be too safe," he said dauntingly, then held up the wire that looked, at one end, to have a small microphone, and at the other, a small transmitter.

Uh-oh.

"Danny," I stated warningly.

I said no more because I didn't intend to say anything else. I thought my warning tone should suffice.

But more, he appeared like he was going to say something before his head ticked, his gaze on me warmed, his mouth grew soft, and he stared at me for a full five seconds like he was a doting boyfriend and I was his doted-upon girlfriend.

This caused havoc on my insides, and I was grateful to him for finally speaking because it meant I had something else to focus on.

"I'm gonna wire you, Evie, so I can not only see what's goin' down but hear it."

"I don't think—"

He interrupted me.

"Babe, let me look after you."

It was then what was happening, what he was intent

on doing, and clearly intent on doing thoroughly, fully dawned on me.

And it felt like something had come up from his cement floors and clamped on my feet, rooting me to the spot as I stared up at him.

No one...

Not ever...

In my life...

Had looked after me.

No one.

"Now, I'm not bein' fresh," he said, "but I need to reach up your shirt and position this." He gestured with the microphone. "I get it in place, you hold it there, we'll tape it and stow the transmitter. You got your shirt untucked at the back, your blazer on, he'll never see. Yeah?"

I nodded slowly.

"Untuck the front of your tee, Evie," he ordered.

I did as told.

And, man.

You had to hand it to him.

He ducked his hand under my shirt fast. He then slid the microphone under the clasp at the front of my bra fast as well. And he did all of this staring right into my eyes, his gaze attentive, his manner efficient.

"Hold that, babe," he murmured.

I lifted a hand and held the microphone in position over my T-shirt.

He pulled his hand out, reached for some tape, ripped off a small piece and then ducked back in.

I took my hand away, Mag kept hold of my eyes as he smoothed the tape over the wire in a practiced manner that took only a few seconds, then his hand was gone.

He gave me the transmitter.

"Hook that to your belt at the back. Turn it on. Cover it with your shirt. I'm gonna go into my room, close the door. We'll test here and we'll test again at the location. You'll switch that on prior to turning into the parking lot. If he's watching you, I don't want him to see you anywhere, in or out of your car, reaching to your back. With me?"

I nodded again.

"Turn it on, hook it to your jeans, and go to Mo's old room." He indicated a door behind me that was closed.

He then strapped on a minimal, wireless headset that wrapped around the back of his head that did not make him look like my ex when he had his headset on while he was gaming.

Something I thought was cute, at first.

Way *not* cute later.

On Mag, it was just *hot*.

"Go, honey," he ordered gently.

I switched on the transmitter, hooked it on my waistband at the back and headed to Mo's old room.

Behind the closed door, feeling kinda like an idiot, but still trying to make a joke (which, yes, would mean making him laugh, *gah!*) I said, "Testing, testing. Sibilance. Sibilance."

I then stood there, definitely like an idiot, because I was hoping I was transmitting, but I had no idea if I was, because I couldn't receive.

Did I open the door to call out and say I'd transmitted?

Apparently not.

For the door opened and Mag, with his jacket on and his hand still on the knob, swung his torso in.

"We're a go," he declared. "Let's bounce. I'll lead you to safe parking where you can hang while I do a drive-by of the locale. I'll text when it's good for you to go in."

I dropped my eyes to my chili-red Rothy's and started walking his way, saying, "Okay."

"Evie."

I stopped and looked up to him to see he had not moved.

"I got you covered," he assured.

He had me covered.

Man.

I nodded.

Then I blurted, "I'm sorry I fell asleep on you. It wasn't you, or *John Wick*. It's just...I keep odd hours and I don't get many chances to sleep."

"Don't think about it another second," he said softly.

"Okay," I whispered.

"Let's get this done," he murmured.

I took in a deep breath, let it go, and nodded again.

* * *

As I sat in a fully lit parking lot of a Burger King on Colfax, I was rethinking my relationship with my brother.

I truly did not believe that Mick would ever do anything that would put me into danger.

Except, I felt in danger.

And the question had to be asked.

Did one make someone they loved feel something like that?

My phone sounded and I jumped so bad, where I hit my back earlier on the counter stung and the dull pain in my forehead thrummed.

The screen declared the call was from Mag.

I picked it up and engaged.

"Okay, I'm having second thoughts," I said as greeting.

Mag said nothing.

"You don't know my brother," I told him. "And I can understand, considering the current situation, which is highly unusual for a first date, or *any* date, though that might just be my experience. You're a commando. You use the word 'mission' when speaking of your employment. Perhaps this isn't out of the ordinary for you. But for me, it is. And I can get why you might not think well of my brother considering what we're currently doing."

"Evan—"

"But he's a good guy. We..." I decided not to get into the whole sad story and adjusted my stream of blathering. "He's messed up but he's a good guy, but...I just..." My voice dipped. "I don't wanna be here, Danny."

He finally spoke and he did it gently.

"Baby, it's not me who wanted to do this. You wanna bag, I'm down."

"He was scared," I blurted. "In lockup. During our visit. He's always cocky. But he wasn't cocky. He was scared."

Mag hesitated a moment before he said, "This is your call, Evie. I'm with you either way. I'm in position, and from the minute you turn in, I'll have eyes on you and whatever happens, if you need me, I can get to you fast. Or I can bug out. Totally your decision."

"What if...if I don't do this and something bad happens to Mick?"

Mag's hesitation was a lot longer that time.

And then he spoke.

"I've known you five hours, Evan. I do not know your brother. I got no foundation in this. No position to defend. But from my standpoint, as it is, it hasn't changed from the beginning. Whatever he got himself into, honey, it's not up to you to get him out. It's his. He has to own it and that includes owning the consequences."

"But he's my brother."

Mag said nothing.

So, I prompted, "Danny?"

"Fuck," I heard him mutter.

"What?" I asked.

"I'd do anything for my brothers," he said, and even over the phone, I could tell he didn't want to say it.

Fuck was right.

I straightened my spine, felt a tinge again where I hit it earlier, but ignored it and stated, "Okay, let's just get this done."

"You'll be good, Evie."

I nodded even though he couldn't see me.

"I will," I agreed. "Thanks. And just...*thanks*. I know I wasn't real gracious about this earlier but I'm, well..." Damn it all, I had to say it. "I'm glad you're here."

"No issues, babe. Now, you got ten minutes to get here, it's a five-minute drive, and I don't think, if he's casing the joint, he'll balk you got here early. But I want you here so I have an eye on you."

My blood pressure spiked, and I spoke words I never in my life thought I'd say unless I was playing an RPG. "If he's casing the joint, he might have seen you positioning."

"He didn't see me positioning."

"But what if—"

"Honey, baby, Evie, get this. He *did not see me positioning*."

I shut up, and this was partly to do with him clearly wanting me to let it go, partly to do with his utter confidence in his abilities, something that shared he was highly skilled in those abilities, and partly to do with double-barrel endearments before my name that were said gentle, but exasperated, and that was cute, and hot.

Damn.

"All right," I muttered.

"Hit it. You get a bad vibe, you bail. I got you covered. You with me?"

"Yes."

"Right. Go. Phone in your back pocket. Keys in your hand. You get out of your car, do not take your bag."

"Okay."

"You got this, Evie."

I had everything.

Always.

Though now, for the first time, I had backup.

"Right," I said.

"Go with your gut. Do not hesitate. Your gut tells you something, you do it. I got eyes on you, and however it goes down, we'll deal, or we'll rendezvous where we need to rendezvous. All right?"

"Yeah."

"Turn on the transmitter and mute your phone then talk to me."

I did as told.

I unmuted my phone and asked, "Got me?"

"Got you."

Oh boy.

Those two words settled, and I had no control over how deep they went.

Which, by the by, was *deep*.

"See you soon, baby," he said.

"Okay, Danny."

I could swear I heard him mutter, "Fuck me, I like that from her," before he disconnected.

I tucked my phone in my back pocket, got my keys from my bag and started up my car.

I spoke to him as I drove to the Storage and Such because I was nervous, because he might expect it so he knew we were still connected, and last, because I wanted that link.

No.

Needed it.

I didn't say much of anything except what I was doing.

Like,

"Pulling out of the parking spot now."

And,

"Indicating to get onto Colfax now."

Etcetera.

I then pulled into the Storage and Such (telling Mag I was doing that) and I did it with my heart beating hard.

Man, oh man, did Mick owe me for this.

Seriously.

The Storage and Such was *not* well lit.

But I found unit six and stopped beside it.

I stayed in my car, letting it idle.

"I'm not a fan of letting a car idle," I told Mag, then realized if I was being watched, they might see my lips move.

I quit talking.

I tried to distract myself with looking around, attempting to figure out where Mag was hiding (he was right, I could not see him anywhere at all, and there weren't a lot of hiding places), assessing the distance and then calculating the time it would take for him to get to me.

I decided there were four different hiding places, and taking into account an average "fast" hundred-meter run (which I assumed Danny could pull off) was about fourteen seconds—and there were other parameters, including the fact he might have to get down from a roof—he could make it to me in between 0.27 and 1.23 minutes.

I could probably hold my own for 0.27 minutes.

I just hoped he wasn't on a roof.

I got bored with this and snapped, "He's late," when my clock struck 11:37.

Two minutes later, a black car with a hood so long, I wasn't sure I'd ever seen that long of a hood, rounded me at my side and angled in front of me before it stopped.

"Shit, shit, *shit*," I hissed. "Why is he cutting me off?"

I needed an earbud.

Mag didn't offer an earbud.

This dude would probably see an earbud, which was likely why Mag didn't offer one.

Shit, shit, *shit*.

The guy in the long car got out.

He was tall, skinny, white, and dressed in jeans and a shirt I couldn't see very well because it was covered by a big leather jacket.

Slowly, I switched off my car and got out too.

I left my bag behind.

But I had my keys in my hand.

He did not hesitate to walk to me.

I braced.

Mag was out there, watching.

He had me.

I had this.

"Evan Gardiner?" he asked.

"Yes," I answered.

"Twenty-two left, thirty-eight right, seventeen left. Trader Joe's bag. Grab it. Keep it safe. I'll text you in a couple of days with instructions."

He then turned to walk away.

Wait.

What?

"Hey!" I cried, starting to follow him.

He turned back. "Twenty-two left, thirty-eight right,

seventeen left." He jerked his head to the sliding steel door on unit six. A door that had a combination lock on it. "Trader Joe's bag. Keep it safe, Gardiner. Or Mick's got problems."

With that, he got in his car, reversed a little, then his massive vehicle chugged forward and rounded the units at the other end, disappearing.

I muttered to myself, "Twenty-two left, thirty-eight right, seventeen left," as I approached the door.

I had to shove my keys in my pocket and get out my phone to engage the flashlight to open the lock.

This I did, and it made a huge, loud ruckus as I lifted the door.

The contents were shadowed, but I could tell there were a lot.

I swung my flashlight around, found a switch, flipped it, there was a hum and recalcitrant tube lights overhead came on. I entered just as my phone rang.

I dug it out of my back pocket, saw it was Mag, engaged and put it to my ear, searching for a Trader Joe's bag.

"Okay, that wasn't too bad," I said.

"Nab the bag, do not look in it, put it in your car, and go. I'll meet you at your place. I'm in position until you pull out," he stated, and I didn't know him very well, but he didn't sound happy.

He also didn't wait for me to confirm.

He disconnected.

It appeared this guy, or Mick, or someone collected a lot of junk.

And thus, it was not easy finding the Trader Joe's bag.

Though I found it in an old cooler.

Mag (and possibly others) was watching so I didn't look in it. I just grabbed it, found it wasn't heavy, but it made a noise that didn't make me very happy. In fact, it made my breathing go wonky.

But I got out of there, pulled the door down, locked it, entered my car, stowed the bag, and got the hell out of there.

I drove five miles under the speed limit on the way home, which might be stupid, but I was freaked and I didn't want to be freaked and in an accident where someone would find whatever was in that bag in my car and I might end up in the hospital.

And after that the pokey.

I needed to focus on something, which I decided, for once, would be my driving.

I would find Mag drove a lot faster for he left his position and he was on my tail the last five miles of the drive.

I swung into my covered spot.

He swung into a guest spot.

When I met him with the bag, he took it from me, and we both jogged up the steps to my second-floor pad.

I let us in.

He closed and locked the door behind us.

He then put the bag on my coffee table, and I stood beside him as he pulled out a wad of plastic sheeting that was stuffed in the top. Sheeting that would remain on this earth long after I was gone, and in its lifetime probably suffocate a number of dolphins.

But, for once, I had no mind to that.

What I heard bouncing around in that bag Mag reached in and pulled out.

A prescription pill bottle.

"Oxy," he growled.

Oh no.

No, no, no, no, *no*.

He was peering into the bag as he declared, "There's gotta be twenty, thirty bottles in there."

He reached back in and pulled out a little baggie filled with milk-colored crystals.

"Ice," Mag bit off. "Meth," he said when I did nothing but stare at him.

"Oh no," I whispered. "No, no, no, no, *no*."

"There's maybe a hundred of these in there," he shared.

Oh *God*.

"And this," he stated, reaching in and pulling out a brick of white covered in plastic wrap and crisscrossed with duct tape.

I'd seen those before.

In movies.

"Coke," he grunted unhappily. "Two of these in there."

I closed my eyes.

I opened them and quipped, "Man, you can get a lot of drugs in a Trader Joe's bag."

"This is not funny, Evan," he clipped.

I pressed my lips together.

He was right.

So right.

Something else.

My brother was totally down with putting me in a dangerous situation.

I had never done drugs.

Considering my father, I'd never even smoked pot.

Except for my father's (and brother's and sometimes stepdad's) pot, I'd never even *seen* any illegal drugs.

I had no earthly clue how much all that was worth and how badly a variety of unsavory characters would want to get their hands on it.

I just knew it was probably worth a lot.

And it was sitting on my coffee table.

I also had no clue why the dude in the long car, since he knew the combination to the lock and where the drugs were, couldn't just grab them himself.

Nothing about this was right.

Nothing made sense.

I'd never had a good feeling about it.

Though now, that feeling was way worse.

But right then, the worst part was, I had a Trader Joe's bag filled with illegal narcotics on my coffee table after having a short, but scary conversation with a shady man in the middle of the night at a storage facility.

And my brother put me right here.

Mick put me *right here*.

I didn't know what I was feeling, or I couldn't quite process *all* I was feeling.

"It's still your call, but now, I'm gonna strongly advise you to let me call Hawk, who will in turn call Slim and Mitch, covering your ass while he does it, and this means you hand this over to the cops without any blowback on you," Mag declared.

"Thank you, I really appreciate your help, but now I think we need to call it a night," I told the Trader Joe's bag.

I felt Mag focus his attention on me.

I did because his attention not only had a feel, but a temperature.

And that was set at *sweltering*.

"Evie—"

Woodenly, I turned, looked up at him and cut him off.

"This is a family affair."

He stared at me like I'd grown a second head before his face softened.

His tone had softened too.

"Evie, baby, honey, I get where you're coming from, but do not let him drag you under."

He did not get where I was coming from.

His parents were still together, he spoke of them fondly, and he probably didn't like his sister's fiancé simply because he was an older brother and he'd *never* like his sister's fiancé.

Now my older brother...

Well.

To wit, he had no *fucking* idea where I was coming from.

"I really...I mean...I know this was a hassle for you and you didn't want to do it, so I thank you, *a lot*, for taking my back. But I'll take it from here."

"Babe—"

"I'm not a babe. I'm a grown woman," I suddenly snapped.

And I knew why.

There he was, literally tall, dark, handsome, but also...*nice*.

Thoughtful.

Willing to go that extra mile for someone he barely knew.

And the extra mile he went for me included one-way radios and extra ammo.

I couldn't even imagine the state I'd have been in that night if he hadn't been there, looking out for me.

And there it was.

A grocery bag filled with illicit drugs that his kind and protective nature helped me procure because my brother gave someone my phone number and told that someone I'd take care of things.

I needed to get Mag gone.

Now.

For his own good.

"I see you're freaked," he began.

"Oh, you do?" I asked sarcastically.

He moved closer but didn't touch me.

However, he did bend down to me from his spectacular height in much the way he'd probably have to bend to me in order to do something awesome, something he was probably very good at, something I'd probably enjoy immensely—kiss me.

But he wasn't going to do that.

He was going to talk to me about the situation surrounding the drugs on my coffee table.

"Don't let him make you this person," he advised.

"You have no idea what kind of person I am."

"You know I had a woman and I had her a long time," he stated. "This is why I know about Urban Outfitters and Anthropologie and the fact those shoes on your feet are made of repurposed water bottles. That," he jabbed a finger at the Trader Joe's bag, "outside its carrier, has nothin' to do with the kind of person you are."

"What I know is, I might have told Lottie a little bit about me, but you were wrong about why she set us up. It isn't about *you* sorting me out. It's about *me* stopping you laying waste to the female population of Denver with your toxic charm," I retorted.

He swung back, his face freezing stone cold.

"I know men like you like to think your shit doesn't stink," I kept at him. "And this is such a firm belief you have, it won't matter what I say. But as you can see," I flipped a hand toward the bag, "I have bigger things to concern myself with. I don't have the time to rehabilitate a manwhore."

"A manwhore?" he whispered.

"Do you deny you've fucked half of Denver?"

"Yeah, I deny that," he bit out. "Lottie called me a manwhore?"

"And how would *you* refer to a *woman* who engaged abundantly in the activities you engage in *abundantly*, then scrape off the poor souls to make way for your next victim?"

"Gotta say, Evan, you give dual personalities a whole new meaning," he replied, his expression now openly hostile.

Outwardly, I shrugged.

Inwardly, I screamed.

"So, are we done?" I asked.

"Fuck yeah, we're done," he snarled. "Good luck, babe. You're really gonna fuckin' need it."

He delivered that.

And as I'd learned earlier, the man could move fast.

So it took no time at all for the door to slam behind him.

I went to it.

I locked it.

Then I turned my back to it.

And I slid down it.

Knees bent, hands flat to the floor at my sides, my gaze was glued to the bag on the coffee table.

I was a crier.

I just was.

I cried when I was sad and when I was stressed. And when I was on my period, watch out. The waterworks turned on for just about anything.

But I had a number of reasons to cry right then.

The weird part about it was, even with where Mick put me, what was on my coffee table, and the scary uncertainty of my future as pertains to that grocery bag...

I had a feeling the biggest reason for me to cry had just walked out my door.

And as such, I did not cry.

It was silent.

But I dropped my head and my body shook with the sobs.

CHAPTER FOUR

Rock Chick Zone

MAG

Mag walked into the office suite early the next morning and noted immediately that his luck hadn't turned.

And he didn't give a fuck.

He was so pissed, he hadn't slept a second.

And somehow, he was more pissed than how *excruciatingly* pissed he was the night before with all that shit Evan had spewed at him.

So when he saw Mo was standing outside Elvira's office with not only Elvira, but Tex MacMillan (for fuck's sake, fucking *Tex*, a certifiable lunatic)...

And when he saw Hawk at the top of the space, which was set up theater style with the men's units forming rows on each level so they could do their desk work and keep an eye on the screens that lined the wall at the front, and Hawk was for some fucking reason standing with Kane "Tack" Allen of the Chaos MC...

Mag didn't pause.

He walked left, direct to Mo.

Mo had not missed his arrival.

No one had.

Everyone was watching him make his way to Mo, he could feel the focus.

Including Tex, Elvira, Hawk, and Tack.

Mag didn't even slow.

It was, unsurprisingly, Tex who spoke first, "Shit, boy, you got a face like thunder."

Mo, who didn't talk much, just stared at him, but Mag could tell he was alert and concerned.

They'd been coworkers awhile, buds all that while, and roommates for a few months.

Mo knew him.

Mo also knew he had a blind date with Evan last night.

And Mo wasn't liking what he was seeing.

Something Mag gave not one fuck about seeing as he did not like what he was *feeling*.

Mag didn't even glance at Tex.

He kept his gaze locked with Mo's as he said, "Lottie gets the bright idea to fix me up with another one of her bitches, you tell her to think twice about it."

Mag felt the attitude coming off Tex, and it was intense, this because Lottie was his stepdaughter, and he might have a whacked-out way of showing it, just as he had a whacked-out way of doing anything he did, but he loved her more than life.

"And you tell your woman," Mag continued giving it to Mo, "if she has a problem with how I live my life, she can fuckin' talk to *me* about it. Not share her judgment about what I do with my dick with anyone who'll listen."

"Jesus," Mo murmured.

"Now hang on—" Tex started.

Mag looked to Tex and clipped, "You are not in this."

"You're talkin' 'bout my Lottie," he leaned toward Mag threateningly, "I *am*. And Lottie wouldn't talk smack about you. She'd never do that. Especially not to you. You're her boy."

"That's what I thought, but apparently I was wrong," Mag returned.

"What happened?" Mo asked, regaining Mag's attention.

"We'll just leave it at the fact me and Evan will not be having a second date," Mag told him. "Now talk to your woman because I am *so* not down with the dirty she did me."

And he wasn't.

He was tight with Mac, Mac being the best woman he'd ever met, so what she did hurt like fuck.

"Tex is right, Lottie'd never talk trash about you," Mo said. "So . . . what happened?"

"I'm not getting into it," Mag replied.

This was, unfortunately, when Elvira entered the conversation.

"Boy, you cannot come in here, verbal guns a'blazin', throwin' down with Mo *and* Tex, and not give us a full picture."

Elvira had a point.

Elvira also wanted to know what was going on because Elvira had a pathological need to stick her nose into everything.

Mag was tight with Elvira too. Until he'd met Lottie, Elvira was the best woman he'd ever met.

Since Elvira didn't make one of his brothers happy by falling in love with him and treating him like gold, she'd been demoted to the second slot.

"You aren't in this either," he told her.

"Well, you walked right up and interrupted a convo that I was enjoyin', seein' as we're connivin' a kickass wedding gift from Mo to Lottie," she shot back. "So, you didn't want me in this, you should have asked for a private word."

"Do we have an issue?"

Terrific.

Hawk *and* Tack had moseyed down to their huddle.

"No issue," he grunted to his boss and swung his eyes to Mo. "You heard me. It's done."

"Mag's claiming that Lottie did the dirty on him and talked trash about him to the girl she set him up with last night," Elvira chimed in.

Mag drew a sharp breath into his nose.

Hawk *and* Tack leveled their eyes on him.

"I would share, personal shit on personal time," Hawk declared. "But seein' as Elvira dragged Tex in first thing in the morning, fired up about something for Mo's wedding, and they ignored me earlier when I said personal shit on personal time, I'll simply have to repeat *personal shit on personal time*." His gaze swung through Elvira and Tex as he finished, "All of you."

"You don't sign my paycheck," Tex stated.

"I know it would be a challenge, and I haven't had one in a long time," Hawk began, eyes on Tex, "so I'd look forward to it and I'd best it if I had to lock you down and kick your ass out."

Tex straightened. "I haven't had a challenge in a long time either, turkey."

"Well then, looks like hump day just turned into thump day," Elvira remarked, appearing like her Wednesday just took an upswing.

"Mag," Mo called, and when Mag looked to him, he repeated, *"What happened?"*

He wanted it?

"Lottie told her I was a manwhore."

"Oh shit," Mo muttered.

"Uh-oh," Elvira mumbled.

And there it was.

Fuck him.

"Right," Mag bit off.

"Gotta say, if the shoe fits . . ." Tex trailed off.

Mag turned his attention to Tex.

"Tex, help me out and shut the fuck up," Hawk said, obviously catching how Mag was staring at Tex.

"Brother," Mo said, and Mag turned to him. "I'll talk to her, but just sayin', she was concerned about how you were workin' through your issues after losin' Nikki, but if Evan took it there, that was Evan. Lottie would never use that word talkin' about you."

"I got somethin' to share about my history with a woman I'm seein', it's mine to share, Mo," Mag fired back. "For fuck's sake, you know that."

"A woman you're seeing?" Mo asked.

Goddamn it.

Elvira spoke up.

"Wasn't last night your first date?"

Mag looked to her.

"Oh shit," she whispered. "You liked her."

Liked her?

No.

Was way fuckin' into her the second he laid eyes on her—and damn, the woman was all kinds of pretty—and that just grew from the minute she threw him attitude, instead of crawling up his ass or tease-flirting or acting like she didn't give a shit if he found her attractive when she totally did.

She was herself.

Take her as she came.

And in the time he spent with her—cracking her head on the counter, falling on her ass, throwing him more attitude, eating three slices of pizza, half the boneless wings, her fair share of cheesy bread, half a cannoli as well as a half slice of cheesecake to falling asleep and making cute snoring noises he knew, if she was sleeping beside him, they'd wake him up and make him want to fuck her, to being funny and sweet and open and honest and most of all, liking his eyelashes of all fucking things—he'd seen a lot of sides of Evan Gardiner.

And was way into them all.

Except the last.

"Maybe Lottie can do some damage control," Tex suggested, unfortunately reading what Mag had been unable to hide.

Yeah.

That was how into her he was, he couldn't even hide it.

"Unnecessary," Mag grunted, and again looked back to Mo. "Though I'll pass on to you, her brother is a problem. We didn't go out because she cracked her head on the counter and she needed to ice it, which was good and bad. Good, because I was there to take her back when she had to go meet some shifty character who drives a freakin' 1965 Lincoln Continental and told her to keep safe a grocery bag filled with meth, oxy, and coke or her brother would have a problem. Then she kicked my ass out, after I gave her good advice about that, telling me it's family shit. And that's the way she wants to play it..." He shrugged. "Though I figure now, with the way

Mac is, she finds this out, it's your shit. All I know is, she made crystal clear it isn't mine."

"Are you fucking kidding me?" Mo said low.

"I wish I was," Mag replied.

"All right, no," Hawk stated, taking another step down, which put him *in* the huddle. He was looking up at Mo. "Hear this, Mo. I'm happy for you. You and Lottie are a great match. But her bein' yours, we are not entering the Rock Chick Zone."

Mag had read those books because Lottie was in them and he'd wanted fodder to give her shit about, as was their way.

In the end, they were funny, so he kept reading them, even after finishing the one she'd had a costarring role in.

And he was seriously down with what Hawk said. Those Rock Chicks had bumpy rides.

And their men being dragged right along with them? Jesus.

He wanted no part of that kind of shit.

Except for the fact that for some reason, Evan was currently keeping safe thousands of dollars of drugs.

"I think that ship's sailed," Elvira muttered, eyeing up Mag and Mo.

"Lee Nightingale lost hundreds of man hours on that Rock Chick shit. I'll repeat, that is not happening here," Hawk said to Elvira.

"Well, all right!" Tex boomed. "We'd hit such a long, boring patch, I thought I'd have to eBay my grenades. Trust my Lottie girl to stir things up."

Mag noted at this juncture that Tack was watching all of them wearing a shit-eating grin.

"Call Slim," Hawk ordered Mag.

Slim being Brock "Slim" Lucas, one of Hawk's posse that included Tack as well as Mitch Lawson.

Mitch and Slim were cops.

Tack was *not*.

"I'm not in this," Mag reminded his boss.

"Call Slim," Hawk reiterated.

"She'd not thank me for that," Mag told him.

"I don't give a fuck. I don't even know this woman and I know she's in over her head. She can thank you later, when this is done and she's still breathing," Hawk replied. "Call *Slim*."

"I'll look into it," Mo muttered.

"Jesus Christ, did you not hear me?" Hawk bit off. "This crew is not taking on the next generation of Rock Chicks."

"I got leave coming, I'll look into it."

Everyone turned to see Auggie at his station, leaned back in his chair, his legs stretched out in front of him, crossed at the ankles, his arms crossed on his chest, watching their show.

Fucking Auggie, also obviously a coworker, and a bud practically since they met.

Hawk's posse included Slim, Mitch and Tack.

Mag's crew was Mo, Auggie, as well as Axl and Boone, the last two out on assignments.

Being on Mo's crew, Aug was also in line for a Lottie fix-up (as were Axl and Boone).

But all Mag could see right then was Auggie, who scored more pussy than Mag just by catching a woman's eyes and quirking a smile.

If Evie caught sight of Aug, she wouldn't crack her head into a counter after she dropped her lip gloss.

She'd walk into a wall.

"You're not lookin' into it," Mag told him.

Auggie's dark eyes shifted to him and they were amused.

Motherfucker.

"Which one is she?" Auggie asked.

"What?" Mag asked back.

"Which one of Smithie's girls?" Auggie gave detail to his question.

As far as Mag knew, he, Axl and Auggie had been to one show at Smithie's club, when Lottie went back to work after the sick-fuck who'd fixated on her was taken out of commission, Mo couldn't be there, so they were in his stead to provide moral support.

And Evie did not dance that night.

In fact, upon seeing her, Mag was very interested in going one night to watch her dance.

Two minutes into meeting her, he had to force himself not to think about it or he'd go caveman, that being locking her in his bedroom and keeping her there until he convinced her to stop dancing, and she wouldn't like that.

Now, he was thinking about Auggie seeing her dance.

And *he* didn't like that.

"You been back?" Mag asked.

"No," Auggie answered.

"She wasn't on that night," Mag told him.

"Mystery pretty," Auggie said. "Best kind."

Mag ground his teeth.

He then turned to Hawk.

"If anyone's on her, I'm on her."

And if she didn't like it, fuck it.

Hawk was right, she was in over her head.

If she didn't realize that, that wasn't his problem.

Her shit needed to be dealt with and she had no clue.

So, he had to wade in.

He should never have left last night.

He should have called Slim his damned self.

Now, he was going to take another crack at talking her into doing it.

And if she refused, he'd make the call.

Tack spoke for the first time.

To Hawk.

"I think you're fighting a losing cause here, brother."

Hawk didn't even look Tack's way.

He stared at Mag.

Then he said, "Personal shit on personal time."

"Gotcha," Mag muttered, wondering, since his day involved desk work, which he hated, how he'd wait until after it was done to track down Evan and lay into her ass.

"Shit gets twisted, Mag," Hawk continued, and Mag refocused on him, "her trouble worsens—"

"I'm gonna get her to call Slim," he assured.

"What I was gonna say is," Hawk went on, "you get approval before you use company resources."

Tack started chuckling.

Tex guffawed.

Elvira said, "Well, hump day just turned into bump day."

She then held out her fist to Tex.

Who did not hesitate to bump it with his own.

Fuck.

CHAPTER FIVE

Give Them Harmony

EVIE

The sun wasn't even up in the sky before I rolled out of a bed I'd eventually put myself in after I'd stopped blubbing.

But I didn't get that first wink of sleep.

I grabbed my phone off the charging mat and went to my texts just to torture myself.

My plea to Mr. Shade of the Long Car,

> **Please instruct on where to take this bag.**
> **ASAP.**

. . . still had the red UNDELIVERED warning next to it.

I had hit TRY AGAIN so often, I probably wore off my fingerprint.

But I did it once more anyway.

The message failed to send.

I realized I wasn't breathing properly so I forced myself to do that thinking I had limited options of what came next.

But, even if it was akin to banging my head against a wall, I was going to explore them.

I showered, didn't wash my hair, and pulled on my Wonder Woman tee, some frayed jeans, my red Chucks and a sloppy cardigan.

I then took the Trader Joe's bag I'd shoved the plastic sheeting back into and then hidden under my dirty clothes in my hamper, grabbed my bag and keys and went out to my car.

It wasn't even seven o'clock in the morning, but I didn't care.

The weather was chilly.

It was late February in Denver and that could mean anything from the possibility you could lay out to a blizzard hitting.

We'd had a mild spell.

That, apparently, was over.

With the bag stowed in my trunk, I drove to my mother's.

I was in such a state, I didn't even sigh when I saw my stepfather's big truck sitting next to my mother's SUV in their drive.

The gas-guzzler family.

I got out, locked up and jogged up to their front door.

I then leaned on the doorbell and didn't let up until the door opened.

Rob, my stepdad, wearing a faded tee and even more faded pajama bottoms, looked at me, his expression went from annoyed to alarmed, and he asked, "Jesus, Evie, you okay?" at the same time he was urgently pushing open the storm door.

Rob was a couple inches taller than me, relatively built with a bit of a beer belly, and good-looking, I supposed, for a stepdad.

He was also three years younger than my mother, something he didn't know about until two years after their wedding.

He'd thought he was three years older.

Mick had let that slip, and Rob had lost his mind.

I had to hand it to him, he wasn't angry because he was younger than my mom and had some idea that the man in a relationship should be older.

He was angry because she'd lied to him, kept up that lie for years, married him amid a deception, and he was not down with that.

I was there during one of their many fights on this subject and heard him say (or shout) that it wasn't only a lie she'd told and didn't intend ever to divulge the truth. And it wasn't the age, he didn't care about the age.

It was that she didn't trust in his love enough not to care about the age herself.

I had to say, I was with him on all that.

Sadly, thus began the cheating, and I suspected that wasn't about being married to an "older woman."

His strike back was messed up, and I *way* did not condone it.

But what Mom had done was messed up too.

It sucked he was a cheater, because there was a lot to like about him.

He was nice. He could be funny. He was responsible in the sense he'd been gainfully employed the whole time I'd known him with the goal of working toward a decent retirement. He treated his own kids from his first marriage great and seemed at his best when his mingled family was together. He got irritated when I did stuff for myself that required tools, and that wasn't an "I'm a man" thing; that was an "I'm your stepdad and your real dad is a waste of space so better late than never you having someone who gives a shit" thing.

And he thought my sister was wasting her life and someone should shake some sense into my brother.

"Is Mom home?" I asked, moving in when he moved out of the way.

"She's still sleeping. I was about to jump into the shower. I'll wake her up in a sec," he said, closing the door behind me. "Now, answer me, sweetheart. Are you okay?"

I looked right into his eyes and stated, "Mick's got some trouble."

His face morphed right to pissed and he bit out, "That fuckin' guy." He got a lock on it and said, "Hang tight. I'll get your ma."

I hung as tight as I could when I felt like I was going to fly apart.

I also realized I hadn't made myself coffee, or stopped for one, which, after a night with no sleep, was a mistake.

It took some time, but Mom eventually came out with her mass of dyed-blonde hair falling in attractive, messy waves around her face and shoulders, and she was wearing a long, satin, sexy nightgown the likes she'd worn to bed her whole life.

They were also the likes no kid ever wanted to see her mom in, no matter that kid was now twenty-seven years of age.

"Jesus, Evie, it's barely seven" was her greeting.

Most of the adult population was awake and getting ready for work at "barely seven."

I didn't get into that.

I was about to launch in when she continued.

"And for God's sakes, I keep telling you," she jerked her head impatiently at my body, "you're never gonna find a man dressing like that."

I shut my mouth and stood immobile, staring at her.

She crossed her arms on her chest and prompted, "Well?" This before she looked to Rob and informed him, "Baby, I need coffee."

Rob was not pleased about this thinly veiled order to serve her and he communicated that by asking, "Carol, are you lookin' at your daughter?"

She gave him narrowed eyes. "Yeah."

"Your son was arrested again two days ago," he went on.

Mom turned to me. "Is this about Mick?"

"Of course it's about Mick. It's always about Mick," Rob answered for me.

"I don't under—" Mom began.

But Rob threw a long arm out my way, finger pointed, and he exploded, "*You* don't understand? *She* didn't make that boy!"

Mom turned fully to Rob and shouted back, "Don't shout at me!"

"Jesus Christ, you're a piece of work," he clipped.

"Fuck you, Rob. You wanna talk about a piece of work? I bet that brunette you're boning is a piece of fucking *work*," Mom shot back.

"Oh no, your girl is not showin' at our door first thing in the morning looking freaked right the fuck out and you use whatever you can grab hold of to continue to shirk responsibility for that fuckwit son you raised," he retorted.

"Do not talk about Mick that way!" Mom yelled.

Rob turned to me.

"Why are you here, sweetheart?" he asked.

"I—" I started.

"Listen, Evie, Mick's a big boy and he's made his own decisions for a long time," Mom cut me off to say. "They're not on me."

"And they're not on Evie either," Rob declared.

She rounded on him and snapped, "This is family business, Rob," making me wince because those words were regrettably familiar.

"You don't got my ring on your finger?" Rob asked.

"It isn't worth dick," Mom fired back.

Rob assumed an expression like she'd slapped him then opened his mouth.

"*Stop it!*" I shrieked, and they both turned to me.

Mom looked infuriated, and not just at Rob, at me.

If someone was going to be shrieking, she liked it to be her.

Rob looked even more concerned, mostly because I was a crier, not a shrieker, and he'd been around for five years, so he knew that.

Mom tried to assume a Mom Tone.

"Calm down, Evan."

No way I could calm down.

I was in a mess not of my own making.

And maybe the nicest guy I'd ever met walked out my door last night because I'd been a raving bitch for the purpose of him doing just that to save him from the likes of *this*.

"Mick gave my number to some shady guy who's making me guard a bag of meth and coke and oxy, waiting for instructions, and if I don't keep that stuff safe, something is going to happen to Mick," I informed them.

Mom's face paled.

Rob bellowed, "*Fuck!*"

"Why are you here?" Mom blurted, her entire demeanor

now panicked, and my body jolted as if I'd been sucker punched.

Rob slowly turned to Mom, his face a mask of fury.

He thought better of whatever he might have said because he then looked back to me.

"Call the cops," he ordered.

"Don't!" Mom cried, and Rob's head ticked in shock. "Just do what they tell you, Evan," she commanded me.

"Mom—" I began.

"Carol, have you lost your mind?" Rob asked.

"No," she snapped at him. "Mick wouldn't put Evie in danger." She again looked to me. "Just do what they say, it'll be done, and Mick will be safe."

Mick will be safe?

"Mom, I'm in possession of a grocery bag filled with *narcotics*," I said. "Because of *Mick*."

"Call the cops, Evie," Rob urged.

"Do not call the cops, Evan," Mom clipped. "Mick trusts you to handle this. Just handle it."

"I cannot believe what I'm fuckin' hearing," Rob declared, scowling at my mother.

"Stay out of it," Mom returned.

"Mom—"

"You know your brother," she said to me. "If this was problematic, he wouldn't lay it on you."

"I'm in possession of a grocery bag filled with *drugs*!" I exclaimed.

"Just stay cool and handle it," she retorted.

"Time to go shopping, baby," Rob said with supreme sarcasm. "Get yourself a new outfit so you can be all dolled up when they present you with your Mother of the Year award."

Mom's frame went into attack mode. I knew this since I'd seen it a million times.

And then she attacked.

"I will, love of my life," she snarled, "and right after that, we'll pick up your Husband of the Year award. That is, if you can tear yourself away from screwing everything that moves."

"I have not stepped out on you since Alice," he growled.

"*Do not say that woman's name in my house!*" Mom screeched.

And there we were.

"Right then, this is all about you," Rob returned.

"You can't just snap your fingers," Mom lifted a hand and did just that, "and trust again, *Rob*."

"Tell me about it, *Carol*."

I didn't have time to stick around for the show.

I'd seen it often enough, anyway.

And I wasn't that big of a fan.

So I turned around, walked out the door, headed to my car and was mildly surprised when Rob came jogging out into the chill in his bare feet and pajamas, calling, "Evie!"

I stopped at the door of my car and watched his approach as my mother stood in the door to their home and screamed, "*Rob! We were not done talking!*"

Rob ignored her, rounded my hood and stopped in front of me.

"I'll call off work, go with you to the station. Be with you when you turn those drugs over to the police and report this," he offered.

I stared up at him, and it wasn't mild surprise he'd left Mom's scene to see to me.

It was shock.

"And what about Mick?" I asked.

His voice grew gentle when he replied, "Sweetheart, I

think the time is now that you need to stop asking yourself that question."

I had a feeling he was right.

This wasn't posting bail, something Mick always paid back.

Eventually.

And this wasn't helping Mick move when his latest girl-friend kicked him out, an event where Mick always did something nice in return, even if he could just afford a twenty-dollar gift card to Anthropologie.

Or this wasn't Mick borrowing my car when his broke down.

Or Mick begging me to talk Smithie into letting him be a bouncer (something Smithie didn't do because he didn't hire anyone with a record if they hadn't been clean without any charges for less than six months, but Smithie, being Smithie, even though the effort was futile, ran a check on him anyway in an attempt to help me out).

So as annoying as all this was with Mick, and how over it I thought I was getting, it was just a part of being Mick's sister.

Now, Rob was right.

I should stop asking myself that question.

The problem was, now, I sensed Mick was in serious trouble.

And if I didn't look out for him, it'd be on me if that trouble landed on him.

And I didn't know if I could live with that.

"Evan, really, your best course of action with this is to give that shit to the cops and let them sort it out," Rob pressed.

"I'll think about it," I mumbled.

"Please, I'm beggin' you, do that," he said, and I

blinked up at him at the earnest tone of his voice. "And anytime, day, night, I'm at work, whatever, if you want me with you when you make the right decision, I'm there."

Well...

Wow.

"Thanks, Rob," I whispered.

"You take too much on, Evie," he whispered back. "I lose sleep over you."

He did?

Oh God.

I was gonna cry.

I had no idea.

"I'll...think" was all I could say.

He nodded.

He then turned and started to round my car but stopped at my front bumper.

"I love her," he said.

I didn't move, even to speak.

"I know it isn't healthy, not for either of us, the way we treat each other, but I can't walk away, can't cut her loose, even though the good we had turned bad, because I love her," he declared.

"I can't really talk to you about this right now," I told him.

Or ever.

"I know. I just want you not to have to think about one more thing. It's fucked up, but it's what we got, it's the way we are, we both choose to stay, and it's not yours to take on. You with me?"

That was as bizarre as it was sweet.

I nodded.

"Do right, Evie," he bid.

He had conflicting ideas as to what Mick thought was right.

But between Rob and Mag, that was two votes for the cops.

Rob jogged to the sidewalk and stood there in his pajamas while I got in my car and drove away.

And there it was.

My limited option exhausted.

I wouldn't go to my sister because I didn't want her embroiled in this.

And I couldn't go to my dad because there was no way he was up this early, and I could knock on his door until my knuckles were bloody and he wouldn't get up.

What he probably would do when he found out was be furious at Mick but not be much help otherwise.

I didn't even know what I expected from Mom and Rob.

Maybe just not being alone in this.

I sorta had Rob.

But Mom was...

Mom.

I was halfway home when I got a call.

It was Charlie, my other boss.

I stripped four nights a week, Sunday, Monday, Wednesday and Friday.

Twelve additional hours a week (that sometimes stretched to more like twenty, if Charlie was in a bind), I filled in on-call, site-support work for Charlie at his company, Computer Raiders, a tech support business.

I'd taken the job because I was a tech kind of girl, it paid okay and it could be fill-in stuff for the time I didn't actually have on my hands to earn extra money, which anyone could use, but I always needed.

Since I had not done what I normally did over coffee of a morning—assess my all-important day planner— what I'd forgotten was that I was on call that day for the

Raiders, from seven to one thirty, with a half hour lunch break.

"Damn," I muttered, looked at the clock on my dash, saw I was officially open for business, grabbed my phone and took Charlie's call. "Hey, Charlie."

"Hiya, Evan. Texting you an address and emailing the sitch. Printer company, their system is down. Sounds like a virus."

Charlie liked us to wear black jeans and his black Computer Raiders golf shirt when were on duty.

I was thinking I forgot deodorant.

"I'll get on it, ASAP," I semi-lied to him, with "ASAP" being once I went home, changed, put on deodorant, and I didn't want to push it, but I had to, so also after I swung by a drive-through to get coffee.

"Thanks, Evan. Later."

I bid adieu, made the trek home in full fret about whether to stash the Trader Joe's bag in my apartment while I was out on a call or keep it with me, decided to keep it with me, but brought it in when I quickly changed clothes and took it back out when I left.

If any of my neighbors saw me carrying that bag back and forth, they'd probably wonder what was going on with me.

I couldn't think of that.

I had coffee to procure, a virus to clear and a system to bring back up that hopefully didn't have too much damage done to it by whatever wunderkind out there created a virus rather than putting their mind to something positive, life affirming and world enhancing.

I was in the midst of doing this, with a hovering printer-company manager staring anxiously over my shoulder, protesting too much that no one was allowed to get outside emails on company computers, which hinted that he was likely the culprit who opened a file with a virus, when the first call came in from my dad.

I got three more after that while still working.

I had to wait until lunch, which I ate at Mad Greens in an effort to deflect the pizza debauchery I'd engaged in the night before (which reminded me of Mag, which reminded me of the ugly things I said to Mag, which made me fight crying into my salad) to call my dad.

"Evie, sunshine of my life," he said in greeting.

Dirk Gardiner, my father, reminded me of that Bob Seger song "Beautiful Loser."

He was lovable. Affable. Gracious. He was "yes, ma'am," if a woman was six or sixty, and "no, sir," if a man was the same. And it was charming.

He'd wanted to hit it big in the music industry but sustained the one-two punch of not really having the talent and definitely not having the drive.

If he went somewhere, he wanted to stay at the Four Seasons, and since he could by no means afford that, he just didn't go at all.

He'd wanted a wife and family, the love and laughter, but no part in taking care of it.

And somehow, with me staying in contact, and my sister being Daddy's Little Girl, he got a lot of the former without much of a hint of the latter.

Though he wanted more, always wanted more.

He wanted it all.

And it was somehow the world's fault he didn't have it.

"Hey, Dad," I said, and shoved a huge forkful of salad in my mouth, because Charlie had another job for me, and he needed me to get it done before I was off at one thirty.

And I needed to get it done, because I'd grabbed my day

planner when I was home changing, and I had Gert that afternoon too.

"Your mom called," he shared.

Great.

I swallowed my salad and began, "Listen, Dad—"

"Bring it here, I'll unload it."

I stared at my greens.

"No problems," he continued.

"Are you . . . being serious?" I asked slowly to confirm.

"Sure. I got you covered, kid," he replied nonchalantly. "Give you a split, eighty-twenty. Me bein' the eighty, 'cause I'll be shifting it."

For once in this situation, I made a quick decision.

"Dad, that's not gonna happen."

"Serve him right. Stick in his craw, his old man did what he couldn't do."

So Dad assumed these were Mick's drugs, he was dealing, and this was not only Dad finding a way to profit off this current situation, which was unsurprising, it was a way to best Mick, which also wasn't surprising.

Dad's version of a win-win.

What wasn't, I noted, in any of that, was any thought to me.

Okay, I needed to check my planner and see when my period came last, because I thought I just got done with it, but I felt like I was going to start sobbing again.

Instead of doing that, I declared, "I'm not having this conversation."

"It'll get it off your hands and you won't have to worry about it," he pointed out.

"Yes, and not only will Mick have issues if I do that, and from what I can tell, they'd be very *serious* issues, *I* might have issues since this guy knows I have it and then I won't have it and he'll suspect I did what you're thinking of doing with it."

"Hadn't thought of that," he muttered.

Of course he hadn't.

"'Bye, Dad," I snapped.

"Evie! Wait!" he called.

I wanted to hang up.

I wanted to hang up.

I wanted to hang up.

"What?" I asked.

"Let this be done, girl. Let this be the last shit Mick unloads on you. Listen to your old man for once, yeah?"

"Yeah," I muttered.

"Look after yourself. I'm in a new band, we got a gig, come see me play. I'll shoot you the info in a text."

Another band.

I hoped it lasted, for his sake. Even if it was just local gigs.

But I knew it had no hope of lasting, because nothing my father had a hand in lasted.

"Right. Great. Looking forward to it," I said by rote.

"It'll be all right, Evie. You always land on top, doncha?"

At another time, in perhaps thirty years, when I had the time, I would have to ponder this.

Ponder how anyone could think that their daughter working two jobs, one of them stripping, to pay for her tuition, her rent, her food, to get various family members out of jams, who it was taking years to get her systems engineering degree because she was out of school more than she was in it because, if she had the money to pay for it, she didn't have the time to go to class, was landing on top.

I had a good car, because I worked hard to buy it.

I had a nice apartment, because I worked hard to have it.

This work, by the way, was mostly taking off my clothes and dancing on a stage with my body slicked with oil and strange men shoving money into the only remaining garment I wore.

I wanted a degree in something that fascinated me, a job making good pay, a husband (someday), a family (someday a little later), love, laughter, vacations, birthday parties, graduations, weddings and a decent retirement in a condo by a beach.

Oh, and to take off my clothes only in privacy for the rest of my life.

That's what I wanted.

I had thought that wasn't asking too much.

But maybe I thought wrong.

Maybe I should start taking selfies.

Of course, I'd have to have an Instagram account, something I did not have (and wasn't actually on social media at all, mostly because I didn't have the time for it).

But I could take apart and put together a radio by the age of six, I was changing the oil in my father's car by the age of eight, and I'd figured out how to do that myself.

I could start an Instagram account.

"Evie?" Dad called.

"Yeah, Dad. I always land on top," I said.

"That's my girl. See you soon, my darlin'. Later."

I put the phone down realizing he did not tell me to call the cops.

He also did not say, no matter when, day or night, he'd be at my side if I went to the cops or something else cropped up with this situation.

So, two votes for cops from two men in my life who weren't blood.

One vote for no cops from my mother.

And one essential abstention from my father.

Last, the person I really needed to talk to about all of this, my brother, I couldn't talk to because whatever he said could incriminate him.

I didn't know what to do with all of that.

I didn't know what to do at all.

What I knew was, I had to finish my salad, hit my call, and go get Gert.

It was grocery day.

* * *

"Evan, what's up? You aren't right."

I looked down to Gert, who was in one of those motorized, grocery-store chair-carts.

This was because she couldn't walk very far.

Into a restaurant when I took her to Chili's or Applebee's, yes.

Around a King Soopers, no.

"I had a bad date last night," I evaded, telling the truth, but not all of it.

She shook her head and scooted along the aisle toward the fruit juices.

Gert was all about fruit juices.

Being "regular" was a big thing for her.

"Boys these days, they don't know which end is up," she decreed.

Mag knew precisely where the ceiling was.

This thought made my heart feel heavy.

"Was he one of them metrosexuals?" she asked, reaching for the prune juice.

I took it from her and put it in her basket, thinking that Mag kind of was, being fit and well turned out.

Though, my guess, all that messy, sexy hair flew in the face of metrosexuality.

"There's a new one, you know," she said, not waiting for me to answer her question, as was her way.

Gert was alone a lot.

As in, almost all the time.

So, when she had company, she *talked*.

"*Spornosexual*," she continued. "Not so much about the grooming, all about the body. I wanna see me one of them. Was he one of them?"

Okay.

That sounded more like Mag.

"I'm afraid I'm not keeping track of all the terms for dudes these days, Gert," I admitted in an effort not to label Mag with the ridiculous word of "spornosexual."

"Well, I got lots of time on my hands and I know it all," she replied. "You have questions, ask me. I got answers. These days, everything is confusing. You gotta do your research. I know what heteronormative is, and you don't wanna be that. I know cisnormative, and you don't wanna be that either. And binary and nonbinary, and not that stuff you do when you're in class with your bits and bytes."

She then laughed and took the endcap probably a little faster than the King Soopers management wished their scooters to go.

But the next aisle was cookies, so she had reason.

"How'd the date go bad?" she asked.

Not because my brother is a jerk, surprisingly, but because I was a bitch, I did not answer.

"He just wasn't my type," I said.

To that, she stopped on a scooter squeal and looked up to me.

Gert had curly gray hair, two missing teeth, three sons

and a daughter who lived in different states and did their best from far away to take care of their mother, who flatly refused to move closer to her children.

And she fell in love with computers the minute she saw her first one in 1981 (she knew the exact year, and by the by, it was August).

In other words, we were kindred spirits two generations apart.

She budgeted everything from groceries to gas to electricity.

But she paid Charlie for tech support, because now, she lived on her computer with her email friends and her Facebook groups and her online forums, and if her system was down, her entire life was interrupted, and she was even more alone than her normal alone.

This being how we met.

And when I went to fix her computer and saw the state of her, and her house, bimonthly grocery shops and more than occasional trips to the likes of Cracker Barrel and Olive Garden, not to mention, me talking her into letting me clean her pad every once in a while, became part of my schedule.

I also talked her into giving up her yearly support payment to Computer Raiders, which felt disloyal to Charlie, but if something came up, she had my number. I didn't charge, but that didn't mean she could afford a trip around the world.

But for Gert and her fixed income, one thing loosening up for her meant a lot.

Another reason for my presence at the grocery store and our eventual trip to some family restaurant chain.

We'd have our usual discussion about it, but I'd be the one paying for both, and Gert would be all about the gratitude in order to hide her relief that she could pay her winter gas bill and maybe afford a haircut.

"That's it. You're in the doldrums because he wasn't your type?" she asked.

"Do you want the marshmallow Milanos?" I asked back to deflect.

"Evan, talk to me."

I focused on her to see she was very focused on me.

She was also worried.

"He was a great guy," I said softly. "And I messed it up."

"How'd a sweet, pretty girl like you mess it up?" she returned softly.

"It's a long story," I told her.

"Well, I got all day. But I know you don't," she said. "Still, I got all day, every day, and everything else on my body is goin' south, some of it literally, but my ears work just fine. So, you wanna talk, I'm an old lady, my husband's dead, but I remember the way it was and that it was hard work, finding a man."

"I'm actually not in the market for a man, Gert. It was a blind date. I just . . . liked him."

She tipped her head to the side. "And you can't fix what you messed up?"

Mag had exited the premises with a slam of the door.

I doubted it.

But for his sake, I wouldn't even try.

I shook my head.

Gert motored toward the Milanos, mumbling, "Shame."

She had that right.

"Think about you," she said, grabbing a pack of the toasted marshmallow Milanos. "I think about you all the time. Minute I met you, I was surprised you hadn't gotten yourself claimed. But that happens a lot."

She kept motoring.

And talking.

But I grabbed another pack of toasted marshmallow Milanos, and a double dark chocolate, both her favorites, because she'd be through the pack she nabbed in a day, but she also wouldn't take three because she knew I'd eventually be buying them.

I tossed them in the cart, and she talked through it.

"Good ones, they fester, and I know why. And it's a fool reason, men not wanting a woman who's got a head on her shoulders and herself sorted. They gotta play the hero. They gotta be the fixer. They can't be the one with the problems 'cause it's all a competition for them and they can't have their woman bestin' them at somethin'. So the smart ones, the adjusted ones, they go to waste. And the men pick the crackpots, then moan that their woman is a hot mess when they looked right past that one who'd give them harmony."

This sounded startlingly like my mother and Rob.

She shot me a semi-toothless grin and finished.

"I was a hot mess. My Stan sorted me out. Maybe you need to get yourself some trouble. Boys'll swoop in like vultures."

One could say I didn't have to search far for that.

I gave her an uncommitted grin.

She reached out and touched my hand.

"You'll find somebody, Evie. Someone perfect. I gotta believe that," she said. "This world, lettin' a girl like you be alone for too long, it'd be a world I don't understand."

I took hold of her hand and gave it a squeeze. "Thanks, Gert."

She clicked her teeth, I let her go, and she rounded the next endcap on two wheels.

Because that was the chip aisle.

And she did this saying, "Up for Applebee's?"

The thought of sitting in Applebee's attempting to enjoy a brisket quesadilla with that grocery bag in my trunk gave me the shivers.

Even so, I had a one-word reply.

"Always."

* * *

By the time we'd unpacked groceries, enjoyed our dinner, I got Gert back to her house, and I was on my way home, I had an hour to figure out where to stash the stash, get to Smithie's, gunk up my face and hair and get onstage.

I was going to have to be quick with the mascara.

The entire drive home, I did not come up with a good place to stash the stash.

I didn't feel safe leaving it at home. A shady guy knew my phone number. Who knew what else Mick told him, who that guy was talking to, and regardless, he knew my name and the Internet made all sorts of information people shouldn't have available in minutes.

I didn't feel safe leaving it in my car in Smithie's parking lot.

He had a secure parking lot, with lights and cameras.

Nevertheless.

Since I wasn't going to pop it by my dad's because he'd sell it, my sister's, and get her tied up in this, and definitely I wasn't going back to Mom's because I didn't want a scene, but also I didn't want to face Rob's disappointment that I wasn't making his version of the right choice, I decided to leave it in my car.

Best-case scenario (as such) was hiding it under my makeup table at Smithie's.

But I wouldn't take it into Smithie's.

I'd never do that to Smithie.

It seemed, all the way around, I had no good choices in this with anything.

In order not to have any neighbors seeing me yet again lugging around a Trader Joe's bag, probably by now expecting me to pet it and mutter about "my precious," I left it in the car as I went in to change out of my Computer Raiders uniform and into civvies to head to the strip club.

I stopped at the line of mailboxes to grab my mail and then dashed up the steps.

I opened my door, flipped on my light, took one step in, my mail fell out of my hands and I stopped dead.

My apartment was a mess.

No.

It was a *disaster*.

The stuffing from my vintage couch, my Urban Outfitters armchair and my cute, boho velvet Target floor cushion was everywhere.

My World Market toss pillows were decimated.

It looked like every door to every cupboard in the kitchen was open, the contents all over the countertops, and if those contents were breakable, they were broken.

My vinyl was skid marks across the floor.

My books were in a jumbled pile.

Keepsakes and sentimental knickknacks were also on the floor, some of them in pieces, because my shelves had been pulled down.

My TV was resting on its face on my rug.

Hanging planters and standing pots were down, dirt in mounds and sprays all over the floor where the containers had broken.

They'd even ripped my macramé pieces off the walls.

I was so shocked by what I saw, I couldn't move, couldn't think, my mind was a blank.

And then I let out a truncated scream when fingers curled around my upper arm and I was yanked the one step I'd taken into my apartment, out of it.

I was again inert and shocked to silence when all I could see was Mag's face, as well as his finger pointing in mine, and he was growling, "Do not move from here. In the door-frame, where I can see you."

I forced myself to nod.

Cautiously, with a gun in one hand, he pushed my door fully open and entered my space.

Okay, all right.

I'd been robbed.

No.

Um.

Okay.

All right.

Someone had come after that Trader Joe's bag and de-molished my apartment!

Oh my God!

The instant I started reacting to this—this reaction being beginning to tremble from head to toe—Mag was back.

Without a word, he shut my door, took my hand and dragged me to the stairs.

He then dragged me down them to his truck that was parked in guest parking.

He'd beeped the locks, had the passenger-side door open, me maneuvered into it, and when I didn't immedi-ately move to haul myself in, he picked me up, *again*, and dumped me in the seat.

When he was about to close the door, my hand shot out, fingers splayed to catch it.

"Danny, that bag is in my trunk," I whispered.

"It's been popped," he rumbled unhappily. "Your trunk is empty."

How...?

I'd only been away from it for maybe five minutes.

Whoever they were, they'd been waiting for me.

"Oh my God," I breathed.

The drugs were gone.

"Oh my God," I repeated.

"Belt up," he ordered.

"Danny—"

"Belt up, Evan."

"Danny!"

All of a sudden, my face was framed in both his hands, he used them to yank me his way, our foreheads collided, I felt the first strum of pain there since hitting it yesterday, and his eyes filled my vision.

"Keep it together, Evie."

I stared into his eyes.

"Are you getting it together?" he asked.

I was not.

I nodded.

"Good. Belt up. Let's go."

I nodded again.

He let me go.

I settled back and belted up.

Mag slammed my door and jogged around the hood.

I had no idea why Mag was at my apartment complex.

I had no idea where we were going.

But I was very ready to be anywhere but there.

CHAPTER SIX

One Day at a Time

MAG

Mag was driving very carefully in order not to freak Evie out even more than she already was.

He did this while at the same time attempting to lock down the feeling boiling inside him.

This was a problem.

A problem about which he was aware.

His anger issues.

Not that what he just saw done to Evie's pad and car wasn't something to get angry about.

Really fucking angry.

But, since he got out of the military, he had trouble managing his temper.

Now, even more than normally, he needed to keep a lock on it.

"My keys," Evie murmured.

He glanced at her to see her face was pale and tight, and she had a death grip on her little bag in her lap even though it wouldn't go anywhere because the long strap was crossing her body.

"Sorry, baby?" he asked as gently as he could and then looked back to watch where he was driving.

"I think...I think I dropped my keys when I dropped my mail."

He felt her eyes on him and glanced at her again to see they were round and filled with fear.

Seeing this, he tightened his fingers on the steering wheel so hard, he felt the tension as mild pain up the insides of his forearms.

"And...and, Danny, we didn't lock the door!"

Her voice was rising.

She was losing it.

But she didn't know they didn't need to lock her door.

There was nothing anyone would want in there.

Not anymore.

If her living room was a disaster, her bedroom was a catastrophe.

Mattress shredded. Drawers pulled out and broken. Clothing strewn everywhere, and a lot of it was ripped in the frenzy. Lamps smashed.

Whoever had gone in there had started up front, got tweaked the longer they searched and didn't find anything.

So they got ugly at the back.

"On it," he said to Evan, releasing his grip on the steering wheel and using his thumb to maneuver the buttons to get to his phone on the computer on the dash.

Auggie, by virtue of his name, was the first on the list.

So Mag hit go.

"Yo, brother," Auggie greeted. "Did you go—?"

He didn't let Auggie finish.

"Listen, I got Evie with me. Her place has been tossed. I

got there a coupla minutes after she did, and she'd just seen it. I pulled her out of there, but she thinks she dropped her keys. Can you call Lottie or Mo, get her address, get over there, get her keys and secure her place? And a call would be good to Hank, or Eddie, Mitch or Slim."

Auggie repeated Mag's earlier words, "On it," and immediately disconnected.

"Thanks," Evie whispered.

"Not a problem," he replied.

Evan said nothing.

Mag did not share that Hank, Eddie, Mitch and Slim were cops.

He'd get into that later.

For now, he assured, "It's gonna be all right."

"Unh-hunh," she mumbled.

She didn't believe him.

But it would be all right.

Seeing as he was going to make it that way.

The feel of the cab was unpleasant, anger coming from him, fear from her, which only served to notch up his anger, they both remained silent the rest of the drive to his place.

He guided his truck into underground parking, slipped it in his spot, and shut it down.

He angled out of his seat quickly, and after he'd rounded the bed, he saw Evan was already out.

He reached his hand to her, and she took it without hesitation, holding on to his fingers like she was dangling over the side of a building and he was the only thing keeping her from falling, her fingers squeezing his so hard, they bunched together with a sting of pain.

Mag's teeth clenched and he had to force them to release to say, "You're safe, Evie. Yeah?"

She looked up at him and nodded, but he knew she did not get behind her affirmative.

He tugged her to the elevators, and they were in them, Evan still holding on tight, when his phone rang.

He dug it out of his cargo pants, saw the screen said, Mo CALLING, and he knew that Auggie had been communicating.

He took the call by saying, "Hey, brother. She's with me, I got her and Auggie's on the way to her pad."

Mo's two words were so weighted with anger, they felt like boulders landing.

"She okay?"

"No."

Mo didn't reply.

That was good because Mag wasn't in the mood for conversation except to say what he was going to say next.

"I need you to talk to Hawk, Mo," Mag said. "You with me? Brock or Mitch, Hank or Eddie, I don't care who can do it. I want it arranged. You know what I mean. I want to talk to him. *Yesterday*."

"I'm with you," Mo replied.

Mo then disconnected.

And Mag had a feeling he'd be having a sit-down with her brother ASAP.

The elevator doors opened, and Mag got Evie out of it, down the hall and into his condo. He then took her directly to the fridge.

Still holding her hand, he opened the bottom-drawer freezer, pulled out the bottle of Fireball he had in there, closed the freezer with his shin and moved her to the cupboard.

He had to release her to do what he was going to do next, but considering she still had a grip of steel on his hand, he knew she needed that connection. He got close, lifted her hand to his chest, pried her fingers from his and then pressed her hand, palm flat against his heart.

"Stick with me," he murmured.

She was staring up at him and nodding.

She kept her hand where it was as he reached to the cupboard for a shot glass, nabbed it, opened the Fireball and poured her a shot.

He covered her fingers over his heart with one hand as he held the glass to her with the other.

"Shoot this," he instructed.

"I...I can't. Smithie doesn't like us to drink on the job. And I...Danny, I gotta get to the club."

She wasn't thinking clearly.

"Evie, you're not dancing tonight."

Her eyes got large.

He ignored that and repeated, "Drink this. Fast. It'll warm you up, smooth you out."

She shook her head. "I have to get to Smithie's."

"Baby, right now, you need to look after you and Smithie'd be the first person to say that. Now take the shot and let's—"

"I can't lose out on my tips."

"Evie—"

"I need my tips."

"Honey—"

"I think I need a new TV and...and..." She took a deep breath, and he thought she was doing it to get her shit together, but then she screamed, "*Everything!*"

He set the glass down and rounded her with his free arm, wrapping his fingers around her hand at his chest and keeping hold.

It was a good call.

She lost it.

Tears *and* struggling.

"Calm down, honey," he murmured, trying to contain her struggles without hurting her.

"It's all gone!" she cried.

"I know it's a lot to ask right now but you need to chill out, Evie. We're gonna sort this."

She suddenly stopped moving except to tip her head back, her pretty, warm brown eyes shining with tears, and she screeched, *"Everything I worked for! Gone!"*

Yeah.

It was gone.

Her cute, personality-plus boho pad.

Her clothes.

Her trunk jacked open on her car.

Even her medicine cabinet and linen closet had been raided.

All because of her *fucking* brother.

He let her go and lifted his hands out to the sides.

"Okay, then let it out," he offered. "Hit me. Wail on me. Scream in my face. That shit was fucked up and you need to let it go, so let it out, Evie. Hit me with it. I can take it."

She stared at him several long beats, but in the end, she didn't pound on his chest or shout in his face.

She crumbled.

Mag caught her.

She sobbed against his chest, shoving her face in while she was doing it, her fingers latched onto his tee at his sides, twisting it so he could feel the fabric tighten against his skin.

Maybe Brock or Mitch, Hank or Eddie getting Mag in to see her brother wasn't a good thing considering, in that moment, he'd gladly beat the absolute *shit* out of him.

"I don't...I-I don't have renter's insurance," she wailed against his chest.

Fabulous.

She tipped her head back and showed him her pretty face was still pretty, even red and wet with tears.

"They've got the drugs, Danny."

"I'm gonna sort it out," he told her.

"*How?*" she cried. "They're gonna hurt Mick."

Someone was gonna hurt Mick, and he had no issue with this.

In fact, he wanted to be first in line.

Before he could say anything, she tore from his arms, taking two steps back, shouting, "God! It doesn't matter, does it? It just doesn't matter!"

"What doesn't matter?" he asked quietly.

She threw out both arms wildly. "*Anything.* Anything I do. How hard I work. How low I have to go to crawl out from under the *piles* of *shit* life lands on me. Do you know what my dad's solution to this problem was?"

"No," he answered cautiously, though he knew by her face whatever it was, he wasn't going to like it.

"Take that bag to his house and he'd unload those drugs. Eighty-twenty split. He gets the eighty, of course," she said snidely.

Yeah.

He didn't like it.

Jesus.

Seemed like her dad was worse than her brother.

"Evie—"

She rushed him but not to get close or fall back into his arms.

To nab the shot of Fireball.

Once she tossed it back, in their current scenario, he

really did not want to think about how cute she was when she breathed out dramatically with her eyes going big, but it had to be said, she was cute.

She slammed the glass down on his counter and looked up at him.

"Okay, that didn't work. I don't feel very smoothed out," she announced.

"Evan," he whispered.

Her face started crumpling, but she drew in a sudden breath through her nose and shook her head angrily.

"Right so . . . right," she began confusingly. Then, unfortunately, she said more words, ones that made sense, just not ones he liked hearing. "So I'll go to Smithie's and I'll slither all over his stage and stick my ass in strange men's faces and earn their bills. I'll ask if he'll give me another shift, maybe two, every week, and after, oh, I don't know, a year of that, I'll be able to replace my furniture, my TV, my dishes. But enrolling for summer semester is out of the question. *Again.*"

For the first time, he wished he hadn't unloaded all his crap after he bought Mo's. He'd had a couch. And a recliner.

At least she'd have somewhere to sit.

"I need to . . . to call Smithie, tell him I'm gonna be late," she declared.

"You can't go to work tonight, Evie," he told her. "You're in a state."

And you might be in danger, he did not finish verbally.

"You saw my place, Danny. I can't *not* go to work."

"Yes, you can, because for the time being, you're gonna be staying here."

She blinked.

It just came out of his mouth.

But now that it was out, he liked the idea.

A whole lot.

If she was close, he could keep an eye on her.

"I'll talk to your apartment manager. Get you out of your lease," he said. "Mo's bed is still in his room. If you don't have rent to pay, you can save to set yourself back up, and you'll have a TV you can watch and a place to sleep."

She stood unmoving and stared at him, those brown eyes again huge.

And cute.

"Now, I'm gonna call Smithie and let him know you're not gonna be in tonight and why," he continued. "You're gonna get hammered if you want. Or I'm gonna get whatever food you want delivered and you're gonna eat yourself into a food coma. Or, if you got more crying to do, you can have at it. Or all three. But you're not stripping tonight. You're lookin' after you 'cause *I'm* gonna be looking after you."

"I can't move in here," she said.

"You can and you are," he returned.

"Danny, I...well..." She seemed at a loss for words before she found some. "That's very sweet. Incredibly sweet. And I don't want you to take offense, but it's also crazy."

He didn't want to remind her that Mick wasn't the only one fucked now that those narcotics were in the wind.

And he didn't want to say what he had to say next.

But he picked that one.

"Your bedroom was worse than your living room."

For a second, she didn't move.

Then she did.

To reach to the Fireball and pour herself another shot.

She threw it back and winced a little but recovered faster and put the glass down.

"Okay, now I'm feeling it," she muttered. "My belly's getting warm."

She called her stomach her "belly."

And her brother probably knew that, and still, he put her in this spot.

To cover his own ass.

He could not focus on that.

He had to focus on her and her brown eyes.

"We'll go to your place tomorrow, get what's recoverable, bring it back here and plan the cleanup effort," he stated. "Tonight is about mentally dealing. With me?"

Evan shook her head that she wasn't with him.

"Danny, I can't move in. We barely know each other."

"And I'm barely home."

Her brows ticked toward each other.

"So what do I care you're here?" he went on.

"Say I consider this, and I'm not really considering this," she stated quickly. "But say I do, I still wouldn't because I couldn't live somewhere and not pay rent."

"Yes, you could."

"Danny—"

"Six months rent-free," he said.

"I'm not haggling over living arrangements I'm not agreeing to," she returned.

Right then.

Shit.

He had to say it.

"Then I gotta tell you, Evan, that I can't let you live anywhere else because I just don't have that in me seein' as you're in more danger than your brother 'cause he's got cops guarding him and you got nothin'. But me."

More big eyes and these he didn't like.

"I'm in more danger than my brother?" she asked.

"That bag is gone, baby," he said carefully.

"But, when he gets back in touch with me, I can just tell Mr. Shade of the Long Car someone took it."

"And how do you think that'll go?"

He saw it dawn on her how that'd go and then watched it land on her, her hand reaching out to grab his counter in order that she could physically take the weight.

"Whatever your brother is into, we need to get to the bottom of it and sort it out," he said to the side of her head, considering she was staring down at her hand on his counter. "And by 'we,' I mean me."

She looked up at him and her voice was soft and shaky when she replied, "I can't move in with you and I also can't ask you to wade into this garbage."

"And here I'll note that you didn't ask."

She pushed away from the counter. "Danny—"

He cut her off.

"Evie, tell me, is it gonna be booze, food or tears? I haven't had dinner, so I'd pick number two with a little of one. But I didn't get my apartment tossed today so it's lady's choice."

She studied him and she did it so long, he was about to say something.

But she beat him to it.

"Why?" she asked.

"Why what?" he asked back.

"Why would you offer to help me, give me a place to stay, get involved in this mess?"

"There are a lot of reasons why," he evaded.

"Tell me two," she bossed.

That cut through his anger, because from the start, he liked her version of attitude.

Though he didn't have an easy answer because a lot of

it had to do with wanting to get into her pants. That said, he also wanted to get to know her better, either before or after getting into her pants.

But more of it had to do with the fact he was just not that guy who could handle knowing someone was in trouble, he could help, and then not help.

Especially a woman.

He went with, "Because I like you."

"Why?" she asked again.

But now, he was confused.

"Why do I like you?"

"It was just last night, Danny, so I remember being a raving bitch to you."

"Evie—"

"And I shouldn't say this, because I should keep you safe..."

Keep *him* safe?

Before he could cut in, she kept going.

"But I didn't mean it. I had to latch on to the only semi-negative thing I knew about you, so I did. I mean," she tossed out a hand, "it's not fair to label you something I'd lose my mind if you labeled a woman the same way."

And again, before he could utter a word, she got in there.

This time to mutter, "Though, it's uncool a man's thought of as a *man* if he sleeps around and a woman is considered easy."

He went careful but he didn't stop himself from reaching to her, using a finger to hook her belt loop at the side of her black jeans, and tugging her a little closer.

He considered it progress in a variety of ways when she let him.

"The only semi-negative thing about me?" he teased,

not about to show how relieved he was that she didn't mean the shit she'd hurled at him last night.

She'd just been overemotional.

And trying to "keep him safe."

He still didn't get that.

But he'd get into it later.

"Danny, I can't stay with you," she said quietly. "Even more now."

"Why even more now?" he asked.

"If you like me."

Oh shit.

He felt his spine stiffen and his lips were the same when he asked, "You don't like me?"

"I mean, you know...because...," she lifted both hands between them and flipped them out before not answering his question, which, thank fuck, answered his question in the way he wanted it answered, "it'd be awkward."

"I'll be a gentleman," he muttered, watching her bite her lip.

Then he watched those lips whisper, "Danny."

No one called him Danny but his mother, his sister and Mo's sisters.

He'd been that in high school.

He'd earned the name Mag in the Marines.

Danny had died somewhere in between.

Every time Evie said it, it felt like a resurrection.

Like he could be that kid again who didn't live knowing what absolute, unqualified shit some people out in the world lived.

Especially women.

But in this instance, with his finger in her belt loop, her close, he felt her calling him that name in his throat and chest and regions south.

He had to focus, so he lifted his gaze to hers.

"You're not comfortable staying here, then I'll take you wherever you wanna go, but a caveat to that, baby, is that, if where you wanna go I don't deem safe, we're coming back here," he offered.

But she stood there and said nothing.

"So, I'm guessing from what little you said, your dad is out," he prompted.

Suddenly, she couldn't meet his eyes and she was stammering again.

"I . . . maybe I . . . well, what I mean is, maybe I can stay tonight, in Mo's old bed," she said the last four words very fast. "And tomorrow, I can figure out what I'm gonna do."

She didn't have anywhere else to go.

She didn't have anyone to look after her.

He remembered then all she'd said about her family.

"Are you keeping them safe from this shit?" he asked, in case he'd assumed wrong.

"My stepdad, Rob, has guns, but if he knew this degenerated the way it has, he'd take them to the county jail in order to try to shoot Mick and at this current moment, I can't deal with *two* family members in the pokey. One was already too many."

At least her stepdad didn't sound like a jackass.

Though she'd said the man was a cheater, so strike that.

It was then he noticed what she was wearing.

"What's Computer Raiders?" he asked.

"My second job," she muttered.

What?

"You got a second job?"

"Tuition doesn't pay itself."

He stood solid as it hit him, *she did not have anyone looking after her.*

Mac had told him she was twenty-seven, so not the usual age of a kid out of high school hitting a university with her parents' help.

But she also didn't demand he take her to her mom's and her dad sounded like a dick.

So, she didn't have her parents' help.

She didn't notice his reaction.

She spoke. "Okay, so, um, we have a plan. I'll sleep on it tonight, here, thank you for offering. And I'll come up with a plan to tackle this situation tomorrow."

He'd take that because he knew she'd sleep on it here for the foreseeable future.

But if he had to see to her doing that one day at a time, then he would.

"Yeah, we have a plan," he agreed.

"Is there a drugstore close? I should get a toothbrush."

He tugged her belt loop and brought her a little nearer.

But he didn't push it, stopped and said, "You hang with your new pal, Fireball, and I'll go out and get you one. You had dinner?"

She nodded. "But I can go with you. And we'll get you something to eat."

He'd boil some pasta.

"I'm covered."

"Danny—"

"Babe, I got food here. I'm good. You want a toothbrush, I'll get you a toothbrush. Then we can hunker down and regroup to tackle tomorrow."

She nodded then looked him up and down, turned her head to take in the room, came back to him and stared at his chest a beat before she lifted her eyes to his face.

"Why were you there?" she asked

"Where?"

"At my place after I...after what I said last night?"

It was moot now, why he was there.

"I think I mentioned I like you."

"Danny," she whispered.

He decided to let her in on his plan.

Kind of.

"We'll get you through tonight. Then we'll get you through tomorrow. And onward. One day at a time, Evie. Now call Smithie and let him know you're not gonna make it tonight."

"He's gonna freak," she muttered. "He doesn't like his girls in jams."

Mag knew the feeling.

"He'll be more pissed you kept it from him. Call," he urged.

She nodded, then, when she bent her head to open her little bag, he reluctantly let her belt loop go.

She stepped away to make her call, so Mag pulled out his own phone and texted Mo.

Word?

"It's okay, Smithie," he heard her say as he turned to the pantry to find some pasta. "I'm with Danny." Pause then, "He's a friend of Mo's." Pause and then a soft, "Yeah."

That made Mag grin.

And his night continued its upswing, which was the only way it could go, when he got Mo's reply.

Hawk's making the calls.

Hawk would get him in to see her brother.

Then Mag would find out what the fuck was going on.

He'd take care of it and make Evan safe.

And then he could focus on other things concerning Evie.

Like her second job.

Her fucked-up family.

And getting her back to school.

CHAPTER SEVEN
Do Over

MAG

To say Mag was antsy and getting more pissed by the second was an understatement.

He, Mo and Hawk were standing in a room at the county jail, waiting to be shown to another room that had Evan's brother in it.

And they'd been standing there for over half an hour.

Evie was home, with his buds Boone and Axl, the bottle of Fireball and zero knowledge this was what he was doing.

When he'd received word that Hawk had arranged the meet, he'd called Boone to ask him to come keep an eye on Evie while he was at the jail.

And, of course, Boone had brought Axl so they both could get a good look at her, assess her suitability for Mag, as well as take her back while Mag was away.

Regardless of the fact that Boone and Axl were Hawk's boys, both were built, and it was unmistakable they could handle themselves, it took Evan visible effort to allow him to walk out the door to see to some vague "business."

She was still freaked.

It was natural.

But it served to piss him off even more.

He did not like leaving her.

He did not like keeping his whereabouts from her.

He needed to get this done, find out what was happening, form a plan, go home to her and share where he'd been and what was going on.

And all that started with, at some point, clapping eyes on Evan's brother.

"As much as I appreciate you sorted this meet for me, Hawk, I got a woman at home who started this fucked-up shit with me at her side and didn't like me leavin' her tonight when it got ugly," he growled at Hawk, who cut his eyes to Mag. "If this is not gonna happen, I gotta get back to her."

"Let Slim do his thing," Hawk replied.

Mag opened his mouth right when the door opened, and Brock "Slim" Lucas stood in it.

Brock looked to Hawk, to Mag and back to Hawk before he proved he was adept at reading people when he said, "I better not regret this."

"He's my man, Slim," was all Hawk said as reply.

Four words from Hawk served two purposes.

The first, Brock nodded, jerked his head to the hall to indicate they should follow him and moved out of the door.

And the second, Mag was reminded that his behavior reflected on Hawk, so he had to keep his shit tight.

Mag glanced at Mo, whose eyes were locked to Mag, his expression blank, but as usual with Mo, his bud found alternate ways to communicate.

And the stiff line of his humongous frame, the tension in his neck, veins popping there, shared how he felt about one of his woman's friends being in a situation.

Mo wouldn't be anywhere else, not with someone Lottie cared about finding trouble, not with Mag in the mix, and Mag was glad he was there for those purposes.

But more, even as tall and built as Mag was—six four and clearly someone you'd think twice about messing with, Hawk a couple inches shorter, but having that same look— Mo was gargantuan, and one look at him would put the fear of God into anyone with half a brain.

The jury was out as to if Mick Gardiner had half a brain.

They'd soon see.

They walked down a hall, into a secure area and Brock led them into a small room with a table and four chairs. Three on one side. One on the other.

Chained to that table was a man who Mag knew would be relatively tall when he stood, maybe six foot, a little over.

He was also undeniably Evan's brother.

Her same straight, reddish-brown hair.

Her brown eyes.

Her slender frame.

There were obvious differences outside gender.

Evie's hair was long, falling in thick sheets over her shoulders.

She was also all kinds of pretty and this guy was not all that good-looking.

And her brother had an olive cast to his skin, whereas Evie's was flawless porcelain.

Last, this guy was straight-up skinny, and although Evan was slender and had smallish tits, she had a generous ass.

Before he'd seen her that had not been Mag's thing. He was a legs man (something she totally had) and a close second on that was tits.

He was not an ass man.

Now, conjuring up the image of her in the face of her brother, he wondered what he'd been thinking all these years, because with Evie, he was all about her ass.

Mick Gardiner got a load of what was entering that room where he was about to have a late evening chat, and after Mo strolled through, he hid his alarm behind douchebaggery.

"What? Has the government picked me to be disappeared in order to force me to perform covert military operations?" Mick asked, presumably referring to the uniform Hawk did not require that they all had adopted of cargo pants, military boots and tee, or in Mo's case, a compression shirt that left little to the imagination of how much he could bench press.

"Uncle Sam wouldn't take you," Hawk replied as he moved behind the chairs and jerked his chin up at Mag, his way of saying, *I'm already done with this guy, sit down and get on with it.*

Mick's attention went to Mag.

"I wouldn't have picked you to be the leader," he said to Mag. "Boss." He indicated Hawk with his head. "Enforcer." He indicated Mo. "Sidekick." He tipped his head to Mag.

"I'm dating your sister," Mag shared, ignoring the slight and folding into a seat opposite the asshole.

The man's eyebrows rose but his body went stiff, probably so he wouldn't shift in his seat and give something away.

"I was with her last night when she had her meet with

the guy in the Continental," Mag told him. "And I was with her today when she got home to find her apartment trashed."

Mick turned white.

But he did not have this reaction for the reason Mag would suspect—his sister's apartment got trashed, and this indicated she might be in danger.

No, it was because, straight from his mouth, "She was supposed to go meet Snag alone."

Mag stayed silent in order to take a very long, slow breath into his nose.

Once he'd accomplished that, he said, "The trunk on her car was also jacked. That'll need to be repaired. Though that's probably covered under insurance. But her apartment was not."

Mick sat still and said nothing.

Mag decided to move to something this dick might care about.

"The Trader Joe's bag was in her trunk," Mag informed him.

"Fuck, shit," Mick muttered, looking away.

Christ.

As suspected, Evie's brother was dirt.

"Now, as you can guess, I give zero fucks about you," Mag told him, regaining his attention, the man's eyes forming into slits. "We're here to find out how much trouble you landed your sister in."

"Snag needs that bag," Mick said.

"I can imagine. Your problem is, it's gone. What needs to be communicated is that it's your problem, not Evan's," Mag replied.

He leaned forward. "You don't understand. When the time comes, *Snag needs that bag*."

"I *do* understand," Mag returned. "What *Snag* needs to understand is that if he wanted it, he should have taken it himself or chosen more wisely who he entrusted it to."

"He couldn't—" Mick began but stopped and jumped when Mag pounded his fist on the table.

Mag felt Mo get closer to his back.

Hawk didn't move.

"You are missing," Mag said low and slow, "how I do not give a fuck what your problems are. I'm here for Evan and only for Evan. She is out of this situation. It no longer concerns her. It never did. And the only person in this situation who knows the players is you. So, you either communicate that or you share with me who needs that message delivered and I'll communicate it. This is what we'll be talking about. What you need or this Snag asshole needs is of no interest to me. Now, how do we extricate your sister from your shit?"

Mick leaned deep into the table and hissed, "That bag gone, I am dead. Do you get me? I . . . am . . . *dead*. You gotta find that bag."

"Do you have a hearing problem?" Mag asked.

"Evie is not gonna want her brother dead," Mick spat.

"Evan is experiencing some epiphanies regarding her family," Mag shared. "You wouldn't know this, so I'll educate you that that kind of thing happens when you open your apartment door and see everything you worked for reduced to garbage because your brother is a piece of shit."

Mick sat back hard, his chains clanging.

"Now, guide her to seeing the light and prove that maybe you got something worth the loyalty she's given you and tell me how to *extricate her from your shit*," Mag pushed.

"I tell you anything, I'll be put down faster than I will be when they find out that bag is in the wind," Mick returned, and the chains clanked again as he tossed out both hands, which were cuffed to hooks in the table. "And newsflash, soldier, I haven't forgotten where I am, you know, cameras and tape recorders and shit. So, anything I say here can be used against me, and first, I'm not a dumbass, second, I'm not a rat, and third, if by some miracle I survive this shit, I don't want anyone thinkin' I'm either of those things."

"So, in an attempt to cover your ass, you're throwing your sister to the wolves," Mag noted and finished, "Again."

Mick tipped up his chin three times to indicate the three men in the room with him and replied, "Seems she's got protection."

"I'm telling her every word of this chat," Mag shared.

Mick couldn't quite hide his flinch.

So he cared.

But did he care enough?

"She's already asking herself serious questions about her relationship with her brother, you don't help me help her, she's not going to have a relationship with her brother," Mag continued.

"If I tell you, she won't *have a brother*," Mick returned.

"Considering she lost nearly everything today because of you, her life goals put on hold because her brother is useless piece of trash, I'm wondering how broken up she'll be about that," Mag stated.

Mick said nothing, but he was stewing, just not in a good way. He was pissed at having to take Mag's insults.

Mag held his gaze.

Mick remained silent.

Quietly, his voice rumbling with disbelief, he asked, "Are you honestly gonna let me walk out that door without the tools I need to get your sister safe?"

"Evie always lands on her feet."

Mag flattened his hand on the table and leaned into it.

He felt Mo get closer.

He felt Hawk go alert.

But once he did that, he stopped.

And then he said, "The thing you don't get is, the people in our lives that we love, if we're worth anything, anything at all, we bust our asses to make it so they aren't in a situation where they have to land on their feet 'cause we made it so they're always on solid ground."

Mick's face twisted before he replied, "Well, then, it seems it's lucky she's now got you."

"Yeah, seein' as I gotta help her survive the likes of you," Mag returned.

The flinch he got at that was not at all hidden, but before Mag could hone in and work that, Mick's face set to belligerence and he taunted, "Tell her I said hi."

"I will, right after I tell her you didn't give that first fuck you cost her everything and didn't think once about anyone but yourself, not even to ask how she's doing, which, by the way, is not very good."

With that, Mag pushed up and walked right out of the room.

Mo and Hawk followed him.

Brock was waiting outside the door.

They moved farther down the hall before they stopped and huddled.

Hawk gave him a look and Mag braced because he could tell his boss was sliding into guru mode.

He'd worked for Hawk for years and the man deserved mad respect. He was a good boss, a loving husband and a doting father. He was also intelligent, experienced and returned the respect he had if it was earned.

And he was an excellent teacher and generous with his knowledge.

But Mag wasn't sure he was in the mood for Hawk to go guru.

"You gotta play this the way you feel you should play this, but with that guy, you might want to think about giving to get," Hawk advised.

Mag shook his head. "Evan strips to pay her bills and put herself through college. She does that and still has a second job. There might be a few things she can salvage from her apartment, Hawk, but it won't be much. That's an annoyance for a guy who makes the cake you do, a setback for a guy who earns like me, but it's a disaster for Evie."

Mag lifted a hand and stabbed a finger in the direction of the room they'd just left and carried on talking.

"*He* put her there. He knew it was a possibility she'd be there or in some other situation that'd have her shit twisted, and he didn't give a fuck. I'm not gonna offer him protection or ask Brock to get the cops to swing him a deal if he takes care of his sister. He's her blood. He shouldn't need to get something to give that to his sister. I'll sort her shit and whatever happens to him is not my problem. And I'll find a way to get Evan to that same thinking."

Hawk did not argue this, and Mag knew it was because he agreed, he just wanted Mag to consider the options.

Mag looked to Brock. "You know someone on the street called Snag who drives a Lincoln Continental?"

"My beat isn't narcotics anymore," Brock answered. "But I'll ask around."

Mo entered the conversation. "You get answers, you give them to me."

"Mo—" Mag started.

Mo turned to Mag. "For now. You take care of Evan. While you do, I'll be lookin' into shit. Your focus now is her. I'll work with Aug, Boone and Axl to make it so, when that can shift, you hit the ground running."

Mag nodded then gave his attention back to Brock. "Appreciate you arranging this."

"Not a problem," Brock murmured. "Hate to say this, bub, but you're gonna have to bring her in. She needs to make a statement."

Mag hated to hear it, but he knew that.

"I'll talk to her," he replied, then cast his gaze between all of them. "I gotta get home to Evie."

He got nods and chin lifts.

Then he took off.

*   *   *

Mag was standing at his door, saying good-bye to Boone and Axl.

Evie, they'd told him, had crashed an hour before.

Probably the Fireball.

And spent emotion.

And the fact, with two jobs, one she worked that was physical and ran into the dead of night, she had to run herself ragged.

"Thanks for lookin' out for her," he said.

"If you need anything..." Boone stated.

"She's gonna need help with cleanup of her pad," Mag told him.

"When you dig in, call, I'm there," Boone replied.

"I'm in too," Axl said.

That meant, whatever went down with them while he was away, Evan had earned their approval.

Not a surprise, she was kind of a dork, but it was seriously cute.

He nodded.

Boone lifted a hand, Axl lifted his chin, and they took off.

Mag shut the door and locked it.

He was turning out lights and telling himself it would be invasive to check on Evan to make sure she was sleeping when he heard the door to Mo's room open.

He arrested when he saw her in the sliver of the door she hadn't opened all the way.

Boone or Axl had given her one of his tees to sleep in.

Christ.

Yeah, she had great legs.

"Hey," she said, opening the door farther and leaning against the jamb.

Oh yeah.

Great fucking legs.

"Can't sleep?" he asked.

"I..." She gave her head some short shakes then asked, "You went to go talk to Mick, didn't you?"

Shit.

Busted.

"We'll chat about this tomorrow," he told her, moving her way.

"He didn't do anything to help, did he?"

He stopped in front of her and murmured, "Evie."

"It's okay," she said.

"It's really not," he replied.

"I'm used to it," she mumbled.

"You shouldn't be," he returned.

She sucked her lips between her teeth.

"You gonna be able to sleep?" he asked.

"Sure," she lied.

Damn, he wanted to hold her.

There, in the doorway to Mo's old room.

Or take her to his bed, stretch out beside her and hold her all night.

Give her something solid. Give her proof not everyone in her life was a dick.

He didn't do either.

He walked back to the kitchen, nabbed the toothbrush and tube of toothpaste that he'd picked up for her, brought it back and handed it to her.

"Didn't think to ask your brand," he said.

She was staring down at the stuff in her hand, seemingly frozen to the spot.

"Evie?" he called, and her head came up.

"Toothpaste is toothpaste," she replied, her voice husky. "It's just sweet you remembered."

At least he gave her that.

Though, from the look on her face, it seemed, for her, it was a fuckuva lot more than toothpaste.

"Danny, I don't know how I can thank—" she began.

"Stop, baby," he murmured. "Anyone would do what I did when they walked up to you with your apartment like that."

"Not anyone."

That was definitely her experience.

"You're a good guy and now I feel like an even bigger bitch I was so ugly to you last night," she whispered.

"We're beyond that," he reminded her.

"Okay," she said unconvincingly.

"Try to get some sleep," he urged.

"Okay," she repeated.

"If you can't, my room's right over there." He pointed

to the door in the unit opposite hers, across the kitchen. "Knock, honey. I'll get up, we'll chat, watch some late-night movies, whatever."

"Okay," she said again, though he knew she wouldn't disturb him just like he knew she probably wouldn't get any sleep. "Thanks again, Danny."

"Don't mention it, Evie. Rest well."

"You too."

Slowly, she slid out of the door, closing it behind her.

Mag stood staring at it, the feelings boiling inside him again.

He'd developed coping mechanisms to handle his temper.

Talking to Mo, Auggie, Boone, Axl, some of them or all of them.

Working out.

Finding someone to fuck.

And last recourse, getting drunk, though sometimes that could bite him in the ass.

He could call any of his friends and they'd talk or come over and listen.

Mag didn't do that.

It might tweak Evie.

Not to mention, at this juncture, with her life a mess, she didn't need to learn he was all kinds of fucked up.

So instead, he turned off the kitchen light, walked to his room and went to bed.

* * *

Mag woke because he smelled bacon.

He stared at his pillow, then he threw back the covers, angled out of bed, walked to his door and pulled it open.

Yeah.

Fuck him.

That was what he'd hoped to see.

Evie, in his tee, in his kitchen, cooking breakfast.

If she didn't want him to see her legs, she'd be in her clothes.

She wanted him to see her legs, her in his tee, and all that communicated.

Thank Christ, today was starting a helluva lot better than yesterday.

She was standing at the stove.

She turned at the sound of his door opening, her mouth moving like she was about to say something, but when she clapped eyes on him, she went completely still, her gaze glued to his chest.

Mag slept in loose shorts.

He worked at his body because he liked doing it.

He did it because it helped him keep his emotions in check.

And he did it because it was a requirement of his job.

But right then, he was fucking glad he did.

"Mornin', Evie," he said, moving out of his room.

She blinked rapidly, her eyes shifting down to his abs, lower, then skimming quickly up.

He never would have imagined he'd wake up the morning after last night (and the one before) and walk out to his kitchen grinning.

But that was what he did.

He buried the grin, leaned a hip against the counter of the island, crossed his arms on his chest, which made her drop her eyes to it again before they speeded back up to his face, and he caught his lip twitch before he asked, "You manage to get any sleep?"

"A couple of hours," she replied.

"Good," he muttered.

"I, uh . . . thought I'd start my thank-you process by making you breakfast," she told him.

He quirked his brows. "Your thank-you process?"

"It has multiple layers. Or it will. I haven't decided what those are going to be yet. But," she indicated the frying pan with her fork, "it starts with breakfast."

He smiled at her. "Baby, you don't have anything to thank me for."

At least, not yet.

"On that, we disagree," she mumbled, turning back to the pan. "It's good you're up, how do you like your eggs?"

"However you make them."

She looked at him again. "What's your favorite way?"

"Eggs are eggs, babe. Whatever way you wanna make 'em, I'll like."

She was going to say something, but toast popped up and that took her attention.

So he said, "Gonna go brush my teeth. Then I'll be back, and I'll help you finish breakfast."

Her attention returned to him, but he pivoted, walked to his room and through it to the bathroom. He used it, washed his hands, did the brush thing, the floss thing, splashed water on his face and pulled his wet fingers through his hair.

And he absolutely did not tug on a tee on his way back to the kitchen.

She had plates down, a stack of toast started, bacon resting on a paper towel by the stove and was scrambling some eggs when he returned.

"Just sit down, Mag, and let me serve you. If you help, it won't be a thank-you," she ordered, not glancing his way.

But...

Mag?

She had not once called him Mag, unless it was right after he told her to do that, but then she went right back to Danny.

Seemed in those hours she didn't sleep she'd made some decisions about how she was going to move forward on some things.

Though not all the right decisions.

Making breakfast in his tee, correct.

Calling him Mag, incorrect.

He saw the coffeepot was full, so instead of heading to a stool at the island, he moved that way.

Which was closer to her.

"Just gonna get a cup of joe," he told her.

"I can get it for you," she offered quickly, turning his way. "How do you take it?"

Fortunately, he'd gotten close by the time she turned his way so he could get up in her space.

Something he did.

Her eyes got wide, then they dropped to his chest, grew lazy, he grinned, and they shot back up to his face.

"Mag, I—" she began.

"Danny," he muttered, looking at her mouth.

Her head ticked, and she said, "But I thought you liked to be called—"

She again didn't finish, seeing as he lifted a hand, slid his fingers along the side of her neck and up into her hair behind her ear.

Yeah, that hair was as soft as it looked.

"Didn't sleep much either, worried about you and if you were getting any rest," he told her.

"Well, I...that sucks. I'm sorry. I—"

She stopped talking when he slid the tips of his fingers through her hair and down the line of the back of her neck.

"I gotta work today, but you can stay here," he said. "I'll talk to Mo. They got a security system at their pad. Mac danced last night, so she's probably asleep, but when she gets up, you can hang with her. Around lunch, I'll come and get you and take you over to their place."

"Mag—"

"Danny," he corrected, running his fingers under her ear, feeling her shiver, fighting another grin, then he stroked her throat with his forefinger and kept talking. "When I get off work tonight, I'll come get you and we'll pop in at the police station. Make a quick statement. Give them what we got to help them do their jobs."

"The police?"

He didn't address that.

He kept rolling.

"And then we'll grab a bite and go to your place, check it out, see what we can salvage, form a plan of attack for cleanup. Boone and Axl said they'd help."

"They did?" she whispered.

"Yeah," he confirmed.

"That's nice," she kept whispering.

But now she was watching his mouth.

"You like them?" he asked.

Her brows twitched.

"Who?" she asked his mouth.

He couldn't beat back the smile at that.

"Boone and Axl."

"They were great," she mumbled, again, to his mouth.

He dipped his head closer to hers.

She swayed toward him.

Oh yeah.

He slid his hand again to the back of her neck and murmured, "How 'bout, since you're closer, you pour me a cup, and I'll finish these eggs."

"What?"

She was still solely focused on his mouth.

"Evie?"

"Mm?"

"Honey, you keep lookin' at my mouth like that, I'm gonna be forced to give you a good morning kiss."

She did not take her eyes from his mouth, but Mag didn't give her a good morning kiss.

Evie lifted her hands, latched on to either side of his neck and yanked him down at the same time she was surging up, and one thing he could say.

Her aim was true.

With her lips she smushed his lips back into his teeth so bad he tasted that tang you got when you took one to the mouth.

She then let go, jerked away, put her fingers to her mouth and muttered, "Oh God, what's the matter with me? I'm so sorry."

But through this, Mag turned to the stove, shoved the eggs from the flame, turned off the burner, then went right back to her.

"Do over," he said.

She dropped her hand. "Wh-what?"

"Do you want to kiss me?" he asked.

Her gaze dropped to his chest, shot up, but stopped at his mouth before it seemed she had to force it to his eyes.

She wanted to kiss him.

"Do over," he repeated, reaching to her, wrapping his hand around the back of her neck and pulling her closer.

"Mag—" she began.

"Danny," he growled, angled his head and took her mouth.

After her first attempt, he was surprised she opened right away.

Even surprised, he didn't let that opportunity slip.

He slid his tongue inside.

She tasted of coffee and woman, her soft hair all around his hand...

Shit.

This was a bad idea.

Strike that.

It was a fantastic idea.

Terrible timing.

He started to end the kiss, moving his hand to the side of her neck to gently press her away.

But she latched on again, this time to either side of his head, before she plunged her fingers in his hair, curled them around at the back and held him to her, tipping her head and sucking his tongue deep.

Jesus.

Nice.

Evie pressed close.

Mag rounded her with his free arm, pulled her closer and took the kiss deeper.

She whimpered and fisted her hand in his hair, her nails scraping scalp.

He felt that in all the important places and growled his approval down her throat.

They went at it and Mag was feeling it in his cock, which she'd fit her hips to, and his hand was heading for her ass when he heard a key scraping the lock at the door.

He instantly broke the kiss, shoved her behind him, and wondered what the fuck he was thinking that he didn't have weapons hidden all over the house, just as the door opened and Lottie strode in.

Tex strode in after her.

And behind Tex came near on every damn Rock Chick that still lived in Denver.

Lottie looked pissed.

Tex looked for Evie.

And the Rock Chicks looked ready to rumble.

"Fuck," he muttered.

CHAPTER EIGHT

For Now. And for Later.

EVIE

I didn't know what was happening.

"Are you fucking joking with this shit?" Lottie shouted, throwing a hand my way.

Wait, I did know.

I had been kissing Mag, but now Lottie was there, shouting, a large man with wild hair and an insanely long beard that was not lumbersexual, it was ZZ Top, was staring at me, and Mag's apartment was suddenly filled with beautiful women.

"Mac—" Mag started.

"Don't 'Mac' me," Lottie retorted. "She's in your shirt and you're in barely anything!"

I could hear her.

I could see the room filled with people.

But all I could feel was Mag's warm, hard body against mine, taste his tongue in my mouth, feel his lips moving over mine, the heady smell of morning man in my nostrils, the feel of his soft hair on my fingers.

And all I could think was: toothbrush and toothpaste.

He'd been off, talking to my brother, trying to figure out what was going on, how to protect me from it, all of this after I'd said such horrible things to him.

And on the way there, or back, he thought to stop and grab me a toothbrush and toothpaste.

Of course, I spent a good deal of time tossing and turning last night, thinking of my apartment, how I was going to bounce back from this fiasco, the danger my brother was in, the danger I might be in.

But I had to admit, most of the night, I spent thinking of Mag telling me to hit him, scream at him, take it out on him, offering me a place to stay, going out to talk to Mick and coming back with the tools I needed to keep my teeth healthy.

"You think now's the time to make your move?" Lottie demanded, forcing me back to the moment, and I saw she was flinging her arm again. This time, to the people she brought with her. "We swung by her pad this morning. And except for Stella getting her place blown up, this shit is as *real* as we've *seen*."

Stella getting her place blown up?

Who was Stella?

And...

Her place was blown up?

"We'll talk later about how you feel about the moves I make," Mag said in a voice I'd never heard him use. It was low, dangerous and *angry*. Admittedly, I didn't know him all that well, but I hoped it wasn't oft-used in his tonal arsenal. "For now, I'll be having that key back."

"It's Mo's key," she returned.

"It's *my* key seein' as I bought this place from him, and you'll be leaving that key before you and your posse turn your asses around and get the fuck out," Mag shot back.

Uh-oh, times about five hundred.

It was clear that wasn't the way to roll with this crowd.

I knew this because at his words Lottie looked even more pissed, and I did not think it boded well that now the ZZ Top guy also looked ticked *and* all the women, who'd seemed settled in for the show, now looked ready to become a part of it.

I didn't know who I was most scared of.

And although ZZ Top Guy seemed the logical choice just from sheer size and what it might say of his state of mind that he hadn't shaved in at least two decades, Lottie was the frontrunner.

"Okay, let's just all calm down here," I began, moving out from behind Mag, only to have him curl an arm around my hips and yank me hard to his side.

My head bounced.

My hair swayed.

And for a split second, I was stuck on the thought that no one had ever done that to me before.

I didn't like it.

But after all he'd done for me, that kiss, and in our current situation, I didn't *dislike* it either.

What I did, after all he'd done for me, that kiss, and in our current situation, was understand it.

But my attention shifted to the multitude of women and one wild man whose collective gazes had sharpened on Mag's arm around my hips, and not in good ways.

Right, maybe Lottie's friends didn't know he was an alpha-man commando who did stuff like that.

I never in my life thought I'd be in this place, but in order to handle a sudden and unexpected volatile situation, I was in this place.

That place being in a position to have to explain how an alpha-man commando operates.

"He's protective," I said. "He was there when I first saw all the damage. And you've invaded his space. It's a commando thing."

"Say what?" Lottie asked.

In answer, I curled my fingers around Mag's wrist (which, incidentally, didn't move) and shared, "You've invaded his territory. He's claiming his territory and nonverbally sharing what he intends to protect. It's not bad, as such. It's instinctive."

No one looked angry anymore, I was pleased to see.

Though how they'd morphed straight to highly amused, I didn't get.

"She's..." one of the blondes started. "She's..." Her voice was trembling. "Giving us alpha lessons," she finally got out.

When she did, promptly, all of them burst out laughing. And another of the blondes, hers platinum, had a giggle that sounded like tinkling bells (she also had very large breasts and was wearing a suede jacket top that had some lace at the waist, some glitter at the shoulder-padded shoulders, a ragged hem that fell to her stone-washed–jegging-covered hips, enough cleavage for seven women and looked like Calamity Jane met Wynonna Judd, but a Wynonna with platinum-blonde hair).

The lone African American lady, who, incidentally, had an enormous and highly attractive Afro, moved forward, tearing my attention away from the platinum blonde.

"This here, girl," she began, "is the Rock Chicks."

Oh...

Lottie's friends.

Denver's famed Rock Chicks.

In Mag's living room.

Whoa.

"It's a wonder I haven't grown a beard, I've been inhaling so much testosterone for the last however many years," the only brunette noted.

"Their men reinvented the idea of *alpha*," the African American lady said. "Hers," she pointed at another blonde, "took the book, doused it with gasoline, set it on fire, melted steel over the flame, fashioned a knife out of it and wrote the new definition by dipping the tip of that knife in ink then drawing a picture of himself."

"That's an, erm, colorful description," I noted.

"I think the only time I've seen Luke hold a pen was when he signed our marriage certificate," the blonde who had been indicated said. "Though, if he knew he could write with a knife dipped in ink, he'd probably do it more often. Including when he signed our marriage certificate."

Everyone burst out laughing again.

Except Lottie.

She started speaking.

"Mag, Mo told me what went down and I not only did not call you a manwhore, I cannot believe you'd think I said that about you."

Everyone stopped laughing and stared at Mag.

Oh boy.

I turned my head to look up at him to see he was still angry and still focused on Lottie.

"Yeah, then where did she get that shit?" he asked.

"It wasn't Lottie, Danny," I told him, and felt like an absolute heel when his eyes came down to me and I had to say what I had to say next. "Some of the girls at Smithie's talked, and it was, well…*me* who used that term. Lottie just said you had a bad breakup and, and…you needed a woman in your life who would let you be you."

He didn't look any less angry, though it was a mixed bag that he didn't seem angry at me.

"She came in here making assumptions," he explained his continuing anger at Lottie.

"You *are* in nothing but shorts and I'm in your shirt," I pointed out, though I didn't tell him I was in his shirt and not back in my Computer Raiders outfit *because* I wanted him to see me in his shirt making breakfast, my body at odds with my mind as to what was the right thing for Mag in this situation.

My body winning out.

In a lot of ways.

"I'm not fifteen. *You're* not fifteen. And she's not my mom or yours," he returned.

He had a point.

I looked to Lottie. "We slept in separate rooms. Boone gave me this shirt because I didn't have anything to wear to bed. I was making Mag breakfast as a thank-you and it was *me* who kissed *him*. Um, the first time."

"The first time," the platinum blonde said through a tinkly giggle.

I saw Lottie cotton on precisely to why I was wearing his shirt making breakfast. I also caught her lips shifting like she was fighting a smile. All while I felt my cheeks heat at the memory of that kiss.

I hadn't had the chance to process the mortification of possibly giving him a fat lip while trying to kiss him, nor how I felt that Mag gave me a do-over.

Okay, so that do-over was the best kiss of...my...*life*, so that was a plus.

But by kissing him, or letting him kiss me, I was not exactly saving him from the disaster my life seemed always to be, so that was a minus.

"I never made Lee breakfast to thank him for invading my life and commandeering my problems," the lone redhead said.

"I made Hank breakfast, my stuffed French toast, but it wasn't a thank-you for him invading my life and commandeering my problems," yet a different blonde said. "Or was it?"

"Your French toast is *everything*," the blonde with the hubby who would write with a knife declared. "You totally need to make it when we hit that Vrbo in Vail next weekend."

"I'll put the ingredients on the communal grocery list," the other blonde decided.

And then I jumped, though I didn't get very far in Mag's hold.

This was because ZZ Top Guy spoke, and even though I sensed it was his regular voice, it was a *boom*.

"Learn fast" was what he said, and he said it to me.

"Sorry?" I asked.

"In the face of death, destruction, car bombs, grenades, shootouts, etcetera," he rolled a beefy mitt in front of him to demonstrate "etcetera" went quite a long and apparently scary way, "conversation will degenerate to grocery lists or even more ridiculous shit. While you're in the middle of your drama, stay sharp, and by that I mean, don't focus on French toast no matter how good my Roxie's stuffed French toast is. And it's fuckin' brilliant."

This seemed bizarre, but good advice.

"I thought we were here to grab her and take her somewhere safe so she doesn't have to deal with her drama," yet *another* blonde remarked.

"You are not taking Evie *anywhere*," Mag rumbled.

All eyes got wide and focused on him.

"Jet, you're not supposed to say that in *front* of the cranky commando," the one called Roxie mumbled.

"Damn, Roxie. Guess I'm out of practice," Jet mumbled back.

"Evie was making me breakfast and you were leaving?" Mag prompted. "After, that is, you drop the key," Mag said directly to Lottie.

"I'm not leaving the key," Lottie said to Mag. "Mo would be upset if I left his key."

"After, that is, you promise you'll never let yourself into my condo just because you're in a snit," Mag amended.

I could see Lottie wasn't fond of the word "snit."

Fortunately, ZZ Top Guy intervened.

"We got a plan, bud," ZZ Top Guy shared.

"I heard your plan and I'm not in favor," Mag replied.

"That's the girls' plan. Except for Ally and Jules, we never do the girls' plans," ZZ Top told him.

"Hey!" the redhead snapped.

"Gotta say, it's the only rule we got that makes any sense," the African American lady said to the platinum blonde.

"Mm-hmm, sugar," the platinum blonde hummed.

"I've had some good plans," the redhead disagreed.

There were some shuffling feet.

The redhead was not good at planning.

I made note of that.

ZZ Top simply ignored her. "We get your girl. Take her home for some clothes. Take her to Eddie and Hank for a chat. Take her to Fortnum's for a coffee where she can hang and Duke and me'll look after her. Lottie, Roxie and Ava are free, so they're gonna go over and sort out her place. You can come get her when you're finished at work.

We'll make sure she gets lunch. I'm feelin' Mexican, but that part of the plan is up for discussion. You down with that?"

His final words were a question.

A question directed at *Mag*.

Before Mag could answer, I curled toward him, and when I moved, he again looked down at me.

"If you open your mouth to agree or disagree with what *I* am going to be doing with *my* time during *my* drama, it will be *me* who's cranky."

"You're a dork, a klutz, a menace with your mouth and unbelievably cute," Mag responded.

Part of that was true, part of that was mortifying (the mouth part) and part of that made me feel warm and happy.

I ignored all of it, and since none of it actually was a response to my statement, I asked, "Is there a purpose to you saying all of that?"

"Fortnum's is watched 24/7 by Nightingale Investigations, which means it's covered," he stated, then jerked his head to ZZ Top Guy. "Tex may look like he lives in a cabin with no plumbing or electric but lots of explosives, but he'd step in front of a bullet for you. Duke would do the same. You gotta make a statement to the cops and I gotta get to work. And I don't like you having to sort through that mess that's your apartment. It's too much too fast. So it's your life, your time, your drama, but my advice is, go with Tex's plan."

I was 100 percent unsurprised booming ZZ Top Guy had a cool name like Tex.

And as bizarre as it was to admit, I was 100 percent unsurprised he would step in front of a bullet aimed at a woman he did not know.

What could I say?

He just gave off that vibe.

"I kinda need to get into my apartment and see what's what, Danny," I said softly.

He instantly turned his head to our company. "You gonna help sorting her pad?"

"No," the brunette said. "I got shit on today."

Mag looked back at me. "Ally's not there, my advice is, be close to Tex and Duke with Nightingale eyes on you. They'll be cool with your stuff. You can trust them."

I got closer to him and whispered, "I don't know any of these people but Lottie. I can't ask them to help."

For a moment, as he held my gaze, he seemed to be pondering this.

Deeply.

And then he spoke.

"More advice, the Rock Chicks want to adopt you, as crazy as they are, let yourself be adopted."

I felt, having this conversation as we were, in front of them, was highly awkward.

So, I curled closer to him and dropped my voice so much lower, he had to dip down to hear it.

And him dipping down the way he did reminded me that he did, indeed, do that when he kissed me, which reminded certain parts of my anatomy how much I liked it when he did, all of which I had to ignore or this conversation would become even *more* awkward.

"I don't know, Danny. Lottie's my friend and I like her a lot. And this situation is intense. You don't take advantage of friends like—"

He wrapped his other arm around me, pulled me to his front and gave me a squeeze with both of his arms to cut off my words.

Then he spoke his own.

And he did this with an odd light in his bright-blue eyes.

One I'd never seen on him or on anyone.

I read it as happiness.

Even...

Joy.

And then my world would never be the same when he said what he had to say, words that explained that light.

"Baby, you are about to learn that you should expect more from the people in your life than remembering you need a toothbrush. A lot more. And I'm all kinds of down with that."

I looked at his face.

I felt that light shine down at me.

I felt his arms around me, the strength of his body pressed to mine.

I even still tasted him in my mouth.

And having all of that, I knew precisely what I had to do.

For now.

And for later.

So, for now, I nodded.

Mag smiled.

Man, he wasn't handsome.

He was straight-up beautiful.

And I was right.

I knew exactly what I had to do.

So, for now, I smiled back.

"Right, then," I heard from behind me. It was the African American lady's voice, "we're gonna need a whole lot more toast and bacon than that to feed this crew."

"I'm on toast," someone else said.

"I'm on bacon," another voice came.

Mag rolled me to his side and did not excuse himself to

put on his shirt or whisper in my ear maybe I should throw on some jeans.

He tossed his arm around my shoulders, tucked me to his side, and appeared for all the world to be settling in to allow the Rock Chicks to make breakfast at his place.

For everyone.

Lottie had clearly lost her pique and was grinning at us.

"Ally, deliver her to Fortnum's, I gotta go make coffees," Tex ordered.

"Got it," Ally, the brunette, replied.

"I think someone needs to pop out for more bacon," the redhead, who was surveying the contents of the fridge, said. "*A lot* more."

"I'm on that," Roxie replied, and she exited behind Tex.

"I'm Daisy."

I turned my head and saw the platinum blonde was close, and with her was the African American lady.

"This is Shirleen," she continued, jerking a thumb to the woman beside her.

"'Sup?' Shirleen asked.

"Um..." I didn't answer.

Daisy then smiled huge.

"Welcome to the Rock Chicks."

And when I bit my lip, she emitted her tinkly-bell laugh.

CHAPTER NINE
Toothpaste

EVIE

My day had started out crazy.

And moved to bizarre.

And I didn't know how to handle it.

We ate breakfast at Mag's pad (all of us) and the bad part about that was, during some of it, he was in his shower, which meant he left me alone with a number of lovely, funny, clearly kindhearted (but definitely crazy) women.

And I didn't know how to handle myself alone with a number of lovely, funny, clearly kindhearted but crazy women.

I mean, the gals at Smithie's I'd call friends.

But seeing these women around each other, I realized we only gabbed when getting ready or on breaks or when we were swiping off makeup before going home.

I didn't have time to actually be *friends* with them.

Babysit their kids when they were in binds, yes.

Go clubbing or out for brunch?

No.

Form deep, abiding bonds over shared experiences, laughs, good times, bad ones, forging friendships that would endure for eternity?

Definitely no.

And this took my mind elsewhere.

This being to the fact I'd never really had any friends. Even when I was young.

It'd hurt back then, that I was never invited to any birthday parties or sleepovers.

My mom's advice had been, "Try to stop being so...weird."

My dad's was, "They don't like you, fuck 'em."

He'd even used the F-word. I'd been nine.

My teachers loved me because I was smart and I'd started having to be the mature one in my family from a young age, and I think they guessed that and felt sorry for me.

But friends?

Sitting and watching the Rock Chicks I came to the realization I'd eventually buried the fact that I never could make friends.

So I didn't really have any.

As I was ruminating on this, not happily, I learned that Mag fortunately did not take long showers or primp prior to work.

He came out in short order, scarfed down food I did *not* make for him as part of a multilayered thank-you, then he led me to his front door by holding my hand, which felt beautiful.

There, he'd taken me loosely in his arms.

Which also felt beautiful.

He'd then said, "If they get you into a car chase, make sure they drive right to a police station."

Which freaked me out.

"Kidding," he murmured, right before he bent and touched his mouth to mine.

Which felt more beautiful than all the rest.

He'd then left, which was good, even if it was bad, and not only because I liked him, but in this situation, he'd become my touchstone, and not having him around freaked me out more.

The Rock Chicks read my freak-out and thus Roxie shared that their friend Jules was "The Law." I'd been introduced to them all: Indy (redhead), Jet (blonde), Roxie (also blonde), Ava (another blonde), and Ally (the brunette) rounded out Daisy and Shirleen. The Stella they mentioned was Stella of the famous rock band Stella and the Blue Moon Gypsies and she now lived in LA, but she was currently on tour or she'd be there "faster 'n snot" (Daisy's words) to be "in on your action" (also Daisy's words).

"Sorry?" I asked.

"She obviously hasn't read the books," Jet mumbled.

"You probably should read the books," Lottie suggested, making herself some scrambled egg whites at the stove.

From my perusal of his fridge and cupboards prior to starting breakfast, I discovered Mag had an Evan-approved balanced diet of say, a quarter healthy stuff, and three-quarters absolute garbage.

Lottie, as evidenced by those egg whites, was known to treat her body like a temple.

Mo, I had no idea, but he looked like he could drink acid and his body would regard it as fuel.

"She was a vigilante slash social worker," Indy said. "Jules, that is. Now she's a mother slash social worker slash wife slash hot chick slash Rock Chick."

I blinked but said no words.

"Breaking it down," Ava took up the thread. "Go to Indy for hair advice, Jet for recipe advice, Roxie for fashion advice, and Ally or Jules to kick someone's ass for you."

I blinked at her again.

"I'm hair advice too," Daisy claimed.

Jet sucked in her lips and lifted her brows.

Indy carefully shook her head at me so I'd see it, but Daisy wouldn't.

Rock Chick Mental Note Two: Don't let Daisy do my hair.

Then again, Daisy's was currently fashioned into a Farrah-Fawcett-on-steroids 'do, so I could see that.

Shirleen, who was stretched out on Mag's couch, called, "I see you got a commando boy, but just sayin', you come to me if you need the Hot Bunch. I schedule their asses. I'll get one free quick, you need someone shot or trussed up and thrown in a trunk."

I turned my eyes to Ally, who seemed the most sane of the crew.

"Hot Bunch is how we refer, collectively, to our husbands. And they don't shoot at people or shove them in trunks." She paused and finished, "Normally."

Oh man.

"We're harmless," Indy promised. "So are our men."

"Unless you can expire from bein' cool as shit, hot as fuck and havin' too much fun, am I right, sugars?" Daisy proclaimed.

"She's right," Roxie said.

"*So* right," Ava added with a smile.

"In other words," Lottie called from the stove, "we got you."

She smiled at me happily, in her element, with her people, engaged to a great guy, financially stable and thinking she'd finagled an epic setup between two friends that was working fantastically, regardless (or maybe because of) the circumstances.

I just didn't have the heart to tell her she was very, *very* wrong about that last part.

Breakfast done, cleanup done, they took me to my place and made me stand outside on the landing and shout at Indy, Jet and Roxie, who were inside, getting my stuff.

I was disheartened to note that a lot of stuff I called after, they called back, "Do you have another choice?" or "We'll swing by Walgreens."

They packed a measly bag that was, I didn't fail to note the irony, a Trader Joe's bag, with some clothes, Roxie mumbling, "I'll corral Tod and Stevie and do a little shopping," and they took me to Lottie's, where I showered and changed.

They then took me to the police station.

Now, I was no stranger to police stations.

However, I'd never been in one with people who belonged there and not in the way of criminals, witnesses to criminal acts or victims of the same.

Jet and Roxie were married to cops.

Indy and Ally's dads were cops.

This was family.

I met Eddie (a gorgeous Hispanic man who belonged to Jet) and Hank (a handsome boy-next-door type, but he was *way* no longer a boy, who belonged to Roxie).

I also met men named Mitch and Brock, who were particular friends of the Rock Chicks, not to mention "tight" with Hawk, Mag and Mo's boss.

We were brought coffees by uniformed officers.

The girls shot the shit with practically everyone who crossed our paths.

And both Eddie and Hank stood vigil, like I needed moral support, while I gave my statement to a young detective who told me to call him "Gav."

Hank (incidentally, Ally's brother and Indy's brother-in-law, totally all in the family) pointed at Ally when we were leaving and asked, "You got her?"

Which received the little sister response of "Don't be an ass."

"I just asked a question," Hank retorted.

Which gave Ally pause to say, "Is there something I need to know?"

Which I thought might be something *I* needed to know.

"Not yet," Hank answered.

And this was a relief, kind of.

"Then don't be an ass," Ally repeated.

To which Hank moved his attention to Roxie and asked his wife, "Do you feel like moving back to Brownsburg yet?"

She did not respond except to shoot him a bright smile and blow him a kiss.

Wherever Brownsburg was, they weren't moving there, I knew this even before Hank heaved a visible sigh and strolled away.

Roxie linked arms with me and guided me out, saying, "It's part of the reason I love him. Lee and Ally were so wild, the big brother gene got so ingrained in him he can't stop himself. If Lee was here, he'd ask the same question even knowing they both have their shit tight. I mean, Ally's the second-best private investigator in the city, but only because she goes it alone and Lee has a team. Like, in most cases, Hawk calls her first if he needs added firepower."

Added firepower.

Geez.

So, Ally was a PI, she sometimes worked with Mag's boss, and this was why everyone acted like she was Rambette.

I could see this. She was trim and gorgeous and exuded competent badass.

I envied her.

Hell, I envied all of them.

After this, they took me to Fortnum's.

I barely got through the doors before Tex was shoving a coffee drink in my hand (he was, I'd learned, the barista at Fortnum's) and booming in my face, "I call that the 'Textual.' Because, first, you ain't gonna be fuckin' texting when you're drinking that because you'll be about nothin' but drinkin' that. And second, it's my signature and it's got the word Tex in it. Get it?"

"I get it," I replied.

"So, take a hit and tell me what you think," he ordered.

I would take a hit because I liked coffee (though I preferred tea). But I took that hit knowing I was going to tell him I loved it even if I loathed it mostly because he seemed kinda friendly, but he also seemed loony and proud of his coffee, and I didn't want to see how friendly could turn in the way of Tex.

Then, after I took a sip of a latte flavored with almond, cherry and chocolate, my eyes rolled back into my head.

"I'll take that as approval," Tex semi-boomed, then strode away.

I was then seated in a couch that sat under the big windows that made up the front of the store and Ava shoved a pink book at me.

It had the big words ROCK CHICK on the front of it.

"Volume one," she said. "There are ten, but two are novellas, so don't panic."

She then plonked down in an armchair across from me and shouted, "Tex! I need a skinny vanilla, stat."

"I only do deliveries to women whose lives are in danger!" he bellowed what was clearly not a joke. "Get your ass up here, you want a coffee."

She grinned at me and hauled her ass up to the counter.

Ally, Daisy and Shirleen all went to work, Roxie went shopping, and Jet and Indy worked at Fortnum's (Indy owned it) so they got to work too, after introducing me to Duke, a long-gray-haired Harley dude who had a rolled bandana around his forehead.

All this while Lottie and Ava hung with me, sipping coffee.

That was the first time my phone rang.

The screen said DANIEL MAGNUSSON.

I'd have to change that to "Danny."

Right before I deleted it.

I took the call on a "Hey."

"Hey, comin' to you for lunch. What do you want?"

He was coming to me for lunch?

That wasn't part of Tex's plan.

I wasn't sure we should deviate from Tex's plan.

"Um…"

"Culver's?" he suggested.

"What?"

"Fried cheese curds and frozen custard?"

Gross.

"Together?" I asked.

I listened to him laugh in my ear.

God.

Beautiful.

"No, baby," he murmured. "I'll get you Culver's. I'm in the vicinity. Make your week."

My week was made meeting a protective hot guy who could kiss, didn't forget to bring me a toothbrush and had a beautiful laugh I could convince myself I wanted to hear until my dying day.

His week included staking out late-night, clandestine meetings at storage units, me being a bitch to him, having to enter my ruined apartment armed and a sit-down with my brother.

Totally had to get my body with the program in order to save Mag from the disaster that was my life.

"I don't own any workout clothes," I told him.

"You'll get set up again, Evie," he assured.

"No, I mean, even before my belongings were decimated, I didn't own any workout clothes. I took pride in that. If I keep eating like you eat, I'll need workout clothes, and right now, I can't afford them."

He sounded appalled when he asked, "No yoga pants?"

That was when I started laughing.

And again, my body, most especially my mouth, was not getting with the program.

"So, how'd it go at the station?" he queried into my laughter.

"And he slips that in after promises of fried cheese curds and frozen custard and making me laugh," I whispered.

"How'd it go, honey?" he whispered back.

How it went was, I took care of me by reporting a dangerous situation to the police, but I did it feeling like I was hammering nails into my brother's coffin.

"It's done."

"It's gonna be okay."

His definition of okay, with a living, breathing Evie, and

my definition of okay, with a living, breathing me *and* my brother were not the same.

Even so.

"Yeah," I muttered.

"Ask around, text orders, and I'll be there soon."

"Okay."

"Later, babe."

No boyfriend in my life, or even a guy I dated, called me "babe."

I said not a word, except, "Later, Danny."

We hung up, I took orders, typed the longest text of my life to send them to Mag, and once it swooshed away, the bell over the door went, which happened so much, the staff had to tune it out or it'd drive them insane.

I'd heard of Fortnum's and the coffee there (though, again, I was a tea person). I'd heard of the Rock Chick books, though never cracked one open, because even if I loved to read, I never had time for it. I even knew Lottie's friends and family came to see her dance on occasion.

But they were there for Lottie, as well as Smithie, so none of the girls worked their table (because, first, swinging your ass in Lottie's friends' faces: gross, and second, because of that, it would be way weird to work for that tip).

But all this took on new meaning with seeing just how popular a used bookstore with a big coffee bar at the front of it was.

I looked down to the book that lay on the couch beside me only to have Lottie call, "Hey."

I lifted my eyes to her.

"Outside all the shit you wouldn't be okay about, you okay?" she asked.

I forced a weak smile.

"Yeah," I lied.

She studied me.

She was damned savvy and street smart to boot, and since I didn't want her reading me, I didn't want her studying me.

Thus, I turned my attention back to the book.

I was on page ten and a little afraid, at the same time very interested to meet Indy's husband, Lee, when the bell over the door rang.

It was that I was into the book.

It was evidence you got used to that bell going.

Both of these conspired to keep my nose in a chapter called "The Great Liam Chase" instead of looking up to the door.

A mistake.

Because I only had Lottie's murmured, "Smithie, cool it," before I heard my boss shout, *"What the fuck, Evan?"*

I looked up at Smithie, a tall, stout African American man who had a fierce bark, no bite and a heart of gold.

"Smithie—"

"I swung by your place..." he started.

I wished people would quit doing that.

"...and it was a *nightmare*!" he finished.

"She knows, Smithie, she's seen it," Lottie said. "She doesn't need you shouting that reminder at her."

"I'm okay," I assured him with a total lie.

Smithie ran a strip club. He could spot a lie at a hundred paces.

This was probably why he shouted, "You're *okay*? Bullshit! Why didn't you tell me your shit was *this whacked*?"

Perhaps softening the blow to Smithie last night had not been my best course of action.

"Well..."

I didn't finish that.

I liked him. He paid well, offered great health insurance and acted more like my father than my father, which was not a difficult endeavor, but Smithie aced it.

So, obviously, I wouldn't want to drag him into my nightmare.

"I don't...I don't even...I can't..." He was looking around, for what, I had no idea, then he focused on Tex. "Is this shit starting up again?" he asked.

"I hope so," was an answer that further put up for debate Tex's sanity.

"*Ohmigod*," the customer standing in line in front of Tex breathed loudly. "Is this a new Rock Chick?" she asked no one in particular, speaking while gazing at me.

"She isn't a Rock Chick, she's a Smithie's Chick," Lottie corrected.

"Do not pin *any* of this shit on me," Smithie demanded.

"Commando Chick?" Lottie asked Ava.

"Maybe Dancing Chick?" Ava asked Lottie.

The bell over the door went and I'd learned, so I looked right there.

Which meant I got the whole show when Mag walked in wearing his navy cargo pants, his tight navy tee that shared the mayor should consider giving his chest its own zip code (I mean, that morning when I'd seen it uncovered in all its glory—*dayum*) and black boots that looked utilitarian, but he was Mag, so he worked them.

"*Ohmigod*," the customer again breathed.

Mag didn't hear her, or a greater possibility, he was so used to women having that response when he arrived somewhere, he didn't care.

He also didn't care much that Smithie was there, looking ready to blow his top.

Or about anything.

But me.

I knew this as I watched him say a perfunctory, "Yo," to Smithie as he passed him to get to me.

Then he bent right down.

Bent right down!

He then kissed my nose...

Kissed my nose!

He pulled back, grinned gorgeously in my face and said words I'd longed to hear my entire life.

"You're gonna have to eat the ice cream first. It's melting."

"I started coming here after all the other Rock Chicks were done and claimed. I cannot *believe* I'm here at *ground zero* during a new one!" the customer exclaimed.

Mag's brows shot together but he didn't move out of my face.

"She thinks I'm a new Rock Chick," I told him.

"She's wrong," Lottie decreed, snatching the bags out of Mag's hands. "You're a Dream Maker."

Mag had turned his head to aim his grin at Lottie, who was retreating with the food, but, I would note, he did not move from being bent to me.

"Lottie's romantic," I said, and regained Mag's attention. "For a stripper."

That earned me another smile.

Then I got my hand captured and I was pulled out of the couch.

Apparently, Mag and his cargo pants and utilitarian boots and zip-code chest entering the vicinity served to calm Smithie down, and I knew this because his head didn't explode, and he didn't shout anymore.

Instead, he went to Tex, cut the line and ordered a coffee.

Mag sat us at a big table in the corner, everyone joined us, and as food was distributed and tucked into, I watched how they worked this.

Mag was not one of them, but he was Lottie's, so he fit.

I was Lottie's, so I fit.

We sat. We ate. They chatted. Mag flatly refused anyone paying him for their food, he got a lot of, "My turn next time" and "Catch you on the flipside" and it was just...

It was just...

A family get-together in a used bookstore and coffee emporium.

But me?

I'd had a bag filled with drugs in the trunk of my car just yesterday.

My apartment had been tossed, my brother was in mortal danger and I hadn't told my mother, my father or my sister, nor gone to them for help, because I couldn't be sure if they would and I couldn't take the blow if they wouldn't.

And I was realizing my best friend was a senior citizen I took shopping and out to family chain restaurants because I didn't have time to do lunch or go to movies or out to clubs with people my own age.

But furthermore, I was just so weird, no one wanted to hang with me anyway.

And I essentially had to pay Gert to spend time with me (though she would do it even if I didn't grab the check).

It wasn't only my apartment that was in ruins.

My life was.

And it was me who'd led it to that.

"Hey."

I'd gone to a storage unit in the middle of the night even if a man who probably was in the position to know just how lunatic that was advised me against it.

"Hey."

And I helped my brother out, my mom, dad, sister, whoever, all the time.

Whenever they needed it, I was there.

But I didn't let them lean on me.

I let them shit all over me.

"*Hey.*"

It was Mag's tone but also the fact he took hold of my chin and turned my head from staring unseeing at my puddle of melting custard to his amazing face.

"Baby," he murmured when he got one look at me.

My next thoughts came unexpected and tore through me like a bullet.

I want you to be mine. I want that to be my world. That a guy like you would turn out as awesome as you seem and I'd earn your attention, then your heart, and then we'd teach our kids to be smart and protective and funny like you and not anything *like me.*

"Evie, honey," he whispered. "Come back to me, yeah?"

I made myself nod.

He took his fingers from my chin but did it gliding one along my jaw a little in a light, sweet, reassuring touch.

"You're gonna have moments like that," he shared. "When I'm not here, you still got people around. Let them help you pull yourself out of 'em. Okay?"

I made myself nod again.

"This is gonna get sorted, Evie. It seems a lot and it seems scary, but," he grinned a grin I could tell he didn't fully mean, glanced toward the store then back to me and joked, "we haven't lost one yet."

I made myself smile.

He knew I didn't fully mean it either when he vowed, "I promise, it's gonna be okay. Yeah?"

"Yeah," I pushed out.

His face got soft.

Oh *God*.

That look.

That look on Daniel Magnusson aimed at me.

I WANNA MAKE YOU MINE! I screamed in my head.

"Forget the custard," he ordered. "I'll take you for more when you can eat it without it being melted. Eat your curds and your burger."

"Roger that, sergeant."

"I only made corporal."

"What?"

"Nothin'," he said then took a massive bite of his burger.

Why did dudes do that?

It wasn't going to fly out of his hands and make its escape before he shoved the whole thing in his mouth.

He watched me watching him chewing.

And with his mouth still full, he asked, "What?"

"You eat like a frat boy." I said it like a tease so he wouldn't take offense.

He didn't.

He swallowed, smiled (again! gah!) and then leaned close to me. "This is normally fifteenth- or maybe sixteenth-date stuff. You know, when I really got my hooks in you after dazzling you with fried cheese curds and impressing you with my masculinity that I didn't cry when they killed John Wick's dog. But just sayin', that's only 'cause I've seen it so often, the tears for that little fella are done and gone. But heads up, I *am* a frat boy, Evie. I'll prove it to you tonight when we shotgun some beers."

I started giggling.

Mag stopped looking so worried.

I fought crying.

"Eat," he whispered.

I nodded and turned my attention to the burger and curds.

"How long you stayin'?" Mag asked, and I cast my gaze in the direction of his question.

It was to Tex.

"As long as you need me to stay."

These people.

These crazy, kindhearted people.

And then there was...

Me.

"I don't want her leaving you, Duke and Nightingale's cameras," Mag went on. "And I won't be done until around five thirty, six."

"We don't close until seven so you're good," Tex replied. "You get tied up, I'll take her to Nightingale's offices. They always got someone workin' in the control room. She can hang with whoever that is."

Mag nodded.

"We gotta get stuck into sorting out Evie's place," Lottie said to Mag then looked to me. "Ava and me are gonna head out in a bit. You cool with hanging here and reading?"

I nodded.

I'd had other things to do with my day, which was an unusual day off, this being when I did those other things. Like pay bills. Laundry. Go to the grocery store. Clean the house. Check in on my sister to make sure she hadn't done something outlandish to garner attention from the on-line community. Like film herself allowing strangers to do shots off her body (not something I made up in my head, something she passed by me as an "idea that held merit," but it wasn't me who talked her out of it, apparently some-one else did that as their shtick).

I had no house, or laundry, and the bills could wait.

And honestly, if my sister wanted to let random people do body shots off her, what did it matter to me?

"Yeah, I'm cool with hanging and reading," I told Lottie. "And I need to call my insurance company about my car."

"After the police were done with it," Mag cut in, "Auggie secured it. If they need access, let me know and I'll text you the details on where it is."

Before I could ask after that, *any* of it (the police, I knew, his friend Auggie had called them in and they'd done their thing at my apartment and with my car—the other bit, my car being "secured" and Mag giving me the details if my insurance company needed it, I did not know), Lottie spoke.

"We'll just clean up," she assured me. "We won't throw anything away until you have a chance to go through it."

"Thanks," I replied.

"Tex'll listen, Duke too, and I'm just a phone call away, you get another one of those moments," she went on.

So she hadn't missed it.

"I'm okay," I promised.

"Tex'll listen, Duke too, and they're both good at it," she asserted. "But I'm just a phone call away."

"Thanks, Lottie," I muttered.

"He's my boy and you're my girl," she stated, jerking her head in turn to Mag and me, and I stared at her, not sure why she was saying that. "I would not fix him up with anyone who didn't deserve him, and the same with you. Are you understanding me, Evie?"

I nodded.

"You really need to understand me, Evie," she said quietly, but there was a fierceness to her tone.

I *thought* I understood her, but that fierceness to her tone made me wonder.

Nevertheless, I nodded again.

She looked to Duke, who was sitting with us, throwing curds into his mouth like M&M's. "I don't think she does."

"They don't," he said sagely. "Then they do. It's a process that can't be rushed. Don't rush it, darlin'."

Lottie heaved a sigh.

Before he left, Mag did the holding-my-hand-and-guiding-me-to-the-door thing that ended with the lip touch, but he added, "I'm not on anything intense. You need me, baby, you call."

I wondered what "anything intense" was.

I didn't ask because it wasn't my business but also because "intense" seemed an alias for "scary as shit" and I wasn't ready for more scary.

I just, again, nodded.

Mag took off.

Lottie and Ava took off.

I cleared away the detritus from Culver's, then sat down with my book but didn't open it because Smithie was looming over me.

"It's always the quiet ones," he said when I looked up at him.

"Sorry?" I asked.

"Child," he murmured gently, "the minute I looked at you, you broke my heart. That lost look in your eyes. *Damn.*"

Oh God.

I felt my chest rise and fall with the effort to stop myself from crying.

"Look around, Evie," he said. "You've been found."

I swallowed.

Actually, it was more like a gulp.

Smithie bent and kissed my cheek.

When he straightened, he told me, "I got a phone too. You need anything, darlin', you call on me."

As if he sensed I was about to lose it, he didn't offer me any further kindnesses.

He left.

I concentrated on finding my insurance agent's number, calling her, reporting the incident and learning that they'd have to come and look at my car.

I then texted Mag that I needed the deets.

Within a minute, he'd texted me the deets.

It was already at a body shop, waiting for the go-ahead to be fixed.

Not surprising with these good, kindhearted people.

I sat with the book.

Jet took a break and sat with me.

Indy took a break and sat with me.

Tex boomed at me.

Duke studied me like he was trying to figure me out (so I avoided looking at Duke).

Then Roxie showed with two men she introduced as Tod and Stevie, who both wore wedding bands and made it clear in sweet ways that they belonged to each other.

Roxie also had a number of bags, and after she made the introductions and Jet and Indy had wandered over, she said apropos of nothing, "Shut up. I won't hear it."

She then yanked out three pairs of faded jeans (two distressed, all three cool), five tees (and they were *fab*) and two cardigans (slouchy and overlarge, in great colors).

And after all of this littered the seating area I was in, she dumped two big Soma bags at my feet and stated, "Undies, bras and nightwear. And the other stuff is no big deal since we got it all at a vintage store, so it cost practically nothing."

It was the "practically" part of that that bothered me.

Then Tod dumped a big Sephora bag at my feet and

said, "Cleanser, toner, moisturizer and some cosmetics. And shut up, I won't hear it either."

"But I don't even know you," I noted.

"Girl, we got a communal slush fund for shit like this," he returned.

I'd been reading so I did not find this surprising.

Still.

"I—" I started.

"Shut up," Tod said.

"But I—"

"Shut up," Tod and Roxie said in unison.

"But—"

"*Shut up!*" Tod, Stevie, Roxie, Indy and Jet all said once.

I shut up.

Air kisses were then exchanged, even with me, and Tod, Stevie and Roxie took off, Jet going with them to pick up her boys (she had three sons) and get home to make dinner for her family, Indy going to pick up her kids (she had a girl and boy) before she met up with Lee and they went to her in-laws for dinner.

This was when I got call number two from Mag.

"Hey," I greeted.

"How's things?" he asked.

"The Rock Chicks are bossy," I informed him.

"Good bossy, or bad bossy?" he asked.

"Is there a good bossy?" I asked in return.

"Yes," he answered.

Hmm.

"I have a bunch of new stuff and I don't think they're going to let me pay them back for any of it," I shared.

"Then it's the good bossy," he stated. "See you around six."

He hung up before I could say another word.

I folded all my new stuff up and returned it to the bags.

Then I went back to reading.

It happened at close to six.

With perfectly imperfect timing, it happened just when the bell over the door rang and I looked up from reading about when Indy performed with Tod at a drag show and then she, Ally and Tex got into a car chase after shots were fired at the gay bar.

I looked up to see Mag walking in, eyes on me, a smile on his handsome face.

Because of this...

Because I'd spent the day with nice people who looked after me, got me lunch, bought me stuff I needed, handed me orgasmic coffees, instead of what I might have been doing if Lottie and Mag had not intervened in my life: cowering in fear while sorting through the ruin of my apartment...

Because of all of this, when my phone rang and I looked down at it and saw it was my mother calling, I took the call without thinking.

I put it to my ear as Mag approached me, my eyes to him, and began, "Hey—"

"*What the fuck is the matter with you!*" my mother shrieked in my ear.

My blood turned to ice and Mag disappeared from sight, seeing as my mind blanked and I had no vision at all.

"Do you know how much shit Mick is in right now?" Mom asked. "Do you, Evie? *Do you?*"

I did not answer as my phone was slid out of my hand and I watched Mag's long forefinger hit the button for speaker.

And Mom's voice filled the air.

"*Answer me, Evan!* Your brother *fears for his life* because you have *shit for brains*!"

I stared at the phone.

Mom kept going.

"Genius my ass!" she shouted. "Dumb as a rock. Who cares how a radio works? You gotta keep a bag safe to keep your brother safe, *you do everything you can to keep that bag safe!*"

"Listen to me," Mag growled, and my eyes darted up to his face.

Oh boy.

He was using that tone he'd used with Lottie that morning.

Except worse.

Way worse.

"Who's this?" Mom demanded.

"It doesn't matter who this is. You can call this number again when you get the go-ahead from Evan to call this number. And if you don't ever get that go-ahead, you never call this number."

"Fuck you, let me talk to my daughter."

Mag's gaze shot to me.

Yep, I said with my eyes. *That's my mom.*

"This is her mother?" Mag asked to confirm.

"I said, let me talk to my daughter," she ordered.

"Toothpaste," Mag muttered, staring at me.

Damn.

Somehow, I'd given it all away over a tube of toothpaste.

"Evan had her apartment tossed last night. There's little that can be salvaged. She lost almost everything," Mag told Mom.

"Well, my son might lose his life!" Mom snapped.

"It's clear it'd be smooth sailing for you if you were given Sophie's choice," Mag remarked.

"What?" Mom asked.

"We're done," Mag stated.

Then he made that so by disconnecting and went on to move his finger on my screen to do other things.

He then extended my phone to me and said, "She's blocked. She's your mom, that's not my call. I'm just askin' you to give yourself a break from that at least until we know if you've got more than a couple pairs of vintage jeans to your name."

I pressed my lips together and ignored the fact that Tex and Duke had both sidled close during that spectacle.

"Did she know before I told her what happened to your place?" Mag asked.

I shook my head.

"You didn't call her?"

I shook my head.

"Your father?"

I shook my head.

He rolled his head around on his shoulders as he drew breath into his nose.

"Mag—"

"Baby," he whispered, "I can't. I can't right now. Mac called. Said they dropped some of your stuff at my pad. I wanna get you home. I wanna get you fed. I wanna get you settled. I do not want to listen to you make excuses for your mother."

I pressed my lips together again.

"You know that shit's not right, yeah?" he asked.

I said nothing.

"You do know, you just got nothin' else," he said softly.

"Maybe I should go home or get a hotel room tonight or something," I suggested.

Without hesitation, he responded, "I can't do that either, Evie. Really. So please don't make me."

When I made no reply, he reached a hand to me.

I didn't want to take it.

I wanted to run far away from him and his people and that look on his face that he got after just one very short dose of my mother.

I needed to figure myself out.

I needed to sort out my life.

What I didn't need to do was drag a nice guy like Daniel Magnusson along for that ride.

My body had other thoughts.

In other words, I reached for his hand.

He pulled me out of the couch, murmuring, "Grab your book and your bag, honey."

I grabbed my book and my bag as he scooped up the handles of all my other bags.

I then chanced glances at Duke and Tex, both of whom had stony faces and gazes locked on Mag.

I figured this was so I wouldn't see the pity if they looked at me.

"Thanks for everything, guys," I said.

Duke rearranged his expression when his attention came to me.

Tex did not and his look made me glad he didn't know where my mother lived.

"See you tomorrow, darlin'," Duke bid as Mag led me to the door.

"I have to work tomorrow," I told him.

"Then see you soon," he replied.

He would not.

I nodded.

Mag pulled me out the door, to his truck, opened my side for me, stowed my stuff in the backseat and waited until I got in before he closed it.

He was in and we were on our way by the time I spoke.

"Danny, maybe we should talk."

"I did tours. Over there. Afghanistan. Iraq. Syria."

I decided maybe we shouldn't talk but I did not share that verbally.

"You would not...it's impossible to describe..."

He cleared his throat.

I stared at his profile.

"In many cases, women over there are not treated very well."

Oh man.

"Danny, honey."

He glanced at me then back at the road.

"Let me do this."

I closed my eyes and faced forward.

"Please, Evan. Let me take care of you however that comes about."

I opened my eyes.

But I didn't say anything.

He did.

"Please."

"Okay," I whispered.

He reached out, grabbed my hand, held it and drove one-handed.

We were nearing his place when he said quietly, "No matter the circumstances, a mother does not talk to her daughter that way."

"I know," I said quietly back.

He squeezed my hand and murmured, "Good."

And then he finished driving us to his place.

CHAPTER TEN

Pushover

MAG

"Why would we do this?" she asked.

"Just get ready," he ordered.

"Danny—"

"I'm cuttin', honey, and if I beat you, you owe me the movie of my choice and I'm feelin' *Anaconda*."

She looked down at the can of beer she had on its side on the counter of the island with one of his penknives pointed to it, close to the base, as he'd instructed.

"On the count of three," he warned.

She looked to him and opened her mouth.

"One," he began.

"This is stupid," she said.

"Two," he went on.

"I've never seen *Anaconda*. Maybe I'll like it."

"Three," he finished.

He shoved his knife in his can and heard her do the same.

Then he circled it to make the hole bigger, pulled it out, put the opening to his mouth, popped the top and beer gushed into his mouth.

He was busy chugging, but he still managed to look around his can to see she had hers to her mouth and beer was running down her cheeks and chin, soaking the collar of her tee that read, "THAT'S WHAT." —SHE.

Seriously kickass shirt.

Seriously cute Evie.

He finished and had crushed his can in his hand when she started sputtering, careened to his sink, dropped her can and spit beer into it.

"You suck," he told her, smiling. "And it's *Anaconda*."

She looked to him, rolled her eyes and snatched up a dishtowel to wipe her face.

Still wiping, she asked, "Is this your attempt to make my t-shirt wet?"

He tossed his can in the recycling as he walked to her, slung an arm around her shoulders and curled her to his front.

"Dual-purpose time-saver for the consummate frat boy. If you can get 'em drunk at the same time you get 'em wet, you're *golden*."

He couldn't know with Evie if that'd piss her right off or if she'd take it in the spirit he intended.

He was pleased as fuck she took it in the spirit he intended and busted out laughing.

When she did, he grinned down at her and slid his other arm around her.

Evan Gardiner laughing in his arms when all he'd seen from her that day was turned on, confused, lost and looking like she was about to cry.

The turned-on bit was good.

The rest sucked.

This was much better.

She rested both hands holding the dishtowel on his chest and smiled up at him.

Then she informed him, "I hate beer."

That was when Mag busted out laughing.

When he was done, she was still smiling, and Christ.

Christ.

She was pretty.

Suddenly, he heard her mother's voice, the words she said coming at Evie through her phone, and he felt a burn hit his gut.

"And since I didn't totally officially get to make you breakfast, I'll whip up something for dinner," she said.

"I thought we'd Postmate it. Maybe Chinese."

Her face screwed up. "You keep trying to intervene, which is giving me the sense you don't trust my cooking."

"I don't know. Are you gonna force me to eat kale and quinoa?"

"Since I only have what's in your house to work with, and that's not in your house, no. And since I hate kale, no times two. But fair warning, I dig quinoa."

Fair warning.

Giving the impression she'd be cooking for him again.

That was not skittish Evie.

That was an Evie he could get onboard with.

He gave her a squeeze before he let her go, saying, "Have at it."

She started moving around his kitchen as he turned his back to the counter of the island, put the heels of his palms to it, and hefted his ass up on it to watch her.

"Do you have a taste for anything?" she asked.

"Rib eye and loaded baked potato."

Slowly, she turned to him.

"Though I don't have either of those on hand for you to cook," he told her.

She did another eye roll with a headshake, but one side of her lips quirked up.

She rummaged in his fridge and came out of it with her arms full of cheese and meat.

"Bacon cheeseburgers?" she asked.

I'm gonna marry this girl, he thought.

He felt that unexpected, never-had-before thought in his gut too.

It was warm, not hot, like a slug of Fireball.

His favorite shot.

"Danny?" she called.

His voice was gruff when he said, "Sounds awesome."

At his tone, her head did a little tick, meaning her hair did a little swish and...

Yeah.

The thought did not suck that he'd sit his ass on his counter and watch this girl make their dinner night after night for years.

"So, that kiss this morning," he said and the packet of bacon, sleeve of American cheese slices and carton of ground beef hit the deck. He grinned slow at her and murmured, "Baby."

This he did before he hopped off the counter to help her pick it up.

"I got it," she said.

So they wouldn't collide like she for sure would make them collide, he caught her hand and held it. "I'm going in. You stand still."

Pink hit her cheeks and he wanted to enjoy that, but for her sake, instead, he crouched and got their dinner from the floor.

He put it on the counter by the stove then hefted his ass onto it, so he'd be close while she worked.

She proved she was at one with this idea when she found a bowl and set it down beside his hip.

"It was a great kiss, Evie," he said to her bent head as she dumped hamburger in the bowl.

"I'm surprised you don't have a fat lip," she said to the bowl.

"I didn't mean that one, but that one too."

Her head came up and her eyes caught his. "It wasn't."

"It was."

"I'm a klutz. It's embarrassing."

"It's you. It's cute."

She looked down to the bowl and reached for his salt and pepper.

"Evie, I'm bein' serious."

"You're being nice. That's you. You're...nice."

He wasn't sure any woman he'd ever known described him as *nice*.

But he couldn't say it sucked.

"Evie—"

Her head came up and she blurted, "I'm attracted to you. You...you're *attractive*. Now, do you have Worcestershire sauce?"

"No."

"Garlic powder?"

"Maybe. Evie—"

"I'm a mess," she whispered.

"So am I," he whispered back. "Everyone's a mess. Anyone who looks like they've got it together, they're either putting on a show or you're not looking close enough."

"How are you a mess? You're...you're..." She threw a hand up to him and then out to his pad. "Totally together."

Fuck.

They were in fiftieth or sixtieth date territory.

"I seem like I got it goin' on because your life imploded. Trust me, I got my issues and I got my demons."

She fell silent and studied him.

Then she spoke.

"Should we just have dinner and watch a movie?"

He'd give her that play, and it wasn't purely altruistic reasons why he would.

She didn't need to know his issues and definitely not his demons.

Not now.

He'd already let slip a nuance of what he'd seen during his tours.

That was enough.

"Honey, I'll do whatever you wanna do to chill out," he told her. "But first, I want it out there and I want it clear, I liked that kiss. *Those* kisses. Both of them, no matter what you think. I want more. I want to get to know you better. And I wanna look out for you while you're going through this rough patch. We can talk about all that when you're ready. For now, I gotta understand what your day looks like tomorrow so I can have you covered."

She opened his cupboard that had his spices and was sorting through it as she answered, "I'm on for Computer Raiders from seven to one thirty. And then I'm at Smithie's, have to be there by seven."

This was going to be a challenge as he had to work.

"And I need my car for Computer Raiders," she continued.

"I can drop you off when I go to work."

She was shaking stuff into the meat, but her eyes came to him. "I do on-site visits."

Goddamn it.

"Evan, it's almost impossible for me to have a man on you for on-site visits."

"Danny, I can't call off. I'm hourly and it goes without saying, I need the money."

Yeah.

That went without saying.

"Auggie has some time off," he said. "I'll see if he can shadow you. If he can't, I'll call in a favor from one of the Nightingale boys or Chaos crew."

"Maybe I'll be okay," she suggested.

"Maybe you will. Though I'd prefer taking steps to omit the 'maybe' from that statement."

She looked away to dig her fingers in the meat and start smushing.

It came quiet when she asked, "Do you think Mick's gonna be okay?"

He didn't give one single fuck what Mick was.

He did not say that.

He said, "We're pokin' around this mess. We know the street name of the guy you met. I got make and model and license plate of his car and I got friends lookin' into that. I haven't been briefed. I had some roadwork to do for Hawk today and my priority is you. To end, I have no idea what's happening, so I have no idea the level of threat your brother is facing."

She started forming hamburger patties.

He watched her hands work and noted she was not stingy with the beef.

Yeah.

Totally marriage material.

"Right now, he's the safest place he can be, honey," he assured her.

"Mom sounded more...*Mom* than her regular," she explained why she brought up her brother, then asked, "Can you get me a plate?"

He twisted to open a cupboard and got her a plate.

She set a formed patty on it.

"He's a favorite," Mag said carefully.

She dug up more meat.

"Right," he muttered. "Dinner and watch a movie."

Evan looked to him. "She's a favorite."

"Sorry?"

"Mom. Carol. *She's* the most important person in her life. And it bums me out and makes me sound stupid, but honestly, it's just in this very moment that I realized that. And it's not, you know, the healthy kind of making yourself a priority to teach your children to look out for themselves. Their hopes and goals and health and happiness. Not to give too much to someone else so you lose sight of what you need to make yourself feel right. Feel whole. It's all about Carol Bowers. Though, runner-up for Mom is Mick. Honestly, unless Sidney, my sister, is in her line of sight, I think she forgets Sid exists. And she only remembers me when she can bum a couple hundred dollars to replace it in their joint account when she gets a little overzealous shopping and she doesn't want Rob to find out."

Mag didn't trust himself to speak.

She set another patty aside and moved around him to get to the sink to wash her hands.

"It's when you said that about Sophie's choice," she continued. "I thought about that and it's true, kind of. Her first thought, how to get what Carol wants out of a situation. Then she's all about Mick. Honest to God, if she was put in that heinous situation, she wouldn't blink. As long as she was safe, she'd not hesitate to say 'Mick.'"

"Is this maybe why he's such a fuckup?" Mag asked, trying to go as delicate as possible, but considering the subject, delicacy was virtually impossible.

"I never went so far in my head to try to figure it out. But maybe. Mostly, he's a lot like Dad, even though he'd be major ticked I said that. Life's a party. Bills to pay?" she asked sarcastically, making her way back around him and bending to open his cupboard to grab a skillet. "What? And I need to make money to pay those bills? What? There are concerts to see and I have to be the guy who brings the best bottle of tequila to the party so everyone will think I'm hot shit and come to me to get a shot. The government is *way* too in our business. Drugs should be legal. Prostitution should be legal. A good time should be lawful to be had by all and damn the consequences faced by those subjugated to it or those on the periphery of it who want no part of it."

They were skimming close to her stripping and Mag wasn't going to take it there.

If she wanted to talk about it, he was game to listen.

No judgments.

But her Computer Raiders getup wasn't as cute as that tee she had on.

Noting that, if it was his choice, she'd be off Smithie's stage and fixing people's computers full time.

And earning her degree the rest of it.

It wasn't his choice.

"So yeah," she went on. "I think Mom spoiling Mick and doting on him, and making me, and in some cases Sid, pick up his slack made him lazy and selfish and thoughtless. But I think for him it's in the genes."

She pulled out the leftover slices of bacon that weren't cooked that morning and arranged them in the skillet.

She turned on the gas, adjusted it and looked to him.

"Do you think I should prepare for something really bad happening to my brother?"

"I honestly don't know," he told her.

She stared at him.

Then she asked, "What aren't you telling me?"

"Not something I haven't said before. The place he's in he put himself in and no matter what your mother said to you today, it isn't on you."

"What *else* aren't you telling me?"

Shit.

Damn.

"Evie—"

"I know he knows the bag is gone, Danny. Mom made that clear. And I figure it was you that told him when you went to go see him. How was he? Was he freaked?"

He gave it to her straight.

"Yes. And, baby, what I don't wanna say, what I told him I'd tell you, but I've been struggling with telling you is, he didn't give a thought to you. Even knowing he'd landed you in shit, he was all about him."

She looked down to the frying bacon.

Fuck.

Her fucking family.

He hopped off the counter, opened a drawer, grabbed a fork and moved in behind her.

He slid one arm around her to hold her to him and used his other hand to shift the bacon so it wouldn't stick.

"I've made a mess of my life, Danny," she told the bacon.

"Join the club, Evie," he said into her ear.

"I'm sorry you think your life is a mess," she whispered.

"And I'm sorry yours *is* a mess," he replied. "Though I'll note, strongly, it's not of your making."

"How do you...?" she didn't finish.

"What?" he asked.

"Nothing."

He wanted to push.

He didn't push.

He just moved bacon around in a skillet.

"After dinner, do you mind if I blow off the movie to go through the boxes Lottie and Ava brought around?" she asked.

"Whatever you want, baby," he murmured.

"Thanks," she mumbled, reached out and took the fork from his hand. "I got it from here."

He did the only thing he felt it was cool to do in that moment.

He pressed his hand against her stomach and his jaw against the side of her head.

Then he let her go and went to the fridge, saying, "I won't offer you a beer."

She shot him a grin. It was small, but it was real.

"What do you drink?" he asked.

"Cold-pressed juice."

She was right there with him, boneless wing for boneless wing.

So he was surprised by her answer.

"Really?"

"No." Her smile was now bigger. "You think I'd pay six bucks for a juice?"

He did not.

He wanted there to be a time when she wouldn't think too much about that.

But now she did.

"Though I've treated myself on occasion and they're yummy," she muttered.

"You had beer at your pad," he noted.

"No, I had *ale* at my pad," she corrected him. "I drink ale. I drink stout. I drink craft beer where the operative word is 'craft,' as in craftsmanship went into the making of that beverage, which is far elevated from just *beer*."

"So, you're a beer snob," he teased.

"Absolutely," she said without shame.

He made a mental note to buy some decent beer.

This he did while he popped the tab on a Bud and headed back to resume his seat on the counter.

"Don't think I missed how you lost at shotgunning and wiggled out of *Anaconda*. Totally watching that your next night off."

"Can I admit something to you?" she asked.

"No judgment here, Evie, ever," he answered.

She gave him a long look and he really hoped she saw what he wanted her to see.

"Scary movies freak me out. I don't sleep great anyway. But a scary movie can mess me up for weeks," she said. "Even bad ones."

"I'll pick something else," he replied immediately and then went alert when her body jolted.

They were having another Toothpaste Moment. He saw it.

"You're a pushover, Daniel Magnusson," she said softly.

She totally had no issue with scary movies.

"I'm really not, Evie," he replied in her same tone. "Not normally."

Oh yeah.

The way she was looking at him?

They were totally having another Toothpaste Moment.

He smiled at her.

She smiled back.

Quickly.

Then she turned to the bacon.

CHAPTER ELEVEN
The Test of Us

EVIE

The next morning, I was in the bathroom, brushing my teeth, when I heard it.

I finished quickly, spit, rinsed, wiped and headed out.

Just as I suspected.

Mag was standing at the counter in nothing but his loose shorts that ran long, almost to his knees, and he was beating something in a bowl.

But when I hit the space, he turned to me, his expression telling me he was about to smile and say some good morning–type words, but his body arrested when he clapped eyes on me.

I had to admit, my new sleep set was cute.

Shorts and racer-back cami, ivory with black flowers on them.

But he'd only given my body a cursory glance.

He was staring at my head.

"You're making breakfast," I accused.

"Well...yeah."

I stomped his way, stating, "I can't offer a multilayered thank-you if you keep doing things for yourself. You helped clean up after dinner last night."

"Babe, you cooked."

I stopped beside him where his body was still turned to the counter, somewhat twisted my way, his hand on the spoon he was using to mix what was in the bowl, and I slammed my hands on my hips.

"Yes!" I snapped. "But it doesn't say 'thank you' to fry up messy burgers then make you help me clean up after. Cleanup is the worst part. And it doesn't say 'thank you' to wander into the kitchen in the morning and have you serve me food."

He didn't respond verbally.

He lifted his free hand and tugged at the hairband I'd used to put a topknot in my hair so I could brush my teeth and wash my face without it getting in the way. A hairband that was oddly precious to me seeing as it was one of the few things the bad guys hadn't destroyed.

Mag pulled it out and my hair came tumbling down.

I felt all of that in my nipples.

"Fuck me," he whispered, his eyes wandering my face and hair in sultry admiration.

And I felt that right between my legs.

So of course, being me, I attacked.

I heard the spoon Mag had been using in whatever he was making in that bowl clatter soggily to the countertop as he caught me in his arms.

He'd learned, fortunately for him.

Thus, he clamped one arm tight around my waist, his other hand he wrapped around the base of my head, controlling it, tilting it to the side, then his mouth came down on mine.

Hard.

I opened my lips and his tongue instantly invaded, and tasting him, receiving the signal he couldn't wait even an instant to taste me, I pressed tight, fisted both hands in the back of his hair...

And went at him.

He returned the gesture.

We did some shuffling around, Mag to press me back into the counter so he could fit himself deeper into me.

Me turning him so I could do the same.

Him turning me to regain the dominant position.

Me approving of this nonverbally because it gave me a cleaner go at his back, which I was headily exploring with one of my hands, doing this moving south.

Mag realizing he'd limited his exploratory options by pressing me to the counter, so he whirled me again.

My fingers were caught in the waistband of his shorts.

His hand was going up inside my cami.

All of this we did without dislodging our mouths.

There was nothing *nice* about it. Nothing *sweet*.

It was hot and sexy and reckless and intoxicating.

It was careless and freeing and exciting and *magnificent*.

I'd never experienced anything like it. Never been lost to a kiss, to the feelings that kiss created, to *a man* like that.

He was stroking the side of my breast with the pad of his thumb while I was pressing even closer, like I wanted to climb him, feeling him growing hard against my belly, when I tore my mouth from his.

"Yes, Danny," I breathed, giving him permission to stop the torture at the side of my breast and just *take it*.

"Christ, you're gorgeous," he whispered, staring down at me with hooded, dilated eyes, moving his hand, cupping my breast, now using the pad of his thumb to take a swipe at my nipple.

Oh God, that felt good.

I moaned, my head falling back, and locked him to the counter by giving him my weight, seeing as my legs couldn't hold me up anymore.

"*Gorgeous,*" he growled.

Then his mouth was back on mine, he was sucking my tongue into his, circling my nipple with his thumb while I tried to burrow into him, wiggling against his hardness, attempting to force my hand down his shorts to get to his ass.

He groaned down my throat and then ripped his mouth from mine.

When it didn't go somewhere else, I blinked up at him.

His head was turned to the door.

"This is not happening," he snarled.

He was wrong.

"It" was happening.

The door was opening.

And there we stood, me practically fused with Mag, his hand up my cami, my hand in his hair, the other one unsuccessful, but obvious in its bid to get to his ass, while Mo, Axl, Boone and another guy I hadn't met yet strolled in.

Mag took his hand from under my cami, but he didn't allow me to move away. He wrapped that arm around me and I figured he did this because he liked me where I was, but also because, from what I could tell, he was fully erect, there was significant promise to that erection, and it wasn't something he wanted his buds to see.

"Explain," he barked to his friends.

Mo was looking at his feet.

The rest of them were grinning audaciously at us.

"I'm not hearing any words," Mag warned.

"You see," Boone began, "there's a pool."

I was not keeping up.

I'd barely processed the fact the activities had been interrupted.

Why was Boone talking about a pool?

"It's a Rock Chick thing," Axl explained as he sauntered in further. "We all got in late, our slots on when you two are gonna seal the deal aren't for two weeks, Lots said you guys were goin' at it yesterday morning, and we're dudes, so we know the drill, consequently we figured we had to instigate some evasive maneuvers early in the morning."

Mo's head came up. "I didn't place a bet. I'm here 'cause I got an update. These jackasses just wouldn't let me knock."

Oh God.

I didn't have one frat boy on my hands.

I had *four*.

I looked up at Mag and snapped, "You need to confiscate keys."

"No kidding," he said angrily, but his gaze was still aimed at his buds.

"Mag's making pancakes," the one I had not met yet, who I assumed was Auggie, declared.

"Fuck yeah," Boone replied happily.

"I'm not feeding you all pancakes," Mag declared.

"Am I on Evan today or what?" Auggie asked. And before Mag could answer, he went on, "That's a marker. And my payback is your pancakes."

"His pancakes are freaking brilliant," Axl told me.

"Totally got the touch with pancakes," Boone muttered.

They were all milling about, taking stools at the island, or leaning into it. Axl even rounded it to head to the coffeepot.

All while Mag and I stood in each other's arms, staring (or more aptly, *glaring*) at them.

Most women, maybe every breathing one on the face of the planet, would not be crotchety at the company I was keeping right then.

This was because Boone was a tall, dark-blond, green-eyed Adonis.

Axl had a full head of silver hair, prematurely that color or he was born with it, I didn't know, but it was fabulous, and coupled with his ice-blue eyes, he was a sight to behold.

And I couldn't be sure, it was a fantastical thought, but from the sheer perfection of Auggie's swarthy good looks, he might actually *be* a Greek god roaming the earth.

Even so.

Them being there, I was crotchety.

Rationally (and such thoughts were not coming to me fast enough around Mag), I should be glad for the interruption.

Attacking Mag first thing in the morning was not conducive to me eventually gently extricating myself from his life, after, of course, I gave him what it was clear he needed, the opportunity to look after me while things were uncertain.

But I was far from glad for the interruption.

I felt it before Mag demonstrated he had a lock on his condition, his demonstration taking the form of putting his hands under my arms, twisting and planting my ass on his counter, then pulling himself up beside me.

And once he had us where he wanted us, he honed in on Mo.

"You got an update?" he prompted before he turned to Axl. "Pour a cup for Evie. She takes a shot of cream."

Axl was grinning hugely as he muttered, "Gotcha," and reached for another mug.

Mag looked back at Mo.

"Yeah?" he pushed.

Mo glanced at me and back to Mag.

I read what that meant.

"Oh no," I said. "I get to know. I'm not kept in the dark."

"She's not kept in the dark," Mag confirmed.

Mo's barrel chest expanded, and he blew out a sigh that I was pretty certain wafted my hair back before he leaned into a hand on the island.

I braced because none of that seemed a precursor to good news.

"Snag, short for Snaggletooth, street name for Fletcher Gumm," Mo began. "He runs a couple of girls."

I went solid.

That guy I met, a guy *my brother knew*, ran *a couple of girls*?

"He's a pimp?" I asked.

"Yeah," Mo verified shortly. "Evie, did you look into that bag?"

"Danny did," I said.

"Danny," Auggie muttered amusedly.

Mag ignored him and stated, "Oxy, meth, coke, a lot of it."

"So much they'd tear Evan's place apart?" Mo asked.

That was when I felt Mag go solid.

He then hopped off the counter, wrapped his fingers around my knee, and laser focused on Mo.

"We didn't empty the bag," he shared. He looked to me. "Did you go through it?"

I shook my head.

He turned back to Mo.

"Well, Boone and I had the occasion to chat with a few of Snag's girls last night," Mo said.

Great.

Absolutely fabulous.

My brother's crap meant Mo and Boone had to find then chat with prostitutes.

"Snag is in the wind," Mo continued. "But one of his girls said one of his *other* girls had a john who had something she decided she wanted. Snag found out about it. He commandeered it. Word got out she stole it, and now she's dead."

"Oh my God," I whispered.

"Though, before she was taken out, she shared Snag had it. Now he's in the wind."

"What is it?" Mag asked.

"That, I don't know, the girl who shared all this didn't know, and who's looking for it, she also didn't know," Mo answered.

Great.

Absolutely freaking *fabulous*.

"So, maybe they found Snag, who led them to Evie, and they got it back and this is all done?" Mag suggested.

"Maybe," Mo said ominously.

"You know more?" Mag asked.

"Dick," Mo told him, shaking his bald head.

"So, we continue efforts to find Gumm at the same time wait and see if they make a move on Evan, or her brother, to know if whatever it is, is back where it belongs," Mag deduced.

"Yeah, without any other leads, those are the plays we got," Mo replied.

No one was happy with this, I could feel, including me.

But it was only me who sat there, paralyzed.

I didn't know what to do or say or how this could possibly be worse than what it was before.

A woman was dead.

I felt Mag's fingers give my knee a squeeze and heard him murmur, "Evie."

I focused on him. "You guys have to stop."

"We will when we know you're safe," he replied.

"A woman is dead."

I watched Mag's mouth grow tight.

"It was in the bag," I said. "Everything that was in that bag when I got it was in it when it was taken. I'm done. I don't know anything. I'm out."

"There's a scenario to that where you're not out," Mag noted.

My voice was rising when I cried, "How can that be? I'm not in that life!"

As it was clear I was becoming more freaked, Mag repositioned to stand between my knees, where he now had both hands with fingers squeezing reassuringly.

"Baby, hang tight, yeah? You're in a good place. You're covered," he assured.

I forced myself to breathe steadily and stared at him.

He watched me do this before he continued.

"If who got it is not who it was taken from, you were in the chain of possession, and they won't care you're not in the life."

"I didn't know I even had *it*, whatever *it* is."

"They don't know that."

"Well, Mick can get the word out to tell them that," I snapped.

After which, Mag looked over his shoulder at Mo.

I did too, and saw Mo wore an expression that was more terrifying than his usual Resting Terrifying Face.

"He won't," I whispered, and Mag turned back to me. "Mick won't. He's occupied covering his own ass, which means conceivably throwing me under the bus, if needs be."

"Evie," he said softly.

It was that softness. His voice, deep with a lovely timbre normally, going soft, it was like his voice box had been touched by the hand of God.

And his face, staring at me with tenderness and understanding.

And his friends, coming over to give him shit but this after two had been out last night trying to sort my problems and one was going to spend his day off covering my ass.

It was all that.

All that which finally made me lose it.

"Welcome to my world, baby," I stated snidely, and watched Mag's expression go alert and his head twitch while doing it. "Last night you got a dose of the honey sweetness of my mom. The night before you got to spend quality time with the stand-up guy my brother is. It's too bad I have to *strip* tonight. I could take you round to meet my dad. You could get high with him, his favorite pastime. So much so, I don't think I've spent a minute with him my entire life where he wasn't at least half-baked. Or we could find my sister, who's probably wrestling on film in a vat of pudding to up her followers. But that's okay. You can come watch me slither around all oiled up to earn tips for giving assholes hard-ons."

"Evan," he whispered.

"I'm trash," I stated.

His face got hard. "Don't say shit like that."

"I am." I leaned his way. "I'm *fucking trash*."

He lifted both hands and framed my face, putting his in mine and growling, "Do not say that shit."

"You are so blind," I mocked. "So *fucking* blind. I've fooled you. But it's not surprising seeing as I've spent twenty-seven years fooling myself. I can't get out of it. I can't find my way to a different life. Straight up, Mag, listen to me. I like you. You're a good guy. So listen to me. You need to get out now. Save yourself because there's no saving me. They're gonna drag me down, and if you're anywhere near, they're gonna take you with me."

"Find somewhere else to be," he rumbled, not at me, I knew, because the guys moved, though apparently Mag's pancakes were really that good because they didn't leave.

They went to his room and shut the door.

"Look at me," Mag said.

I turned my gaze from watching his bedroom door close to his face.

"I like you too, Evan, and I'm not blind to shit," he declared.

"You need to let me go."

I meant his hold on my head and just…

Me.

He did not let me go.

He made a speech.

A speech that was such, I hung on every word.

"We're gonna sort this shit out and then we're gonna date in a way you put a bag with clean panties and a nightie in my truck 'cause you'll be spending the night. That is, before you got your stuff at my place, and I have mine at yours. I'll make you breakfast. You'll make me dinner. You're gonna get your goddamn degree. You're gonna find a job you dig. You're gonna build the life you want, Evan. Don't know if I'm gonna be a part of that. Just know, as of now, I feel the deep need to explore that possibility. And this is not a damsel-in-distress situation where I'm blinded to dick, intent only on saving the little woman. It's because you like my eyelashes, you give a shit about the planet, you knew your brother was gonna get your ass in a sling but you moved to protect him anyway, you got no issue making the first move to go after what you want and you make fucking great bacon cheeseburgers, even without Worcestershire sauce."

"You're the nicest guy I've ever met," I whispered.

"And this is a bad thing?" he did not whisper.

"Can't you see I'm trying to protect you?" I asked.

He slid his fingers back into my hair and curled them around my head.

"Trust me," he stated, his tone now guttural, and those two words landed like punches in my gut, sharing inexorably that this conversation just took a dread turn. "This goes the way I want it to, there'll be a time I got no choice but to land my shit on you. I'll fuckin' hate it, only slightly more than you will when you hear it. This is not the test of us, Evan. *That* will be the test of us."

I stared in his intense blue eyes.

And got it.

"Afghanistan. Iraq. Syria," I said softly.

"You know what a rape house is?"

Oh no.

No.

That was when I lifted my hands and grabbed his head.

"Yeah," he grunted. "Well, I've seen one."

"Danny," I breathed, my eyes stinging, the tears coming.

"So, you want it straight-up, Evie?" he asked but went on before I could answer. "Your brother and his shit is chump change to what I've seen men do to women."

"Honey," I whispered.

"And I'm gonna fuckin' get you clear, Evan, are you hearing me?"

I nodded.

"And you are not fucking trash. I know trash. And that is not you. And not simply because, in every instance I ran up against trash, it had a dick. But that *does* include your fucking brother."

"Okay, sweetheart," I said soothingly.

"Don't talk that shit to me or anyone ever again, Evan. Yeah?"

I repeated my nod.

"We done with your episode?"

"Yes," I said.

"You have 'em whenever they come. Let 'em fly. And I'll talk you down. You still with me?"

"Yes, Danny."

With all that was happening, it was more than the fact I was a crier that I couldn't stop it.

So the tear dropped from my eye to run down my face.

Mag shifted a hand and caught it with his thumb, then spread the wet over the apple of my cheek.

"Now, I'm making pancakes," he declared.

A sharp giggle escaped me that wasn't humor, as such, even if it kind of was.

"Okay," I replied.

He started to move away but then didn't and both his hands shifted so he could rub his thumbs over the apples of my cheeks.

"I got a really bad temper," he admitted quietly, these words filled to the brim with shame and even fear that I knew to my soul he should not feel.

And thus, I held on, with hands and eyes, and listened.

"You gotta know that before either of us make moves

to lock each other in. I wasn't like that before. I can't say I never got mad. But I never got mad in a way it was like I was outside myself, watching me lose it, and I had no control over how bad it got. I've been in fights. With guys. It used to get physical. And I lost my mind on Nikki a couple of times, just shouting, but she knew about it so she took it and it killed me, knowing she accepted that about me and I couldn't control it. I found coping mechanisms. I haven't totally lost it in a while, but I feel it sometimes, boiling under the surface. And I've researched it so I know it's not something that will ever just go away, unless I medicate, and my job, I can't do that. So...that's what..." he drew in a big breath and finished, "you gotta know."

"All right," I said softly.

"It gets bad, Evie, I gotta stress that."

These words made something inside me move, a weird fluttery feeling.

It was around my heart. A tightness there I never really felt because I'd lived with it my whole life.

But right then, in a colossal shift to the world as I knew it, it just...

Loosened.

"You heard my mom talk to me the way she did last night."

"Babe—"

I pressed in at his head.

"Listen to me, Danny, please?"

He shut his mouth.

"She's never seen what you've seen, and she's like that. And I've been taking it my whole life, knowing there's no reason. I just did it because she's my mom and I'm supposed to love her. There's a reason why Nikki understood.

You're a good guy, Danny. Now it's your turn to trust me, because I won't lose track of that."

I was then still holding his head and he was still in my face, but *way* in my space.

He'd wrapped one arm around me and pulled me to his body, his other hand at the back of my head, and we were making out again.

It was getting heavy, what with my special somewhere pressed against his rock-hard abs, when, yet again, his buds spoiled the fun.

"This is not getting me pancakes," Auggie called.

Mag broke the kiss only to mutter against my lips, "I'm gonna kill these fuckin' guys."

I smiled into his eyes.

The anger slid out of his.

He then kissed my forehead and let me go, turning to Auggie and saying, "Newsflash, asshole. The reason they're good is you gotta let the batter rest."

"This dude is Julia Child with a Bronze Star," Boone noted. "His pancakes are good but he's a virtuoso at the grill. He can even make pizza on that fucker."

It was good to know Mag could cook, but...

"Bronze Star?" I asked Mag.

"That's like, eightieth-date territory, baby," he muttered.

"Right," I whispered.

He turned his head from the batter and grinned at me before he leaned in and touched his lips to mine.

"So, Evie," Axl said, sliding the cup of coffee he'd poured me earlier on the counter by my hip. "Just in case you got time, I brought my laptop. It's acting up."

"I'll have a look," I told him before I took a sip of coffee.

"She's not free tech support, dickhead," Mag growled.

"Yes, I am," I decreed.

"See," Axl jerked a thumb at me. "She is."

"Is it in your car?" I asked.

Axl nodded.

"Go down and get it," I ordered. "I'll have a look while Danny's cooking."

"On it," he replied and took off.

"Babe," Mag called.

I gave him my eyes.

"Seriously" was all he said.

"It's okay. Promise" was how I replied.

He blew out a sigh.

My bag at the other end of the counter rang.

Auggie grabbed it and brought it to me.

It was Charlie.

I had a callout.

I heard the sizzle of butter hitting a warm griddle, the promise of goodness.

And I felt my heart beat.

Free.

And there you go.

Life goes on.

And sometimes, I was now learning, it was good.

CHAPTER TWELVE
The Dream Team

EVIE

"So, she's got nothin', and we're on a break, and she's at Target, buying Legos."

Auggie was on the phone.

With Mag.

Sharing about our day.

"She then makes me drive her to the goddamn county lockup, not so she can lay into that asswipe brother of hers. So, she can lay those Legos on Bobbie. You know, that cop who sometimes runs the desk there. Because Bobbie's kid was sick."

I stood in the hall outside the dancers' dressing room at Smithie's club, hands on hips, ordering, "Stop talking, Auggie."

Auggie ignored me.

"Yeah, Evie doesn't have a couch, but Bobbie's kid has a new Lego set," he told Mag. "Then she gets a call from some old lady whose got somethin' jackin' with her computer. And just sayin', brother, you're up for dinner at Gert's next Tuesday. And so am *I* and Boone, Axl, Mo *and* Lottie. I tried to get us out of it, but the woman talked so much, I couldn't get a word in."

I put my hand out and demanded, "Give me your phone, Auggie."

"Yeah," he said into the phone, continuing to ignore me. "So, Gert's one tough cookie and she pretty much thinks Evie walks on water, which means, when the woman takes a breath, I tell her what's goin' down, and Gert loses her goddamn mind."

I squinted my eyes at him at that reminder and remained in my stance, hand held out, glaring at him.

"This is probably why she let slip that Evie has been single-handedly feeding her for the last two years," he continued.

Which was when I moved, shouting, "Auggie! Stop!" at the same time launching myself at him and going for his phone.

He just rounded me with an arm, tucked me to his side and twisted his torso away, all the while still...freaking...*talking*.

"Yeah, so heads-up on that too, brother. Gert didn't wanna accept, but she's in a financial sitch so she can't really argue too much. This means I'm on grocery duty next. I volunteered Boone, Axl and Mo and Lottie, but you're up after she gets through the lineup."

"Auggie! I have to start getting ready! Stop messing around! Give me that phone!"

"Yeah," he said into the phone he was not giving me. "So now I don't know whether to be terrified of the chick Lots has lined up for me or jump the gun and just walk into the dressing room and ask her to marry me. But after the Lego argument, where Evie essentially threw down in a goddamn *Target* about her right to buy a sick kid a present, I'm leaning toward terrified."

The Lego argument was not my finest hour.

People stopped to watch.

But he'd actually thought he could tell me I couldn't buy something, stating he'd buy it and I could say it was from me.

Of course, he was right. I should save my pennies to buy a new mattress, so I had somewhere to sleep.

But he'd actually *thought* he could *tell me* I couldn't buy something...

And I'd listen.

And obey!

I stared at his perfectly angled, perfectly stubbled jaw.

"Sure," he said then offered his phone to me. "Mag wants to talk to you."

I snatched it out of his hand, pulled out of his hold and walked two paces away before I put it to my ear and said, "Auggie doesn't get any more of your pancakes *until the end of time*."

Mag's laughter spilled into my ear.

Okay, that made me feel better.

Slightly.

Reminders of his bodacious pancakes made me feel even better.

Though not enough.

Auggie had shared all my secrets with Mag!

"And, you know, since we're spilling our hearts out to each other, either directly, or through intermediaries, you should know that Gert's my only friend. She's seventy-nine, is an aficionado of Olive Garden and her children don't live close. Girls my age never got me. I would say this is a boon for you, since you don't have to pass some girlfriend test. But Gert loves me and she's gonna look you over with a keen eye. And if you aren't on your best behavior, she'll begin a campaign to surgically excise you from my life."

Through chuckles, Mag said, "I can win over a seventy-nine-year-old woman."

"You don't know Gert. She's very opinionated. The first words she spoke to Auggie were, 'God, I hope you're not Evie's new boyfriend. You're way too pretty to be good for any woman.'"

Mag burst into laughter again, through it forcing out, "Fuck, I wish I was there to see that."

"I do too," I replied, turning my eyes to Auggie. "It would serve him right."

"Baby, three things," Mag said.

"What?" I asked.

"First, girls didn't like you not because they didn't get you. But because they saw all the guys wanted a shot at you and they were jealous."

"That's what moms are supposed to say. My mom just told me to stop being so weird."

I heard a sucking void of sound over Auggie's phone and rethought sharing that with Mag.

"Second," he eventually said, his voice sounding tighter, but he was persevering, "stop buying Legos for people's kids. You got somethin' like that you wanna do, you tell me. I'll swing by Target, get it, and you can do the giving."

Hang on a second.

What?

Not Mag too!

"Last, you can tell Aug he's off duty. I'm headed to Smithie's right now. I'm on you and I'm your ride home."

I stood stock-still.

"Evie," Mag called.

I remained standing stock-still.

"Evie," Mag growled.

"Hey," Auggie said softly, suddenly standing close.

"You're off duty," I said stiffly. "Mag's on his way."

The phone was out of my hand, I heard Auggie mutter, "Evie's having a moment. I got it. See you soon."

Then Auggie's black eyes were so close, nothing else existed.

"Talk to me," he urged.

"He's on his way," I whispered.

"Yeah," he said.

"He can't watch me dance, Auggie," I told him. "He can't see me dance."

"Hey," he said then grabbed my neck on either side "Hey, hey, hey," he repeated, and I knew why.

The damned tears were building in my eyes.

"My boy thinks you're the shit, babe," he said.

Another "babe."

Yeesh.

I didn't have it in me to get into that.

Mag was *on his way* and he was going to *see me dance*.

"I gotta get out of my head, you know, to do it," I shared. "I gotta be like, a different Evie in order to be able to go out there. I'm not like Lottie. She's talented and she's proud of her abilities, of her body, she understands the world where this exists. She puts things in boxes. She uses them to get what she wants and she's at one with that. I'm not... that's not me."

"I can get that," he replied.

"I won't be able to get out of my head if Danny's watching."

He kept his hands on me even as he straightened and declared, "I'll stay."

I shook my head. "No, no, no. You spent all day with me. You need to go home or do something *you* want to do."

"I'll stay, look after you, drive you to Mag's after."

"Auggie, I can't ask you to—"

"Evan, he's going to keep it in check, for you. But he's gonna like watchin' you dance for a bunch of horny assholes about as much as you're gonna like him watchin' you dance for a bunch of horny assholes. I'll stay."

"No. Seriously. I wouldn't feel right if—"

"You know, Duke called Hawk last night."

Uh-oh.

I wasn't sure that was good.

I closed my mouth.

"Now, Hawk was there when Mag talked to your brother. So, Hawk gets an earful about how your ma talked to you. And so, Mo, Boone, Axl and me get a call to haul our asses to the office last night. We get there and Hawk is *pissed*."

Oh man.

I hadn't met Hawk yet, but by virtue of his name, and him commanding a crew of commandos, I had a feeling him being pissed was not a good thing.

"He's got a daughter, you with me?" Auggie asked.

I nodded.

"He also had another daughter, who, while he was deployed, got shot in a drive-by shooting. His wife had a brother who was bad news. His wife refused to give up on that brother. She got shot too. Neither of them survived."

"Ohmigod," I breathed.

Poor Hawk.

"So, to say he's not down with you getting shit on is an

understatement. Before, he was resigned to one of his boys getting tied up in some messy shit. Now we're under orders to handle it."

Which meant now, even a man I'd never met was looking out for me.

"And the list of people I owe keeps getting longer," I mumbled.

"You know, that's what those assholes put in your head and you got it stuck so deep in there, you don't see you don't live that life. You gonna make Gert pay you back for taking care of her? You expect Bobbie to do something for your brother in exchange for Legos?"

"Of course not."

"Then shut it down about owing shit, Evan. This is what people do in life, that is, if they're worth dick. Sometimes you give. Sometimes you get. The measure of a person is how gracious they can be when they're in the position they have to receive."

"You know, you're actually more annoying when you're being nice," I told him.

He smiled, wide and white, then folded me in his arms and gave me a tight, brotherly hug complete with a kiss on the side of my head.

Then he let me go and shoved me toward the door to the dressing room and said, "Go. Get ready. I'll explain things to Mag."

I moved to the door to do as he said, but turned at it and called, "Auggie."

He already had his phone to his ear, but he turned his head to me.

"Thank you."

He jerked up his chin and then said, "Mag? Yeah. Evie and I had a chat and she's not at the place where she's down with you bein' here while she dances. I'm on her tonight. I'll bring her to you after." A pause and then, "No, yeah, really, brother. Evie needs this and I got her. Okay?"

His attention focused on me and he nodded.

"Cool, Mag," he said. "I'll call when we're on our way to your place."

I heaved out a breath, mouthed "thank you" to him again, and then pushed in the door.

My shoulder was practically dislocated when I was yanked inside.

"What in the holy hell-blazin' *fuck*?"

I blinked at Ryn, another dancer, who was scowling at me.

A half second after, I saw I was surrounded by Ryn, Pepper and Hattie, with Lottie behind them, arms crossed on her chest, foot out, a smug look on her face.

She'd instigated an ambush.

"Uh, *hello*, Evan?" Ryn called my attention back to her. "I've cozied up to you in a fake lesbionic, tip-inducing wonder scene more times than I can count, and you don't pick up the phone and call when your brother lands you in deep shit?"

"I mean, seriously," Hattie said then looked at the other two girls. "We look out for each other. Am I right? Sisterhood."

"You're right," Ryn replied.

"Breaking this down," Pepper entered the three-way conversation that just happened to involve four people. "We're hurt you hung with the Rock Chicks and let them clean up your pad and you didn't call on us."

They were hurt?

I liked them.

I knew they liked me.

But when I needed help and I didn't call, they were *hurt*?

Wow.

"Well, I didn't really—" I began to share that was not at my instigation, or my choice, but that was as far as I got.

"It's us from now on," Ryn declared. "The Dream Team. The Rock Chicks are cool and all, but we're next gen."

"So, you know, Lottie says there's more stuff to go through and you have to sift through some of it, so we're gonna go do that tomorrow." Pepper flipped a hand at the three of them, as well as me. "All of us. We'll meet at your place at noon. I'm bringing lunch. And tonight has been declared a benefit for the rejuvenation of Evie's pad. All the dancers are giving you their tips. Even Carla and Dominique."

I opened my mouth.

"No," Hattie said quietly, and that was Hattie. She was gorgeous and she could dance almost as good as Lottie. In fact, she'd studied dancing for years and wanted to go professional, but life, as it was wont to do, got in the way. But offstage, she was quiet. Even timid. "Don't, Evie. And you know why."

I did.

My life wasn't the only life that had a mess in it somewhere, either on the surface, or buried deep.

I'd taken all their backs before.

Including Carla and Dominique.

"You should know," I said to Pepper, who I knew Lottie was in the throes of fixing up with Auggie. "Auggie's out there. He's on duty to look after me tonight."

"Fabulous," Pepper told the ceiling.

"Maybe you should dance in a mask," Ryn teased Pepper.

"You're the one who likes masks," Pepper retorted to Ryn.

Really?

What did that mean?

Interesting.

"I wonder if Boone likes masks," Hattie remarked.

"I'm not getting together with Boone," Ryn told Hattie.

"Well, I'm not getting together with Auggie, so it doesn't matter if he sees me dance," Pepper told Ryn.

"I'm totally not getting together with Axl," Hattie declared, giving a visible little shiver that had a lot to do with her being pathologically shy around guys.

"You are, you need this," Ryn, always a boss, said.

"You need Boone too," Pepper cut into Ryn's bossing. "You need to settle down. You scare me."

What?

Why was Ryn scaring Pepper?

"I'm fine," Ryn returned.

Pepper looked to me. "She is not."

"What's—?" I started, but Lottie spoke up.

"You women better slap on some makeup and pull on your G-strings or Smithie is gonna get involved and no one wants that," she said. "He's been threatening to pull you, worried you'll be at risk when you're onstage," she told me, and that made *me* shiver. "We talked him out of it. But tips gotta be made. There's furniture and plates and whatnot that need replaced. So, let's get at it."

She then clapped.

That was Lottie.

Queen of Smithie's in a variety of ways.

We were just fortunate she was benevolent.

And thus, we all headed to our mirrored dressing tables. Carla and Dominique were already out there. They both had kids, so they started early and ended the same.

Pepper also had a kid, Juno, cute as a button, sweet as heck, and hilarious, but it was her dad's week to have Juno, which meant Pepper went late, which was good for Pepper. Tips were better the more time the horny assholes had to get drunk.

"You're totally going out with Boone, you can't help yourself. You're curious," Pepper muttered to Ryn along the way.

"You're totally going out with Auggie, and I'll bet your tips break records tonight, you trying to impress him," Ryn muttered back.

I sat down at my vanity and looked to Hattie, who was sitting next to me.

"Axl's very handsome and he's really nice," I said.

"That's the problem," she replied.

"You've seen him?" I asked.

She nodded, leaning toward her mirror to slather on some foundation. "He worked the crowd during Lottie's sitch."

I hadn't noticed.

Then again, I'd actually been able to take some classes back then so if I wasn't working, I was in class or studying, and alternately concerned about Lottie, so I hadn't noticed.

"I think they get why we do what we do," I assured her.

She turned to me. "I don't care if he gets it. *I* get it. And honey, just sayin', what you've told us about your family, what Lottie shared about what's going down, it's only you who doesn't get what we do. You aren't them. Your family, that is. You're doing it for your own reasons. A means to an end. And you don't owe anyone an explanation about that."

She was right.

Really right.

I'd just never thought of it that way.

"You're right," I spoke the words out loud.

She shot me a grin and, "I know," and turned back to her mirror.

I turned to mine.

Because they were going to give me their tips tonight, it was Friday night, the biggest tip night that I danced.

My lowest Friday night take had been five hundred dollars.

My highest was over two thousand.

That meant my fellow dancers...

Strike that.

Friends were probably going to refurnish my living room that night.

So, I had to be right there with them.

* * *

After counting, I tried to shove the envelope in my little purse.

It didn't fit.

"How much?" Auggie, at my side driving, asked.

I had to clear the frog out of my throat before I answered, "Nearly eight thousand. And that doesn't include my tips from tonight."

"Jesus," he muttered.

"It was a good night and Lottie always makes a bundle, but I think Smithie chipped in."

"Undoubtedly the man wanted it under the radar, but you should know how people feel about you, so I'll tell you I saw him slipping Lots some cash."

Of course.

Best boss in the world.

A man who owned a strip joint.

And that was just the way.

You just never knew.

The most stand-up-appearing guy could be an absolute slimeball.

And a strip club owner could have a heart of pure gold.

"Pepper turned it up a notch tonight, I noticed," I remarked.

"Babe," he said.

Then he said no more.

I turned to him, and after his chat to me and that brotherly hug, I couldn't quite keep the earnestness out of my voice.

"She's really sweet. And I know she has a kid and some dudes balk at that, but I've babysat her often, and Juno is *everything*."

"Pepper's also got a dickhead ex who fucks with her whenever he can and makes opportunities if they aren't available, and as such, she's not feelin' lettin' another guy in her life right now, but more, into her kid's life. We haven't set something up and it's not about her kid. I want kids. I want lots of kids. Kids are kids. They're in your life, you love 'em like your own. So it's not about Juno. It's not about Pepper. It's not about her dancing. It's what Pepper needs in her life at the present and that's not me."

"Wow, Pepper has shared a lot."

"I got the sense she didn't want me to think she was blowing me off," he muttered.

"That's Pepper. She's thoughtful," I told him.

He glanced at me and I saw a hint of the flash of his white smile before he looked back to the road and asked, "You're not gonna give up, are you?"

"No," I answered.

"Evie, darlin', I'm not gonna be that stalkery guy who pushes shit with a woman when she's not in that zone."

"Auggie, something I'm learning, you can get caught up in your life and not realize what zone you need to find until life forces you to pay attention."

He was silent a beat before he said quietly, "Point made."

We didn't dive deeper into that the rest of the journey back to Mag's.

Auggie had the code to get into the underground garage, and as he drove to guest parking, I saw my Prius, its trunk looking good as new, parked next to Mag's humongous truck.

Something about that gave me a delicious shiver.

Auggie escorted me up and used his key to let us in.

The condo was dark, except for the light of the TV, which shined on Mag, who was stretched out on his side on the couch, up on an elbow in some throw pillows.

His eyes were on us.

Auggie walked me to the living room area, stopped us and stated, "She's safe home. Now after watching her and Lots and Pepper dance, I'm going home and washing my eyes out with soap."

Mag grinned and said, "Owe you."

"Yeah, you do," Auggie replied, turned to me, kissed the side of my head again then bid, "Later," pivoted, and walked back out the door.

I heard the lock go.

"He still has his key," I told Mag.

He grinned, this time at me, and then murmured, "C'mere, baby."

Seeing him stretched out like that in the light of the television, I could no sooner stop myself from walking to him than I could stop myself from eating a Toll House cookie fresh from the oven, no matter how hot it was and knowing it would burn my tongue.

I dropped my bag and the envelope of cash on his coffee table on my way and watched him shift before he executed a cool move, which included him pushing up, grabbing my hand, tugging me down so I landed on him but somehow ended up mostly *under* him.

It was far from lost on me how good it felt, having his weight on me.

But I'd just danced, it was three o'clock in the morning, and in order to let Auggie off the hook, I hadn't showered, just toweled down and cleaned my makeup off before I put my clothes back on and we took off.

I was tired, not exhausted.

But I'd just danced, I felt icky, and I didn't want to go where Mag was clearly taking me.

I also had this niggling disappointment he was intent to take me there.

I'd thought he'd stayed awake to make sure I was home safe, which was sweet.

It seemed he did.

But also, so he might get himself a little somethin'-somethin'.

"So," he murmured, his gaze moving all over my face and hair, and I knew what that meant.

Then he surprised me.

His eyes came to mine and he asked, "Gert?"

"If you pass inspection, she'll love you."

"She treats you right, I already love her."

He wasn't going to make a move.

He was talking about Gert.

He was being *Danny*.

God.

What was I going to do with Daniel Magnusson?

"So what's the drill after you dance?" he asked. "Are you jazzed and need to chill out watchin' TV or somethin' or do you just crash?"

I noted in those choices he did not offer a heavy make-out session, which would probably lead to a little somethin'-somethin'.

Yeah.

What was I going to do with my Danny?

"I see my Prius is back in action," I noted.

"Yeah, saw to that probably around the time you were shouting at Aug in a Target," he teased.

He saw to that.

While his friend was watching out for me.

"You know, I had a plan," I whispered.

His head cocked as he asked, "Sorry?"

"Yesterday. I'd formed a plan," I told him. "I was going to let you do what you had to do, and then I was going to exit your life, finding a way to do that permanently."

He had been relaxed and mellow.

At my words, he was no longer relaxed and mellow.

"I didn't think I was good enough for you," I went on.

"We had this conversation this morning, Evan," he said irritably.

I lifted a hand and ran my finger along his jaw, a lot like he'd done to me the day before to soothe me when I was having bad thoughts.

His expression shifted from annoyed to alert at the same time it was gentling.

"I'm getting the sense," I said softly, "that would have been the biggest mistake of my life."

"Baby," he whispered.

"Too soon?" I asked.

"No," he answered quickly.

At the swiftness of his answer, I was beginning to know what I was going to do with Daniel Magnusson.

"Sometimes, I'm tired and I need to crash," I answered his earlier question. "Sometimes, I'm jazzed, and I need to hang to chill out. But I didn't shower before I left tonight so I could get Auggie home and that means I feel kind of ick, so I need to shower and then go to bed. The girls are meeting me at my place tomorrow at noon to sort through some stuff."

"Which girls?"

"Some of the girls from work." I grinned. "The Dream Team. Pepper, Hattie and Ryn."

"Lottie's fix-ups," he muttered.

"Yeah," I confirmed. "They're my friends and I really didn't...until tonight, when they got in my face, hurt that I didn't call on them when things got crazy, I realized that I hadn't put that together. They gave me their tips tonight. Because of them, in one night, I have enough to set myself back up."

He didn't appear as elated as that news should make him.

"It was super nice," I told him.

"Have you done that for them before?"

My gaze moved to his forehead.

"You've done it before," he said.

I moved my eyes back to his. "We look out for each other."

"So, it was just your turn."

"Yeah," I mumbled.

"I gotta say, I'd hoped you had the day off so we could relax and do somethin' fun, like go see a movie and then I could finally take you out to dinner. I figure it'll suck, but in the end, it'll put your head in a good place, if you know what's goin' on with your pad."

"I'll treat you to a movie and dinner after we sort through my pad."

"You're such a brat," he returned. "I'm paying."

"Danny—"

"And I'll obviously be with you so I can look these women over for the sole purpose of giving the guys shit about them."

I stiffened. "They're awesome."

"Yeah, and the boys are dragging their feet, like I did, and as it panned out," he gave me a bit more of his weight before he took it away, "that was a stupid mistake."

"Well, I made it too."

"You so did. As you can see, I'm a nice guy."

I started laughing.

He touched his mouth to the laughter on my lips.

Then we were both off the couch because Mag made that so.

And as was his way, he walked me to the door to Mo's old room, holding my hand.

He stopped outside it, let go of my hand, but took me in his arms and brushed his lips against mine again.

That wasn't the goodnight kiss I'd wanted but considering how it went with us, it was probably the wise choice.

"Shower, crash, I'm on breakfast duty tomorrow," he said.

I narrowed my eyes at him. "*I'm* on breakfast duty tomorrow."

"Compromise, we'll go out and hit brunch somewhere before we meet your friends."

That was totally doable.

"Deal," I agreed.

He grinned at me, bent and touched his lips to mine again, gave me a squeeze, murmured, "Sleep well, baby," then he let me go and walked back to the living area.

"You too," I called right when the TV went off.

I went into the bedroom, through it, right to the bathroom.

And during my shower, I didn't think of all that had befallen me.

I didn't think about the girls at the club and how much it meant, what they did tonight and how they made it clear what they felt about me.

I didn't think about arguing with Auggie or how I belatedly realized he'd given me my first brotherly hug that did not come attached to gratitude that'd I'd done something to earn it.

And I didn't think about Mag, our episodes that morning (both of them), his sweetness that night, and how warm it felt, not scary, not anxious, that every moment shared he might be the one.

No.

I didn't think of any of that.

I thought of a woman named Nikki and how in the hell she'd let go of a guy like Daniel Magnusson.

CHAPTER THIRTEEN

Force of Nature

EVIE

The next morning, I was at Mag's coffeemaker, scooping in coffee, when the door to his bedroom opened, and he appeared in it, messy-haired, sleepy-eyed and cranky-looking.

Even with that last, my mouth watered.

Because he was messy-haired (and that hair!) and sleepy-eyed (and man, those eyes).

And *bare-chested*.

"You fuckin' suck," he declared.

That killed the mood and my eyes went squinty.

"What?" I asked irritably. "Are we now in a competition about who's going to start the coffee?"

He didn't answer.

He walked right up to me, pulled the coffee scoop out of my hands, tossed it on the counter, swept me in his arms and laid a wet one on me.

He might be messy-haired and sleepy-eyed, but he'd brushed his teeth.

Yum.

He also smelled all musky *man*.

I *loved* that.

It was getting heated, I liked that heat, and then he ended it.

I was blinking up at him as he was smoothing the hair away from my face, staring down at me, now lazy-eyed, but always gorgeous, when he said, "I want you to think today about alternate sleeping arrangements tonight after I treat you to dinner and a movie."

Was he...?

I continued to blink up at him.

Was he asking me to take the day to consider having sex with him tonight?

I mean...

How sweet was that?

"If I sleep with you," he went on, "I might be able to exhaust you so I can beat you to the kitchen and make you breakfast without any backtalk."

The "exhaust you" part gave me a tingle.

The "backtalk" part made me squint my eyes at him again.

"You know, many men would want the little woman making them breakfast," I pointed out.

"What I know is, many men are morons. You're a man at all, you take care of your woman. You beat that competitive streak, I'll even bring you breakfast in bed."

That sounded *awesome*.

I did not share that.

"You know, most women can take care of themselves, say, by feeding themselves, say, by *cooking breakfast*."

"Now you're just bein' ornery," he groused.

"Who uses words like 'ornery'?" I asked.

"I do, when I'm trying to beat back the need to carry you to my bed and eat *you* for breakfast."

Oh...

My.

My legs went weak, my fingers dug into his shoulders, and I whispered, "Danny."

"Torture, all that's you across my condo, and I'm alone in my bed," he muttered.

Oh my God.

He was so...

Into me.

I moved my hand to fiddle with a loose, dark curl at his neck and promised, "I'll think about alternate sleeping arrangements tonight. But just to say, I don't consider sleeping with someone until at least the sixth date. So, since we're already living together, which I figure puts us at least in ninth- or tenth-date territory, it's looking good for the both of us."

He gave me a squeeze, a grin and a murmured, "Good to know, honey."

"And if you're treating dinner and the movie, I'm buying brunch."

His cheerful, I'm-gonna-get-me-some expression morphed back to cranky.

"Follow me, my handsome Danny, out of the '80s, into a bright future," I urged on a tease.

"How is it, when you act like a dork, the need to bang you strengthens?" he asked.

"I have it on good authority me being a dork is cute."

He dipped his head to me, his eyes changed to something profoundly beautiful and equally profoundly *hot*, and he whispered against my lips, "That good authority knows what he's talking about."

He then kissed me.

I kissed him back.

It got heated.

But he ended it, turned me in his arms, let me go and put a hand to the small of my back to give me a little shove toward my room, saying, "I'll finish coffee. You get ready for brunch. I'm starved. Keep your bathroom door closed, honey, and I'll leave your cup on the nightstand."

I did as ordered because I was hungry too.

And because I wanted to be out in the world with Mag, doing normal things normal people do.

Normal *couples* do.

And because it was dawning on me that I'd never had this.

"This" being what just happened in Mag's kitchen with Mag.

I didn't even have it with my ex.

The confidence to tease and boast, that last, even in jest.

To talk frankly about impending intimacy with no hint of anxiety because I knew to my bones with the way we kissed, it'd be good for me and for him, because he was into what I had to offer.

I'd never been that sure.

I'd never felt that confident.

I'd never felt this way before at all.

Not with what just happened with Mag in his kitchen.

Not before that, waking up, raring to take on the day, a day where I knew I was waking up to him, and time with friends, rather than a day to endure or exist through until I was again asleep.

And I thought, maybe Mag had been right.

Maybe what Lottie wanted for us wasn't about her looking after her boy.

Maybe it was about her guiding me to what I needed to see about my life, my place in it, what I deserved and the people around me the way they should be seen.

The bad.

And the good.

And the hope.

And the fact I deserved a time like I just had with Mag in his kitchen.

And I deserved a guy like Danny Magnusson in my life.

* * *

"Okay, well, apparently, this jackhole didn't have it out for your shoes, which I gotta say is too bad because no one needs this many pairs of Chucks," Ryn declared, standing in my bedroom with one of my navy Chucks held up in one hand, one of my burgundy Chucks in the other.

"Chucks are timeless," Hattie chimed in.

"Agreed," Ryn replied, finding the mates and returning them to my shoe shelves in the closet. "But there's not a single high heel in this joint."

"I only wear heels when I strip," I told her.

Ryn looked at Pepper, openly befuddled, and asked, "Is that even possible?"

"Don't ask me," Pepper replied. "I had to buy under-bed storage so I had more space in my closet for my heels. The bitches at DSW send me birthday cards."

I looked to Hattie and laughed.

This had happened to me a lot that day.

Laughter.

Including during brunch, something that Mag alternately teased, joked and audaciously flirted his way through, to the point my sides hurt from laughing so hard.

It was kind of our first, real, official, going-out-somewhere-together date.

And it was the best I'd ever had.

On that happy memory, Mo strolled into the room and pointed at a box that I'd gone through that Ava and Lottie had filled with decimated knickknacks.

Perhaps it was the girls (and Smithie) being so generous, therefore I knew the road to restoration would not be as painful as I thought.

Perhaps it was my epiphany that morning, with the various and sundry ones I'd been having the last few days.

Perhaps it was because I was in the best mood I'd been in for as long as I could remember.

But there was no mourning, just an understanding that the box was filled with nothing but what was now garbage. Understanding that Mo had carried a great many boxes of the same down to his truck.

All those little bits and bobs I'd collected over the years held no meaning to me anymore.

They were just things I'd bought along the way to make my space pretty.

And I wasn't going to thank whoever did this for the opportunity.

But, silver lining...

It felt fitting that, where I was now, how I felt now, about a lot of things, that I had the chance to start from scratch.

"This for the heap?" Mo asked.

"Yes, Mo, thanks," I answered.

He bent, hefted it up and looked to me. "The bed of my truck is filled. Lottie and me are takin' it to the dump. We'll come back and get some more of the furniture. Yeah?"

Obviously, Mo and Lottie showed as well to help.

"Yeah, Mo, thanks again," I replied.

He jerked up his chin, disappeared, Lottie appeared in his place and it struck me again how perfect they were for each other.

She was a little thing, slender, slim-hipped, slightly above average height, lots of blonde hair, and even in a sweater and jeans and minimal makeup, she was top to toe feminine.

And Mo was tall, broad, bald and aggressively masculine.

Even in a lineup with choices, I'd pick those two to be together.

So maybe, the world just worked as it should.

Maybe, out of the crap, goodness rose up, and you just had to be aware enough of what was going on around you to see it.

I mean, they used manure to fertilize plants and flowers.

Was I right?

"We'll swing by Fortnum's on the way back and bring coffees. You girls in?" she asked.

"Totally," Hattie said. "Do they do chais there?"

"Tex would disown me if I asked for a chai," Lottie declared. "Runner-up?"

Hattie shared her runner-up and we all gave our orders (mine, it went without saying, was the Textual).

Lottie took off.

And Pepper got up from the ruins of my mattress to show me the picture of a couch she'd pulled up on her laptop.

It was orange velvet, had a slight curve and tucked upholstery at the back rest that gave it a ruched look.

It was *the bomb*.

I then saw the price tag, and it was also an eighth of the

money they'd given me last night and I was mentally budgeting about half of that for a new sofa.

"You absolutely need this," she declared.

How would Mag feel about an orange-velvet, curvy couch?

"Babe," the man in my thoughts called, and I looked to the doorway. "Pots and pans proved indestructible, those are put away. Your plates and shit are mostly a wash, though a couple of cups withstood. And your vinyl was a mess, but I sorted it and most of it survived. Your Fleetwood Mac *Rumours* was cracked and Pearl Jam *Ten* was scratched, which sucks. But the rest is good, so I boxed them. We'll haul them to my place."

I had not noted he had a turntable, but although I was not emotionally attached to my knickknacks, I was to my vinyl, so I was down with having it in a safe place.

"Thanks, honey," I said, then bid, "Come have a look at this couch."

He moved into the room.

And we all watched as he did, and I had a feeling it wasn't only me who enjoyed the show.

He looked at the laptop.

And his change of expression nearly made me choke on the effort of swallowing the bubble of laughter that surged up my throat.

He then looked at me. "Are you being serious?"

I started giggling and replied, "Not anymore."

"Christ," he muttered, but then cupped the back of my head, bent to kiss my forehead, let me go and sauntered out, warning, "It's gonna be noisy 'cause I'm gonna be vacuuming."

And he disappeared down the hall.

"I just had an orgasm because *that man* announced

without a single hint of whining that he was going to *vacuum*," Pepper decreed.

"I had an orgasm with the forehead kiss," Hattie shared.

"I hope he doesn't know you don't own a pair of civvy high heels," Ryn noted.

"Danny doesn't care about high heels," I told her.

She studied me a second before she looked to the hallway and murmured, "I'm rethinking putting off Boone."

We heard the vacuum go on.

"And I'm rethinking putting off Auggie," Pepper said, and when I looked to her, I saw she was also gazing at the hallway.

Hattie said nothing.

And I wondered if Axl could break through that shyness.

I hoped so.

Pepper closed her laptop and went to help Ryn with tidying my shoes as I folded down to the carpet beside Hattie, who was going through the pile of clothes that Ava and Lottie had set aside.

"These I think are mendable or still wearable," Hattie said, pointing to a pile. She shifted her finger to the other pile. "These are—"

She didn't finish because she jumped, I jumped, and the air went static because we heard the terrifyingly loud sound of glass shattering along with a gunshot over the noise of the vacuum.

Then another gunshot.

Mag!

I bounded to my feet, ready to head that way, but Hattie grabbed my hand, waylaying me, all while Ryn rushed the door.

She was closing it when she flew back as it flew open.

And there was Snag.

In my bedroom.

Pointing a gun at Ryn.

"Back the fuck off," he growled to her.

She slowly backed away.

Oh God, oh God, oh God.

A gun.

On Ryn.

And where was Mag?

He turned the gun on me.

I pushed Hattie away from me.

"You. Come. Now," he ordered.

I didn't hesitate a second.

I went to him.

He grabbed my upper arm in a painful grip and dragged me down the hall.

I whimpered when I saw the spray of blood on the wall in my living room, the vacuum resting on its side, still whirring, and Mag's feet in prone position coming out from behind the remains of my couch that had been pulled from the wall in preparation of being removed from the apartment.

"Did you shoot Danny?" I asked tremulously, something snaking through my gut, so poisonous, I feared I'd throw up, at the same time the urge was so strong to pull away and go to Mag, I was struggling with beating it back.

But if I pulled away, the girls might be in (more) danger.

And if he took me away, they'd be free to call 911 to get help for Mag.

"Shut the fuck up," Snag answered.

And then, even if I was willing, he dragged me out my front door with an excruciating yank on my arm.

*   *   *

"*Where is it!*" Snag shouted in my face.

"*I don't know!*" I shouted back for the *millionth* time.

He then backhanded me so brutally, the chair he'd tied me to tipped over and skidded several feet.

And I lay on my side, tied to that chair in that cold warehouse that didn't have any fucking windows, seeing as they'd all been broken out, so it definitely didn't have heat, and I didn't know what to focus on.

The pain radiating out of my cheekbone, or the same thudding in my head where it'd cracked against the cement floor when I tipped over.

Or, through all this, the agony of seeing Mag's feet that way on my floor.

In my reality, I saw Snag's shoes fill my vision before he crouched over me.

"I gotta know where that fuckin' bag is, bitch," he snarled.

"Someone stole it from my car," I told him, again, for the *millionth* time. "I have no idea where it is."

"Your dad's a dealer."

I closed my eyes tight.

I opened them and said, "Not anymore."

"Stupid cunt," he bit out. "Like father, like fuckin' son. It's a joke, those two, both of 'em losers, both of 'em tryin' to outdo each other on the street."

Oh my God, Dad.

Oh my God, *Mick*.

Oh my *God*, why was this my goddamn *life*?

"You look in that bag?" Snag asked.

I opened my mouth but caught myself from saying "we," just in case (and I couldn't think about it another way or I'd unravel) Mag was okay, and that spray of blood was a figment of my imagination.

And then I said, "I looked into it. I saw the drugs."

"And you didn't get any bright ideas to give it to your dad to move it?" he pushed.

"No." I shook my head, my cheek scraping against the floor. "No. Mick told me to do what you said, and I did that. I kept it safe and waited for instructions."

"Not safe enough, if, like you said, it got stolen from your car."

"I just had to run in and change clothes. I didn't want my neighbors wondering why I was toting around a Trader Joe's bag everywhere I went."

"You dig through that bag?"

I shook my head again. "No. No. Just looked into it and saw what was in it and that's all I needed to see. I didn't want anything to do with it. I texted you that night to tell you I didn't want responsibility for that bag. The texts wouldn't deliver."

"I had occasion to put my phone outta commission."

I could guess.

"I need that bag, Gardiner."

Suffice it to say, tied to a chair in a warehouse after being kidnapped and...and...whatever happened to Mag, I absolutely could guess that too.

"I don't have it," I whispered, "I swear, I don't—"

I didn't finish because I heard a weird *thunk*.

Then I heard Snag mutter, "What the—?" as he rose away from me.

After that, I heard running feet before a muted explosion that preceded a hissing noise.

Another *thunk*, and through smoke forming from something on the floor, I saw a figure moving through the warehouse, all the way at the other end.

Then I scrunched my face tight when a gunshot blast assaulted my ears.

"I can see you, motherfucker!" Snag shouted.

Another muted explosion, a hiss, more smoke, and I opened my eyes and started coughing, noting visibility was decreasing rapidly.

I still saw *two* shadowy figures moving through the space.

Another *thunk*, explosion, hiss, gunshots and then someone leaped over me in my chair.

Blinking against the tears forming in my eyes, choking on the smoke, I saw through it what appeared to be Boone hitting Snag in the back with a savage shoulder tackle that sent Snag flat to the ground, landing on his front. Such was the fall, Snag's gun flew out of his hand, and I heard it sliding across cement.

Boone hesitated not a second in landing a knee in the man's back, to Snag's grunt of pain.

He then took his head in both hands and slammed it against the cement floor.

Snag went still.

Whoa.

That was when I felt movement at my wrists, which were zip-tied at the back of the chair.

"Hang tight, baby, try not to breathe," Mag was saying. "Get you out to fresh air and cleaned up soon's I can."

But I didn't really hear his words, seeing as a sob tore jaggedly up my throat the minute I heard his voice.

My wrists were freed, then my ankles were freed from where they were tied to the legs of the chair, then I was up in his arms and he was jogging through the smoke.

But I heard his grunt of pain when he lifted me

He'd carried me before and he did not grunt.

Oh God.

What did that mean?

He set me on my feet outside, but his hands didn't leave me.

He held me steady as he said, not to me, "Get me some goddamn water."

I was crying, blinking, struggling to pull in breaths, at the same time desperately trying to focus on him through my blurry vision, and woefully failing.

"If you got saliva, spit out that smoke, honey, you with me? Spit it out. Let your body do what it does to take care of you."

I bent to the side and spat. My nose was running, my eyes were killing me, but I could spit.

A lot.

Mag must have sensed I had myself steady on my feet because his hands left me, and when I straightened from spitting, immediately I felt what seemed like a wet wipe on my face.

I instinctively rubbed against it, trying to get it toward my eyes.

"Stay still, Evie. Gotta dab, not rub. Let those eyes do their work. Let me get that smoke off your skin."

I nodded but then jolted, bracing to run when I heard a vehicle pull up beside us.

Mag caught me and cooed, "It's Axl, baby. It's just Axl. It's okay. He's bringing water."

I heard a door slam and then Axl saying, "Water," and a bottle was put to my lips.

"Don't drink. Swoosh and spit," Mag instructed.

I did that.

He gave me more.

I did it again.

"Be still again, honey," he ordered. "I'm gonna run this down your face and pat it dry. Yeah?"

I nodded.

He did that.

He did it again.

My shirt was soaked, it was cold outside, but I began shivering violently and not because of either of those.

"Blanket," Mag grunted.

I heard retreating footsteps, but more importantly, Mag was coming into view.

Instinctively, I reached up and grabbed either side of his face, and in doing so, I knocked off the headset with microphone he was wearing, and it fell down his back.

"I thought—" I started.

"I saw him through the window, read his intent, saw he had a gun. He saw me, raised his weapon and I got off a shot. He returned fire, clipped my shoulder. When I fell back, cracked my head against the wall. I was out less than a minute but long enough for him to take you."

My eyes moved to where his words were referring, and I saw the stain, I saw the hole, and I saw the white of the bandage through the hole in his navy thermal.

Good *God*.

"Your shoulder."

"It's fine."

I jolted again when a blanket landed on my shoulders and Mag moved instantly to pull it closed at the front as I looked behind me to see Axl.

"It was through and through. It's battle dressed but he needs a doctor," Axl shared unhappily.

My eyes shot to Mag. "Then let's go do that. *Now*."

He didn't answer, seeing as all our attention was taken by movement coming from the warehouse.

It was Boone, dragging Snag out of the door by a leg, Auggie strolling casually after them.

Snag was recovering, I could tell, and struggling to get control of his body, something it was apparently hard to do when someone was dragging you across asphalt by your ankle.

I was so immersed in this, I didn't feel it at first.

It took Axl's low warning, "Mag," for me to feel it.

And then I felt it.

Which was right before I saw it.

Mag's temper.

Unleashed.

He sprinted toward Boone and Snag, and Boone instantly dropped Snag's foot and stepped aside.

"*Stop him!*" Axl thundered, jogging that way.

"I'm not gonna fuckin' stop him," Auggie called.

"I'm not either," Boone said.

"Stop him" meaning stop him from tearing Snag apart. Mag was bent over the man, he had Snag's shirt fisted in one hand and his other was just fisted and landing in Snag's face.

Repeatedly.

Oh God.

"He can further harm *himself*," Axl clipped.

Oh God!

"Danny!" I shouted, rushing toward him.

Mag did not stop, going so far as to violently shrug off Axl, who was trying to catch his arm.

That couldn't be good for his shoulder.

"*Danny!*" I screamed.

Boone caught me before I made it to them, and held me, but I struggled against him, because, up close, Snag's face was quickly turning to mush, but more, I could see a dark stain that now looked wet growing at the shoulder of Mag's thermal.

"Danny!" I cried.

"Brother," Auggie murmured. "Hawk."

My gaze darted to Auggie and then my head jerked right at the same time Boone shifted us so he could look too.

At what I saw, I stood suspended.

Two men were getting out of a Camaro, with Mo coming out of his truck behind it.

But I scarcely saw Mo or the man coming out of the passenger side of the Camaro.

This was because I fancied a gigantic swirl of dust like out of a Robert Rodriguez movie curled behind the man folding out of the driver's side of that Camaro.

He took his time ambling across the asphalt in such a way it seemed life had gone slow motion.

He was the epitome of a lean, mean commando machine.

He was probably around Auggie's height, Auggie being the shortest of the bunch, if six one could be considered short.

He had dark hair not liberally sprinkled with silver.

But in the sea of hotness I found myself floating in after I met Mag, this guy was on a different level.

If he'd ever had frat boy tendencies, he'd strangled them, spat on the corpse and then set it ablaze.

He was what Mag and his boys would become in a few years.

He wasn't *all man*.

He wasn't *all commando*.

He might be an avenging angel.

There were no words to describe precisely what he was.

But what he was, he was that 100 percent.

"You doin' all right?" Hawk asked me, his eyes assessing my person efficiently, and he did not hide his displeasure at seeing the sting in both my cheeks that was clearly visible.

"Y-yeah," I replied, seeing as he was freaking me out by being a human-size force of nature, but also, I'd dropped the blanket in the dash to Mag and I was freezing.

Hawk turned his head to the man standing beside him, Hispanic, also intensely good-looking, and without a word said by Hawk, that guy jogged back to the blanket.

Hawk then shifted his attention to Snag, who Mag had stopped pounding, but the man was still on his knees, his body lax, held up by Mag's fist in his shirt.

"Are you conscious?" Hawk asked.

"Fuck you," Snag spat, and I was pretty sure a tooth came out along with spittle and blood at his words.

Yuck.

I noted tears were also running out of Snag's eyes from the smoke, but that was currently the least of his worries.

"I see your situation has not impressed itself on you," Hawk remarked.

At that, Snag just spat, his head lolling to do so, his aim to the ground by Hawk's feet.

It was then Boone let me go, so Hawk's man, who went to retrieve the blanket, could give me said blanket.

Boone helped pull it around me and I held it close to my front.

Hawk watched this as if my comfort was the most important component of this wild scenario, and I decided I liked Mag's boss.

He then turned back to Snag.

"There are few in your line of work who do not know who I am," Hawk noted.

"Everyone knows who you are, motherfucker," Snag replied.

"So, I take it, you put your hands on Evie not knowing she has my protection."

Aw.

That was sweet.

And it meant something to Snag. Even in the bloodied mess Mag had made of his face, he looked freaked.

He struggled to hide it, failed, but still managed to accuse, "She took somethin' of mine."

"You gave it to her, dumbfuck," Hawk returned.

"To look after," Snag retorted.

"All right," Hawk said, putting both hands on his hips, and I imagined the sky lifted several inches, "I'm done with this. Outside the narcotics, what was in that bag?"

Snag blinked. Then it appeared he was trying to think.

Finally, he said, "Nothin'."

Hawk's gaze slid to Mag and he nodded.

Once.

Mag pulled an arm back.

Not the arm attached to his injured shoulder.

That one he was using constantly to hold on to Snag, dammit.

"Okay! Okay! Call off your asshole!" Snag shouted. "I'll tell you."

Mag's arm dropped but this gave me occasion to look at his face and I saw his mouth was pinched with pain and he'd gone slightly pale.

However, I felt, regrettably in this scenario, that I should not rush to coddling the man I was living with, albeit platonically (for now, and that happy change in circumstances was indefinitely delayed, stupid Snag!), and instead stayed still and kept my mouth shut.

When several seconds ticked by in silence, Hawk prompted, "I'm not hearing you tell me."

"It's a gun," Snag said then hastily added, "Not my gun."

"We know it's not your gun. We know one of your girls took it off a john. We know that girl is now dead. What we wanna know is, whose is it and why is it so fuckin' important?"

"I tell you, will you let me go?"

Hawk heaved a beleaguered sigh.

"I see you haven't come to grips with your situation. This isn't a negotiation. You're gonna tell me, and your choice is whether you tell me easy, or you tell me hard. And how you choose decides how we disappear you after. If we do that nice, or if we do that nasty."

Oh man.

I looked to Mag, who was focused on the man in his hold.

"Now," Hawk carried on, "I work hard, my boys work hard, downtime is scarce, we were all enjoying our Saturdays, and we find ourselves here, dealing with you. And the longer you make us stay here, the more my mood deteriorates. So let's cut the dicking around and tell me about that gun."

"It was used in a murder," Snag said.

Oh no.

"And the guy who was murdered was a cop."

Oh no!

My gaze cut again to Mag, but he was now scowling over my head at Boone.

"*Names,*" Hawk barked.

"Man, you are signing my death sentence if you make me—"

"*Names!*" Hawk roared, I jumped, and Boone slid an arm around my belly and pulled me back into his body.

"Cop was Tony Crowley. Who done him was," he seemed to be breathing funny before he pushed out, "Cisco."

"Shit, fuck," Auggie clipped.

I had a feeling Cisco was even worse than being a cop killer and that was pretty damned high up on the bad guy scale.

"Jorge, Axl, Aug, deal with this asshole," Hawk ordered. "Boone, Mo, take care of Evie and Mag. Communicate. I want a huddle in the office as soon as this current shit is sorted."

And with that, Hawk turned and strolled away.

CHAPTER FOURTEEN
Do Right

EVIE

I sat on Mag's couch, staring at Mag's view, thinking about Mag.

As well as Mag and me.

And what Mag meeting me meant to Mag.

My father was a drug dealer.

My brother was a drug dealer.

And Mick's bullshit got Mag shot.

Shot!

Got him shot and his friends spending their Saturday afternoon throwing smoke grenades (or whatever those were) and tackling people.

Against my wishes not to be separated, but with Mag assuring me he'd be okay and sharing he wanted me at his place, where he knew I was safe, Boone had taken Mag to someone called Dr. Baldwin.

And Mo had taken me to Mag's place, on which descended Lottie, Ryn, Hattie, Pepper, and Tex. That last for protection seeing as Mo had stayed long enough to have a conversation with Tex in the hallway and grab a new shirt for Mag before he took off.

Not long after, a new addition to the cadre of hotness that seemed ever-growing showed.

His name was Dutch.

He wore a leather jacket with the Chaos MC patch on the back.

And Mag's friends were commando-hot, but Dutch was rough-biker-boy hot.

Such was the situation, however, regardless of this new hot guy in our midst, Ryn, Hattie and Pepper were all about me.

Getting ice for my face.

Cleaning and slathering Neosporin on the scrapes on my cheek.

Pouring me shots of Mag's Fireball.

And alternately bitching out loud or fretting quietly about the fact I'd been kidnapped at gunpoint and they'd run out to find Mag recovering from being unconscious with a bullet wound to his shoulder and a spray of his blood on the wall.

All courtesy of Mick Gardiner.

All courtesy of *me* because I didn't do what was right.

Needing the love of a family so badly, a family that didn't love me, I'd done what was weak.

I needed to go.

The first available moment I had, I needed to stuff what I had left in as many Trader Joe's bags as I could find, grab the money the girls gave me, empty my bank accounts, write a variety of notes that would never come close to sharing all the feelings I had for a variety of people, especially Mag.

And get the hell out of Dodge.

Get these people safe.

And escape my dysfunction.

I didn't know where I would go, but I was thinking Canada.

They said people were super friendly up there and I could do with some friendly.

Amid melancholy daydreams of moving to Canada, Lottie plopped down on the couch in front of where I was twisted toward the window.

She was staring at me intently.

I liked her, a lot.

But I'd never let her in.

I'd never really let anyone in.

I was too busy trying to win my fucking family.

What I'd done was drag her and her man into a mess where their friend got shot.

Shot!

And I owed it to her to give her what it was clear she wanted to do in that moment.

I just didn't have it in me.

"Lottie—"

I should have known that she'd be stronger than me and not easily put off.

"I've seen this before," she declared.

"I really can't—"

"You're at a place where your primary instinct is to let them win because that's been your go-to all your life."

I shut my mouth.

She kept talking.

"You're at a place where you're gonna let them continue to control the thoughts in your head and the decisions you make for your life. And this next is gonna be harsh, but I'm not gonna apologize for that because I'm sensing this is a crucial moment where you're gonna make a decision that's gonna define the rest of your life and you need to make the right one. So here it is. From the time you became an independent adult, all that is *on you*."

I sat completely still, struck, even stung, but deep down I sensed it was a hurt I had to feel, and I let myself feel it as I stared at her.

"I've been watching you and how you hold yourself apart," she went on. "You're interested in people. You're the first to offer if someone needs something. But they drilled it in your head for so long that you're unworthy, and it hurt so bad, you protected yourself from maybe finding out what they convinced you is true out in a world without them. And I get it. That kind of conditioning is hard to shake. But if you think for even a second on it, you scared the piss out of them."

I did?

"What?" I whispered.

"You're pretty and you're sweet and you're funny and you explained what a transistor was to your dad when you were six. You were better than him when you were *six*. And he didn't see that as something to be proud of. He didn't see that as something to nurture. He didn't stop at nothing to forge the path for you to find the you that you were born to be. Your mother failed at the same thing and did worse. Your brother fuckin' hated all you were because he was already small, and you made him feel smaller. And they all made moves to hold you down. They made moves to make sure you didn't understand your gifts and how beautiful they are. They made sure to minimize you so you wouldn't reach your full potential, because if you did, you might see what wastes of space they all allow themselves to be. And as a kid, you got no defense. But Evan, as an adult, that's a different story."

When she stopped talking, I realized how heavily I was breathing.

She started talking again.

"Now I see you sitting here, letting them twist shit in your head. Talking yourself into seeing all that's going down as *on you*. When you did one thing. You made a tough decision. Look after your brother and get mired in shit or don't look after your brother and mire someone you love in shit. There was no right decision to that, Evan. You didn't make the wrong one. You just made *a* decision. And you'd be in a place right now, beating yourself up, no matter which way that swung, and *he* put you there. You should not have had to make any decision at all. Do not take that on. Do not let him take away any more of what you fought to have."

She reached out and took my hand in a firm grip.

And she kept going.

"I know you were sitting here, planning to bolt. Planning that, when I heard you today, gabbing with your girls in your bedroom about shoes. I saw a man who digs you sorting through your vinyl, smiling at himself because you like Metallica. I saw the Evan and the life she had that was *meant to be*. Not a single fucking soul in this room, or out of it, outside members of your family, are pissed at you about what's going down. What we'd be pissed about is if you bolt."

"Danny got shot," I whispered.

"Yes, he did, and he survived, and I'll tell you right now, you got a battle on your hands and it's not what you think. The battle you got is that he allowed that man to get to you and he's killing himself right now he let that happen. Now you got a *real* important decision to make. You can give in, let them win, or you can fight for what you deserve. You can take off and leave Mag where he's at in his head right now, or you can be here and stand strong for your man. What's it gonna be, Evan? What *really* makes you? Who *really* are you? What life do you *really* want to lead?"

"I wanna get my degree," I told her quietly. "I want to stop stripping. I want friends to go to movies with. I want a life not defined by my family." I pulled in a breath and said, "I want Danny."

She shook my hand. "Then *fight* for that."

I felt something weird, like an electric hum, skating up my spine.

"You want Mag, so you understand all there is to have if you have him," she continued. "Nikki wanted him too. It's Mag's to tell you and I'd normally let him do that, but I can't now. Both of your futures are at stake."

I thought I'd been listening closely.

But now that she was talking about Mag, my ears hurt, I was listening so hard.

"He's shared," she told me. "Mo's shared. She loved him. She wanted a life with him. She also wanted to dictate what that life would be and made a faulty play for the purpose of protecting what they had. She wanted Mag to quit his job and do something less dangerous. In other words, she demanded that Mag not be Mag. Which means, in the end, she didn't love Mag. Not more than she loved herself. And there's one single thing I'll give to your family. They taught you, if you love someone, you let them be who they are."

She squeezed my hand tight, didn't let go and didn't stop talking.

"*That* is why I chose you for Mag. And I think the world

of you, Evie, but it would disappoint the fuck out of me you gave him a hint he could lay his hands on something that beautiful and then took it away."

"I need your sister to ask her husband to find a way to get me in to see Mick," I blurted.

Her head twitched and she asked, "Say what?"

"I need Jet to ask Eddie to find a way to get me in to see Mick."

Slowly, she smiled.

"And I need my phone," I went on.

But since I could get my phone myself, I got up and found it.

MAG

Mag walked with Boone into the office suite with his arm in a sling, a bottle of painkillers in his pocket and a need to kill somebody.

He looked right immediately, toward the wall of windows beyond which was the conference room, and saw Hawk was not fucking around.

Tack was there, as was his son, Rush, who had taken over from Tack as president of the Chaos MC.

Brock and Mitch were there too, as was Lee Nightingale and his right-hand man, Luke Stark.

Axl and Auggie were in the room, Mo was standing outside.

"Evie okay?" he asked Mo.

"Hangin' at your place. Tex and Dutch are on her inside and Rush's got Joker and Jagger keeping watch outside."

As Mo was saying this, Hawk joined them.

"A word, Mag," Hawk said low, then walked up the steps and out of view of the conference room.

Mag followed.

When he stopped, Mag stopped with him and immediately said, "I'm good."

"No, you're not," Hawk replied.

"You gotta know, you can't take me off this, Hawk," Mag told him.

"I'm not gonna take you off this, Mag. I'm gonna tell you, your mind doesn't work like theirs."

Mag didn't know what to say because he didn't know what Hawk was trying to say.

Hawk explained.

"You can think you got everything covered, but you don't got in you the dark they got in them so you can't ever know what they're gonna pull."

Now, he understood.

He just didn't agree.

"I was vacuuming, Hawk."

"You were armed. You had Evie and her girls working in the back, so you were her line of defense. And you couldn't begin to think some jackass would open fire on a Saturday afternoon in an apartment complex in Platt Park."

"I should have been prepared."

"You were."

"He got the drop on me."

"He got a lucky shot in, and if he didn't have that luck, he'd be handcuffed to a hospital bed. That's not the way it went down and you gotta shake that off so you can have your head in the game."

It sometimes seriously fucking sucked when Hawk went guru.

Hawk got close. "You know, Mag. You're pissed and

kicking yourself in the ass, and I'll tell you, I'd be the same. Feel that and set it aside. Get outta that headspace, because you know. You know it's not the measure of a soldier the battle he finds himself in or the chaos that becomes of that battle. It's how he comports himself in it. I'd say don't let me down. I'd say don't let Evie down. But what's important here is you not letting your emotion get the better of you and letting yourself down."

They locked eyes and they did it a long time.

Mag broke it by nodding.

Hawk nodded back and carried on.

"Goes without sayin', Brock and Mitch are all kinds of interested in finding the gun that killed their brother and linking it to Cisco. That guy's off the street, his operation in disarray will be a big win for the DPD, not to mention the citizens of Denver. So it's done clean, they want this punted solely to them and I'm of a mind to agree."

Mag opened his mouth.

Hawk lifted a hand.

Mag shut his mouth and ground his teeth.

"It's theirs. This is their brother, think on that," Hawk said quietly.

Fuck.

Again, he was right.

"That said, the cops are not gonna turn down some friendlies having their ears to the ground. And word has to get out that Evie has nothin' to do with this. But Brock and Mitch don't have to know how close to the ground we're gonna get to have our ears to it."

And finally, Mag's bad mood started lifting.

Slowly, he grinned.

Hawk's lips twitched and then he said, "Let's get in there."

Mag agreed by turning and walking down and into the conference room with his boss.

EVIE

"Evie! Sunshine of my life! What's shakin'?" Dad asked in my ear.

"Well, my apartment was tossed on Wednesday," I replied conversationally while pacing Mag's condo with my phone to my ear and six pairs of eyes following my movements. "I lost nearly everything. And that bag of drugs was stolen from my car, after someone jacked my trunk to get to it. Oh! And today, I was kidnapped and the man I'm seeing was shot."

Dad was completely silent.

I let that last for several beats before I continued.

"You didn't ask, but just so you know, Mag's okay and so am I. I had to be rescued by a team of commandos who threw smoke bombs and also got shot at. But they saved me. After, you know, Snag tied me to a chair and hit me while he interrogated me."

"Evie, my darlin'," Dad murmured, and I had to give it to him, he sounded mortified.

But he said no more.

"And Snag had some fun things to share while we were enjoying our time together, Dad. Including you and Mick being in a competition to be the worst drug dealer in Denver. Which leads me to ask, does the dispensary know you're still dealing, Dad?"

"Evan, now—"

"No!" I snapped. "I was *kidnapped at gunpoint today!*"

My father again fell silent.

I did not return the favor.

"Now, you get on your goddamned phone and you sit down with your loser friends and you share that I do not have that bag. I didn't want that bag in the first place, but now it's gone, and it's got *not one thing to do with me*. You do that and you spread that wide and you ask them to keep that message rolling through the underbelly of Denver and I keep silent about your extracurricular activities so you can continue to hang with your brethren at the dispensary. You don't do that, I've had occasion to meet a number of policemen during the Adventures of Evie this week. And I think they'll be very intrigued to hear how my loving father makes his cash."

He assumed his not-oft-used stern fatherly tone.

"Evan, listen to me—"

I didn't listen to him.

I carried on lecturing.

"And one last important note, your line of credit at the Bank of Evan Gardiner is closed. I need a new mattress and a new couch and new plates, but I also need to ascertain if Mag actually *is* into women wearing high heels, because if that leads to sexy times, I'll consider it."

Before he could say a word, I disconnected.

I then blocked his number, after which I scrolled up to my mother and hit go.

She answered with, "I am not talking to you."

"Good," I retorted. "Because I'm no longer listening to your abuse, but I have a few things to say."

"My *what*?" Her voice was rising.

"I was kidnapped at gunpoint today, Mother."

Another moment of absolute silence.

"I was tied to a chair, interrogated and hit," I shared. "The man I'm seeing, a man I've come to care about a lot in a short period of time, was shot. He's fine. He then went on with his friends to rescue me. But that was my day, the culmination of a week of having to deal with the *shit* that *Mick* landed me in."

"Jesus Christ," she whispered.

"Your son is a drug dealer, and if you choose to champion him regardless of the ridiculous and felonious decisions he makes about how he's going to lead his life, then fine. That's your choice. But I'm no longer going to bail him out and I'm no longer going to bail *you* out when you overspend and use me to continue lying to your husband. It is truth that betraying the trust of intimacy between spouses is the worst betrayal you can make. But sustained and deliberate lying is also the betrayal of intimacy spouses share, so I do not condone Rob fucking you over, but wake up, Mom. Not only did you start it, you keep doing the same."

With that, I hung up, and since she was already blocked, I didn't have to complete that chore.

So, I stopped pacing, stood there and stared unseeing in front of me, remembering my conversation with Mag while I was making us hamburgers.

It had been on the tip of my tongue to ask him how you scraped off family that was bleeding you dry.

At that time, I hadn't been ready for his answer because that would lead to expected action and I wasn't ready for that either.

Now, apparently, I'd figured it out.

And I didn't know what to expect, but my hope was, it would make me feel free.

It didn't.

It made me realize in a profound way what I did not have, all they'd taken from me, my complicity in that, and the fact those conversations were utterly no fun, and having them might just be the last thing they'd forced my hand to do.

I felt something land on my head and I jumped.

When I looked up and around, I saw it was Tex's hand.

"That wasn't easy," he low-boomed. "But you stuck to your guns. I'm proud of you, girl."

His words.

Those words.

No one had ever said them to me.

And so, in hearing them for the first time at age twenty-seven, I couldn't stop it.

I burst out crying.

But unlike the many times I'd done it before, the instant it started, I was engulfed in a bear hug that communicated caring, warmth and pride.

Which made me cry even harder.

Those arms didn't loosen.

My phone in my hand rang and they still didn't loosen when I forced it between Tex and me to look at the screen.

It said "Stepdad Rob."

"It's my stepdad," I mumbled.

"I think you've had enough for today, darlin'," Tex advised in what I read as a Tex Gentle Tone. And I read that because it was kinda loud, but it rumbled in his chest in a way I just knew, if a baby was resting against that chest while he spoke in that voice, the noise would make no difference. That baby would be lulled right to sleep.

I looked up at him. "I don't think I should draw it out. I just want to have it done and move on."

"Your call, Evie," he said.

I nodded.

He let me go.

And, swiping carefully at my eyes with one hand (because I felt I had a shiner, maybe two), I took the call with the other.

"Rob," I greeted and didn't let him get a word in, especially when I heard my mother wailing in the background. "No offense, but I said all that needed to be said to Mom."

"Okay, Evie, all right, sweetheart." He was speaking fast. "But please don't hang up because I don't know what's happening. She's in a state like I've never seen and she's sayin' you been *kidnapped* and *shot at*?"

"No. I was just kidnapped while cleaning up my apartment that was searched, nearly everything in it destroyed, and the man I'm seeing who was helping out, he wasn't only shot *at*, he was *shot*. Through and through to the shoulder."

"Holy fuck," Rob breathed out.

"And I'm in a mood, so take this as you will, I wouldn't normally get involved, but Mom knew. She knew my apartment had been destroyed and she didn't give a fuck. She phoned me and hurled words at me, ticked I didn't keep those drugs safe for Mick. They got them, after jacking up my car to steal them from my trunk. I'll grant she couldn't know that would move onward to me being kidnapped and Danny shot. But since Mick is a drug dealer and he involved me in his work, it isn't a big surprise either."

"Did you know?" he asked, not me.

"Is that her? Is that my Evie?" I heard Mom ask in the background. "Let me talk to her."

"Did you know about her apartment and those drugs being taken?" Rob pushed.

"Let me talk to her, darlin'. I gotta know where she is. I gotta see with my own eyes my baby's all right," Mom pleaded.

"*Woman!*" Rob roared so loud, I had to take the phone away from my ear. "*Did you know she was in this kind of danger?*"

"Rob—"

"*Answer me, goddamn it!*"

"*Don't talk to me that way!*" Mom shrieked.

He was back to me. "Evie, are you okay?"

"I have friends around me."

"Your man?"

"I'm told he'll be fine."

"*Let me talk to my daughter!*"

"I gotta go now, sweetheart," Rob said. "But I'm gonna call a little bit later. Please, answer when I call, and just to say, it won't have anything to do with your mom."

"What does that mean?" Mom demanded.

Lottie was motioning to me, so I said, "I'll think about it, Rob. Good luck. And good-bye."

I was about to take the phone from my ear to disconnect, but I didn't when he said softly, "Love you, Evie. You're a good kid. From the minute I met you, wished you were my own."

Tears filled my eyes again and my voice was husky when I replied, "Thanks, Rob. That means a lot."

"Take care of you and I hope we speak soon."

"Okay."

"'Bye, sweetheart."

"'Bye, Rob."

On that, I disconnected and focused on Lottie.

"She didn't do the block so maybe the stepdad isn't a total dickweed," Pepper muttered.

I heard her but more, I heard Lottie say, "Eddie's got you in."

My heart jumped, and before I could lose the will to go forward with all this, my mouth moved.

"Let's roll."

I grabbed my bag off the kitchen island and marched to the door, feeling bodies close in on all sides.

So I stopped, looked around, and I was right.

Bodies were closed in on all sides.

"You guys can take off," I said carefully to Pepper, Ryn and Hattie, going carefully because they all were wearing determined expressions. "Thank you for, well…everything today and it sounds lame, but truly, I'm really so sorry this got out of hand the way it did. Now you need to go home, chill out, and this can be Lottie, Tex, me and hottie biker guy."

"I'm going with," Ryn stated.

"Me too," Pepper decreed.

"I'm not leaving your side," Hattie declared. "Except, of course, when you talk to your brother, if the cops won't let me in, but I'll be waiting for you in reception after you're done."

Hattie really was all kinds of cute.

Axl was in for a world of goodness.

I didn't focus on that.

I started, "I really don't think—"

"Clue in, Evie," Ryn interrupted me. "This is how it's done, sister."

I stared at her.

I stared at Pepper.

I stared at Hattie.

I looked to Lottie.

She was smiling.

I didn't have a lot of experience with this kind of thing, but from Lottie's smile, it seemed Ryn was correct.

This was how it was done.

"You said something about rolling?" Lottie prompted.

I nodded, turned and barely took a step when I was brought up short by hottie biker guy standing in front of the door with his long legs planted and his arms crossed on his wide chest.

When he caught my eyes, his deep voice rolled out.

"Guts me to do this, you bein' on this tear, and I don't know you, but seems like it's been a long time comin', I still gotta say we do not have the go-ahead to ride."

"I'll take responsibility for Evie makin' this play," Tex said.

Aw.

I loved Tex.

"Not sayin' she can't make this play," Dutch said to Tex. "Just sayin' she's gotta make it when her man lifts the house arrest."

Say...

What?

House arrest?

"Are you being serious?" I asked.

His gaze came to me. "After I got shot, found my woman tied to a chair in a warehouse with her face lookin' like yours, I set a man on her to look out for her with the simple instructions to keep her safe in my crib, and he did not follow those instructions, I would not be happy."

"Danny's more enlightened than you," I probably lied.

"You *do* know I know your man?" Dutch asked, and in so doing, sharing that he knew I was lying.

I tried a different tack.

"Please?"

"Babe..."

Gah!

Another "babe"!

"I feel you," he went on. "Sounds like your family is the

pits. But need to remind you what you been sharin' with your biologicals. You got kidnapped today."

"You'll keep me safe. Tex'll keep me safe. And when we get there, we'll be in a place crawling with police. I couldn't be safer than there."

Dutch didn't respond.

"Please?" I tried again.

Dutch stared at me.

"I need to do this," I whispered. "And I need to do it before I lose the courage to get it done."

He continued to stare at me before he muttered, "Fuck," pulled out his phone, engaged it and then said into it, "We're riding. Evan has something to say to her brother. We're heading to County." He then disconnected and leveled his eyes on me. "Shit goes down, you do as told. Don't make me regret this."

I smiled at him.

Big.

And through it, I said, "I won't. I promise."

He studied my smile, his expression changed to something that made my nipples tingle, then he wiped it and said, "Let's ride."

MAG

"I'm feeling a more active role in this situation," Lee Nightingale stated.

"Lee—" Mitch began.

Lee looked to Brock. "Your woman was kidnapped." Then to Tack. "*Your* woman was kidnapped." And finally to Mitch. "And your *kids* were kidnapped. Now, my woman was kidnapped, *twice*, so I suspect our shared experience with this kinda bullshit would lead us all to a place we...did not...*fuck around*."

"No one's gonna fuck around, Lee," Brock assured.

"All right, we'll just break up on the understanding we always got. You do what you do and me and my men will do what we do," Lee returned just as his phone rang.

Rush's phone was ringing too.

Lee ignored his.

Rush didn't do the same.

"Your boys, or Chaos, or Hawk's soldiers do anything to fuck with bringing down Cisco," Mitch began, "and bringing him down clean, I gotta say, respect, but there will be issues. Tony was a good man. Tony had two kids and his wife was pregnant when he was capped. And Cisco is a thug who somehow managed to convince people he's a boss and none of us at this table are unaware of what that's meant on the streets of Denver."

Before Lee could respond, Rush's low conversation ended and he rapped his knuckles on the table, getting everyone's attention.

And Mag did not feel good about the fact Rush's eyes were aimed at him.

"That was Joke," Rush said. "There's a convoy rolling out of your condo. Seems your woman engineered a sit-down with her brother."

Instantly, Lee nabbed his phone.

Mag blew out a sigh.

Then he stood.

And walked right out of the room.

EVIE

"Just so you're prepared, when you enter that room, your brother will be chained to the table," Hank told me.

God, I thought.

"Fine," I replied.

"No physical contact," he went on.

"Again, fine," I said.

He stopped outside a door and looked down at me.

"Eddie's in with him now and Eddie will remain in that room with you. He'll try to be unobtrusive, but he will not leave. I'll be watching through the one-way. And Evan, I gotta share how far this not-being-a-private chat goes. Anything he says that might incriminate him or anyone he knows, or any information he provides about criminal activities, he will be further interrogated about after you leave. Do you understand?"

I looked right in his attractive, whiskey-colored eyes and declared, "I know a policeman was killed, Hank. I know my brother was in possession of the gun that did that. I know *he* knew he had possession of that gun, and instead of turning it over to the police, he kept it safe for whoever to do whatever they intended to do with it. So, if he incriminates himself about being involved in this sorry business, that isn't on me."

His face gentled and he said, "I'm not asking you to get him to talk—"

But I didn't let him finish.

"If you were, I'd say yes. This isn't about that, but if you want to make it so, I'm in."

His chin shifted to the side in surprise before he replied, "Just do what you came here to do and what comes of it, does, Evie."

I nodded.

Hank turned the handle on the door and shoved in.

I heard my brother in the middle of saying something, ending with, "...this harassment bullshit. You can't let every asshole and their brother come in and—"

He abruptly stopped when he turned his head to the door that Hank had gotten out of the way of so I could fully push open and he saw me walk in.

He then paled, jerked in his chair like he was intending to stand, making his chains rattle and Eddie warn, "Cool it, Gardiner."

I felt the tightness in my cheek, how it was pushing up into my eye.

I also felt the burn in my other cheek, and I knew that graze against concrete broke skin.

I had not had a look at myself, but I could tell by Mick's reaction the results of my short time with Snag were dramatic.

I glanced in Eddie's direction where he was standing, arms crossed, in the corner.

He gave me a nod.

I moved in.

"Evie," Mick whispered, reaching both of his bound hands across the table as I sat down opposite him.

"I've had an interesting day, Mick," I told him, purposefully resting my hands in my lap.

"Sweetheart, honey, oh God, what the *fuck*?" He started this with coos and ended it with clips.

"You did this to me," I said.

He blanched further on a flinch and moaned, "Evie."

I guessed that was the end of my line because I leaned deep into the table and screeched, "*You did this to me!*"

Mick dropped his head.

I stared at the top of it, but I didn't see it.

I saw the spray of Mag's blood on my *fucking living room wall*.

"You know, the whole time I was captive. The whole time he held a gun on me. The whole time he was tying me to a chair. The whole time he was asking me the same question over and over and *over* again until he got sick of it and lost it and hit me. The whole time I was lying on my side in an empty warehouse in the cold, tied to a goddamn chair, all I could think about was one thing. When Snag shot Danny in my living room, if Danny had survived."

"God, this got so dicked *up*," Mick told the table.

"Look at me," I bid.

He shook his head.

"*Look at me!*" I shrieked.

He lifted his head and now his face was red, so were his eyes, and they were bright with wet.

Once upon a time, that look would register on me.

Once upon a time, that look would bring me to heel because I so badly wanted to be everything a sister should be to my brother.

It was no longer that time.

"He shot my boyfriend in my living room."

"Evie, I had no idea—"

"You knew."

He shook his head again. "I didn't. I had no idea. Things were hot for Snag. They were up in his shit, thinking he had what was in that bag, so he needed to unload it for a while, and he promised me he'd get clear and take it off your hands as fast as he could. No one was supposed to know you even had it. He told me he'd be sure when you grabbed it no one was around. He promised me you'd be safe. I swear to God, Evie, he promised me."

"So, you admit it. You did this to me. You did it to Danny. You did this to us. You put us right in the line of *literal* fire, and for what? A favor to a friend? A friend who's a pimp?"

"I owed him."

"You owed him, and as usual, *I* paid."

"Sweetheart—"

"Fuck you," I bit out.

He blinked in shock, going so far as to sit back heavily with the weight of it.

"Were those drugs in that bag yours?" I asked.

He began to look shifty and then he sounded it.

"I don't know what you're talking about."

God, I was sitting there looking like I did and telling him about my day, and he was covering his own ass.

How had I not seen this before?

It was a new definition of love being blind.

"Liar," I whispered. "You're in the clink and you not only needed someone to look after a murder weapon you promised some piece of slime you'd keep safe, you needed someone to look after your stash."

"I was just paying on a marker I owed. That's it. I got nothin' to do with anything that mighta been in that bag. I was just paying a marker."

Such a *liar*.

"You're dead to me," I told him.

His eyes got big and he leaned forward, again reaching out with his hands. "Evie, don't say that."

"Leave me with one good memory, Mick. If you know anything, anything at all, that will find the man who killed that cop, you tell Detective Chavez." I jerked my head in Eddie's direction.

Mick's face closed down and he spat, "I'm not gonna rat."

"I can't imagine why not, considering you're a complete rodent."

He looked stunned, wounded, and then he looked ticked.

"Well, fuck you too, Evie," he snarled.

Really?

Really?

This was where we were now?

Trading *fuck you*s?

I gave him a long stare before I replied, "You didn't have to say that, Mick, considering you've been doing that all my—"

I didn't finish.

The door opened and Mag walked in.

His arm was in a sling.

His face was murderous.

And his attention was focused on Mick.

"Honey," I called.

He looked down at me and grunted, "You done?"

I looked to Mick and decided I was.

So I stood, leaned into a hand on the table that separated us and gave him the words he gave me.

"Do right by your sister, Mick. Do right."

With that, I pushed away, nodded my thanks to Eddie and moved to Mag.

He took my hand, and connected, we walked out of that room.

Well down the hall, I started, "Danny—"

"We'll talk when we get home."

I looked up and saw how hard his jaw was, therefore asked tremulously, "Are you angry with me?"

He stopped abruptly, released my hand, turned to me, cupped my face and bent so his eyes were so close to mine, another inch, and I could give him butterfly kisses.

"No, I am not angry with you," he decreed roughly.

But that was all he said.

So I replied, "Okay."

"Okay," he grunted, took control of my hand and started us walking again.

"Were you watching?" I asked.

"Got there around the time you made him look at you. Determined to give you space to do what you needed to do. Got done doin' that when he said, 'fuck you.'"

Well, one good thing about that, he already knew my brother was a douche canoe.

"So, I'm your boyfriend, huh?" he asked.

Oh shit!

He gave me a look I couldn't quite read, though I knew it wasn't bad, before he pushed open the door that led into reception.

We both stopped dead when we got into the waiting area.

It was crowded.

Not just with Lottie and Tex, Ryn, Hattie and Pepper, and Dutch and his two hottie-biker buddies.

But now also Mo, Boone, Auggie, Axl, a dude that at first glance I thought was Hank's twin and another hot guy I would almost immediately know was Luke, Ava's husband, seeing as she, Indy, Jet and Roxie were coming through the front doors as we entered reception and Ava went right to him and got a lip touch.

The other dude was Lee because he and Indy did the same.

Most of these people, I barely knew.

All of these people were mine.

Suddenly, I couldn't wait for Gert to meet Mag, Mo, Lottie and the guys.

She was going to love them.

"I'm hungry!" Tex boomed. "I'm also feelin' Mexican. Anyone up for Las Delicias?"

"Does anyone ever turn down LD?" Indy asked.

"I'm callin' Nancy," Tex stated, making his way to the door. "You call the gang," he ordered Indy. "I'll get the tables and extra chips and salsa."

Then he was gone.

Guess he was hungry.

I looked up to Mag. "We should get you home."

He looked down to me. "Feedin' you first."

"Honey, you were shot today."

"I'm fine."

"Danny—"

"Baby, what did I say this morning?"

That morning felt like ten years ago.

"Which part?"

"About a man who takes care of his woman."

I clamped my mouth shut.

He seemed okay with me calling him my boyfriend.

But was I his woman?

I didn't ask that.

But Mag asked a question.

"Do you like Mexican?"

"I love it."

When he got that answer, he smiled.

CHAPTER FIFTEEN

Drop

MAG

Mag let himself and Evie into his condo, flipped on the lights, then made sure the door was locked behind her before he moved in, tossed his keys on the island and went direct for the Fireball.

His shoulder was killing him.

As the doctor ordered, he should have popped a pill and rested after Baldy got done with him.

He did not.

Now it wasn't early, it wasn't late, and he'd take a painkiller, but only when he knew Evie was settled after the day she'd had.

They'd not had the dinner he'd wanted to treat her to prior to taking her to a movie.

They'd had a chaotic dinner where people from the Rock Chick and Chaos crews descended from all around Denver, which meant around five hundred were in attendance, and the only reason it didn't drive him around the bend was how obvious Evie made it that she was enjoying herself.

She made this more obvious by babbling at him the entire way home about how Axl and Hattie, Boone and Ryn, and Pepper and Auggie were dancing around each other, but she could tell the girls, and the guys, were interested.

Also, how great Lottie and Mo were together, how happy she was for them and how she couldn't wait for their wedding.

As well as how, after starting to read that *Rock Chick* book at Fortum's, she thought Lee would scare her with his over-the-top "alpha-ness," but it was Luke who freaked her out.

And how she thought people in a motorcycle club were supposed to be terrifying, but Joker was "so cute" with his wife and kids.

She'd only quit babbling at him when she started talking on her phone after getting a call in the elevator.

He didn't know she was such a talker, but he didn't mind the babbling. It indicated she was getting more comfortable with him and he was all kinds of down with that.

Not to mention, it communicated she seemed to be happy about just about...*everything*.

In fact, the best part of the night was her babbling, seeing as he spent the dinner sitting next to her with her face the way it looked, his arm in a sling, putting up with people not in their crew sending them pitying looks, probably thinking they got in a car wreck or something.

Mag never thought he'd wish for a car wreck, but he'd prefer that to the reality that he'd let it get to the point where Evie had been dragged from her home, then tied to a chair and beaten.

He found the Fireball wasn't in the freezer, it was on the counter.

Apparently, Evie and/or her girls had helped themselves to his crutch.

It was not as good at room temp as when it was chilled, but he wasn't going to quibble.

He was pulling down shot glasses when Evie said, "Thanks, that's really appreciated. You take care too. 'Bye."

He had his hand wrapped around the bottle but his eyes to her when she took the phone from her ear.

"My apartment manager," she explained. "He shared he was not entirely at one with the police coming and going, dusting for prints and the like. And he was definitely not at one with gunplay on the landing, but he assured me the window is all boarded up, my door is secure, and he's promised to have that window replaced Monday, latest Tuesday. Even so, he was worried there might be something of value in there some other hooligan, his word, might wish to commit a crime to take from me and that boarded-up window might not be much of a deterrent. But since Lottie and Ava brought over my jewelry and three pairs of my Chucks, and the rest I don't care about, it'll all be good. Except the Chucks that were left behind, and no one will take those. Though I'd like to swing by tomorrow and grab my vinyl."

She paused to take a big breath, then finished.

"And the rest of my Chucks."

"We'll do that," Mag told her, and finally turned his attention to pouring the shots.

"*I'll* do that. I'll ask Boone or Auggie or Axl to go with me," she said, approaching him at the island. "You're gonna drink that shot you shouldn't drink after losing a goodly amount of blood today, then you're going to go lie down, and tomorrow, you're going to rest all day."

He had to admit, she was taking all of this a fuckuva lot better than he'd ever have called it.

He also had to admit, it might have something to do with the blood loss, more to do with the pain, most to do with the emotion of the day, but he was fucking wiped.

Dead on his feet.

And last, he had to admit, she was normally cute when she was bossy.

But no way in fuck was she going anywhere without him until he had visions of her lying on her side, tied to a chair, with an asshole holding a gun crouched over her under control in his head.

"We'll talk about it tomorrow," he muttered, using his glass to push her glass toward her then taking his, and he downed the fire.

He put the glass down and refilled.

"Danny," she said softly, reaching out and wrapping her fingers around his wrist. "Maybe you should go easy on that."

He couldn't go easy on it until he knew she was settled and he could swallow a pill, which would probably knock him out.

This was because it was boiling inside him.

Christ.

And he didn't want to let her down. Hawk down.

Himself down.

But he was either going to shoot that shot or throw it across the room.

He was about to tell her she needed to let him do what he needed to do when her phone rang again.

She'd set it on the island.

She looked down at it.

He looked down at it.

It said STEPDAD ROB.

Seeing as she'd shared over dinner, and everyone who'd been witness to it had crowed how awesome it was (and Mag wished he hadn't missed it), Mag was in the know about her activities that day in regard to her family.

In the know and down with every decision she made.

So, he was not all that down with the stepdad phoning.

Evie looked up at him.

"I think he's worried about me and he's the only one who's given a shit throughout all this, so I think I should talk to him real quick just to let him know I'm okay."

Legos and groceries and heading out in the dead of night to meet some asshole in a Lincoln Continental, Evie was always taking care of someone else when she should be looking after herself.

He didn't like it.

But it was her, and one thing he'd learned in his life, you had to let people be who they were.

So he jerked up his chin.

He did the shot when she let him go and turned away to grab her phone.

"Rob?" she greeted. "Yeah, I'm okay." Pause and, "Yeah, Danny's here. We've had dinner. We're just about to settle in, watch some TV and get some rest." Pause then, "No. I haven't told Sidney. Mostly because I didn't want her worried but also because there was nothing she could do. But I've... well, for various reasons, I've cut ties with Mick and Dad."

She stopped talking then whirled to Mag, and her eyes were big.

Cute.

Mag ignored other things about her face, including the fact one of her eyes couldn't get as big as it should when she made that face, and he focused on that cute.

Strike that.

He latched on to it like it was a lifeline.

"You did?" she asked with unhidden surprise. "I-I...really don't know what to say. But I think this is good. It probably doesn't feel good, and I know she's my mom, but you deserve better."

When she stopped speaking, Mag wasn't sure, but he thought he caught her mouthing *He left her*.

"What?" she asked into the phone. "Yes. But not tonight. I know you're worried but I'm really all right. I'm with Danny and he's," she ducked her chin, "proven adept at taking care of me."

Mag felt some tension release in his neck and instantly his shoulder felt better.

It wasn't the Fireball dousing the burn inside.

It was those last words Evie said.

She turned a little away and spoke again into her phone.

"Maybe we can set that up sometime later. I do want you to meet him but right now he's not a super big fan of my family so maybe we can give him a little time, I'll work on that with him and we'll figure something out." Pause then, "Yeah." Pause and, "That means a lot, Rob. Truly, it does. And you being how you've been through all of this means a lot too. I'm sorry it led to what it did between you and Mom, but sometimes things happen for a reason."

She looked to Mag as she ended it over the phone with her stepdad.

"Me too, Rob. Thank you. Love you and talk to you later. Try to get some sleep." Pause and, "'Bye." She dropped the phone from her ear and announced, "He left Mom and he wants to meet you."

"You're right, I'm not a super big fan of your family, so I'm all in to break bread with Gert, who digs you and shows it, but that dude's gonna have to wait," Mag replied.

"Gotcha," she mumbled.

Mag poured another shot and downed it.

Evie watched.

When he was done, she suggested, "Maybe we can lie down and watch a little TV."

"I was vacuuming."

Her head ticked.

"Sorry?" she asked.

"It was not a priority to vacuum. It was a priority to cover your ass. And I was vacuuming. Not covering your ass and look at you."

"Danny," she whispered.

But he couldn't escape it no matter how hard he tried to block it out with her voice and her hair and her cute that he was learning could transcend almost anything.

Except that purplish-red along her cheekbone that was swelling upward and partly closing her left eye and the striated grazes that were already scabbing over that ran about an inch long under her right eye.

He poured another shot, saying, "You were probably out of your mind scared."

"I was, that he'd hurt you."

In surprise at these words, his gaze lifted again to hers.

"Please, sweetheart, let's stretch out in front of the TV." She shot him a grin. "I'll watch *Anaconda*."

"She lands on her feet," he muttered.

"What?"

"You land on your *goddamned feet*!" he thundered,

turned, and sidearm-threw the shot glass with such force, it embedded itself in the drywall opposite, liquor splashing a thin stream the entire way, fire searing through his shoulder as he did it.

He then pivoted back to her.

"It's *my job*," he thumped his chest, ignoring the new throb of pain that sent through his shoulder, "to keep you on solid ground."

He stood there, his chest rising and falling, and each time it did, a nag of pain shot through his wound.

His arm was in a sling and he was staring at the woman he was set to make his, who looked like she'd followed her heart in the wrong direction and hooked up with O.J. Simpson.

Christ.

Christ.

And as she stood across from him, staring back, not speaking, he knew he'd really blown it by letting his fucked-up lack of control get the better of him.

Again.

She'd already seen it once that day.

Christ.

That was, he knew that until she asked, "Do you have a TV in your room?"

His chin jerked into his neck.

"Say again?"

"Well, I'm not about to get carried away in shenanigans that might tear your stitches, but you'd promised alternate sleeping arrangements tonight and I don't want to be alone, I want to be with you. I also want you to lie your ass down and get some rest. So, do you have a TV in your room?"

"Yeah," he answered.

"Right then, I'm gonna go put my pajamas on and you

are *not* going to take that shirt off without me helping so
don't even think about it. I'll do your boots and socks too.
But you can do your jeans. And I hope you have ice cream,
because I was too stuffed for sopapillas, but now I need
something sweet, and I want ice cream."

After delivering that, she walked to the island, took the
shot he'd poured her, downed it, then turned and strut-
ted away, aiming words for him toward the room she was
heading to.

"Be out in a minute." She stopped in the doorway and
looked back to him. "And if you clean up that Fireball, I'm
sleeping in here."

"I made the mess, I'll—"

"Shut up, Danny," she ordered quietly.

He shut up.

"Do you have ice cream?" she asked.

"Yeah," he answered.

"Good, honey," she muttered, then disappeared into Mo's
room.

Mag stared at the empty doorway a beat.

Then his head dropped, and he stared at his boots.

He pulled his shit together, put her shot glass in the sink,
the Fireball in the freezer and walked to his room.

He had the bedside lights lit and the TV on low and was
sitting on the side of his bed, toeing off his boots when she
walked in wearing another pair of shorts and a cami, these
in a swirly pink and green pattern.

She stopped in front of him and put her hands on her
hips, her eyes surveying his thermal.

She then decreed, "We're either gonna have to stretch
the neck of that beyond recognition or cut it off."

He picked door number one.

"No scissors, honey, this is my second-favorite Henley.

Don't make me shoulder that blow. I already lost my favorite one today to a bullet."

One side of her lips twitched, and she clicked her teeth.

Clicked her frickin' teeth.

Fucking hell.

Was he going to laugh?

She approached.

And no.

He was not going to laugh.

Because somehow, even after them going at each other in his kitchen three mornings in a row, she was entirely unaware of the effect she had on his cock.

Especially when he could see her acres of legs.

He knew this when he *couldn't* see her legs, but he had a close-up of her tits since they were in his face seeing as she was up close and personal, clicking off his sling.

"Baby?" he called, his voice tight for two reasons, amusement and his effort to fight his dick getting hard.

"Yeah?" she answered.

"You don't want me to tear my stitches, it'd be good you got your tits out of my face, 'cause if you don't, things are about to get the good kind of physical."

She hopped back.

He grinned up at her, and since she'd unclipped it, he slid the sling off his arm.

"You're aware I wanna fuck you," he noted, feeling his own lips hitch as he did.

"Uh...yeah."

"Well, that's because you're cute. And it's because you're a dork. It's also because your heart's way too big for your own good. But just sayin', it also has a lot to do with the fact you got mile-long legs, a great ass, perky tits, a lot of hair and you're pretty as fuck and all of that is standing in my bedroom right now."

"Right," she mumbled, her cheeks coloring.

He stood, which brought him up close and personal again, but in a way he could control his reaction, and he cupped her jaw, tilting her head up so he had her eyes.

"I want you at my side tonight too," he told her. "We'll watch TV. We'll sleep. That's it. I got some pain, and after ice cream, I'm gonna take a pill to control it that'll probably put me out. So, we're not goin' there tonight. We're not goin' there until I can make it be what I want it to be the first time between us. But you're in my bed, and to be clear, in the future, feel free to turn me on whenever the spirit moves you, but just for the time being...cut a guy some slack."

"Okay, Danny," she whispered.

"In other words, efficiency in taking off my shirt and then you can get the ice cream and I'll change into my shorts."

She nodded.

He bent and brushed his lips to hers before he sat back down.

She scraped him with her nails on his stomach and his lat, which felt too good, but he let it slide as he watched her bite her lip with concentration while she stretched the fuck out of the collar of his thermal getting it over his head without making him raise his other arm.

Then it was gone.

She stared at the big bandage on his shoulder.

"It's gonna heal fine," he promised.

Her gaze came to his and she repeated, "Okay, Danny," before it was Evie who cupped his jaw, bent and touched her mouth to his and then straightened.

"I'm gonna clean up too," she told him. "So, take your time and call when you're done."

"Right."

She shot him a soft smile and he watched her legs and ass as she walked out of his room.

He got his jeans off, his shorts on, retrieved the pill bottle from his jeans, put it on his nightstand and was sliding his arm back into the sling when he called, "Babe! Do me a favor and grab the pillows off Mo's bed! We might need 'em!"

"Gotcha!" she called back.

He finished with his sling, piled his pillows on one side and stretched himself out on the bed, propped up.

He didn't want to admit what a relief it was to take a load off.

But it helped significantly with the pain.

Evie came in with the pillows, left, and then the lights went out beyond his door and she came back with the carton of Tillamook Birthday Cake ice cream.

"I approve of your ice cream selection," she announced, sliding into bed beside him. "Birthday Cake is the best, with Malted Moo second runner-up."

"Monster Cookie," he parried, taking the spoon she offered.

"Oo, nice one," she muttered, digging in.

She'd put her hair up in a knot at the top, but tendrils were falling down her cheeks.

Yeah.

Just all kinds of pretty.

"Babe," he called.

She looked at him and answered, "Yeah?" before she shoved a huge-ass spoonful of ice cream in her mouth.

And only Evan could make shoving a huge-ass spoonful of ice cream in her mouth something that gave him an almost overwhelming urge to bang her breathless.

He wanted to lock onto that thought.

But he saw the purple, the swelling, the scabs.

Okay.

Focus.

He had Evie and her bare legs in her pajamas lying in his bed with him, holding a carton of ice cream between them.

And repeat.

He-had-Evie-and-her-bare-legs-in-her-pajamas-lying-in-his-bed-with-him-holding-a-carton-of-ice-cream.

He pulled in a deep breath.

And then he whispered, "It gets worse than that."

"All right."

All right?

"Honey, you gotta—"

She shook he head. "Stop it, Danny, we'll handle it when it happens. We've handled enough for today, doncha think?"

Yeah.

He thought.

More than enough.

"And we're here," she continued. "We might be a little worse for the wear but we're here. Let's just eat ice cream, watch TV, I'll get you some water to take your pill and then tomorrow is another day." She smiled. "And another day off because I can't strip with a shiner."

His eyes moved over her face thinking that he already knew he could fall in love with this woman.

What he was figuring out was he was about to head into free fall.

And he was not going to reach out a hand to grab hold of anything.

It was coming clear he was good to just...

Drop.

* * *

Mag opened his eyes and saw dark.

But he felt nagging pain in his shoulder.

He also felt Evie's head resting on the other one and her arm along his gut.

He was still up on the pillows, and it hit him that he'd fallen asleep in the middle of ice cream. Then she'd obviously turned out the lights, switched off the TV, and snuggled up to him on top of the covers, probably so she wouldn't disturb him.

And she hadn't.

He hadn't woken up.

He also hadn't taken a painkiller, which right then he knew was a mistake.

Last, he was a stomach or side sleeper and he needed to move, but couldn't, because Dr. Baldwin told him to sleep a few days in the sling, on his back, elevated.

But he was uncomfortable.

The only good thing about his position was Evie cozied up to him, though she'd trapped his arm against his side with her warm softness.

To try to fool his body into a semblance of comfort, he stretched his legs and carefully pushed his arm under her so he could wrap it around her.

He didn't go careful enough.

Her head moved on his shoulder, her body shifted against his, pressing closer, and her hold across his stomach tightened.

Fuck.

Just that from his Evie and he was getting hard.

She tipped her head back and he felt her push her face to his neck.

"You awake, honey?" she mumbled.

"Go back to sleep, baby," he replied.

She moved again, which meant he had more of her weight, including her tits pressed to his side.

Jesus.

"You sound really awake," she said.

"I'm fine. Go back to sleep."

She lifted her head. "Are you in pain?"

He moved his hand to run the tips of his fingers soothingly along her back.

The problem with that was, her cami had ridden up and his fingers hit soft, smooth skin.

Christ.

"I'm good, promise," he lied.

She misinterpreted the tightness in his voice and shifted again, murmuring, "I'm gonna go get you a pill."

But Mag curled his arm around her and clamped tight. "Don't want you to move."

"Is my moving hurting you?"

Everything about her was agony right then, but not that way.

He should have known he wouldn't be able to make it through a night with Evie in his bed.

He'd agreed to it because she didn't want to be alone.

And because he wanted her in his bed.

"No," he grunted.

He must have communicated something in that grunt because her voice went soft and sweet in a way he felt right in his dick when she whispered, "I think we're gonna get up to some shenanigans."

That tone in her words?

Her body pressed to his?

Oh yeah, they were.

She pushed up as he turned, and when her mouth slammed into his, she only smushed his lips a little against his teeth.

But to be fair, it wasn't all her.

He was right there with her.

Though Mag didn't mind because, right after, when he offered his tongue, she sucked it deep.

As usual with his Evie, the heat shot through the stratosphere the moment they tasted each other.

He'd never had that with a woman. That zero to ten thousand with a taste.

But there it was again.

In his bed.

This meant the sling had to go.

He pushed away, she heard the click of the clasp, whispered, "Danny" uncertainly, but he slid the fucking thing off, tossed it, and went back in.

He took her mouth, tangled himself up in her and her protests were gone.

When she was pressing close, seeking his now rock-hard cock with her hips, her hands all over his back, in his hair, and her mouth got greedy, he put his hand up her cami to go for her tit and he knew he already had her way in the zone when she didn't let that happen.

Oh no.

Her arms went right up so he'd pull the cami off.

This he did, then cupped her breast and lifted it, bending to it, the nag in his shoulder only a nuisance in his bid to get his mouth around her nipple.

He pulled deep, felt his gut tighten when it budded on his tongue and felt the sound of her moan blaze right through his balls.

Her nails scraped his scalp, her other hand dove into the back of his shorts and curled into his ass.

Fucking hell, she was hot.

Sweet and hot.

He returned to her mouth and she breathed, "Danny," against his lips, rubbing up against him, using her hand at his ass to press him closer, and on instinct, his hand went to her belly, down into her shorts, and in.

Oh yeah.

Fuck yeah.

His Evie.

Sweet.

Hot.

And *wet*.

She whimpered and started riding his fingers before he even got one to her clit.

"Baby," he growled appreciatively.

"Yes . . . yes, that feels . . . *nice*," she gasped.

Nice didn't cover it.

It felt so *nice*, he wanted more.

So, he glided a finger hard over her clit and up inside her sleek wet.

Her head fell back, her nails dug in and she started riding *that*.

Christ.

She was perfect.

That said . . .

"Evie," he slid his finger out and lazily circled her clit, "let's slow it down, honey."

Her response was to slide her hand that was in his shorts over his hip and latch onto his dick.

All right.

Fuck yeah.

Guess they weren't going to go slow.

With her hand at his cock, he was way down with that too.

She stroked.

He groaned.

She kissed him.

He took over and pressed her to her back.

He returned to finger fucking her and she jacked him while they went at each other's mouths like kissing was going to be outlawed.

He was about to call it and move on to the next portion of the festivities, his choice, going down on her, when she moaned a warning, needy, "Danny," against his mouth.

All right.

He'd go down on her in the morning.

He rolled off, at the same time tearing her shorts and panties down her legs.

She went after his shorts as he went after a condom in his nightstand.

They were both naked and she had her mouth all over his chest and neck, her hands all over his stomach and nipples as he tore it open and rolled it on.

And then Evie...

Christ, his Evie...

He barely got the condom to the root, and she was up, swinging on to take a ride.

Mag couldn't stop his smile.

He did stop her from taking over by angling up, ignoring the flash of pain in his shoulder, and grabbing her hips as he rolled them in the bed.

When he had her on her back with him on top, between her legs, he ran his hands over her ass, down the backs of her thighs, lifting her knees.

She dove between them and commandeered his cock.

There was humor in the thickness of his tone when he said, "Baby."

"Hurry."

"This isn't a race," he pointed out.

"It's been a long time, Danny. A *long* time."

Well then.

It was his job to take care of his woman.

And something like that needed to be taken care of immediately.

He took her mouth, wrapped his fingers around hers at his dick, and they both guided it where it needed to be.

Their hands moved away, and with a slow, smooth glide, he was seated deep in her tight sleek wet.

Good Christ.

Good Christ.

Yeah.

She was perfect.

His Evie, she fit like a glove.

In so many ways.

Mag slid his mouth to her ear and whispered, "You good?"

"Yeah," she panted, her hands roaming his back, hot and urgent. "You?"

"Oh yeah."

"Honey?" she called.

"Yeah?"

She turned her head and nipped his earlobe with her teeth, which sent a shiver down his neck and over his back before she begged, "*Move.*"

He smiled against the skin of her neck.

Then he moved.

He didn't want it wild, and not because of his wound.

This was good. This was right. This was *them*.

The beginning of *them*.

He wanted them both to be present. He wanted them

both to be aware. To fall into the experience in a way they'd remember it.

Evan had other ideas, he knew it when she jacked a long leg up high and pressed it tight to his side, wound her other leg around his ass, clamped on with both hands, also at his ass, and squeezed her demand.

She wanted it that way?

Mag was all about giving his girl what she wanted.

So, he let go and rode her wild, the forearm of his healthy side in the bed to hold some of his weight, his other hand between them to make certain she got there.

She got there, fuck, and it sounded almost as good as it felt, with her dragging her nails up his spine and moaning his name low and long, her pussy closing like a fist around his cock.

And all that meant she took *him* there, his world minimizing to his bed, his woman, their connection, groaning his orgasm into the skin of her neck.

When he came down, he heard her heavy breaths mingling with his labored ones, felt her cunt still spasming around his dick, and the fire in his shoulder made itself known.

This meant he rolled, keeping them connected, so she was on top, and the pain eased.

Her breath breezed across his throat, her hair had come out of its knot and was all over his face, and her little tits pressed against his chest felt almost as good as her pussy wrapped around his cock.

"You didn't answer," he told the dark ceiling, "so I will. It's official. I'm your boyfriend."

She was still a second before she giggled and tilted her head to press her nose against the underside of his jaw.

"Should I make you a plaque?" she asked.

"I'll set it on my workstation," he answered.

She giggled again.

He gave her ass a squeeze, lifted her off and rolled her to her back beside him.

He pressed a kiss to her chest before he rolled the other way, moved through the dark to the bathroom, dealt with the condom and switched on the lights. Blinking away the bright, he had the lights on only long enough to check his bandages to make sure there was no blood and in their "shenanigans" he didn't do any further damage.

All he saw was white, so he switched off the lights and rejoined Evie in bed.

She cuddled into him and he took her in with his hands, noting she'd put her cami and panties back on, not the shorts.

"You need your sling," she whispered into his throat.

"Yeah," he agreed reluctantly.

"Do you need a painkiller?" she asked.

"Yeah," he told her even more reluctantly.

She didn't say dick.

She kissed his jaw, slid away, left the room and he found the sling and was putting it on when she came back with a glass of water.

He clicked the thing in place. She handed him the water then reached beyond him, her body brushing his, to nab the bottle of pills.

She shook one out, handed that to him too, then did the reaching thing again to put the bottle back.

All of this even though that bottle was closer to him and he could do it.

But he sensed he shouldn't.

This was Evie.

Like him, she needed to be taking care of somebody.

He slugged down the pill and she grabbed the covers to pull over them when he was setting the glass aside.

They settled back in, just as they had been when he woke, except with the covers on, and Mag found nothing uncomfortable about it anymore.

"That was really...*wow*," she whispered to his chest.

He smiled into the dark and tightened his hold on her.

"Danny?" she called.

"Right here," he answered.

He couldn't see it.

But he could feel it.

His brief answer was another Toothpaste Moment. He knew it with the way she stiffened, then settled, offering him more weight.

So he was shocked as shit when she shared, "You're really *so* not my type."

He took a beat.

Then busted out laughing.

She lifted her head and he felt her watching him through the dark.

He stopped laughing when she laid her hand on his cheek, he felt the new vibe of the room and stared at her shadowed face.

"Words obviously don't suffice. But thank you for getting shot for me."

"Baby, it shouldn't have gotten—"

She interrupted him to say, "You see it as a failure. What you need to see is, I'm a woman who spent her whole life twisting myself into knots trying to make people I loved love me. And now I find myself with a man who's not only willing to take a bullet for me, he does that and ends the day throwing a shot glass across the room, angry at himself because someone harmed me." She moved her hand to stroke his jaw and continued, "I see it from your perspective, honey. What you need to do is see it from mine, what that means to me, especially with the life I've led and then," she dipped to brush her lips against his before she finished, "just let it go."

Just let it go.

With a guttural noise, he slid his hand into her hair and held her mouth to his.

The kiss he gave her had depth, it was wet, but there was only a little heat because they'd both just come, she'd gotten him over his fuckup, she'd had a tough day, and he needed to let his girl sleep.

So, he ended it and tucked her face into his neck.

"You good?" she asked.

"So good," he answered.

"Good," she whispered and snuggled closer. "'Night, Danny."

"Goodnight, baby."

It didn't take long before the pill started working, but Mag fought it.

Until he felt Evie slide into dreamland.

Only then did he let go and join her.

CHAPTER SIXTEEN

Cinnamon Marshmallow Clusters

EVIE

I woke up with Mag's mouth on my neck and his hand gliding over my belly.

When I opened my eyes, I saw dark and I didn't know if it was because it was still night or it was early morning.

I didn't care what it was, not with Mag touching me the way he was.

"Honey?" I called sleepily, reaching for him.

"You were snoring," he murmured against my neck.

Oh my God.

Oh no.

Snoring was bad.

I knew people who broke up with a partner who snored.

And there I was, snoring during our first sleep-together!

"Fuckin' cute," he kept murmuring as his fingertips slid under the elastic of my panties and skated across skin.

Oo.

That felt nice.

Apparently, my snoring wasn't a turnoff.

My hands encountered skin too (which almost felt better, but not quite) as I whispered, "Only you would think snoring is cute."

"Mm," he hummed.

Okay.

He was in a mood.

And I was totally in that same mood.

Oh *yeah*.

My hips shifted to give nonverbal instructions to his hand.

But it only served to make Mag give verbal instructions.

"Take these off," he growled, tracing his fingers to my hip and tugging my panties.

I did not hesitate a nanosecond.

He pulled away and removed his sling.

I got those panties gone.

He tossed the covers from us and rolled back to me.

Just...

Lower.

Oh.

My.

God.

Yes!

An important thought pushed through my sleepy-morning-sex-Mag-was-about-to-go-down-on-me haze and I started, "Your..."

I was going to finish *arm* but didn't because his mouth closed over me.

Yes.

Yes.

Yesyesyesyes*yes*.

He was good at that.

Right from the get-go!

I slid my fingers in his awesome hair.

Mag ate me, and he did it tremendously, and he kept doing it until I exploded, bursting into molecules, and it felt so good, I didn't care I was nothing but a loosely connected mass of happy atoms, floating in the air.

When I was still coming down, he rolled off and up to lie back on the pillows.

I rolled over and *on*.

"Baby," he murmured, his hands tracking up the tops of my thighs that were straddling his hips.

"Condom," I mumbled, sliding my hands all over his freaking phenomenal chest.

Good to look at.

Way better to touch.

"That was for you. You don't have to—"

I put my lips to his and demanded, "*Condom.*"

He didn't make me ask again.

In fact, I had to lift up because he reached to his nightstand.

He then pulled out a ribbon of condoms that, in the shadows of the rising sun (it was dawn, I still didn't care), looked about a yard long.

I would have laughed.

But I was too focused to laugh.

I took them from him, tore one off, released it from its sleeve and took my time at his cock, gliding it on, among other things.

"Jesus," he groaned, his hands now at my hips, thumbs digging into my hip bones, his gaze hot and bothered and roaming all over me. "Taste you. See you. Feel you. Smell you. Too much. Stop playing and claim that, Evie."

He was good with his mouth, I wanted to give him good with my hand.

But his dick was so hard, so hot, it felt so damned good, I knew it felt even better inside, so I wanted to *claim that*.

Claim *him*.

So I did.

Positioning him, I bore down and as I did, his hips surged up.

Powerfully.

Whoa.

Wow.

He felt amazing inside, the way he filled me.

Beautiful.

I rode him and I clenched him, and I touched him with a single-minded purpose.

Mag was about dual purpose, however, his thumb finding my clit.

I bent over him again, moving on him, and shared, "I wanna watch you come."

"Yeah, and I wanna watch you come."

"But if I come before you come, I won't be able to concentrate on watching you."

His words were deep, a little rough, but amused when he noted, "This isn't the last time we're gonna do this, baby."

Oh.

Right.

Well then.

Onward.

My clit was still so sensitized by him going down on me, not to mention the friction against his cock and the banging at the base, in the end, I came before he did, and I missed his show.

But.

Whatever.

I'd have another shot.

I was careful not to collapse on him when it was over. I just rested against him, making sure to shift my weight to his healthy side.

Though I did burrow my face into his neck since he smelled good.

"Your arm?" I asked.

His hands felt nice, light, sweet, and tender as they roamed my skin and he answered, "Weird, I don't feel it when you're fuckin' me or I'm eating you."

I giggled into his neck.

Then I got serious.

"You need to put the sling back on."

"In a minute."

"Danny—"

He wrapped one arm around me and gave me a squeeze. "In a minute, Evie. All right?"

I drew in breath, held it and let it go.

It was hard, letting that breath go, and with it, letting the conversation do the same, seeing as he hadn't sprained it, he'd been shot, and we really shouldn't be engaging in these activities so soon after that occurred.

Engaging in them repeatedly.

But he was a grown man.

And it was his decision.

That was something I'd learned the day before.

My decisions were my decisions.

And the people around me made their own decisions.

And those were *theirs,* and whatever came of that, I had to let it go.

He didn't say anything.

I didn't say anything.

And all of a sudden, I felt weird.

We were just lying there, still connected (though I was losing him), post sex.

Good sex.

No, great sex.

Sex during which I hadn't thought for a second about if I was doing something he liked (or not), what he thought of my body...nothing entered my head at all but enjoying him, giving him me...

And connecting.

I knew he liked it.

I definitely knew I liked it.

It was natural.

It was like bickering with him practically the minute he first walked into my apartment. It was like giggling at him being sexy and flirty and playful over brunch. Or sitting next to him at Mexican last night, Mag with his good arm around my chair, both our chairs tucked close, me with my boyfriend, him with his woman, and we'd only really had one date.

It was us.

I didn't know if I'd ever been an us with anybody, not even my ex.

But Mag and I had been us since the beginning.

On this realization, I relaxed against him and enjoyed the moment.

That was, I enjoyed the moment until he tightened his arm around me for a second and muttered, "Gotta clean up. Be back."

I slid off and he slid out of bed.

I found my panties in the sheets and had them on by the time he got back.

He stood, naked and beautiful, in the dawn's early light beside the bed and donned his shorts and sling before he got back into bed and claimed me, pressing me down his healthy side.

"Do you need a pill?" I asked.

"No. Before bed only," he answered.

"But if you're in pain..." I let that trail.

"Got a high threshold for pain," he told me. "But even if I didn't, I need sleep to heal, I need the pain gone to sleep, so before bed only and only for a few nights. Painkillers will fuck you up and my life just took a good turn, not gonna let dick fuck it up."

Oh my.

He'd been shot yesterday, and he thought his life had taken a "good turn."

That turn being me.

Oh man.

I liked that.

A *whole* lot.

"Okay, then I'm going to make breakfast in bed for you."

His body started shaking so I took my head off his shoulder, pushed up and looked down at him.

Yes, he was laughing.

"What?" I asked.

"No fair. I get shot for you, and you get a leg up on the breakfast game."

My face must have registered my thoughts because his arm moved in its sling, he winced, then he took his other arm from around me and cupped my cheek.

"You didn't shoot me," he said softly.

"Danny—"

"Stop it. Now."

I closed my mouth.

"I don't blame anyone but Fletcher Gumm for this," he declared. "And I won't ever blame anyone but Gumm for this."

"It could have been worse."

"It wasn't."

"It could have been catastrophic."

He slid his fingers back into my hair, pulled my face to his and said low, "It wasn't."

I took in air and nodded.

"We done with that?" he asked.

"I reserve the right to feel bad, freak out or otherwise react to it for the foreseeable future. Though you're allowed to get angry about me doing that if that lasts longer than, say, ten years."

He burst out laughing, doing so pulling my head further down, which meant my body went down with it, and he tucked my face in his neck.

He then rounded me with his arm, tensed it and kept it that way to hold me close.

When he got control of his hilarity, he agreed, "Okay. Ten years. Starting now."

I smiled against his skin.

"So, today, breakfast, your turn 'cause I wanna make a few calls, and you're right, I should take it easy. Then we'll hit your pad to get your vinyl and anything else you wanna grab—"

"Danny—"

"It'll fuck with me, but you can carry," he grunted.

Okay, I could do that.

I said no more.

"We'll grab some lunch, hit the grocery store and stock up then back here to take a load off."

"Sounds like a plan."

"Evie?" he called.

"Hmm?" I answered.

"Baby," he said in a much different tone, and I closed my eyes. "You had a big day yesterday."

I opened my eyes.

"Yeah."

"You wanna talk about it?"

"I...don't think so."

"If you do, not sure you can miss it 'cause you're layin' on me, and I won't be much farther away all day, so just sayin', I'm right here."

God.

He was just...

So nice.

I turned my head, pressed a kiss to his shoulder, then pushed up again to look down into his extraordinary eyes with his amazing curly lashes.

"It's soon," I whispered, "but I don't care. Fair warning, if by some awful happenstance Lottie needs a kidney, I'm giving her one of mine."

"Only if mine isn't a match," he whispered back.

Oh boy.

Yeah.

I liked that too.

A whole lot.

There he was, my boyfriend.

There I was, his woman.

This being so, I kissed him.

It was sweet, and it was wet, and it lasted a long time.

But it didn't go anywhere.

Because Mag had been shot the day before and we'd been active enough since then.

It was time to make breakfast.

I was hungry.

And I had to take care of my boyfriend.

* * *

Late that afternoon...

After breakfast.

After going to my pad to pack some things (the blood splatter was still there, but I was pretty proud of the powers I'd discovered I had that I called on to ignore it).

And after unloading my stuff at Mag's, going to lunch, the grocery store, and back to Mag's, whereupon I made a double batch of my cinnamon marshmallow clusters as a thank-you to the boys for throwing smoke grenades and rescuing me.

After all of that, I walked out of Mo's old room where I'd gone to use the bathroom to see Mag stuffing his face with marshmallow clusters.

I also looked down at the cookie trays (Mag had cookie trays, I'd found, because, in his words: "I kick chocolate chip ass"—something I was keen on discovering), and I saw one half of an entire tray was decimated.

Such was my surprise, coming to a stop beside the island, I asked the question no girl should ask her brand-new boyfriend.

"How long was I in the bathroom?"

"Babe," he said in a garbled way, seeing as his mouth was full, but even so, he had another cluster on deck in his hand to shove into it, "these are *outstanding*."

"I can tell. You've eaten a quarter of them," I remarked.

He grinned, cinnamon-marshmallow-toothed and not caring. I knew this because he shoved the next cluster in.

"Danny!" I snapped. "Those are for the boys!"

"Make more," he replied, still with mouth full.

"I can't. I'm out of cereal. And marshmallows. And butterscotch morsels."

Though, not chocolate ones, we'd bulked up on those for future chocolate chip goodness.

"We'll go back to the store."

Yeesh.

"Danny, it boggles the mind I have to keep reminding you of this, but . . . *you were shot yesterday.*"

"So?"

So?

"We've been busy all day. You need to rest."

"I can rest when we get back from the store, while you're making more of these," he replied, grabbing another freaking cluster.

"Danny!" I cried.

"Get over here. You're bein' cute. I need to kiss you," he demanded.

"No." I shook my head. "No way. You're going to taste like cinnamon and marshmallow and butterscotch and chocolate and *you* and all of that in a kiss is going to mean we'll do other things that don't include you *resting.*"

He gave me a look that was a combo punch of sweet, sexy, playful and incendiary before he declared, "Now you really need to get over here."

"Stop being sweet and hot," I bossed.

"Stop being cute and fuckable," he retorted.

"I see we're at an impasse," I remarked.

"Yeah, it's impossible for you not to be cute or fuckable."

"And it's impossible for you not to be sweet and hot."

His expression changed again, and it was not one that made my panties catch fire.

It was one that made my heart squeeze.

"Baby, come here. I promise I won't do anything that will end up with us on the floor, goin' at it."

I studied him closely, and only after I ascertained the veracity of his assertion, I went there.

When I got there, he rounded me with an arm, which was good, seeing as his other one was in a sling and this meant he couldn't eat more clusters.

For my part, I rounded him with *both* arms.

"Where'd you get that recipe?" he asked.

"I made it up."

His brows rose. "Seriously?"

"I wanted something sweet, I didn't have the patience to make cookies, and I didn't have Rice Krispies to make treats, but I did have the marshmallows, morsels and Cinnamon Toast Crunch. Those clusters are proof necessity is the mother of invention."

"No, they're proof you really are a genius."

I grinned up at him.

He stared down at me.

He then stated, "Okay, I lied. I'm totally gonna start something."

I frowned and began to pull away, warning, "Danny."

Even one-armed, he was stronger than me.

That said, he also had other tools to use to get what he wanted.

And he used them, saying, "Baby, you pulling hurts my shoulder."

I stopped pulling immediately.

He cinched the arm he had around me tighter, pressing me to him.

But I saw the satisfied look on his face.

"Was I hurting you?" I asked dubiously.

"Not really, but just to say, I have no shame using guilt if it means I'm gonna get laid."

I felt my entire body twitch in surprise at his words.

This was before I dissolved into laughter.

"Christ," he whispered in a way that made my laughter fade to just giggles. "You're pretty normally, but when you laugh, your eyes make these little upside-down crescent moons and I've never seen anything so pretty."

I stopped laughing altogether.

"Danny," I whispered back, feeling things, many, *many* things and feeling them deep.

"Even banged up, it's gorgeous."

I melted into him, repeating my whispered, "Danny," and getting on board with the notion of starting something.

His head was coming toward mine, this already my most favorite thing I could see, when a knock sounded on the door.

His head went right back up (not even close to my most favorite thing), his eyes went to the door, and I fought shifting out of the way in case electric-blue bolts of lightning shot from them and annihilated the door.

"Group text," he growled at the door. "I'm gonna tell all of them at once we did it so they'll stop fucking with us."

In another life, say the one I'd been living about five days ago, I would balk at a guy I was seeing stating he was going to send a group text to our friends to share we'd had sex.

In this one, in order to stop the interruptions, I was totally down with it.

He bent again, this time damnably quick, kissed my forehead then let me go and prowled to the door.

He looked through the peephole.

Then he did something bizarre.

His long body swayed back, like he was trying to avoid a blow.

Oh no.

"Who is it?" I asked carefully.

His head turned to me and he didn't answer.

He said, "I'll get rid of her."

Her?

Her who?

He repositioned so when he unlocked and opened the door (and he did this last not very far), he hid whoever was out there from view.

"Now's not a good time," he said, his voice void of, well...everything.

"Oh my God, Mag! It's true! You *have* been shot!" A woman exclaimed with unhidden shock and panic.

"I'm fine, Nikki. But now is—"

Nikki?

His ex?

That sway from the door like he was trying to escape pain.

His ex was outside.

And seeing her brought him pain.

It felt like my insides had started shriveling.

"Why are you up? Why aren't you resting? And don't give me any of that macho shit. You need to lie down. And I'm going to make that so. Get out of my way."

"Nikki, dammit—"

"Out...of my...*way*," she demanded, he abruptly pivoted, and he did so because she was pushing in.

Oh yeah.

My insides were shriveling.

Mag might think I was pretty.

But she...

Nikki...

His ex...

The one he loved who broke up with him and it sent him into a tailspin...

She was a knockout.

Tall. Blonde. Blue-eyed. Perfectly symmetrical features. A hint of a honeyed tan even if it was February, which meant she probably skied or snowboarded or was a runner or a rock climber or something interesting and outdoorsy.

She was trim, long-legged and had some serious flesh up top.

And she was totally put together.

She didn't look like she was about to walk into the Met Gala.

But for a Sunday afternoon, she was something, with a skintight tee and high-waisted jeans, a kickass bulky knit cardigan that only served to show how slender yet busty she was, tasteful jewelry and high-heeled booties.

She was also, outside the tall part, everything I was not.

For instance I was in a pair of vintage, low-rider jeans Roxie had bought for me, my baseball tee (that I was thrilled had survived) that had a snarling kitty on the front peering up through water at a tiny swimming mouse with PAWS at the top, and my bright red Chucks.

She was further, I realized at that juncture, frozen to the spot, staring at me.

One thing we had in common. I was doing the same at her.

Then her face got hard, her lips started to sneer, and she didn't seem as beautiful anymore as she did a sweep of me with her eyes and then turned to Mag.

"Really? Another one? The day after you took a bullet?" she derided.

Mag stood there for a second, staring down at her.

I stood there for that second, staring at the both of them, realizing, physically, how utterly perfect they were for each other.

Nikki stood that second too, glaring daggers up at her ex-boyfriend.

Then Mag spoke.

"Not that I wanted this to happen, maybe not ever, but definitely not now," he started. "Nik, this is Evan, we're seein' each other and it's serious. Evie, honey, this is Nikki. My ex."

We're seein' each other and it's serious.

Evie, honey…

We're seein' each other and it's serious.

Evie, honey…

It's serious.

With these words clamoring gleefully in my head, I forced my body to move, but I'd been so motionless, it jolted when I did. I still carried on, covering the distance between us with my hand raised.

Mechanically, she took it.

I gave her a little squeeze, let go, and mumbled what was part truth, part lie, "Um, this is awkward and I'm sorry about that, but, erm, nice to meet you," all while she gazed at me with a mixture of incredulity and pain.

Mag didn't help either of those when he positioned himself by my side and slid an arm around my shoulders.

He didn't go for the gusto, curling my front to his side and rubbing it in.

But he did make a point.

"I'm fine," he told Nikki. "I don't know who told you, but they shouldn't have."

As he spoke, her eyes drifted up at him, hazy and wounded.

"Why not?" she asked quietly.

He did not say it was no longer her business.

He said, "But when you found out, you should have called."

"I...this...I..." She shook her head, her long, golden hair brushing this way and that on her shoulders.

She was out of it, unable to process the situation she was in, and my heart went out to her.

She then seemed to focus, but it was on Mag's condo.

And as she looked around, something came over her.

When it did, she said quietly, "Even this is temporary. It isn't even really yours."

"Nik—" Mag began in a tone that shared he clearly understood these odd words.

She turned her attention to him, and she was herself again, the woman who walked in with a purpose, feeling she had every right to be there.

Oh man.

"You should be resting," she declared then her eyes came to me. "He should be resting."

"I—"

I didn't get any further than Mag had.

"Don't let him give you any of that 'I have a high threshold for pain' garbage."

Uh-oh.

Someone was pissing on her patch with her *I know how he's playing this, because, you see, I know him through and through, including how to deal with him, so let me instruct you for the time you have with him before I take over again* bullshit.

The "take over again" part being something she thought she was going to do when she showed at the door five minutes ago.

That was when I felt something come over me.

"Pain is pain," she went on.

I stood there, silent.

She continued with her lesson.

"So, you really shouldn't let him hand you any of his commando crap."

"Nik—" Mag tried again.

Her eyes shot right to him. "Has she been struck mute?"

Uh-oh.

I felt it happening.

Now something had come over Mag.

Time for me to intervene.

"Uh, just to say, Nikki?" I called, and she looked to me. "Danny's the one who sustained the injury. He knows how it feels. He also knows where his pain pills are. I've told him to rest, repeatedly. If he refuses to do that, he's a grown man, it's his choice."

But something *else* came over her the second I started speaking.

And it was back to wounded when her gaze shifted to Mag.

"Danny?" she whispered.

"Fuck," he muttered.

"Okay—" I started.

"*Danny?*" she shrieked so loud, I winced.

Good God.

"Nik—" Mag began yet again.

"Fuck you!" she shouted.

Oh boy.

"We're not doin' this," Mag growled.

"Danny? Danny?" She mocked then tossed a hand my way. "You let some woman you've known, what? *A day?* You let *her* call you *Danny?*"

It was a guess, but I figured he hadn't let Nikki call him that.

"Let's go back to the beginning of this visit where I said now's not a good time," Mag stated. "And just to add, with this shit, it's never a good time."

She turned to me.

Oh boy!

"Just so you know, we were together a long time. We talked about marriage. Kids. And between us breaking up and you, there've been about a hundred other *yous*," she shared.

I was really glad I knew that already or that would have been a blow.

Something she intended.

Jeez.

Seemed like Mag's ex was kind of a bitch.

That was when Mag curled my front to his side and bit out, "Nik, stop it."

She didn't take her eyes from me.

"So, just sayin', those hundred *yous* have yet to replace *me*."

"I have a feeling that's changing as we speak," I muttered.

"You'd be wrong," she snapped.

"Just to make shit clear," Mag said, and I looked up at him to see, surprisingly, he was addressing me, "me and Nik, *we* didn't break up. She dumped me."

"Okay," I said slowly, not super sure why he was making that point.

I turned my attention back to her, seeing as she turned her attention back to Mag to declare, "I did not dump you. I left and told you when you got yourself sorted to come back."

"No, you didn't leave. You kicked my ass out and told

me *not* to come back until I made the changes in my life that you required," he returned.

All right.

Damn.

Just…

Damn.

He was holding me, but I'd seen enough of them, what with my mom and Rob going at each other all the time.

I knew what a lovers' quarrel looked like.

And this conversation had suddenly morphed into that.

I didn't like it when Mom and Rob did it.

But I *really* didn't feel like being an innocent bystander during one that involved a guy I was falling for and had a strong suspicion I could spend the rest of my life with.

I started to shift away to give them some privacy and at the same time reevaluate my own circumstances, which might require me buying stock in Kleenex before I moved in with Tex, but I got nowhere as Mag's arm around my shoulders clamped so hard, a smidge harder and there'd be pain.

"Mag, it's for our future," she retorted.

"Nik, honest to fuck, can you be standing right there lookin' at me as I am right now and think we have a future?" Mag returned.

"It's for the best," she shot back.

"It was for *your* best," he volleyed.

"It's for *our* best," she rejoined.

God.

I really did not want to be standing right here.

"I was done havin' this conversation months ago, I can say without doubt I'm seriously done havin' it now," he told her.

"It isn't done until it's done," she stated.

"By that you mean, it isn't done until you get what you want," he translated.

I wondered if I closed my eyes, held my breath and concentrated hard enough, if I'd become invisible so I could spirit away.

Second choice, spontaneously combust.

"By that I mean, *we* aren't done," she fired back.

Oh God.

I looked to the floor and kept my eyes there, especially after I felt Mag go completely still.

I knew what that meant.

And as it meant what it meant, why wouldn't he let me go?

I wouldn't make a fuss.

I wouldn't cause a scene.

Okay, so, he was the nicest guy I'd ever met, he was great in bed, he was funny, he thought I was pretty, he liked John Wick and Metallica, and he took a bullet for me.

All huge positives in brand-new boyfriend material.

So, sure, we'd known each other all of five days, but I still knew I'd grieve his loss longer and harder than I did my ex-boyfriend who'd been in my life over two years.

But he'd loved this woman. He'd wanted a life with her.

So, if that would make him happy, and he had a shot at getting that back, I wasn't going to insert myself into that.

I was, however, definitely buying stock in Kleenex.

"Nik, fuck, I..." Mag started quietly.

I tried to carefully pull away.

He held tight.

Why wouldn't he let me go?

"That's why you're here," he kept talking quietly. "Whoever told you I got injured told you about Evie."

She did not confirm this.

Though I'd figured that out around the pissing-on-her-patch part of the conversation.

He continued speaking.

"Babe, we're done. It doesn't matter what got us there, it's over. I've moved on."

I stopped pulling and blinked at the floor.

"Mag—" she began.

"Don't," he cautioned.

"You've said that before," she told him.

Hmm.

"I haven't."

Hmm!

"Well, you *have* said you're not someone to quit on something you believe in," she retorted.

I figured that was the truth.

"Nik, really, don't. Let's end this here."

Okay, now I didn't want to be standing there for a different reason.

"Mag—"

"Honestly, what's done is done. You should move on too," he advised.

She shared her own advice.

"Well, then I should warn you, if I do, I won't be available when you come crawling back."

"Okay," Mag stated, but it wasn't in agreement to what she'd said. I could tell he was gearing up to deliver more, and his tone was strange.

So strange, I tipped my head back to look up at him.

And I saw from his profile his expression was also strange.

There was pain.

Not *pain* pain.

The kind you get when you really didn't want to say

something that was going to hurt somebody, but you didn't have a choice.

This being why he'd swayed from the door.

He knew there was a possibility she'd see me, and he'd eventually be pressed into the position he was in right now.

This made me ridiculously happy at the same time my heart was now going out to Mag.

I opened my mouth to offer my own advice, that being leave what he was about to say unsaid, invite her departure again, and let his future actions speak his words.

But I didn't get out even his name.

"I didn't want you in here because Evie's been having a rough go of it lately. I didn't want her to put up with whatever was gonna happen with you, but you took that choice away, operating under some assumption I'm seein' I gotta disabuse you of."

Oh no.

Totally time again to intervene.

I pressed my hand to his stomach and said urgently, "Danny."

"She made me dinner the other night, Nik, bacon cheeseburgers, and when she came out of the fridge with the shit to cook, I knew I was gonna marry her."

Uh.

Say…

What?

My mouth had dropped open, I just couldn't close it.

He looked down at me, and when he did, he appeared uncomfortable, even awkward, it was insanely adorable, then he looked back at Nikki and when he spoke again his voice was gentle.

"I'm sorry. When we talked about that when we were together, marriage, kids, I'm seein' now, they were just the logical next steps. You're a good woman, we had good times, a lot of them, and we just had a lot of time in. It was what we were supposed to do. I got caught up in that. Don't get me wrong, you meant somethin' to me, Nik. You meant a lot. Not havin' you hurt like fuck, you meant that much. I just didn't get what I was supposed to feel until I saw Evie with an armful of meat."

Many women would prefer this epiphany to happen when the sun was shining on her face or the wind was blowing through her hair.

But I'd totally take it happening for Mag when I was carrying an armful of meat.

He looked down at me again, still awkward, still adorable, and muttered, "Too soon, I know, it just had to be said."

"Not too soon," I whispered, pressing close to him.

His eyes moved over my face, the awkwardness faded, and his lips hitched.

"So," Nikki broke into our moment, "I see you finally let it overpower you."

We both looked to her, and she, regrettably, continued speaking.

"I didn't want to say anything," she said to Mag, not nicely, which meant she hadn't actually misinterpreted the things with her next words she wanted us to think she'd fake-misinterpreted. And she proved this when she said to me, "I thought it was rude. But I obviously don't have to tell you, what with your face like that, his temper is off the charts."

She . . .

Did not.

"Evie," Mag called.

She . . .

Really...

Did not.

Mag's hold on me got tighter.

"Evie," he repeated.

"Are you insinuating that Danny did this to me?" I asked quietly.

"Evie," Mag said again.

"In an effort to drive a wedge between us, are you *honestly* implying Danny would take his hands to me?" I kept at her.

"Baby," Mag muttered.

But Nikki just ticked her head to the side in one of those bitch moves that always happened prior to what was about to happen, happened.

And then that happened.

I tore from Mag's hold and went after her, nails bared.

There wasn't a lot of space between me and my target, and she was stunned immobile at my actions, so my chances at taking her down were significantly increased, but I forgot how fast Mag moved.

Thus, I didn't manage to get at her because Mag's arm hooked around my belly and he dragged me back three steps, those being *Mag's* steps, which were about five of mine.

Unable to instigate a smackdown catfight, I bit at her, "You should be ashamed."

"I'm feeling a lot right now, but shame isn't part of that," she retorted.

"This doesn't surprise me because, from the minute you pushed in here when Danny didn't want you to, to now, you've displayed nothing but spoiled, selfish tendencies. Then again, you dumping him because he wouldn't come to heel, I should have already known that."

"He's got issues," she hissed. "I was trying to help him with his issues."

"It work for you, helping him with those by breaking his heart?" I returned.

Her torso shot straight.

"Evie," Mag said in my ear. "Stand down, baby."

"So...what? You two have been together how long? Days? Weeks? And you've got all the answers?" she asked me.

"Nope." I shook my head. "I have none. Zero. Zip. Though I know one of them is not walking away."

Her head jerked like I'd slapped her.

I didn't care.

Because she wasn't kind of a bitch.

She *was* a bitch.

"And another," I carried on, "is not trying to force him to be someone he's not."

"Evie, baby, honey, *stand down*," Mag urged in my ear.

He'd delivered his double-barreled endearment, so although it was hard, I clamped my mouth shut.

"Nik—" he began, but she lifted a hand, shaking her head.

"Yeah. Yes. I get it, Mag. I got it the minute I heard her call you Danny."

And without another word, she turned to the door, opened it, and disappeared behind it.

We both stood, Mag's arm still around me, presumably staring at the door (it was presumably only on Mag's part because I couldn't see him, I was staring at the door) and we did this for a long time.

Then the realization dawned on me that for the first time in my life I'd gone on physical attack against another human being, which was mortifying.

It was also why I pulled from his arm, took several steps away, turning to face him, but staring at his feet while I tucked hair behind my ear and babbled.

"Well, that was an interesting afternoon's diversion. But I think now I'm willing to go to the grocery store because we *definitely* need more cinnamon marshmallow clusters after that."

And ribeyes and the makings for loaded baked potatoes, because if I could make this man think he wanted to marry me over hamburgers, I was totally broiling him a steak.

"Babe," he called.

I lifted my eyes to his.

"No pressure," he said softly. "After what I just said. It's just, you're, well…Evan…" He cleared his throat. "You're just the shit."

"You're more the shit," I told him.

He grinned and his discomfort started to melt away. "I didn't invent cinnamon marshmallow clusters."

"Well, I didn't forgive you in less than twenty-four hours for saying douchey things to me."

"I didn't charge your ex, going for blood."

"I didn't take a bullet then arrange a commando rescue."

His grin got bigger and he slightly lifted up his sling. "I'm seeing a variety of pluses for this wound. First, you keep climbing on top, and second, I can drag it out for years, squeezing it for all its worth."

"I like the top."

His expression changed and so did his voice when he shared, "Baby, when I'm fighting fit, you'll beg for the bottom."

I shivered.

Mag didn't miss it.

The hot look in his eyes could melt steel.

Even so, I shivered again, and my nipples got so hard, they ached.

"You really should rest that arm," I whispered.

"Later."

"Danny—"

"Evie, either get in my bed or I'm gonna carry you there. What's it gonna be?"

We stared at each other.

He got fed up with it first and took a step toward me.

So, I turned and dashed around the island.

Straight to his room.

CHAPTER SEVENTEEN
Special

MAG

Tuesday morning, Hawk sat at the head of the conference table in his offices.

Mag sat to Hawk's left, Jorge to his right, Aug next to Jorge, Mo next to Mag.

"So, we got word. Cisco does not have that gun," Hawk declared.

Mag's eyes moved to Jorge, seeing as Jorge was likely behind procuring this information considering he grew up on Mamá Nana's patch, Mamá had a soft spot for him and Mamá Nana knew everything about everybody because a large part of her operation was trading information.

"Though, it probably goes without saying, Cisco is actively looking for that gun," Hawk went on.

"Shit," Auggie muttered.

Mag just concentrated on controlling the boil in his gut because this meant there was a gun floating around out there that killed a cop.

And the man who killed that cop was Cisco, who wasn't that smart, case in point, the continuing existence of this gun, a gun registered to him that had, if tales being told were true, his prints on it. So he'd clawed his way to where he was because, after Benito Valenzuela was put out of commission, there was a void in the power structure of Denver crime and Cisco wasn't squeamish about how he went about filling it.

The longer that gun went unfound, the more chance he could get desperate.

This meant Evie was likely still in the line of fire—Cisco's fire—because that man would leave no stone unturned to cover his own ass.

They'd had a seriously fucked-up Saturday.

Their Sunday was marred only by Mag having to lay it out for Nikki.

And yesterday, Hawk and Smithie had been in touch and told them they were still not to pitch up for work.

This meant he and Evie spent half the day in bed and half the day on the couch with only a quick trip to the grocery store to buy steaks and stuff for loaded baked potatoes and for her to make more of her clusters breaking up these activities.

They'd watched *Anaconda*.

She'd laughed her way through it.

Then, when she learned he hadn't seen *Harry Potter*, she'd had a hilarious fit and made him watch the first two, before he begged her to let him stop.

She'd also gone down on him on his couch, and what she lacked in finesse, she *way* made up for in spirit, so he knew he could totally work with that and get off on it, and he knew this because he did.

Spectacularly.

And they'd fucked three times, twice with her on top, once with him powering into her on his knees, her in front of him on all fours on his bed, her sweet ass in his hands.

He'd taken a pill both nights and slept like the dead.

Now, he had niggling pain, and in truth, he knew he should take it easy and not fuck his Evie so much.

But he was finding it impossible to keep his hands off her.

Because the woman crafted a mean burger.

But she broiled a spectacular steak.

And now, he was learning they couldn't just get on with life.

This being her, back at work without protection (Boone was on her now as she did her Computer Raiders gig). Getting her apartment back in order. All so she could set the new course of her life that didn't only include the addition of him.

The good news about that was, this meant she had to continue to stay at his pad.

But that was all the good news to be had.

"Mag," Hawk called his attention.

He gave it to the man.

"Whatever this means, you should know, her father has been active," Hawk shared. "He's all over dropping it in any ear that will listen that his daughter has dick to do with this. He's sharing wide it's the brother's fuckup, and Evan needs to be left alone."

"Yeah, he's all over that after his daughter was kidnapped and the drugs he was hoping he'd get his hands on are gone," Mag returned.

Hawk did a shrug. "Yours to do with what you want. But you should know it so you can decide what to do with it."

Mag nodded, knowing it fucked with him, but he had to tell her that her dad was trying to look out for her.

He was doing it too late.

But she should know.

"You're on light duty," Hawk continued.

"Yeah," Mag muttered.

"And it's now clear we've thrown down for Evan," he went on. "Nightingale's nosing around. Rush has got some of his Chaos boys doin' rounds, asking a few questions. And none of that would be happening if Evan wasn't part of the equation. That's some firepower at her back that isn't gonna be missed. But that doesn't mean she shouldn't be covered. That said, I wanna see you further down the road to recovery before your duty changes. It's gonna sting, but you are not at one hundred percent, so you gotta take a backseat, look after Evan in ways only you can do, and I'm assigning Jorge and Mo as leads on this."

That simmer in his gut roiled.

Dr. Baldwin had told him he wanted at least two weeks, better three, with his arm in that sling, and after that, only light use, no exercise, for another week before he got into the nitty-gritty of restrengthening muscle and working his way back to normal range of motion.

He hoped like fuck this would be all over by then.

But in the meantime, it was going to mess with his head that he was unable to take an active role in dealing with this for Evie.

But Hawk was right, Mag knew it, and he could think with his dick a lot of the time, but not when it put the team at a disadvantage.

And in this case, Evie at one.

What she needed was for him to be there when she wasn't working so she knew she had someone who gave a shit.

What she didn't need was for him to go macho gung-ho in protection of his woman and maybe get hurt (worse) or fuck up and make things worse for her.

But considering he was macho gung-ho regularly, not being that for Evie was going to suck.

"Gotcha," Mag said just as Hawk's eyes went to the door.

That meant all the men's eyes went to the door in time to see Elvira opening it and swinging her torso in.

"Right, well, I got me a girl calling herself Sidney Gardiner in my office," Elvira started, and Mag's gaze instantly shifted to the glass wall, across the suite and through the glass to Elvira's office to see a woman standing there who had a heavy hand with facial contouring and such an artfully messy knot on the top of her head, he knew it probably took her an hour to do it. "And she's demanding some answers from her sister's new man."

"We're done here," Hawk declared.

Relieved, Mag got up, as did everyone, but only he moved quickly to the door.

Evie's sister's eyes were going everywhere, to him, beyond him to the other men, and back to him, but he had her full attention when he walked into Elvira's office.

"Sidney?" he asked, offering her a hand to shake.

She stared up at him and breathed, "Holy crap, I'm totally going nerd."

When she seemed unable to get over her shock her sister could bag a guy who looked like Mag, Mag's patience took a serious dive, and he stopped offering his hand in order to put it on his hip.

"What can I do for you?" he asked coldly.

She did the looking around thing, now not only to him, and beyond him, but also to his shoulder before she again gave him her eyes.

And then, even though they had the same hair color and similar features, it was only then, for the first time, that she looked just like Evie.

This being when she squinted her eyes at him.

"You can explain to me why my sister is in mortal peril and no one thought to tell me about it," she snapped.

Well.

Shit.

"I think your sister should—" he began.

She gave him The Hand, and when she did, he heard Elvira make a gulping noise behind him that sounded like she was both strangling and laughing, and Mag stopped talking.

"No. Nope." Sidney shook her head. "She's yours so you know Evie. You know she takes it all on and she doesn't share dick. So, you're the new guy, this once, I'll educate you. It's on *you* to clue me in when shit gets real for my sister. Even her waste-of-space ex tore himself away from his joystick in order to drop a text when Evan was up to her eyeballs in their bullshit. He did that even if he never got shot because Evan insists on enabling Mom's crap, Dad's crap and Mick's garbage."

Mag was so surprised this was what she was there to say, he had absolutely no clue how to reply.

Though he didn't have to, considering Sidney wasn't done.

"Now I know bloodshed has caused Evie to reevaluate things. Mom's in a snit. Rob's left her. Dad's in a panic and worried like fuck for Evan. And Mick's being all dramatic talking about Evie signing his death warrant and bitching that she told him to fuck off, which she should have done," she leaned toward Mag, "*years ago*. But, as you can see, in all this, the one name that doesn't come up is," she leaned back and jerked a thumb at herself, "*mine*."

"Mm-hmm, share your truth, sister," Elvira encouraged as she moved to take her seat, not only for comfort, but because it was a better audience position.

Sidney looked to her and gave a sharp, sisterhood nod.

"Sidney," he called, got her attention and carried on, "it's really not up to me—"

"*Wrong,*" she interrupted him.

Okay.

Now he was getting ticked.

"I don't even know you," he bit out.

"Did you know I exist?" she asked.

"Yeah," he answered.

"Did you know she hasn't involved me in this?" she pushed.

"Yeah," he grunted, seeing where this was going and nipping it in the bud. "But it was dangerous, she didn't want you involved, and that was her decision to make."

"How about this, hot guy," she started. "Considering it was dangerous and it not only involved my sister, but my fuckup of a brother, who fucking cares what she decides? I should know."

It sucked to admit she was correct.

He then said what he did not want to say because, even if it was right, it might mean headache for Evan. "You should be telling this to Evie."

"Well, I'm not, seeing as I'm telling it to you."

"Sidney—"

He didn't go on because she suddenly looked to her feet, the carefully arranged tendrils of hair that framed her face drifting, then she looked up and Elvira made another noise.

But Mag braced.

"My sister was kidnapped," she whispered.

"She's fine," Mag said softly.

"She was kidnapped because my brother is an asshole."

Mag had nothing to say to that.

"She doesn't tell me this shit not because she wants to protect me," she continued. "She doesn't tell me because I wasn't hired out by Dad to fix all of our neighbors' computers when I was eleven. She doesn't think a lot of me and the choices I make in my life and I'm okay with that. It's her opinion, she's entitled to it. Does it hurt? Yes. Can I allow that to change who I am and what I want to do with my life? No. I don't want her stripping and not because I look down on strippers. Because that's not Evie. But do I say anything? No. But when my sister's boyfriend gets shot and she gets kidnapped, it doesn't matter what choices I make in living my life, I *should know*."

"Give me your number."

She seemed visibly relieved.

Mag was not, visibly or otherwise, for a variety of reasons.

He got into one of them.

"How did you know who I am and where to find me?"

"Dominique, one of Smithie's girls, is a friend of mine."

Well, that explained that.

Mag pulled out his phone.

Sidney opened her massive designer bag and pulled out hers.

They exchanged numbers and then Mag shared a few things of his own.

"This dramatic, or otherwise, just so you know, this kinda thing is not gonna happen to Evie in the future. She's come to a few realizations about your family and acted on those."

"Yeah, Mom shouted through the phone at me for a whole half an hour about her part in those realizations and how she blames Evan for Rob leaving her."

Not a surprise.

Fucked up.

But not a surprise.

"What I'm gettin' at, Sidney, is Evie is coming to some realizations about your family so maybe coming here and throwing down with me shouldn't be the only thing you do in regard to looking after your sister and your relationship with her."

"Mm-hmm," Elvira hummed.

Sidney looked to her.

"She's kinda bullheaded," she told Elvira.

"I hear that. My sister's a nut and works my nerves regularly. My brother isn't much better. If they got their shit together, though, I'd still be all in to listen to them," Elvira replied.

Now it was Sidney humming, "Mm."

Mag didn't have much to do for work that day, being on light duty, which meant desk work, and that meant monitoring the screens to keep track of shit they had going on and running other shit on their systems the guys out in the field called in.

Even so, he was done with this visit with Evan's sister.

"We finished?" he asked.

Her attention returned to him and he saw right away she wasn't.

Fuck.

"Rob's a good guy and he's worried sick about Evie," she shared. "He also needs to look you over and," her eyes did a sweep of him, "I'm seeing you're the kind of guy who would understand where he's coming from with that. So, it'd be cool you didn't make him wait too long to do that."

"I'll consider it and talk to Evan," he muttered.

She nodded.

Then her gaze went to Elvira, to Mag, back to Elvira, she looked uncomfortable and Mag braced again even as he said, "Whatever it is, spit it out."

"Maybe we can have some privacy," she suggested.

"It's my office," Elvira pointed out.

"She's gonna nag my ass until I share it with her anyway, so you might as well just say it," Mag told Sidney.

"I don't nag," Elvira said to Mag.

He looked to her. "You nag."

She considered that a beat before she shrugged one shoulder and owned it. "Okay, I nag."

Mag returned to Sidney and raised his brows.

"Okay then, no offense, I mean, really, this is the case with about ninety percent of the population," she said fast.

"What's the case?" Mag asked.

She shared the case and she did it again fast.

"Evan is smarter than you. Like *way* smarter. Like there's gonna be times you'll feel like Forrest Gump kind of smart."

Mag opened his mouth to say he already knew that, but Sidney kept going.

"Her ex, he couldn't deal. He's a programmer. He was a TA in one of her classes. He thought his coder shit didn't stink. He didn't become one with his games because he descended into that like people do who get lost in it. He did it because he's a loser and he's weak and she made him feel more of both of those because she is who she is, and in the end, he didn't have the strength to cut her loose so he made it so she'd do it."

"I'm not him," Mag pointed out.

"It's hard on her, to, you know, *relate*," Sidney said, and Mag grew tense.

"I'm not findin' that the case," he said low.

"I mean," she threw out a hand, "yeah. She can be normal, and she can be real, but you know, she shouldn't have to be that all the time because she's not normal. She's special. And there's gonna be times you're gonna feel that, and if you don't get off on her being special, then *you* need to cut her loose because she should be with someone who does."

She's special.

Well...

Shit.

Mag was shocked as all hell, but he was finding there might be one member of Evan's family who he could put up with.

"Trust me, I'm into your sister," Mag stated.

Sidney looked him right in the eyes.

"She's gonna make more money than you."

Mag stood still.

"I see you got your shit tight with this operation," she said, tipping her head to the windows behind Mag. "But, I mean, if she wanted to, Evie could figure out how to put rockets in space. Like, every one of her teachers wanted to have a sit-down with Mom and Dad to share she needed to be in different classes, maybe even go to different schools, be more challenged to even come close to meeting her potential. She's gonna get her degree, I know it. And then everyone is gonna want her and they're gonna pay big to have her because she turned down like, a bazillion academic scholarships because, you guessed it, Mom's crap, Dad's crap and Mick's garbage."

She stopped talking and Mag did not start.

That was because he was fighting the need to tear Elvira's office apart.

She'd turned down scholarships?

"Mag," Elvira said carefully.

Mag took in a deep breath.

"Mag, hon, keep it together." Elvira was now talking soothingly.

"What's going on?" Sidney whispered.

"Now I gotta educate you, girl, seein' as you don't tell a protective alpha guy who's fixed on your sister to make her his that your parents and brother fucked up her life even *more* than he already knew they did without, you know, cushioning that info. Or maybe not sayin' that shit at all unless he's somewhere he can rip a punching bag off its chain and toss it out a window," Elvira replied.

"Oh," Sidney mumbled.

"Mag."

Mo was now there, probably due to Elvira giving him the signal.

"I got it locked down," he growled.

He felt Mo stay close.

Mag forced himself to focus on Sidney.

"I know she's special," he stated. "I don't know much about computers, and I don't wanna know. She doesn't know how to disassemble a gun, and she probably doesn't wanna know. It doesn't matter she could figure it out on her own. That doesn't signify. She's gonna have her strengths, I'm gonna have mine. That's life. That's a relationship. I couldn't give a shit how much money she's gonna make just as long as she's happy in how she makes it. What's gonna happen is I'm gonna teach her how to shotgun a beer and she's eventually gonna make me watch all the *Harry*

Potter movies. That's not gonna blow us up, it's what's gonna keep us strong. Because that's how I'm gonna make it happen."

And again, Sidney was reminding him of Evie because she had big eyes and was muttering, "All righty then."

"Now are we finished?" he asked.

"Sure," she said.

"Talk to your sister," he ordered.

"Will do," she replied. She then gave an airy wave and said, "Laters," before she started heading out.

"Later, girl," Elvira called.

Mag got another look from Evan's sister, a happy one, before she walked by him.

He then felt Mo get close.

"What happened?" Mo asked.

Mag looked to Mo.

"Evan was offered academic scholarships. And she's stripping."

Mo's lips tightened.

"Yeah," Mag grunted.

"Keep on," Mo grunted back.

"I got no choice, worse, neither does she."

"Just to say, my desktop at home is givin' me fits," Elvira put in.

Mag cut his gaze to hers. "Call Computer Raiders and request Evie."

She was smiling broadly when she replied, "Will do."

"You good?" Mo asked Mag.

But it was Elvira who spoke.

"I'm inviting that sister of Evan's out for a cosmo," she declared.

Mo looked over his shoulder at Elvira then back to Mag.

"You're good," he said.

Then he strode out of the office.

"Mag," Elvira called.

"What?" Mag answered, his attention still on his friend's departing back.

"Boy, look at me."

He looked at her.

"It isn't right, and it isn't good, how it came about, but since it did, you got an opportunity to do something normally you would not. That is, help your girl to be all she's meant to be. And Mag, as much as it sucks she got delayed in her path to that, and how, if you give her that, you'll always be the one who gave it to her. That's a beautiful thing. And if she's as smart as everyone says she is, she's not gonna miss it."

Hawk could go guru because he was good at it.

With work shit.

Elvira could do it because, as she'd just demonstrated, she was good at it too.

With life shit.

"Thanks, Vira," he muttered.

She gave him a scrunched-nose smile.

And with nothing for it, Mag got back to work.

* * *

Evie was sitting next to him in his truck, giggling.

He was surprised about this because, not five minutes ago, both of them were standing outside his truck, bickering.

She did not like that he was driving with his arm in a sling.

He did not allow anyone to drive his truck but him and there was no way in hell his ass was going to be in a Prius unless he was unconscious or so weak from loss of blood, he didn't have it in him to fight it.

When he'd shared these things, the last bit got her ass in his truck.

And now she was giggling.

"What's funny?" he asked.

"You came home early to make Gert chocolate chip cookies," she answered, still laughing.

"I told you I was gonna win her over," he reminded her.

"Bribing her with cookies is the way to go," she replied. "Especially your cookies. I didn't decimate them like you did the clusters, but I nabbed one and you're right. You kick chocolate chip ass."

He was glad she thought that, because, "Babe, there's a dozen left at home, all for you."

That got him nothing.

He glanced her way and saw he was wrong.

It hadn't gotten him nothing.

She looked like she didn't know whether to smile big or bust out crying.

He decided to help her make that decision.

"What's my cookie bribe for you gonna get me?" he asked.

When he glanced again, he saw she was now grinning.

Mission accomplished.

"You're oversexed," she teased.

"Me bein' oversexed means you're oversexed so is that a complaint?"

"No," she said quickly.

That was when he busted out laughing.

She curled her hand around his thigh in the middle of it, and when he shot her another glance, he saw her grinning at him.

Shit, fuck.

He had that from her, and he had to do what he had to do, and for her, he had to get it out of the way.

So, he set about doing that.

"Right, one piece of bad news and two pieces of interesting news."

"Oh boy," she mumbled.

"Bad news fast, Cisco was not the one who nabbed that bag out of your car. So, he's still...whatever he is."

"What is he?" she asked, sounding curious.

"A bad guy."

She didn't ask any further questions about Cisco.

Yeah, his girl was smart.

"The interesting news is, first, your dad is doin' what he can to make sure the people in that sphere know you got nothin' to do with this."

She had no reply to that, but her hand still on his leg twitched.

"The second bit of interesting news is your sister came to my office today and—"

Her nails dug in through his jeans, which was one reason he stopped talking.

The other one was her shouting, "What?"

Her hand disappeared and he heard her digging in her purse, he knew for her phone, so he talked fast.

"It was not a bad visit, Evan. Listen to me, I think—"

She cut him off to say, "Hang on, honey, it's ringing."

Mag sighed.

"Yes, it's your sister," she snapped into the phone. "Yes." Pause, "Yes, and I am not okay with that." Longer pause and then, "No, he told me you..." Pause. "What? I don't care if you approve." No words, then, "Sidney, you can't just walk into Danny' place of business and—"

There was a very long pause before she spoke again.

"It was for your own good."

More silence.

Then, exasperated, "I was trying to protect you!"

Mag made a turn through nothing coming verbally from Evie and then she spoke again.

"Don't be sweet when I'm mad at you. If you have something to say, say it to me. Don't interrupt Danny's work." Pause and, "I call him Danny. He's Mag to everyone else." Silence and then, "We can't. Some other time. We're having dinner with Gert."

Her next was quieter.

"Yes, Gert. And yes, that means what you think it means."

Mag started smiling.

"I think you knew that before you went to his office and interrupted his day," she went on. "And no, I can't chat about this now because we're on our way there." Pause, then, "No, I'm not talking and driving, and yes, I pay my insurance, so I know my driving record. Danny's driving." A heavy breath and then, "Tell me about it. But he refuses to ride in my Prius, and he won't let me drive his truck." Her voice was pitched higher when she said, "Only you would approve even *more* of that ridiculousness. Okay, I gotta go. 'Bye and love you."

Mag knew on the other end of Evie's line that Sidney was saying she loved her sister back before he saw out of the corner of his eye Evie's phone hand going down.

"So, your sister approves?" he joked.

"Shut up," she muttered.

He got serious and advised, "You should spend time with her, have a long talk. I think she has things to say you'd wanna hear."

"She's part lunatic." Evie was continuing with the mutters.

"Baby, met her once and she did not hesitate to impress on me how deep her love is for you and how you worry her. I got no opinion on how she lives her life because it's not my life and she's not my sister. But from the little I know of her, you might be giving her a bad rap."

He knew she was talking to her side window when she replied, "She wants to escape her way and I want to escape mine. It's just that her way opens her up to being hurt by outside forces, whereas my way opened me up to the same, but by inside ones."

Yeah, his girl was smart.

He didn't have a free hand to touch her like he wanted to so he just said as gentle as he could, "Yeah."

"And since you heard it," she started, "I get in a lot of bust-ups in my car. Nothing serious. I blame it on multi-tasking."

Excellent.

Now he had an excuse always to be the one to drive when he was already always going to be the one to drive, just before, he'd have to squabble with her before he did it.

"Then it's good I'm driving. I'm busted up enough," he said.

"Shut up, Danny," she repeated, though with a smile in her voice.

He gave her that for a beat.

But then he had to give her something else.

"I had two good doses of your family today, Evie, and you made some big decisions on a day some huge shit went down. You seem cool. You seem like you're good to just keep on keepin' on. And that's your MO. But in the now, you need to know that isn't where you're at anymore.

You don't gotta forge ahead because you have no choice. You got someone at your back. You got someone you can unload shit on. And you got someone who can help you process it. That's me, and from what I saw today, it's also your sister."

Her hand was clenching and unclenching his thigh as he spoke.

And she did the sweetest thing she could do when he finished.

She didn't lavish the gratitude or try to tough it out and make him believe she was okay.

She said, "You know, I think about it a lot, how we grew up. And I wonder what was worse. To be a nonentity, treated like she almost wasn't even there, like Sidney. Or to be used, like me."

"Not sure there's a worse in that, baby. They're both equally bad," he murmured.

He knew she'd turned to face him when she asked, "Why don't you like your sister's fiancé?"

"Because she ceases to exist when the NFL is in season," he told her. "I get digging football. I dig football. But I don't lose sight of everything but the television schedule and my fantasy football league for six months out of the year. He refuses to do anything Monday or Thursday nights and all day Sunday. I get it. Enjoy what you like. But with him, there are no exceptions. So, when a good friend of hers got married on a Thursday 'cause folks are doin' that kind of thing 'cause it's cheaper, she had to go alone. And she was in the fucking wedding party."

"Oh man," she muttered. "That's bad."

She was right.

It was.

And that was only one example.

"Obviously my opinion, but my woman's wearing a pretty dress and doin' something that's important, my ass is not in front of a TV. When the US beat Russia in hockey in 1980, that's a game it'd suck to miss. But if you did, it wouldn't be the end of the world. Thursday night football? No."

"Are you in a fantasy football league?" she asked.

"Yeah," he answered.

"Danny?" she called.

"Yeah?" he repeated.

"I've always wanted to play Dungeons and Dragons, the top on my bucket list is going to a Comic Con and by far the best TV show I ever saw was *Stranger Things*."

"Dungeons and Dragons doesn't seem like my gig, babe, but I'd try it if you wanted me to. Though if I don't like it, I'll share and bow out. I'll take you to a Comic Con, got no problem with that. And *Stranger Things* is the shit."

"I'm not a big football fan," she admitted.

"I don't care, though I am, but it isn't my life."

She hesitated a beat, and her voice was quiet when she asked, "You'd try Dungeons and Dragons?"

"I'm warning you, it's probably not gonna be my thing. But yeah, I'll try it."

She didn't say anything for a long time.

Then she said softly, "I think it's going to be hard to get used to it. I'm not sure it was, like, a normal habit, just something I did. I think it was more like an addiction, something I needed. Helping them. Being that person they turned to. I got some kind of fix out of it, and in the beginning, it was a good high. Then, the more I gave, the more they took, and the high didn't feel so good anymore. I want to say it's already a relief, not having them in my life. But as dysfunctional as it is, instead, I already miss them."

"They're your family, baby," he whispered.

"I need to stop being so judgey about Sid," she muttered.

"Yeah," he agreed.

They both fell silent and it also lasted a long time before she called, "Danny?"

"Right here, babe."

"All that said, I think my new addiction is going to be pretty easy to get used to."

He couldn't let that go without touching her, so he moved a knee to the steering wheel to keep his truck steady while he squeezed her hand on his leg.

He only did it briefly, but she was Evie, so she gave him shit about it.

"You steer with your knee?"

"It was just for a sec."

"You need to get over your aversion to my Prius."

"I'll work on it," he lied.

"You're not gonna work very hard, are you?"

"Nope," he told the truth.

She giggled.

And there they were.

Mag let out a breath.

And drove the rest of the way to Evie's friend's house.

*　　*　　*

The woman was literally a little old woman.

Gray curly hair, face full of wrinkles and half his height.

Not even.

Gert stared up at him the minute she opened the door and then she declared, "Oh no. You are not gonna do."

Mag pressed his lips together so he didn't burst out laughing.

She looked to Evie and stated, "Evan, my girl, the pretty ones are always headache, heartache or both. I thought you knew that."

"Gert, Danny made you chocolate chip cookies," Evie told her, then held out the container with the cookies.

Gert cast it a suspicious glance. "From scratch?"

"Yes," Evie answered.

"Not any of that tub of Toll House already-made stuff?" she pressed.

"None of that," Evie promised. "They're really good. Fluffy and soft. He makes them with Crisco."

Oh shit.

The woman, still barring the door, looked up at him with disgust.

"*Crisco?*" she demanded.

"That's how my mom makes 'em," he said.

"Hmm," she hummed, seeing as he'd pulled the mom card and no woman could say jack about what a mom taught her kid.

"Can we come in?" Evie asked.

Gert said nothing to that, but she shifted out of the door and opened it further.

Mag let Evie go before him (and he did not fail to note that Gert took the cookies from her as she passed) and then he was treated to Gert actually doing the fore- and middle fingers to her eyes then to him and back and repeat as he walked into her house.

He was again fighting laughter.

Tonight was going to be fun.

Entering the house put them right in a small living room that was filled with men, and Lottie.

And Boone wasted no time sidling up to him and muttering under his breath, "Beware, brother. She hates, like...*all* of us. All but Mo. And Lots. It's good you're here because no one's talking but Lottie and Gert, and that's because we're all terrified of the old broad."

Gert went around them (slowly), headed straight to an armchair and did this saying, "I'm too old to be serving anymore. You want a drink, the kitchen's through there."

She jerked her head to a doorway, set her container of cookies down on a table close to her chair, and then looked at Lottie.

"So you're the mastermind behind this?" she asked, tossing a hand at Mag and Evie.

"Yup," Lottie answered casually.

Gert was about to say more, but her gaze fell on Evie in the brightly lit room, her face lost some color and her eyes narrowed.

"What on earth? What happened to your eye*zzzz*. Plural!"

"I was kidnapped," Evie shared openly. "That's why Danny's arm is in a sling. The guy had to shoot him to get to me. But he didn't have me for long before Danny and the boys saved me." She threw a hand out to the guys. "And Gert, they used smoke grenades. It was pretty rad."

Gert sat there, the ornery woman façade shocked clean out of her, and she did it staring at Evan.

"It's okay, I'm safe," Evie assured, leading Mag to an open armchair and sitting him in it. She sat on the arm at his side, and she did all of this talking. "They have me under constant guard."

The shock left Gert, and anger replaced it.

"Your brother," Gert bit out.

Evie was about to speak but Mag got there first.

"Her brother," he confirmed.

"That boy's a bad seed," she snapped at Mag.

"That wasn't lost on me," Mag told her.

"I keep tellin' her, he's a waste of effort." Gert was still talking to Mag.

"Think with his latest, he's made that clear to Evie."

"The dad's not much better," Gert decreed.

"I've learned that too," Mag replied.

"And the mom's a piece of work," Gert kept on.

"She's my least favorite," Mag shared.

Gert's eyebrows stretched way up when she heard that, and she tried to fight it, but approval started seeping into her expression, because no one knew better than a mother how uncool it was to be a bad mother.

Then she studied him.

Her voice was softer when she asked, "You got shot protecting Evan?"

Totally, taking that bullet had a number of pluses.

"Not my finest hour seein' as he got to her."

"If there's an A for effort, son, gettin' shot for your girl is it."

Mag said nothing.

"I fell in love with a boy with a mess a' hair who was lazy with a razor," she imparted. "Married him. He spent forty-five years drivin' me up the wall. He's been dead the last ten and I miss him every day."

After delivering what Mag guessed was her official seal, she looked to Lottie.

"Where's the girls for the rest of these buggers?" she asked. "I wanna look 'em over."

It seemed Lottie and Gert *had* been talking, with Lottie doing a lot of sharing.

"They're working tonight, Gert," Lottie told her.

"Well, we best arrange something," Gert returned. "Says a lot about a man, his buddy gets shot and the next thing, he's off throwin' smoke bombs to rescue his friend's girl. Boys like that, these girls gotta be right."

"I did take that into account when I made my matches," Lottie noted.

Gert nodded but she did it in a way she wasn't actually agreeing.

"I can tell you got a head on your shoulders, gal, but you don't got enough life under your belt. This means I'll be in that bookstore drinkin' one of your stepdad's coffees. When I'm there, those girls better be in there so I can check 'em out."

"We'll arrange that," Lottie agreed.

Evie stood and announced, "I'm getting everyone drinks. And Gert, what's going on with dinner? As you can see, your living room is filled with strapping men and they need to get fed."

Gert looked to Mag. "Are you actually strapping?"

Mag grinned at her. "I thought I probably shouldn't meet my girl's best friend while packing."

He thought it was a decent joke, but Gert looked horrified and turned her attention to Evie.

"Am I your best friend?" she asked.

"It's okay if I'm not yours," Evie said as answer.

But this only served to make Gert look even more horrified.

She turned this on Mag. "See to that, son. I can tell with all this company you're fillin' her life up in one way, but a girl needs her girls and those girls should be her own age."

"There's no law that says you have to be my age to be my best friend, Gert," Evie stated.

"Yes, there is," Gert returned.

Mag aimed his smile at his lap.

"What am I, chopped liver?" Lottie asked.

Mag looked up.

But Lottie's comment meant Gert turned her attention to Lottie. "You're an excellent start but a girl's gotta have a *bunch* of girls. Ones who like shoppin' and others that like martinis and all that other stuff. I seen it on *Sex and the City*." She lifted up her hand and counted them down on her fingers. "You gotta have the raunchy one and the prissy one and the professional one and the, I don't know what that curly-haired one was, maybe the messed-up one 'cause, Lord, that girl could do some stupid things."

"I don't like shopping *or* martinis," Evie pointed out.

"Well, girls who like to do whatever you like to do then," Gert retorted.

"I like going to Olive Garden with you," Evie shot back.

"Evan, you know what I mean," Gert replied.

"No, I don't," Evie said smartly. "I can have whatever best friend I want." She turned to Lottie. "No offense to you. You're awesome and I'm so glad you're my friend. And stuff happens for a reason. It just does. And all this bad stuff brought me closer to you and Ryn and Hattie and Pepper. And we can go get martinis whenever you want. But I'll probably drink something else."

"I don't like martinis either," Lottie shared.

"Well then, good," Evie muttered.

"You were gettin' everyone drinks?" Gert prompted.

"Right, what have you got?" Evie asked.

"Beer. Water. Crystal Light. And prune juice."

A chorus of five beers, Mag included, sounded and Lottie ordered a water.

Evie moved in the direction of the kitchen.

Mag started to get up to help her, but he stopped when Gert called, "Danny?"

He didn't correct her on the name. He just gave her his attention.

When he did, she looked deep into his eyes.

"You got the best girl in the world there," she said.

"I know," he replied.

She gave him a long, measuring look.

And then she said, "I want some Crystal Light."

CHAPTER EIGHTEEN
Definitely a Consideration

EVIE

Sunday night (or more aptly, Monday morning), I skedaddled offstage, grabbed my robe, shrugged it on, and when I hit the hall, I paused and gave Boone, who was standing at the end of it, a chin lift.

He returned it, and I rushed into the dressing room feeling bad.

This was because Boone was my bodyguard that night and I wanted to be fast so he could get home, but I also wanted to talk to Ryn so she'd stop avoiding Boone and go out on a date with him.

I was going to work on all the girls, but since I'd had my chat with Auggie, and it was clear Pepper was not (yet) ready to go there, and Hattie seemed a tough row to hoe, I'd decided on Ryn.

I hit the room and saw the girls all there.

That was, all of them except Ryn.

"Where's Ryn?" I asked.

"Don't even," Pepper answered tetchily.

Hattie looked at me and mouthed "Bad."

"Bad?" I mouthed back.

She gave me big eyes.

"What's going on?" I asked.

"She and Boone had a thing," Pepper told me. "So, even before we got the signal, she left the stage, hustled in here, and I can only assume she escaped, seeing as she wasn't here when I got in here."

I moved deeper into the room. "She and Boone had a thing?"

"Yeah, after a lap dance," Pepper replied.

Oh boy.

I couldn't even let Mag watch me strip. Just the idea of him seeing me do a lap dance made me think I'd pass out.

Not that I did lap dances. I'd tried it once, and it wasn't any good for me *or* for the creepy dude who bought it.

Good money.

But serious *euw*.

"I tried to talk to her, but she told me to butt out," Pepper continued. "And she wasn't super cool about it either."

When I turned my gaze to Hattie, she was giving me a look and she repeated her mouthed "Bad."

Oh boy!

"Speaking of," Pepper went on, "are you gonna quit now that you have Mag?"

"We haven't been seeing each other for even two weeks," I told her, heading to my makeup station, and more importantly, my towel.

"You're living together," Pepper noted.

"Out of necessity," I reminded her, shrugging off my robe so I could begin to towel off the oil.

"Not sure I'd move on, I bagged me that one," Pepper muttered.

"You'd have one of your own, if you'd just agree to go on a date with him," I pointed out.

Pepper decided she was finished talking.

I gave Hattie a look.

Hattie gave me a shrug.

I didn't push it further, partly because I wanted to get out there so Boone could get me home, and thus he could get home. Partly because I was fired up to have a chat with Ryn, not Pepper. This meant I wasn't prepared to chat with Pepper and chats like this needed preparation. And partly because I was dying to know what went down with Boone and Ryn, and I could only find that out while interrogating him in his car.

So, I dashed through toweling down, swiping off as much makeup as I could with a few disposable cleansing towels (which I'd ascertained were biodegradable), pulling a brush through my hair, shoving my tips in my bag and throwing on clothes.

I said my farewells, met Boone in the hall, he escorted me out to his black Charger, and we were away home.

I decided not to take the direct approach, but that wasn't the only reason I started with "Thanks for playing bodyguard tonight."

"Not a problem," he grunted, like it was a problem.

Though I sensed the problem was not guarding me.

It was having a *thing* with Ryn.

Even so, I looked to him and said, "It's been days since I've been kidnapped. Not to mention, Danny and me went to my apartment yesterday to check it out. It's still a mess, but I have a window and the mess was the same mess, not a new one. So hopefully I'm out of the woods and you boys will be off Evie duty soon."

He just grunted again, but this time it formed no words.

"You okay?" I asked.

"Sure," he lied.

Hmm.

Time to take the direct approach.

"So, um…Pepper said you and Ryn had a thing. Is everything all right with that?"

He said nothing.

"Not my business," I muttered, turning to look out the windshield.

After a long while, he announced, "We all got it, you know."

I looked to him again. "Got what?"

"Issues," he stated. "After shit we've seen, shit we've done."

"Right," I said softly.

"We share, talk it out."

I was glad they did that.

Boone kept going.

"Mag's told us you've seen him lose it."

Hmm.

"It is what it is, Boone," I replied. "I can't say how right now, but as his friend, I want to assure you, I like him a lot, so I'm determined we'll find our way."

"Me, it's sex."

I blinked at his profile after he shared this in a way he sounded like he didn't want to, he had to, and I whispered, "Sorry?"

"Sex. For me. Outside talking to the guys, that's how I work it out."

"Okay," I said softly. Then quickly, I went on, "You don't have to—"

"And control."

I pressed my lips together.

"You get what I'm sayin' to you, Evie?"

"I don't know," I replied carefully.

"You don't need this shit," he muttered.

That was when I really looked at him in the dashboard lights.

And what I saw was that he was messed up.

"I can take whatever shit you wanna give me, Boone," I told him quietly.

"Yeah, that's you. You lived your whole life taking shit. You don't need mine."

"Well, the shit I took was from people who didn't care about me. You just gave your Sunday night to keep me safe. You tackled the bad guy for me through smoke grenades billowing. In this kind of thing, it isn't tit for tat. But just to say, you've given yours, but that isn't the only reason I'm down to give mine."

He didn't say anything.

"But if you don't want to share, Boone, I won't be hurt. Promise."

"I had it in me, you know, before shit went down when I was in the service. It went into overdrive after."

"It?"

He glanced at me.

He looked back to the road.

Another glance at me.

Then back to the road and, "I'm a Dom."

"A Dom?" I asked.

"A Dominant. A Dom. In sex."

Okay, so we weren't sharing.

We were *sharing*.

"Boone, I—"

"She's a sub."

"Ryn?" I asked in surprise.

"Yeah," he said.

That didn't track.

Outside Lottie (and Mag), Ryn was one of the most dominant personalities I knew.

Then again, I didn't know how these things worked, maybe she was so in charge all the time, she had to find ways to let go.

"You really don't have to share this with me if you don't want to," I told him quietly.

"Am I making you uncomfortable?"

"No, I mean, you just watched me strip for eight hours."

"Yeah." He was back to grunting.

Hmm.

I had a feeling the guys weren't much happier than Mag would be, watching me strip.

Then again, whenever I caught them out in the crowd, they weren't looking at me but scanning the area.

And I was learning, such was the brotherhood, they'd do anything for Mag.

And possibly, for me.

"But like I said, I'm happy to listen if you want to talk," I told him.

"It's not that I wanna, it's that I gotta. Shit festers. I learned, you get it out."

"Well, I'm here to lay it on, Boone."

Another grunt, this time forming the word "Thanks."

Light dawned and I said, "The lap dance."

He gave a jerky nod. "I'm into her. Made that clear. She's putting me off. And that's okay. Her prerogative. Not how my mind works, though."

Oh boy.

"So you kinda already in your head think Ryn's yours, and she's giving lap dances."

Another grunt with his "Yeah."

This was a problem because, like all of us, Ryn worked at Smithie's because she had to.

"It's not the stripping," Boone declared, like he could read my thoughts. "I'm down with look, don't touch. And she's gotta make a living. I'm not that kind of Dom where I inject myself into shit like that. It's the lap dances. That's not in her control, or mine. And that's not good. It fucks with me."

"Well, Boone—"

"You don't give lap dances," he noted.

"Only the girls who are okay to do that, do that," I shared.

"Yeah, so she could not do that."

I couldn't argue that, though I had to admit, even if I sucked at it and it was major *euw*, in times when I was hurting financially, I'd considered it. It mega upped your tips.

Which was why Ryn did it.

She needed the money.

"I hate to remind you of this, honey, but you two haven't even been on a date," I said.

"I know that logically, Evie. But my mind sometimes doesn't work logically. The shit happening with you, I know Lottie wants her for me, and she wanted you for Mag and you two are workin' out great. But more, I'm into her and I know Ryn is attracted to me. And her not wearin' barely anything, straddling some stranger's lap, it's messing with my head."

Another glance my way while I processed a happy quiver at his saying "you two are workin' out great," before he turned back to the road and kept speaking.

"The thing is, I'm not that kind of Dom where play gets into life. But I'm that kinda guy."

"Protective," I whispered.

"Yeah," he whispered back.

"Do you want me to talk to her?" I offered.

"I'm not sure that would help." I watched him smile a smile that I wished Ryn could see because I was going home to all that was Mag, and still, it made me shiver. "She's definitely a brat."

"A brat?"

He glanced at me again before he said to the windshield, "You don't know the life, do you?"

"No."

"Then, if you're interested, I'll let Ryn tell you."

"Okeydoke," I mumbled.

"I'm gonna let other guys take your duty at Smithie's, babe," he shared. "Unless Ryn's not on. Better for her and for me."

"Okay, Boone."

We fell into silence and I didn't know what Boone was thinking, but what I was thinking was that I'd never really had good girlfriends.

I still knew the drill.

If it wasn't yours to share, you didn't share it.

Especially with a guy.

Most especially with a guy your girlfriend was attracted to.

But arguably, Boone was more my friend than Ryn was. It was true; I hadn't known him longer.

That said, he'd tackled a guy through a billowing smoke bomb for me.

Quandary.

Boone seemed to know I was turning this over in my head because he said, "I don't really find it hard to find a partner, Evie. Do I want more? Yeah. But by process of elimination, that's bound to happen. If Ryn doesn't want to

go there, I need to get into that headspace and find someone who does. And I will."

Oh no.

He was going to give up on Ryn.

"She needs the money," I blurted.

"Sorry?" he asked.

"The lap dances. None of the girls *really* want to do
them. But Smithie makes his money on the door and at the
bar. He doesn't take a cut of tips. A lap dance lasts maybe
ten, fifteen minutes and it's fifty bucks, plus a lot of guys
tip on top of that. So, she does it for the money."

The vibe in the car was no longer heavy with his mood.

It was stifling with his mood.

"Is she in trouble?"

Sadly, I had to say, "I don't really know. I could find out,
but I don't think it's girlfriend code for me to pump her for
information to give to you."

"You don't have to pump her for information. I'll find
out."

Hmm!

We drove the rest of the way home, the silence broken
occasionally with idle chitchat.

Boone escorted me up to Mag's place and let me in.

Mag was on the couch, watching TV, waiting up for me,
even though it was after three in the morning. This, what
he'd been doing the first time I came home from Smithie's,
as well as Friday, the first night I was back to dancing.

I *so totally* was falling for this guy.

After cursory greetings, Boone gave me a hug and said
to Mag, "I'm out."

"Thanks, brother," he called.

I heard Boone lock the door behind him as I dropped
my bag on the island and wandered to Mag.

He didn't have his sling on, and I made it clear with my eyes how I felt about that.

Mag just grinned at me and reached when I got close enough for him to do it.

I was on my back on the couch, with him on top of me, his bad arm resting with his hand flat against my chest, and I noted from close up his lashes were just as amazing lit only by a television set.

"Why aren't you wearing your sling?" I asked.

"It's annoying," he answered.

"It's my understanding you have another week with it on."

"Yeah, but for now it's off."

All right.

I'd said my piece.

So I let that go.

"Good night?" Mag asked.

"It's over and I have a wad of cash in my bag, so it is now."

He smiled down at me.

"Ryn and Boone had a thing tonight," I shared.

"A thing?"

"A thing after she gave a lap dance."

His chin lifted slightly with understanding, and his expression turned thoughtful before he muttered, "Yeah. Not surprised. He's into her and he's a certain kind of guy. One who wouldn't be down with some of that even if she's not yet his. I don't think he should be on you at Smithie's anymore. I should have known it was bound to fuck with his head."

I wondered what he meant by "a certain kind of guy."

Did he know Boone was a Dom?

Did the boys share that much?

I didn't ask, because if Boone didn't share, it wasn't my place to do it.

Instead, I said softly, "You guys know each other really well."

His hand at my chest moved up so he could stroke my throat as he replied, "Honest to Christ, if I hadn't found them, I don't know where I'd be."

"Then I'm glad you found them," I replied.

"Yeah," he agreed.

"And Boone and I talked it out and he's of the same mind. If Ryn's onstage, he's not on Smithie's duty."

"Hopefully soon, this'll be all over, so it won't matter."

That was the hope.

Though, since not a thing was happening, dangerous or otherwise, it seemed this was going to drag on forever.

"Shower then bed?" he asked.

I smiled at him and nodded.

He started to push away as I was making my own preparations to get up with him, and in doing so, turned my head and saw his laptop open on the coffee table.

There were Zillow listings on it.

Weird.

"Moving?" I joked after he was on his feet and he'd grabbed my hand to pull me to mine.

"I can rent this pad easy, make a whack," he told me. "And I got some money saved up. I'm not a stock portfolio type of guy. So . . ." He trailed off.

So . . .

Although I had utterly no experience with this, he meant, if you have money—and apparently, he had some money—invest in real estate.

But I looked down again at the laptop and saw he wasn't

looking for a property that might offer future income as a rental, like another condo or a townhouse.

He was looking at homes.

It was then, something I didn't understand at the time, and forgot about it until then, came to mind.

Something that Nikki had said about Mag's place being temporary and not even his.

Thus, even though he'd begun to move us toward his room, I tugged on his hand to stop him.

He looked at me.

"Are you, you know, restless?" I asked.

His mouth cocked up at one side.

"Is that code for 'do I want an orgasm?'" he returned, but before I could answer, he continued, "And just to say, the answer to that will never be no."

I swayed closer to him and his head was coming down in that way I loved.

Still...

"What I mean is, are you wanting to move on from this place?" I clarified.

His head stopped its downward descent and he shook it. "Just moving up."

"Not moving on?"

Now his whole head cocked. "What are you really asking, baby?"

"It's just that Nikki said this place was temporary and it sounded like that was a thing with you. It was also around the time when she thought she might be able to get back in with you."

Mag shifted how he was standing in order to position himself fully in front of me, and as he already had one of my hands in his, he took up the other, so he was holding both.

"Okay, yeah, after I got out of the military, I moved around a lot," he shared. "Crashing on couches. Having a roommate, getting fed up with that roommate, finding somewhere else to be. I met Nikki when I was doin' that and we dated, but we didn't get serious because, I see it, looking back, I was restless. It wasn't good. I also see now that, without the Marines, I'd lost my purpose. I didn't know who I was. I needed some grounding. That was when I applied for the job with Hawk, got it, found the guys." He shrugged and carried on, "And I had my place again. I learned who I was and what I needed to be doing. And I got a job doing it."

"The commando calling."

I said it like it was a tease, and he grinned, but we both knew it was no joke.

"Yeah, I gotta be challenged in that way. I gotta belong to a team. I gotta feel like I'm doin' something with a purpose. A lot of vets have this same issue. When they're serving, their job has meaning. They got into it because of that. And then they're out and it's hard to find that again."

"So, your job has more meaning than just the fact you know what you're doing, you're good at it and it provides a challenge?"

His hands gave mine a squeeze. "Yeah, honey. I can't say a lot more, but Hawk doesn't do business with assholes." He started to study me intently before he said carefully, "Though that doesn't mean we don't run into our fair share of them. They're just not paying Hawk's invoices."

I nodded when he quit talking, deciding to ignore the scary part of what he just said, and when I didn't speak, he started again.

"That was when things settled with Nikki. After I got onboard with Hawk's team. That said, looking back, we never *settled*." He squeezed my hands again. "Now, with it being over, seeing it for how it was between her and me, what she wanted from an us, which was not for me to be a part of that, but the person she wanted me to be, I didn't fit. I love my job. I love my brothers. I respect the fuck outta Hawk. But at home, none of that mattered. So yeah, with her, that manifested itself in a lot of temporary. Finding someplace to be, and it was never right. Then we moved in together, and I gotta admit, we'd break leases, move and we'd do it a lot. And then where we moved wouldn't be right. So, repeat. But this," he tipped his chin to the laptop on his coffee table, "isn't that."

"Okay then, what is it?"

"Bungalows and a couple Denver squares that, if we go the distance, you can boho the fuck out of and they got big garages so I can have some space for my man cave to get away from the macramé."

I blinked up at him.

"You want kids?" he asked.

I bobbed my head mutely.

"Two? Three?" he went on.

I shook my head.

His brows went up. "Four?"

"No," I said softly. "I don't know. Two. Maybe three, because, if the first two are the same gender, I'd want to try it again so I could have both."

He smiled down at me and shifted closer, holding tight to my hands.

"Mo's old room would be crowded for all that," he whispered.

"Yeah," I pushed out.

"Babe, relax," he said on another hand squeeze. "This isn't pressure. And this isn't restlessness. This is me being a thirty-four-year-old guy who's got a wad of cash in the bank who lives in a condo, shotgunning beers, and he's beginning to wonder what fertilizers will make the greenest lawn. It's growing up, honey, bein' smart with my money. And I just happened to meet this girl I like a fuckuva lot, so why not?"

Oh man.

He was on the road to leave behind the frat boy and become a full-blown Hawk.

I felt a highly pleasant internal quiver at that thought and choked out, "Yeah. Why not?"

"And just so you know, that's not gonna be the forever home. I'll always be working to give more to my woman, more to my kids, until the kids are off and it's time to downsize." He got even closer. "What I'm sayin' is, don't let Nikki put shit into your head that that's an issue. It wasn't right with her and I didn't read it, but my behavior stated it clear. We settled but we never settled in and definitely didn't settle down because, if I did that with her, it would be *settling*, and that wasn't what I wanted."

"I don't want that for you either, Danny."

"You know anything about fertilizers?" he asked.

"No clue," I answered, and offered, "I could do some research for you, though."

"That'd take the fun out of it," he muttered.

"It's a lot of change for you in a short period of time, a long-term relationship being over, buying Mo's place and his stuff, meeting me, my issues, then looking at houses."

"So Nikki's shit already got into your head."

"I actually didn't remember it until just now, but maybe, yeah," I admitted.

"Want honesty?" he asked.

I nodded.

"All right," he began. "Your apartment is a disaster. You gotta start almost from scratch. I want you off the stage at Smithie's because that isn't where you wanna be and I want you in a classroom and on the way to the life you should be leading, something you want too. It'd be a lie if I said that wasn't part of a number of reasons I decided to have a look around a real estate website. And I'd be a dick, I was with a woman I was into, she knows how into her I am, and I looked into buying a property without taking into account that her ass might be livin' in it with me. If I get serious about this, we'll go look at places together. Do I think it's time for us to make what we got now official in that way? I don't know. It feels right. I love spending time with you. But where we're at isn't normal. I'd want some normal in before we go down that road. That said, you gotta know, you're definitely a consideration and a major one."

I stared up at him.

This lasted some time.

"That freak you?" he asked.

"No."

"Then why aren't you talking?"

"I'm trying to decide how I'm going to give you an orgasm."

His expression changed, it was a lovely change, then he moved Mag Fast, the TV was off and he was pulling me to his bedroom.

Mag no longer put his sling on to sleep.

Which was good.

Because in the end, I gave him two orgasms (to him giving me three), and as such, we both passed out.

CHAPTER NINETEEN

The Miracle

EVIE

I woke up on my stomach, leg hitched, eyes aimed over the edge of the bed.

It was quiet and dawn was on the room.

It was also Sunday.

Sunday.

The best day of the week.

And I thought that even though I had to strip at the end of it.

It was also a week after I came home from Smithie's to find Mag looking for new homes on Zillow.

With me *definitely a consideration*.

And it'd been a good week. No kidnappings or shootings, and except for Rob texting me in a restrained way I knew he was holding himself back from begging so he could see I was okay (but more, since he mostly knew I was okay, he wanted to meet Mag and decide if he approved), no family drama.

Best of all, Lottie and Mo set a date for their wedding.

And the day we both found out, Mag asked me to be his date.

They weren't messing around and as such, their engagement wasn't going to be a long one.

But it was still months away, and he was so sure of us, I was so sure of us, I was going to be Mag's date.

And he was going to be mine.

I smiled to myself and turned carefully, just in case he was still sleeping.

What assailed my eyes was that he was still sleeping. On his back, the covers down to his waist, his injured arm cocked, his hand resting between his pecs, his hair messy and falling on his forehead, eyes closed, those curly lashes resting on his cheeks.

I'd never seen him asleep, he was usually awake before me.

And it shouldn't surprise me, but somehow it did, how he seemed a new brand of beautiful while he was sleeping.

It was on that thought, it hit me.

He was mine.

This man sleeping beside me was mine.

My boyfriend.

My lover.

My friend.

That beautiful sleeping man was *mine*.

And on these thoughts, I moved into him and pressed my lips against his pectoral.

I felt him stir.

But that didn't stop me.

Oh no.

That was what I wanted.

I slid my lips up to his throat.

"Baby," he murmured, low and sleepy, and I felt wet hit between my legs at that word coming from him like that, aimed at me.

I ran my lips over his rough jaw, pushing my body even further up.

He pressed his arm under me, curled it around, his fingers drifting along my spine and into my hair.

I headed for his lips, but I didn't kiss him.

I looked into his sleepy, beautiful eyes and whispered, "You're handsome when you sleep."

"Yeah?" he whispered back.

"Yeah," I confirmed.

He moved his hand through my hair, around to my face, where he stroked my jaw with the tips of his fingers.

He was like that, Mag was.

He touched.

Affectionate.

Loving.

Not just during sex. Not just when he was trying to butter me up.

He was a guy who held hands.

He was a guy who cuddled.

He was those two things.

Affectionate.

Loving.

"I need to go talk to my brother again," I announced, and his brows shot together with annoyance.

"Evie."

"I have to thank him." I slid my hand up to his face and rubbed my thumb along the stubble at his cheek. "If he wasn't a douche canoe, on our first date, you probably would have thought I was just some klutzy nerd that lectured you on environmental issues within minutes of meeting her and then counted down the minutes until you could be shot of her."

His brows relaxed and his mouth softened.

"Babe, I was into you the second I laid eyes on you."

He was?

Nice.

"Then I demonstrated I was a klutz, this I did spectacularly, after, of course, I lectured you on environmental issues," I reminded him.

"A cute one."

I grinned at him.

"Nothin' wrong with havin' fire and an opinion, Evie," he said. "I know you got a bent to talk yourself down, think things about you aren't as awesome as they are. But just so you know, I was into you the second I laid eyes on you, and I was only *more* interested in you when you started lecturing me and *seriously* into you when you smacked your head into the counter."

My mind wanted to distort that.

Make it negative.

Find some reason not to believe.

But I couldn't. There was no evidence to support it.

He was into me from the beginning and he didn't hide it.

"I was into you the second I laid eyes on you too," I shared.

"Yeah?"

"Yeah."

Both his arms went around me, and in a great Mag Surge, he rolled me to my back, so he was on top.

After he got me in position, his hands went into my cami, sliding up my sides, skin on skin.

I shivered under him.

"Sunday," I whispered.

"Sunday," he whispered back, and the way he said that word made me know he felt the same way about lazy Sundays as me.

I loved that.

And then he kissed me.

It was soft and slow and sweet.

I loved that too.

After a long time of kissing, it wasn't soft or slow or sweet and he wasn't only kissing my mouth.

I wasn't only kissing his either.

Then, after a long time of rediscovering one another (even if we hadn't really lost touch, considering we'd had sex last night before going to sleep), Mag rolled on a condom, hooked my legs at the backs of the knees with his hands, lifted them and lowered his body down on mine.

I pressed my legs tight to his sides...

And then, slowly, his tongue tracing my lips, his eyes holding mine, he slid inside.

God.

Yeah.

Heck yeah.

Totally would beg for Mag to be on top.

We then made love and it was *making love*.

I'd never done it before, and I was an instant devotee.

Or maybe I was just a devotee of Mag.

It was steady and familiar and profound and *beautiful*.

And my orgasm wasn't earth-shattering.

It was gentle and quiet and *consuming*.

And when Mag purred into my neck with his, I sensed his was the same.

He didn't slide out until he had to, and he didn't stop touching me, kissing me, until he felt the need to.

And I knew he felt the need, that need being driven by hunger, coupled with his drive to look after his woman, and move onto the next phase of our Sunday, when he looked into my eyes and asked quietly, "Breakfast?"

"Yeah," I agreed.

We kissed again.

And when we were done, together, we rolled out of bed.

* * *

I sat at a stool at Mag's island, watching him make pancakes (bonus, we had fresh blueberries so they were blueberry pancakes, and side note: I was trying not to slide into a happiness coma that I could say "*we* had fresh blueberries" seeing as *we* went grocery shopping together the day before, again, and Mag made even shopping for groceries fun).

I was also thinking I kinda missed our breakfast game.

We'd settled into a routine.

Mag made breakfast.

I made dinner.

Even before I had to head out to Smithie's, I made dinner. We just ate early, something we could do since Mag was still on "light duty," so he got home around 5:30.

It worked great because Mag was a master at breakfast, and he loved my cooking (we could just say I'd wowed him with far more than my burgers—he'd lost his mind, in a Mag way, when he'd had my spicy noodles).

Still, it had been fun to fight about it.

"What'd you want to be when you grew up?"

Mag's question cut into my thoughts and I stopped watching him wield the pancake flipper (okay, I had to admit, I was part watching his long-fingered, veined hand wield the flipper and part staring at his ass in his shorts). I looked up to his face to see he was twisted at the waist, and his eyes were on me.

"Janet Guthrie," I answered.

His head jerked with surprise. "You wanted to be a race car driver?"

I shook my head.

"She was an aerospace engineer first," I told him. "For her early cars, she built her own engines."

He turned fully to me, openly impressed. "Serious?"

"Yup. She was, like, the whole package. The real deal."

"Shit," he muttered, going back to the pancakes. "I didn't know that."

I reached out, grabbed my phone, poked at it, found what I wanted, and then quoted, "'*You can go back to antiquity to find women doing extraordinary things, but their history is forgotten. Or denied to have ever existed. So women keep reinventing the wheel. Women have always done these things, and they always will.*'"

Mag slid a filled plate in front of me and shoved the butter my way, asking, "What's that?"

"It's a quote from her. Even though the feminist movement was gaining steam back in those days, she wasn't a feminist. Not at first. She just wanted to race cars. She just wanted to go fast. To compete. Her story is actually tragic. She was incredibly bright, and incredibly talented. But no one would sponsor her. You need money to race and she couldn't get anyone to back her. She had the chops. But she also had a vagina."

I did some more poking on my phone and then turned it his way, doing so reaching around it with my finger so I could scroll up, and more, and then some more.

"That's Danica Patrick's entry in Wikipedia." I turned

my phone back to me, returned to Guthrie's entry, showed it to Mag and did some more scrolling, just not much of it. "That's Janet's." I put my phone down. "They both had talent. But that's the difference of thirty years and looking like a model." I finished on a mumble, "Though Janet was no slouch, she was really cute. Still is."

Mag shot me a crooked grin. "I didn't know you were a race fan."

"I'm not. I'm a Janet Guthrie fan."

"Then get on it."

I blinked because his tone had shifted to heavy with meaning, and it did this even though his words didn't make sense.

"I'm sorry?"

He turned around, grabbed his own plate, came back to the island and set it in front of him, standing opposite me.

But he didn't reach for the butter.

He shared, "I've been thinking."

"Okay," I said slowly.

"And I have a plan," he declared.

And it was a declaration.

A serious one.

Seeing as that was so, it was hesitantly when I asked, "What...plan?"

"We're good together."

"We...are," I continued talking hesitantly.

He nodded his head once, briefly, and spoke on.

"I suppose you can make the salespeople at Urban Outfitters super fuckin' happy and drop a load fixing up your place. Or you could move in here and use that money you got from the girls to get back to school."

I stared at him.

He wasn't quite done.

"Bonus, your overhead will be lower since we'll be sharing expenses. That means you can quit Smithie's, take on more hours at Computer Raiders, and the rest of the time, focus on your future."

"Are you asking me to move in with you after we've been seeing each other for less than a month?" I queried.

He looked side to side, then pointedly down at me in my jammies sitting at his island, where my butt had been every day practically since we met, but definitely since we fell into our Food Regime.

What could I say?

I liked to watch his ass in his shorts while he was at the stove and this was the best vantage point.

"Okay, Danny, I catch your point but there are extenuating circumstances to why I'm staying with you," I pointed out.

"Do we fight?"

"No..."

"Gert likes me."

I pressed my lips together because I didn't think it was appropriate that I wanted to bust with laughter, whether it be joyous or hysterical, I didn't know.

His stare grew intense. "Do *you* got some issue with me?"

"Of course not, you're...you're..." I was at a loss for words, so I simply tossed my hand his way and finished, "*You.*"

"That's hardly a ringing endorsement, Evan," he returned.

Seriously?

"Well, you know," I continued, feeling awkward, because I wanted what he wanted, like *a lot*, for many reasons. And the scary part of that was that going back to school was not the top slot like it always used to be when I considered my life priorities (Mag was). But even so, this was too fast even if it was great, and I didn't want anything to mess it up. "I *do* have issue with you putting fresh, hot blueberry pancakes à la Danny 'Mag' Magnusson in front of me then instigating a deep conversation before I even got them buttered."

"Evie," he said low. "Not sure you caught this, honey, but I'm bein' very serious here. And bein' serious, I'll remind you that you woke me up, so I assume you were conscious and reasoning when I was moving inside you earlier."

One could debate the "reasoning" part, considering, even when he was being gentle and taking it slow, having sex with him was mind scrambling.

But I was definitely conscious.

Though I could make an argument all of that was a dream.

Which, of course, was actually a point for *his* side of our current discussion.

"Danny," I whispered.

"A woman you admire couldn't get through the roadblocks of her time. But you can. You've been held back long enough. Don't slip into a position where you hold yourself back out of habit."

I studied his face, took a beat and then said calmly, "I love that you want to take care of me, but—"

That was as far as I got before he interrupted me.

"Yeah, I do. But that isn't what this is about. For me, you're super fuckin' cute, you're a fantastic cook, you're a great lay, you listen, you're thoughtful, you're nice to people, you're interesting, you're funny and you're a massive dork. In other words, I like having you around. I like it in a way, I've made it no mystery, I think we got a future. For *you*, I hope you get some of that back. Though I'm no dork."

He had that right.

"So it's soon," he went on. "You're right. But I know a lot of folks who jumped in fast because they knew there was something there and every single one of them are married and got kids."

He was talking about the Rock Chicks.

Not to mention Lottie and Mo who got super, double extra serious after just a few days.

Though I suspected Mag had an ulterior motive.

"And you don't want me dancing anymore," I stated carefully.

"And *you* don't like to dance," he retorted.

I could not argue that.

But I could still argue.

"Danny, I mean no offense, really, you make me happy, the happiest I've ever been. I love what we're building. But for a step like that, this is way too soon."

He stared into my eyes.

Then he looked down at his plate, muttering, "Right."

"I don't want to hurt your feelings," I told him earnestly.

He again looked at me and I held my breath when he did.

"Just to confirm, you *were* conscious and reasoning when I was moving inside you earlier, yeah?" he asked.

God, it so totally felt as profound to him as it had to me.

And I *loved* that.

"Yes," I answered.

"You ever have that before?" he pressed.

No.

Profound and consuming sex that came naturally and felt beautiful?

Not even close.

I shook my head.

"Babe," he leaned into a hand on the counter toward me, "it's you."

"What's me?" I whispered.

"For me."

I felt my lips part.

Oh...*my*...*God*.

"And this isn't about your burgers, or your steaks. I knew from then," he kept at me, "but every day since then, you made me know it even better."

Suddenly, my breath wasn't coming easily.

Danny wasn't quite finished.

"So, the way I see it, you can drop a bundle on furniture and other shit to set up your pad only for us to keep goin' how we're goin' and we're gonna end up trying to decide whose furniture to keep and what's gotta go, or you can invest in you." He reached for the butter and slid it his way. "Your call."

I watched him slice off a pat and begin to butter his pancakes agitatedly before I asked, "Were you thinking about all of this when you were looking at Zillow listings?"

His eyes came right to mine, and his tone was as flat as his pancakes. "No, I was thinking about all of this, primarily how much I like being with you, while I was moving inside you this morning."

"Okeydoke," I whispered.

He went back to buttering.

"Any word on the bad guy?" I asked.

"Cisco is in the wind," he grunted, finishing with the butter and sliding it back to me. "Got no clue, but I suppose that happens when you're an asshole and a dumbfuck, you kill a cop with a gun that's registered to you and aren't smart enough to wipe the weapon and dispose of it. But what do I know? I just know, now that half of Denver is asking around about that gun, he's vapor."

I didn't butter my pancakes because I was watching Mag slather his with syrup and do it irritably.

And generously.

He had a heavy hand with syrup, but not *that* heavy.

I'd hurt his feelings.

It was me...

For him.

And alternately, it was him...

For me.

And he was right now a guy who'd made love to his girlfriend, then made her pancakes, then opened a locked gate beyond which was the path to her dreams and asked her to move in with him, even if she was already doing that and it wasn't just copacetic.

It was awesome.

It was awesome to go grocery shopping with him and tease him that he bought more Cinnamon Toast Crunch and marshmallows and hinted broadly, "Just to have on hand, you know, in case you wanna spoil your boyfriend."

It was awesome to come home at night after dancing at Smithie's and have him waiting up for me on the couch. It was awesome to then get a cuddle and rundown of where we were both at with our days and in our heads. And it was awesome to go to bed beside him.

It was also awesome he drove all the way to Culver's from work because I had an assignment close to there around lunchtime, and he wanted me to eat the custard when it wasn't melted.

More awesome was when he texted to tell me *Iron Giant* was playing at the Mayan in a retrospective, that was his favorite animated movie, and he wanted to make plans to go even if I'd seen it, but definitely if I hadn't.

But I'd seen it, and it was my favorite animated movie too.

And that in itself was awesome, that we both loved the *Iron Giant*, because he was bar none the sweetest weapon of mass destruction ever.

It was just awesome.

All of it.

All that came with being with Mag.

"So, I'm still in danger," I noted.

"Days pass and nothin' goes down, I got my doubts." He forked into his pancakes, but before lifting them up to his mouth, he looked at me and finished, "I still want you covered for a while."

I still want you covered for a while.

That was Mag too.

He had me covered.

"You're just life," I blurted as he shoved the big bite into his mouth.

"What?" he asked after a couple of chews.

"I...I just..." I shook my head and looked down at my own fluffy purple-speckled cakes.

Breakfast he'd made me.

God.

God.

I'd missed it.

I'd been sleeping beside it for weeks, waking up next to it, *living with it*.

And I'd missed it.

"Evie," he called. "What?"

Okay.

All right.

I'd just shot him down when he'd asked me to start our future together, and although he was not in a happy-go-lucky mood, he wasn't throwing a fit, shouting, growing sullen or acting like an ass because he'd gotten his pride stung or didn't get his way.

Oh God.

Yes.

It was him...

For me.

"Evie," his voice was more demanding, "*what*?"

I lifted my gaze to him, and he slow-blinked when he caught my eyes.

I couldn't imagine what my face looked like after taking a second to actually have a thought about how awesome my boyfriend was, that thought being a world-rocking epiphany.

But from his reaction, I wasn't hiding I'd had a world-rocking epiphany.

"You're just life," I repeated. "I just go on. That's what I do. Day to day. I know as a kid there's something missing at home. I power through. I start school and nobody likes me, I can't seem to make friends, I just power through that too. I grow up and know I'm different, I might be able to make something of myself, but my family weighs me down, and I just power through. My brother asks me for a favor that puts me in danger, and I know it's gonna put me in danger, and yeah. Again. I just power through. I just power through, Danny. That's me. That's what *I do*. So, I missed it. I missed you walking into my apartment. I missed the miracle. You were just life."

His body went absolutely still.

Except his lips.

"The miracle?" he whispered.

Yes.

The miracle.

That hair.

Those eyes.

His chest.

These pancakes.

That *man*.

"Tex told me he was proud of me and Rob told me he loved me," I explained. "Boone confided in me. He trusted me with some deep stuff, and I know you know what an honor that is. The girls got mad at me because I didn't call on them when I was in a jam. You walked through the door of my apartment, Danny, and I was so busy powering through, I missed the rainbows and sparkles that waved in your wake."

"I'd prefer lightning bolts and power surges, baby," he said quietly. "I'm not a rainbow and sparkles kind of guy."

"Okay, lightning bolts and power surges, but if, down the road, we have a girl, you better get onboard with rainbows and sparkles."

Once these words were out of my mouth, I was hit with a lightning-bolt-induced power surge and it was coming from Mag's electric-blue eyes.

The charge crackled between us for so long, it was likely our pancakes were incinerated, but I could not stop looking into those amazing blue eyes.

Before the entire building went up in flames, fortunately, Mag spoke.

"So, you movin' in, Evie?"

"Yeah, Danny."

Without delay, he left his pancakes, and as he rounded the island, I twisted his way on my stool.

He took my face in his hands and I caught his tee in my fists at his waist.

And then he bent to me.

But he didn't kiss me.

He asked a question.

"What's Boone confiding in you?"

"Uh…" I mumbled. I was still unsure, even if the boys talked, that was something they talked about.

"Now I'm understanding Mo's pain when we all claimed Lottie as her brother husbands," he muttered.

A startled laugh bubbled out of me. "Her what?"

"Without the benefits, of course," he assured.

I smiled at him. "Of course."

"So cinnamon clusters for my foreseeable future," he remarked.

"Yeah, for your foreseeable future," I teased.

I watched his eyes smile.

I enjoyed watching that.

And then I got serious.

"I'm a little scared, Danny," I admitted.

"I am too," he surprised me by saying. "But you're worth the risk."

Suddenly, I was a lot less scared.

"Evie?"

"Right here," I stated the obvious.

"You're the shit."

Oh God.

Why did that make me want to cry?

I knew why.

Because I was.

I'd been led to believe differently.

And I'd swallowed that as a matter of course.

But I was the shit.

And not because some hot guy wanted me to move in with him.

Because I just was.

And having that thought in my head was a miracle too.

On this latest revelation, my voice was husky when I replied, "You too."

He touched his nose to mine, which was mega sweet.

And after he did that was when he kissed me.

When he got done (and I was pretty glad he took his time), he also tossed my pancakes in the trash, saying his woman wasn't going to eat cold ones, so he was making a new batch.

I had an issue with this considering the waste of perfectly good food and the state of hunger in the world.

But I didn't say a word.

CHAPTER TWENTY

Sex Shoes

EVIE

"You have to get those."

"You totally have to get those."

"Seriously, you *sooooo* have to get those, you need to get them in every color."

I was standing in the shoe department of Nordstrom wearing a pair of sexy red sandals, staring down at my feet and experiencing some pretty extreme Shoe Peer Pressure.

Ryn, Hattie and Pepper were all over taking care of my "heel problem."

I did not think I had a "heel problem."

I thought I had a driving need to get to Fortnum's because Gert was going to be there soon to look over the girls to make her determination if they were good matches for the guys (but mostly, I figured, so she could get out of the house).

Smithie heard of this so he was showing too, though I didn't know why, since he already knew everyone. Probably because he considered himself our second father, the brand of that Smithie embodied included sticking his nose into everything.

And Lottie was not about to let her handiwork be picked over without her input, so she was going to be there as well.

But most of all, I was finding shopping, not my favorite pastime, was giving me a driving need for one of Tex's Textuals.

I glanced over at Axl, who was standing slightly removed in a zone where he could see everything, but still close enough he could get to us quickly.

He had his arms crossed on his wide chest, making his pecs bulge and the sinews in his forearms ripple. His long legs were planted. And from about two point oh five seconds after he positioned himself, the shoe department suddenly became crowded with females, regardless (or maybe because) of the fact he looked like he'd prefer to be strapped down with someone poking needles into his forced-open eyes.

So, last, I needed to get Axl out of Cherry Creek mall.

I gave the girls a hang-on-one-second finger, walked over to him, and his gaze went from scanning the store to scanning me from my head, past my NASA tee, my faded, distressed jeans, down to my red patent-leather sandaled feet.

"Hey," I said when I stopped close.

"Dig you, babe, but if we're not out of here in fifteen minutes, I'll either kill somebody or fake a heart attack," he declared.

Another "babe" from another of Mag's boys.

I was almost not registering them anymore.

And I had an affirmative.

I needed to get Axl out of there.

But, as to the matter at hand.

"What do you think of these shoes?" I asked, sticking out a foot.

He cast his extraordinary light-blue eyes at my foot.

They came back up to my face.

I held my breath at his expression.

"You don't wanna know what I think of those shoes."

Oh.

All right.

Well then.

"Okay. What do you think *Mag* will think of these shoes?" I asked a different question.

"You two are moving in together," he noted.

"Yes," I confirmed.

"Which, I'm assuming, means you two enjoy getting it on."

I pressed my lips together.

He took that correctly as a positive response, though I wasn't sure it was indicative of the grand scale of just how positive that response was, but I suspected he didn't want to know that part.

"Mag could have a severe case of West Nile virus, and if you were in the mood, you could put those on, and he'd still do you."

I turned instantly and announced loudly to the girls, "I'm getting them."

"Woo-hoo!" Ryn hooted, throwing her hands up and doing a shimmy, making her hair sway and her boobs jiggle, which in turn brightened the day of another male who was shopping with his partner and clearly finding it tedious.

Until now.

I turned back to Axl. "We'll get these and then go get Textuals."

He jerked up his chin and didn't hide his relief.

He also didn't ask what a Textual was, considering I'd introduced all the boys to them and now it was our group coffee drink.

Okay, maybe it was weird, but I thought there was something super cool about having a gaggle of friends who'd assumed a group coffee drink.

I'd never had that.

I really liked it.

And maybe it was also weird that I couldn't wait to introduce the girls to Textuals so they could join my coffee group.

The more, I was finding, the merrier.

I cast a glance at the girls again, and now that the decision had been made for me to get the shoes, I saw they'd risen from their chairs and started to browse.

And this included Hattie.

Though she did it casting sidelong looks at Axl.

Longing sidelong looks at Axl.

Something she'd been doing since he picked us all up for this outing.

And here he was, standing removed, which meant distant, and badass, which meant unapproachable.

Hmm.

I edged closer to him and said, "You know, no bullets have flown for weeks and Hattie's right there. You could probably take five minutes while I check out to have a chat with her. And then, on the way to Fortnum's, she could sit in the front seat."

Those light-blue eyes intensified on me and I saw they could become *ice*-blue eyes.

"What?" I asked.

"You're happy," he stated.

"Yeeeessss." I drew it out.

And I was.

And not simply because no bullets were flying.

Mag asked me to move in on a Sunday, and it was only Tuesday, so it wasn't like in the intervening time we'd arranged for me to get out of my lease, moved my stuff and I'd redecorated his bedroom (because it was a little sparse in there and veritably screamed *MAN!*) and reorganized his cupboards (something, we disagreed, he needed me to do).

But I had my vinyl and my Chucks at his place so it already kind of felt like home.

"People who are happy want others to be happy like they are," Axl shared. "Especially when they're the gettin'-some-on-a-frequent-basis kind of happy. They want everyone walking in a fog of oxytocin, endorphins and pheromones like they are."

"I'm not sure I'm in a fog," I sniffed.

His lips quirked. "Evie, you decided in a split second you're gonna buy a pair of shoes, and with your style, the only time you're gonna wear 'em is when you wanna make Mag jump you. You probably aren't ever even gonna wear those shoes out of the house. You're in a sex-happy fog."

I could no longer debate this issue, mostly because he was right.

"Hattie's really sweet," I cajoled.

"Hattie the way Hattie is, Hattie's gotta make the first move," he returned.

"Hattie's not gonna make the first move," I retorted. "She's crazy shy."

"I know that. And I misspoke," he replied. "I made the first move. And she blew me off. So what I should have said was, she wants to give it a shot, she's gotta make the *second* move."

He made a move?

When did he make a move?

"You made a move?" I asked.

Axl sighed.

He'd made a move.

And she blew him off.

Ouch.

This was disappointing, and sucky for Axl, but it really wasn't a surprise.

"How about I prime her for *you* to make a second move?" I suggested.

"Evie, you and Lots are just gonna have to chill."

Lottie might not be there coaxing me to buy sex shoes.

But I knew she was riding the high of her success with me and Mag, so she'd been on all the guys to step shit up.

I thought about what Boone had said, and asked, "Does this mean you're gonna find someone else?"

"Babe, I'm not gonna go monk, waiting for a woman I want who doesn't want me."

Okay, good.

He wanted her.

Because of that, I leaned closer, took a chance and probably broke the girlfriend code (but for a good cause, and that cause was partly for the good of my girlfriend, as well as my guy friend).

I then whispered, "I think she wants you too."

"Evie—"

I heard my phone ring upon cutting him off, saying, "Axl."

He got closer too.

And he did this to say, "Think about it. Lots put you and Mag together, you met him, you were interested. He wasn't ready to move on from Nikki, had other things going on with his life, and made it clear he had no intention of going there. Would you be all in to put yourself out there?"

The very thought of that made me shiver.

Dammit, I could no longer debate this either, because he was again right.

And now I was all worried about him because he was hanging with us, Hattie was right there, and even though she was into him like he was into her, if he'd made a move, and she'd rebuffed him, this could not be super fun for him to be close to her.

But, and I might have been wrong, she was crazy shy, and he was a commando, so really, it was up to him to pull his finger out.

I decided not to carry on with this (at that time). I'd get back into it with him later.

Instead, I gave him a look, turned, huffed off toward my still-ringing phone, and made a mental note that huffing off in heels seemed way more dramatic than doing it in Rothy's (or the like).

I pulled my phone out of the bag, saw it said DANNY on the screen (obviously, I'd changed his name in my phone, though I'd managed to refrain from changing it to MY HOT GUY COMMANDO BOYFRIEND), and all at once, I plopped down, leaned forward to unstrap my shoes and took the call.

This was unwise.

It meant I lost my balance and nearly fell flat on my face.

But thankfully I shifted my weight fast enough to my ass that didn't happen.

"Hey," I greeted once I was safely seated.

"Hey," he replied. "What's up?"

I felt a gooey feeling in my stomach because he did this. He called just to touch base. Connect while we were apart. Find out what was going on. How I was doing. Discuss dinner options. Reaffirm that he did not want me to move his plates to the cupboard closer to the dishwasher (which was insane, you just took them out of the machine, reached up, and *boom*, plate put away—he had spices and oils there, which was madness—he said he prepared food in that zone, so he needed the spices and oils to be handy, and although this seemed logical, he was still wrong).

"We're at the Nordstrom shoe department," I told him.

"Is Elvira there with you?"

Although I'd heard this name, and knew she worked with the team, I did not know this woman, so I could not fathom why Mag was asking this question.

I still answered, "No."

"I think there's a chair there, upholstered in purple, that's reserved for her."

Ah.

So Elvira liked shoes.

Apparently, a lot.

"And that's the chair she was sitting in when her husband proposed to her," Mag carried on.

Ah.

So Elvira might like shoes but a trip to Nordstrom for her was a sentimental journey.

I grinned and slid the first shoe off. "It's just the girls and Axl and I."

"This means Axl didn't tell her where you were."

I kept grinning but said nothing.

"It also means Axl probably wants to shoot me right now," he went on.

I continued grinning and did not attempt to deny this truth as I went after the buckle on the other shoe and asked, "What are you up to?"

"Fighting the urge to find Mo and hold him at gunpoint to tell me where they disappeared Snag so I can find that asshole and strangle him, because I got at least another week of being benched because of this shoulder and sitting around on my ass is driving me up the wall."

I sat still, one hand with the phone to my ear, bent over, the fingers of the other hand on the strap of my shoe, and I said nothing.

This went on so long, Mag called, "Evie?"

"What does 'disappeared' mean?" I whispered.

It was Mag's turn to be silent.

Oh boy.

"Do I not want to know?" I asked.

"No, you don't want to know," he answered.

Oh boy!

Moving on.

"We're almost done here," I shared. "I gotta purchase my sex shoes and then we're going to Fortnum's. Can you get a break and come over? I'll order you a coffee so it'll be all ready for you."

Mag was again silent.

Therefore, I called, "Danny?"

"What are sex shoes?"

Did I add the word "sex" to "shoes"?

I did.

"You'll find out," I muttered.

It was Mag sounding happy, very happy, when he replied, "Pleased as fuck you're not on at Smithie's tonight."

I was too.

What I was not pleased about was that I was down with Mag's plan to get me where I wanted to be with work and education and life, but this meant I would soon be putting in notice.

I'd taken off the second shoe and was replacing them in their box when the sales assistant, sniffing out a commission, materialized out of thin air.

I handed the box to the assistant and he floated off as I hastily pulled on my footies, shoved my feet into my Chucks and tied them.

All this I did, still connected to Mag, but I did it silently, deep in thought and with the phone pressed to my ear and shoulder.

"Evie, you there?" I heard in my ear.

I grabbed my bag, got up, and just in case any of the girls, who had at this point dispersed widely to peruse the wares, could hear, whispered, "I was just thinking of the impending task of putting in notice at the club."

"You're not gonna lose them, not any of them, honey. You just won't have to be naked when you're around them anymore," Mag replied.

One could say that would be good.

I was walking to the register as I shared, "I wish I'd made friends with them before I was imminently going to quit. I mean, we were friends. But, you know, now we're shopping friends which means we're *friends* friends."

"I know, baby," he murmured soothingly.

"It probably would have been more fun to be naked around them if we'd gotten to the point of *friends* friends."

"Gonna have to share some truths with my girl," he muttered.

"Sorry?"

"Evie, baby, honey..."

Oh no.

It was the double-barreled endearment, but this one didn't sound like it was gonna go all that well.

"...you know I'm into you," he continued. "*Way* into

you. And I'm a one-woman kind of man. You being that one woman, you get that?"

"I get it," I said, pulling my credit card out of my wallet awkwardly since I was doing it one handed, at the same time wondering why he was telling me this, at the same time kinda fretting that he was telling me this at all because I already sorta assumed it.

"But your friends are hot."

I suddenly needed to choke down a giggle.

Mag kept talking.

"So, just sayin', words like 'would have been fun to be naked around them,' especially about a minute after you told me you're buyin' sex shoes, uh...that's a no-go."

I couldn't hold my giggle back and thus let it loose at the same time I asked curiously, "Which one would be your first choice?"

"You actually asking that shit?"

"Axl, Auggie, Boone, and that's a tough call and I reserve the right to switch the order and do it frequently, depending on who's currently being sweet to me and/or keeping me alive."

He burst out laughing.

I shoved my card in the reader, smiling and listening to him do it, and when he was done, I prompted, "Well?"

"Hattie, Pepper, Ryn," he answered.

Surprising.

"Really?"

"I guess I got a thing for the shy ones," he said.

"I'm not shy," I declared, pulling my card out of the reader.

"Baby," he said in a voice that made me want to strap on my sex shoes right then, beam wherever he was, and make him jump me, "you gave yourself a concussion slamming your head in the counter going after some runaway lip gloss the first night you met me."

"I'm klutzy, not shy."

"You're klutzy because you're shy. Or at least you were then. And, just in case you intend to twist that, being that landed you a commando."

"My heart's desire," I teased.

"Yeah, it landed that same thing for me too."

I quit moving.

Entirely.

Because he'd just called me his heart's desire.

Worth a repeat.

Daniel Magnusson just called me his heart's desire!

And I knew, to my bones, that had very little (okay, maybe a *wee bit*) to do with me making him hamburgers.

I was frozen, but Mag's mouth could move, and it did to speak.

"Though I'm down with thinning out my tees, minimally, and my socks, maximally, to give you space for your shit, we're not moving the spices."

Sneak attack!

"Don't say something so sweet it knocks the wind out of me and then get in a dinger about the spices, Danny," I returned. "Everyone knows you keep the dishes by the dishwasher."

"I'm not everyone, Evie. And neither are you. And honey, *that* is what landed you a commando."

Hmm.

"I'll give you that, but you can prepare food at the island. We'll go to the Container Store. Get a spice tray to put in one of the island drawers. That way, they'll be right there for you."

"Babe?"

"What?"

"Straight up, you give me you in sex shoes, you could put the spices in the hallway, and I wouldn't give a shit."

I felt gooey again.

Hot and gooey.

Even so.

"Stop being so sweet when sex shoes are hours *and hours* away."

"Preview at Fortnum's. I'll meet you there in half an hour. Order me a Textual if you're there before me."

See?

Totally got the guys into Textuals.

"Same for me, if you beat us there," I replied.

"Right. Later, baby."

"Later, Danny."

"And, Evie?" he called before I hung up.

"Yeah?" I asked.

"Babe."

He said no more.

I wondered if I was supposed to interpret something from that one word. His tone sounded kinda heavy, but not in a bad way.

However, I was unable to interpret that one word.

Therefore, I whispered, "What?"

"I love it that you're so solid with us, you can give me your order of my boys, and ask mine with your girls, and it ends in you giggling, not getting up in my shit that I rose to some bait, tweaked you and you took that out on me."

"But I asked, Danny. And I did it knowing it was all in fun."

"I love that too. And that was the first indication you feel we're all about trust. That's what I love the most.

You're totally the shit, Evie. And I'm learning you're more of that every day."

Oh my God.

See!

Mag's phone calls were *everything*.

"See you soon, honey," he finished.

He then didn't give me the chance to respond.

He hung up, and I dropped my phone and looked to the sales assistant, who was sliding my bag on the counter toward me.

"I'm so sorry. That was rude," I told him. "Being on the phone while you were ringing me up."

He blinked.

Well then, apparently, people didn't apologize for talking on the phone when someone was serving them.

"It was my boyfriend," I went on to explain. "We just decided to move in together. Accidentally, I just proved I trusted him. Which I'm glad about. And he proved he trusted me back. Which is awesome. Oh, and he's a commando."

"Is he as fun to look at as that one?" the man asked, jerking his head toward Axl.

I glanced over my shoulder at Axl, still standing impatiently, exuding badass and looking gorgeous.

I looked back to the assistant.

"Better."

The man smiled. "Then you're forgiven."

I smiled back, grabbed the handles, lifted the bag his way and said, "Thanks."

"Have fun in those shoes," he bid.

Oh, I would.

I felt my smile change.

He saw it, read it and winked.

My smile got even bigger before I walked toward my posse.

I gathered up the girls and Axl herded us to the exit.

Ryn was leading.

Pepper, Hattie and me were following, with me walking in the middle.

Axl was at the rear.

"Was that Mag on the phone?" Pepper asked.

"Yeah, he calls at least once a day," I answered.

"Sweet," Hattie whispered.

She didn't know the half of it.

"Do you call him?" she asked.

Oh no.

I looked at her. "No. Should I?"

"No," Pepper answered, and I turned my head her way.

"You sure?" I pressed.

"Yes," she answered.

"I mean, I don't want it to be one-sided," I went on. "I want him to know I like him as much as he likes me."

"Babe, those shoes say that and then some," she replied. "You can coast on those shoes for at least six months."

"Then you'll have to buy another pair," Hattie said.

"Yeah, if you buy another pair, and then another one, and so on, you'll never have to be the one to call him for the rest of your life," Pepper added.

Normally, I would balk at owning shoes that, Axl was right, it was unlikely I'd ever wear out of the house.

But if it got me my way with the spices...

"I remember those days, the first blush, when you can't be apart, and when you have to, you connect," Pepper mused, turning her gaze wistfully toward Ryn, who clearly wanted a coffee as badly as I did, because she'd pulled well ahead.

"You can have that too," I pointed out while we made

the turn to go down the short hall to the doors to the parking garage.

Pepper said nothing.

I studied her profile.

It looked sad.

Shit.

I turned to Hattie.

She was watching her feet move.

She looked sad too.

Shit!

I turned to glare at Axl.

He caught my glare and lifted his brows.

He then started and clipped, "Evie!"

This was right when I walked into the door.

Bah!

"God! Are you okay?" Hattie asked, her hand on my shoulder, leaning in to look at my face as I swayed back and blinked.

I might have just slammed into the door and cracked my head, but I started smiling.

Big.

"I'm a klutz," I announced.

"You're maybe the only person I know who would say those three words looking like you just won the lottery," Pepper noted.

I hadn't won the lottery.

I'd worked long and hard.

And then I got my reward.

Because I wasn't like other girls.

Including being a klutz.

And that landed me a commando.

I didn't share this with Pepper, Hattie, or Axl, who was now standing with us.

I shrugged and said, "It's me."

I barely got out the "me" part when we all heard a chilling scream coming from outside.

Woodenly, we turned to look out the glass doors.

Well, Hattie and Pepper and I did.

Axl shoved through us, growling, "Do not leave this area." He then pushed swiftly through the doors, finishing, "Call Mag."

I had my phone out and turned on when Hattie whispered, "Oh my God. Someone's got Ryn."

"Ohmigod, ohmigod, ohmigod," I chanted, whisking my thumb over my screen to go to my calls and engage Mag.

I put it to my ear just as I let out a little scream, right along with Hattie, because we heard gunshots outside.

"What's happening?" Pepper shouted.

I was stuck, frozen, unsure what to do when Mag's voice came into my ear.

"Forget something, babe?"

"Someone has Ryn! And I think they're shooting at—!"

I didn't finish.

My phone was yanked viciously out of my hand.

I whirled on whoever did that just in time to hear both Hattie and Pepper make distinct noises that conveyed the same message.

Fear.

And panic.

My arm was seized, and I began struggling.

I stopped when my wrist was wrenched up my back and I had a different voice in my ear.

"You make trouble, she dies, he dies, you all die."

I stopped struggling.

CHAPTER TWENTY-ONE

The Initiation

EVIE

This just cut it.

I was tied to another chair.

Tied to another...*fucking*...*chair*!

Worse!

All my girlfriends were tied to chairs with me.

Like Steve and Robin from *Stranger Things* when the Soviets got ahold of them, but without being injected with truth serum that made us giggle and everything seem funny.

Tied to chairs, back to back.

I was attached to Ryn. Pepper at my side, Hattie to her back.

Ryn had been brought in later by a set of bad guys different than the three who took Pepper, Hattie and me.

And they didn't handle her very gently.

Not like the guys who took me, Pepper and Hattie were gallant, but the ones who pulled in Ryn seemed pissed off and they were rough with her.

But she was alive, breathing, she didn't appear injured, though she was obviously spitting mad.

Which was good (ish, though not the mad part).

However, this meant they had numbers.

Which was bad (totally).

We'd been kidnapped.

Fucking kidnapped.

All of us.

Me and my friends.

Kidnapped and tied to chairs.

I got my friends *kidnapped and tied to chairs*.

No.

My brother did.

And due to the decree of the meathead who was guarding us that we couldn't talk, I hadn't been able to ask Ryn about Axl.

God, if I was still talking to Mick, I'd quit talking to him. I'd then cut him out of every picture I had that he was in. After that, I didn't know. Possibly sew a voodoo doll of him and stick pins in it. Or perhaps burn him in effigy.

Something.

On this thought, the meathead who kept telling us to shut up if we tried to speak got a call. Since I had a view to the door, I watched as he looked at the screen on his phone and then moved out of the room.

A desolate room, by the way.

Four walls.

Wood floor.

No windows.

And four chairs with our asses tied to them.

Oh, and there wasn't a lot of heat, something I was learning was de rigueur with kidnappings.

It wasn't freezing, but it wasn't toasty warm either.

In fact, my fingers were getting numb from the cold.

They'd put us in hoods after they stuffed us in their cars, so I had no idea where we were.

That was fun.

Not.

I watched him go, and the instant the door closed behind him, I twisted my neck and asked Ryn, "You okay?"

"I take kickboxing. I got a good one to the balls of one of them. So now we can say he's not my biggest fan," she replied.

"But otherwise, you're okay?" I pushed.

"Well, if being tied to a chair but doing it breathing and without any broken bones is okay, then yeah. I'm okay," she said.

Yes.

That was our new definition of okay.

"Axl?" I went on.

There was a beat of silence.

My heart thumped *hard*.

"Ryn!" I hissed, returning my attention to the door.

"There was a firefight. I mean, like, lots of bullets were exchanged. I think he worried I would get caught in the crossfire. And, you know, I was worried too. He stopped shooting, shouted 'cease fire' about a million times, and showed himself, lifting his hands. My guess, he thought, since we were in freaking Cherry Creek mall's parking garage and someone had to have called the cops, seeing as there were people shooting at each other and hitting cars and windows were exploding and such, those assholes might feel in the mood to negotiate before the cops got there. But when Axl showed himself, he didn't have his gun. They opened fire on him and, and…"

As she trailed off, there was a beat of nothing, though

my blood pressure skyrocketed through it, before I heard a muffled sob and felt our chairs move with her body bucking.

Oh no.

No.

I closed my eyes and dropped my head.

"They shot him?" Hattie whispered, her voice not only quiet, but husky with emotion.

So.

Totally.

Into Axl.

"I-I don't know. He went d-down, and . . . and I d-didn't see him again," Ryn told her brokenly.

I lifted my head, opened my eyes and focused on the door.

"Maybe he hit the deck so he wouldn't be shot," Pepper suggested.

"M-maybe," Ryn muttered.

I stared at the door.

"Think positive, sweets," Pepper urged.

Ryn didn't reply.

I continued to stare at the door.

After a few seconds, Hattie asked, "They're gonna come and rescue us. The boys are? They're gonna come get us, right?"

They were.

Absolutely.

They would just because that was who they were.

But Auggie was into Pepper.

And Axl was into Hattie.

Not to mention Boone's brain had already claimed Ryn as his even if Boone as a whole had not.

And I was Mag's.

Definitely.

We were moving in together.

We were discussing the proper placement of kitchen items.

We both liked *John Wick* and *Iron Giant*. And I'd recently discovered, although the film was hotly debated, we both were on the same side and thought *Once Upon a Time in Hollywood* was a masterpiece.

Not to mention, the last time I caught him on his laptop, he wasn't looking at homes. He was looking at awesome, top-of-the-line turntables. This meant he liked vinyl. And I liked vinyl. But more, he wanted to make it so we could listen to vinyl.

Together.

He was going to buy a house and I was going to boho the shit out of it and we were gonna live there, listening to vinyl.

And okay, maybe after Mag asked me if I wanted kids, I'd secretly started daydreaming about little boys with electric-blue eyes and little girls with dark curls.

They were good daydreams.

The best.

I mean, Mag teaching little boys to be men like him?

And Mag spoiling little girls like they should be spoiled?

I'd never had better daydreams and I knew I never would.

Not in my life.

So I had plans.

I had good friends.

I had an awesome boyfriend.

I had a bright future.

I had it all.

Finally.

I had it all.

And goddamn it, I wasn't losing any of it.

"They will," Pepper assured. "Won't they, Evie? They'll rescue us. Right?"

"He hit the deck," I stated.

"What?" Pepper asked.

"Axl," I said. "Ryn, honey, he hit the deck. He's a commando. He'd know once he showed himself that they were going to fire on him, and he'd be prepared. He was thinking five steps ahead. He was thinking, better they take you without any holes in you so when they come and get us, we'd all be all right. That's what happened. Yeah? Okay?"

"Y-yeah," Ryn replied on a sniffle.

"Um, I mean, I don't wanna be Debbie Downer or anything, but *how* are they gonna find us?" Hattie asked.

"I don't know," I answered. "I was in an abandoned warehouse the last time, and I don't know how they located me then. But I wasn't there for very long, so obviously, they have ways."

"I'm totally taking kickboxing courses when this is over," Pepper muttered.

"Me too," Hattie said. "Though they had guns on us and I'm not sure I'd kickbox a dude with a gun."

"It slots in, you know, the instinct," Ryn said, thankfully sounding like she'd gotten herself together. "Even if he has a gun, when someone has you by your hair and it's clear they intend to do something to you that you don't want, the instinct takes over."

Pepper sounded pissed when she asked, "They had you by your hair?"

"When we're rescued, first thing I'm gonna do after I

down five gimlets is go to the Dry Bar and get a scalp scrub and a blowout," Ryn declared.

Okay.

Good.

They were talking about blowouts.

We were all keeping it together.

So we'd have it together when the guys found us.

Right.

Good.

Onward.

"This is a long shot as a bright side, but just sayin'. I hope this serves to communicate that you all need to get the lead out and go out with your respective commando," I announced.

"How about instead, we talk about how we can escape," Ryn suggested.

Escape?

She wanted to try to escape?

I wasn't sure that was a good idea.

"They should have zip-tied us," Hattie noted. "They didn't. I can start picking at these ropes and I'll totally get them undone. I'm hell on wheels when the chains on my necklaces get tangled. I went on vacation once, and they all got messed up in my jewelry thingie. Like, seven necklaces. I had them separated in ten minutes flat."

"I think maybe ten minutes is a bit longer than we should remain tied here," Ryn remarked.

"Gotcha," Hattie mumbled and kept mumbling, "On it."

I was still feeling this was not a good idea.

Before I could impart that, Pepper did.

"Okay, I, for one, do not want to attempt to escape."

"Why not?" Hattie asked.

"They have guns," Pepper replied. "They might get testy

if they show before we get loose, and see we're trying to get loose. I don't want a guy testy at me who's also a guy holding a gun. And anyway, we all came in wearing hoods. We don't know the lay of the land. Whatever's beyond that door might be filled with bad guys. Testy bad guys. With guns. So, Hattie, stop doing that."

"One thing I learned in the movies, if they wanted us dead, they'd kill us on the scene," Ryn told us. "They certainly had enough bullets to make that happen."

I looked to the ceiling.

No effigy for Mick.

Voodoo doll.

Absolutely.

"I'm relatively certain the training the guys had did not come from watching Bruce Willis movies," Pepper retorted. "And sisters, I have a kid. We can just say my main priority right now is the same as it always is. That being, going home to Juno, alive and kicking. So, stop picking, Hattie."

"Right. Juno," Hattie said quietly. "Maybe we shouldn't try to escape."

"Okay, I hear you, Pepper," Ryn said. "It just feels stupid, sitting here, doing nothing but waiting to get rescued."

"Did anyone read those Rock Chick books?" Hattie asked. "Those women got kidnapped all the time. Maybe they're like an...I don't know. A how-to. As in, how-to-behave-when-kidnapped type a thing. Or how-to-know-whether-you-should-attempt-to-escape-or-not."

"Nope," Ryn said. "Haven't read them."

"Me either," Pepper said.

"I only read part of the first one," I told them. "And to where I got, Indy had been kidnapped twice, she didn't know what to do either, but before she figured it out,

Lee rescued her the first time, and Tex rescued her the second."

"Well, you've been kidnapped," Ryn pointed out. "What did you do?"

"I'm learning there are various forms of kidnappings. The last time, after the guy tied me to a chair, he interrogated me then hit me. Although the numbers involved in this one do not make me happy, in ranking them, so far this is better than the last," I shared.

"Well, we got that going for us," Pepper noted. "I've never been hit and I never wanna be hit."

"Me either," Ryn said.

"I hadn't either, until I was kidnapped," I told them.

Hattie said nothing.

In fact, it was weird how Hattie said nothing.

I knew I wasn't the only one who thought that when Ryn prompted softly, "Hatz?"

"I, uh...you know, my dad really wanted me to be a successful ballerina," she said.

I knew she was a dancer, and a good one, what with our occupation and all.

I also knew she'd wanted to go professional with that, and not in a zone where she had to take her clothes off to earn her money.

But a ballerina?

Hattie was naturally curvy. Very curvy. I'd never seen a ballerina that was curvy like she was.

Oh boy.

I didn't have a good feeling about this story.

"How does that factor into whether you've been hit or not?" Pepper asked a question she knew the answer to already, we all knew the answer to it, but she asked it gently.

"Well, you know, early on, it's known whether kids are gonna...make it. Obviously, I...didn't."

"So, he...*hit you*?" Pepper asked carefully.

"He was frustrated. He invested a lot of money and time in my training," Hattie replied.

Pepper's voice had risen when she repeated, "Invested a lot in your training?"

"You are fucking kidding me," Ryn spat.

"Oh, honey," I whispered.

"So, you've got an asshole dad," Pepper started, now sounding fit to be tied. "Evan has an entire asshole family. I have an asshole ex who brought out the asshole in most of my family. Or maybe it was me getting pregnant young and unmarried and them being high-horse, judgmental, Bible-thumping dickheads and they'd just held their tongue before and not exposed it. And Ryn has an asshole brother."

Uh-oh.

Ryn had an asshole brother?

We were Asshole Brother Sisters?

I did not like that.

"Pepper," Ryn muttered warningly.

"How do you have an asshole brother?" I asked Ryn, obviously, case in point, where our asses were at that time, knowing a little something myself about the assholery brothers could get up to.

"He's not an asshole. He just has problems," Ryn told me.

"He's an asshole," Pepper told Ryn.

"It's a disease," Ryn said tetchily.

Oh God.

He had a disease that made him an asshole?

"You're right," Pepper agreed. "It's a disease. Like cancer. But if you get cancer, you don't deadbeat-brother your sister. You get help for your cancer."

"It's a *mental* disease," Ryn stated. "That makes things different."

"It's alcoholism, Ryn," Pepper retorted. "And there's a treatment. I've never had to do it, thank God, but I still know it's no fun doing chemo. But you still do chemo so you can get better and not make the people who love you watch you waste away."

Whoa.

Harsh.

And Pepper wasn't like that.

Thus, I could read from that, Pepper and Ryn had had this conversation frequently and Pepper was growing impatient.

Ryn fell silent.

I twisted my hand until I got it into position to hold hers.

I could only grab on to her ring finger and pinkie with my own.

But I held on.

Her fingers curled around mine.

And she held on too.

"I'm sorry, Ryn," I said quietly.

"He was the best brother in the world," she replied.

"And now, he's not," Pepper noted.

"Pez, cool it, okay?" Hattie said softly.

"I haven't been a good friend," I declared. "I didn't know any of this about any of you. You're all kidnapped because of my brother. You took my back. And I didn't make the effort to take any of yours."

"You get a pass this time, Evz," Pepper said. "Things have been tangled for you. For instance, all of us tied to chairs, waiting for rescue."

That was when I fell silent.

Actually, we all did.

Though part of mine was that I was thinking about her calling me "Evz." She'd never called me that. I'd heard, in passing, them calling each other Hatz, Pez and Rinz, but they'd never called me Evz.

I felt like I'd gone through an initiation.

And passed.

And the crazy thing was, that made me feel good, no matter how tough that initiation was proving to be at this moment.

Ryn broke the silence by saying, "I bet the Rock Chicks didn't just hang around, waiting to be rescued."

"Have you seen Luke Stark or Vance Crowe?" Pepper asked. "They *soooooooo* did."

I had seen Luke Stark but not Vance Crowe.

But more, I'd *definitely* seen Danny Magnusson, Axl Pantera, Auggie Hero and Boone Sadler.

Which meant I giggled.

They all started giggling with me.

We stopped when the door opened and the guy who'd been in with us before strolled in.

Behind him came another guy I hadn't seen before, followed by one of the guys who'd kidnapped Ryn.

The last guy was carrying another chair.

He closed the door behind him.

But it was the middle guy I paid attention to.

Because he scared the shit out of me.

Yeah.

One look at him, he scared the absolute *crap* out of me.

And, unsurprisingly, he only had eyes for me.

He also came to a stop three feet in front of me.

"I gotta say," he began, "I been to Smithie's. And when I went, I was into you even before I knew you were Dirk Gardiner's daughter."

Oh crap times three.

One, this tall, beefy, dark-haired, pug-faced, creepy guy with mean and openly crazy brown eyes had seen me mostly naked.

Two, he was into me.

Three, he knew my dad.

"Um, I don't think you got the memo, bud," Ryn said from behind me. "But we have protection. The serious kind."

The chair was set behind creepy guy, who I was assuming was the infamous Cisco, and creepy guy reached around to it.

He flipped it, sat in it in that man-way where he apparently was forced by the laws of nature to straddle the thing to prove he needed plenty of room for his big balls (which might be indicative he actually didn't have big balls), and he did this stating, "I know you got protection. But, you know, shit is real for me."

And he spoke all these words to Ryn, but he did it staring at me.

Ryn kept talking.

"By my estimation, you got T minus five minutes before our guys bust in here and kick the shit out of your guys."

He leaned into both arms folded on top of the back of the chair.

And he continued to talk to me.

"This will be a problem for them considering every entrance and a variety of scan spots outside are rigged to blow."

As my stomach started to burn, he tipped his head to the side and assumed a smile that made his creepy factor shoot through the roof, which in turn made my skin start to crawl.

Well, one good thing about that, and only one.

It was good we didn't try to escape.

"Did you know you can buy land mines?" he asked me. "Right here. In Denver. Got a guy, out on East Evans. Front of his shop, he does tailoring and alterations. In the back, though. That's where the fun stuff is."

I held his gaze, my stomach feeling sick, my throat feeling funny, like it was drying up while at the same time preparing to conduct vomit.

I did not want Mag to blow up.

I did not want any of the guys to blow up.

I didn't want any of my girls to blow up either.

And last, I, personally, did not want to blow up.

It didn't say a lot about me, but in that moment, I was uncertain if I wanted this creepy guy to blow up, but I was leaning toward yes.

However, so I didn't damn my soul to hell for thoughts such as that, I had to pull myself together and finesse this situation so *no one* blew up.

"I think I know what you're looking for, and I don't have it," I told him.

"I know. Your dad does."

I sat still as a statue and not because I was tied to a chair.

But my eyelids moved.

They did this to do a slow blink.

"Sorry?" I whispered when I could get my mouth working.

"Your dad?" he asked, but it was an answer. "Dirk. Dirk Gardiner. Not sure how it went for him. If Mick told him or if he figured it out on his own. However it went, he knew what you had so he tossed your apartment to find it. He jacked your trunk too."

"Oh my God," Hattie whispered.

But I didn't move.

Didn't speak.

This couldn't be true.

My dad was a loser, sometimes a lovable one, most of the time an annoying one.

But he wouldn't do that.

Not to me.

Not to me.

"So, I think, if I had a kid," creepy guy continued, "which I don't, but if I did, I'd probably give a shit about that kid. And if I had something I shouldn't, and someone wanted it back bad enough to take that kid and do not-nice things to her, and bonus," he threw his hand out, "to her friends, and do this until I got it back, I'd think about handing over what wasn't mine."

"I don't believe you," I whispered.

"You should," he replied.

"My dad doesn't have that gun," I said.

"Yes, he does," he returned.

"How do you know he has it?" I asked.

"Since he told me."

What?

And again...

WHAT?

I...

Could not.

Believe this!

Ryn's fingers curled stronger around mine.

Creepy guy, who I now knew for sure was Cisco, kept talking.

"He also told me he wanted five million dollars and he'd give it back. Now, I work hard, Evan. I mean," another one of those creepy grins, "there's time to have fun. Gotta carve out time to have some fun. But to get ahead in life, you gotta hustle. I've been hustling. Doing it a long time. I'm not gonna hand over money I worked hard for to some lowlife, pot dealer, rock star wannabe player."

His expression changed.

And at that change, my throat decided to conduct vomit and I had to struggle to keep it down.

And when he spoke again, it wasn't conversationally.

It was sinisterly.

"You think I'm gonna give my hard-earned money to some lowlife wannabe, Evan?"

I shook my head. "I've been giving my hard-earned money to a lowlife wannabe for years and it doesn't feel all that great. So, no, I don't think you are, and more, I'd advise against it. It leaves you feeling shitty."

Surprised at my response, he extended his neck and his eyebrows went up.

But I was feeling a lot less terrified.

This was because I was processing.

Processing the latest load of shit my family had landed on me.

It was my father who did that to my apartment.

It was *my father* who figured out what Mick had in that bag with those drugs and he'd frantically ripped apart everything I owned to get his hands on it.

My father.

"So, my brother put me here and my father *kept* me here," I stated.

"Not sure you should turn up at Thanksgiving," Cisco suggested.

I'd already made that decision.

"It's my understanding Dad's been telling people to leave me alone," I noted.

Cisco shrugged. "Sure. He *is* a dad. He just ain't a real great one."

He could say that again.

But I made a decision.

"Untie me and give me my phone," I demanded.

Cisco shot me another creepy smile and replied, "I'm feelin' some of the time we'll share together I don't want you tied, but I ain't givin' you your phone."

"Okay, give me yours."

He stared at me.

"Listen," I said. "I can handle all of this for you in about five minutes. I'll get you that gun and you can let us go."

"Evie," Ryn hissed.

I ignored her. "I assume you have my dad's number programmed in your phone. And actually, that'll work out better. My call coming from your phone. So I'll use that."

Cisco studied me but said nothing.

"Though, I want my phone too, so I can call Mag and tell him not to rescue us," I continued. "You see, I think you're getting an inkling that my family life isn't all that great. But my *life* life *is*. I have a new boyfriend. He's awesome. He's sweet. He thinks I'm the shit and he tells me that all the time. No one has ever told me that, until he entered my life."

Cisco's expression changed again, and weirdly, it changed like he was pissed on my behalf.

I couldn't give that my time.

I was busy finessing.

"We're moving in together. And I have a feeling he's going to give in on where we store the spices. I've also realized I have good friends, the best kind of friends you can have. I'm gonna go back to school. Finally, after a lot of crap, I've got things to look forward to. I have a life worth leading. And I'm gonna lead it. And I don't care what I have to do to make that happen without anyone getting hurt."

I moved my head around to indicate the girls and kept going.

"You don't know us, but we've all been through a ton of shit. Now, you can force us to endure more trauma, and that'd suck, and it'll be hard, but we'll survive. We'll get through. We've done it before. All of us. We'll do it again. Though it'd save a lot of time and a lot of money on therapy if you'd just give me my phone, and yours, so I can handle this for you."

"I'm feelin' you. I think I like you. You got spirit. And no matter what people think about me, I don't get off on hurting folks. At least not folks who didn't do dick to me," Cisco replied. "But you gotta understand why I won't do that."

"I don't," I retorted. "You want that gun. I want out of here. I want my friends out of here. And I want a Textual."

His head jerked on "Textual," but I just kept talking.

"So you promise to let us out of here, I'll get you that gun."

He started to shake his head, so I kept at him.

"I get shit is real for you. You've made shit real for me and my girls. Let's all breathe a little easier. Just untie one hand. I'm not asking for privacy. I'm not requesting the use of all my limbs. I'm good with the phone. I do one-handed all the time. This may affect my car insurance, but even if I've had a few bust-ups, I've never dropped a call."

Cisco held my eyes.

I returned the gesture.

"You can get me that gun?" he asked.

My heart jumped as hope flared.

I nodded, tried not to do it fervently, just confidently, and he watched me do it.

He didn't take his gaze off me when he said, "Get her bag."

Yes!

"Mine's the little brown one," I called when one of the men moved.

It wouldn't be that easy, I knew it wouldn't, but I didn't like how much harder it got when Cisco tipped his head to the other guy and that guy approached Pepper at my side.

I turned my head to watch him do this and my throat closed automatically against the bile racing up it when he pointed his gun at her head.

She emitted a whimper.

I started breathing in short spurts through my nose.

"So, you know," Cisco began, and I looked back to him, "I'll be listening, and if I feel you're gonna fuck me, you'll have her brains all over that nerdy shirt."

"I'm not gonna fuck you," I whispered.

He cocked his head to the side. "You're not a lot like your dad or your brother."

I pointed out the obvious. "I'm the black sheep in the family."

"You're not scared?" he asked.

"I'm terrified," I admitted. "I'm also a survivor."

"Mm," he hummed, watching me closely as the door opened. "Yeah, I think I like you," he decided.

Great.

The guy that came back in untied one of my hands and gave me my phone.

"Speaker," Cisco grunted.

I nodded.

Then I went to Favorites, called Mag and hit speaker.

He answered with a clipped, "Evie. Hang tight. We're—"

"Hey," I cut him off quickly. "You're on speaker, honey. I'm fine. The girls are fine. Everything's fine. Just back off. I've got something worked out with Cisco."

He sounded incredulous, and maybe a little freaked, when he asked, "What?"

"I've got something worked out with Cisco and he's got, uh...wherever we are wired to blow with land mines outside and stuff. So, you know, just stay safe, stand down and I'll call you in a bit with directions of where to pick us up."

"Evie—"

"*Be quiet and stand down, Mag,*" I snapped. "I have it covered. Just *be quiet* and listen for your phone. *Listen to your phone.* I'll call you."

I hoped he was now listening to me.

Really listening to me.

"Mag?" he asked.

Okay, he was listening to me. I never called him Mag. I thought of him as Mag, but when his name was in my mouth, he was Danny.

I didn't exactly know what I was communicating with that, I just wanted to catch his attention and make him really *hear me.*

"Quiet. Listen," I said. "Is Axl all right?"

"Yeah, he's right here with me."

Thank you, God.

"We'll be out soon, and I'll call," I finished.

I touched the screen, but I didn't disconnect the call and I hoped like all hell that Mag didn't say anything, which would mean his words coming through the speaker, because I wanted to get Pepper back to Juno. I wanted the girls to get the lead out and give the guys a shot.

And I wanted to go home to Mag.

Quickly, I put my phone facedown on my thigh and held my hand out for Cisco's phone.

It was shaking.

I didn't think this was bad. I wasn't a trained operative. My hand was going to shake. He'd expect that.

"Get me in your phone and dial Dad," I ordered. "I'll get him to talk to you about where he can hand off that gun."

Cisco looked at me and then he leaned back, opened his jacket and pulled out his phone.

He ran his thumb over the screen then handed the phone to the free guy.

I heard it ringing.

He had it on speaker.

I took in a very deep breath as that guy handed it off to me.

"Man," I heard my father's voice coming over the phone, and for a second, I was shocked silent, because he was using a tone I'd never heard.

Brisk. Bold. Strong.

Deep in the role of player.

I could assume a role too.

Or at least I hoped I could.

Dad kept speaking in that tone.

"I don't wanna be talkin' to you unless you got my money. You got twenty-four more hours before I hand this thing over to the cops."

"Dad!" I cried, all panicky. "Dad!"

Silence.

"Dad!" I exclaimed. "Cisco...Cis-Cis-Cisco! He has me! He has me and my girls! He kidnapped us from *Cherry Creek mall*."

"Evie?" Dad called.

"Dad! Please, just *please*. You gotta get him that gun! You gotta bring that gun to him where he tells you." I whimpered, then, "Please...*No!*" I shrieked. "God, *no!* Don't touch me! Don't touch me again! Don't touch *her!* *Get off her! I'm doing what you told me to do!*" I blew a harsh breath at the phone. "*Dad! Please! Help me! Give Cisco that gun! They're hurting me! Us! Help! Plea—*"

I cut myself off and jerked the phone toward Cisco.

The guy walked it to a grinning-again Cisco, and Cisco took it.

"You heard her," he said to my dad.

But he said no more since I screwed myself up and screamed bloody murder.

Cisco was out-and-out smiling at me when I went quiet, but the girls started making a ruckus.

"Yeah, motherfucker," Cisco was talking loud to be heard over the fake shouting and pleading for help. "An hour. That gun. Glazed and Confused. Broadway Market. I'll have the girls. You have that gun."

He paused a second.

Then he said, "You better," before he disconnected.

All the noise instantly stopped.

Cisco started smiling big again.

I curled my hand over my phone at my thigh.

"That was phenomenal," he shared.

"Glad you approve."

"Totally like you," he declared.

"If you really liked me, you'd take the gun away from Pepper's head."

"Oh, right," he muttered, then jerked up his chin at the guy on Pepper.

The guy stepped away and dropped his gun hand.

I heard Pepper's sigh of relief just as I had my own.

I was running my thumb over my screen in hopes of disconnecting from Mag before they took it away from me.

Thus, I was holding my breath when the guy by me reached in and took it away.

"I was kinda hoping I could keep that," I said quickly, so if Mag was still on the line, he'd hear, know I no longer had my phone, and he'd disconnect.

"You were hoping wrong," the guy grunted.

I shrugged and looked back to Cisco.

When I caught his eye, he asked, "Feel like donuts?"

I always felt like donuts.

Who didn't always feel the need for a donut?

Except now.

Now the thought of a donut made me feel queasy.

He'd ruined my day.

He'd ruined the girls' days.

And now he was ruining donuts.

Shit.

Nevertheless, I forced a grin that even felt like it was a grimace.

And I replied, "Sure."

CHAPTER TWENTY-TWO
Smarty Pants

EVIE

We were driving into the city and I didn't like it.

I didn't like it because I'd been separated from the Dream Team.

The girls were all in different cars.

I was sitting in the back of a shiny black Lincoln town car with Cisco, and we were in the lead.

"So, you have a new boyfriend," Cisco broke the silence we shared where I was tense and he seemed tense too, drumming his meaty fingers on his knee. "Hawk's boy."

"Yeah," I muttered to the window.

"You two solid?"

Oh God.

Apparently, this guy *really* liked me.

Gulk.

"Absolutely, one hundred percent solid," I told him.

He made no response.

Then he asked, "What about that one, the one who was sitting next to you?"

Wait.

What?

Seriously?

I turned my head his way.

"The one you had your guy turn his gun on?" I asked.

He gave me a "you know how it is" tick of his head and a crooked grin.

Bluh.

He also said, "Yeah, that one."

"Well, first, you kidnapped her and then you had one of your men hold a gun to her head. And second, she has a kid, and no offense, but she really loves her kid, so I don't think she'd be big on exposing her to bad influences."

"No offense taken," he assured.

Well, thank God for that.

"And I can't be dealin' with no other man's kid," he declared.

And the utter coolness, and true, real-man-ness of Auggie was all of a sudden proven.

"How about the one you were tied to?" he kept on.

"Ryn's a ballbuster. She'd put up with your stuff for a nanosecond."

His expression turned contemplative as he muttered, "Not big on nags."

I sighed.

Then I cut him off on his next pass.

"And before you ask, no on Hattie as well. She had an abusive father. I think she's had enough violence in her life."

At that, his expression turned inquisitive and focused.

And his voice went soft when he noted, "You don't have a very high opinion of me."

Was he insane?

"You had one of your men hold a gun to one of my friends' heads," I reminded him. "And you had us all kidnapped. Your guys shot at our friend. *And* you threatened to torture us."

And you're a cop killer, I did not say out loud.

"We weren't gonna torture you."

"So when you said you were gonna do not-nice things to us, what did you mean?"

"I was losin' steam on that the minute I walked in," he shared. "Goes against the grain to mess up a hot chick."

"But a chick you consider not hot is fair game?"

His dark, heavy brows jumped together. "Shit, you a feminist?"

"Yes," I retorted. "But it isn't just feminists who aren't fond of dudes messing up chicks of any persuasion."

He twisted toward me.

Fabulous.

Now we were having a full-on conversation.

"Why aren't you scared of me?" he asked.

"I *am* scared. But at this juncture, I'm more scared my dad is gonna do something stupid, screw things up, and put me and my girls back in danger."

"You probably shouldn't have told me that," he warned quietly.

"You know my dad. You're preparing for the same thing."

"Yeah," he admitted, still quietly.

I drew a sharp breath into my nose and looked out the window.

And to the window, I asked, "Can we make another deal?"

"Say it and I'll consider," he offered.

I looked back to him. "If Dad fucks this up, do whatever you intend to do to me. But let the girls go."

"Hate to say it, Evan, but I got more leverage with all of you. Hawk'll cave. Nightingale will too. Chaos would hand deliver that gun to me, tied with a bow if I asked, if it got a woman out of deep shit. Definitely four of them."

Evidence was suggesting I totally had the wrong end of the stick in my thoughts about dudes in motorcycle clubs.

"Right, then, let Pepper go so she can get home to Juno."

I hated making a deal that might keep Hattie and Ryn in deep shit.

But...

Juno.

When he didn't respond, I begged, "Please."

His eyes moved over my face.

I let him do this and I managed it without squirming.

He then whispered, "You really are not shit like your dad and brother."

"No, I'm not," I whispered back.

We stared at each other.

Then finally, he said, "I'll let the hot mom go."

My shoulders slumped and I said with feeling, "Thank you."

"Nerd girl," he murmured pensively, his eyes roaming my face. "Smart girl. Ballsy girl. Who'da thought?"

Okay, I'd successfully held it back, twice.

But I was thinking now, I was going to hurl.

He slid a few inches across the seat my way and I braced to stay strong.

"I got a lotta money, baby," he cajoled softly. "And I wouldn't let anything touch you. That life would be that life and you wouldn't even know it was happening. I'd take good care of you. I guarantee you that."

"In a way, I've had someone in my life who lives that life, I didn't know it, and look where I am, Cisco."

"My name is Brett."

How weird this guy had a normal name and his parents didn't name him Butch or Ebenezer or Boris or something.

He slid back. "And I take your point."

I released another breath and looked again out the window.

"Just to say, life happens, and it molds you into who you are."

He was defending his path to evil villainy.

I did not *think so*.

"Just to say," I told the window, "the same life happened to me and my brother and my brother chose who he is, and I chose something different."

There was a moment of silence before he muttered, "Girl like you could make me see the error of my ways."

I turned back to him at that.

"A girl like me has spent her whole life trying to guide people to the right path. She's failed. Repeatedly. And seriously, she's goddamned, fucking *tired*, Brett."

"You're breaking my heart, baby," he murmured, and honest to God, he looked like the words he spoke were true.

I turned fully to him and slid a bit his way this time, and I did it to say, "You know, when you find a woman who holds a piece of that heart, remember this conversation, and don't tire her out."

We stared into each other's eyes for long beats before he nodded.

I slid away, righted myself in the seat, crossed my arms on my chest and watched out the front window.

I heard his movements and knew he was on his phone, but as far as I was concerned, our conversation was over.

I had other things to occupy my mind.

I was assuming Mag had heard our conversation, so he, and the guys, were going to have something planned for Glazed & Confused. And I knew they knew what they were doing, but I was still worried because I didn't know if Cisco's guys knew the same.

I could almost guarantee my dad was going to be at Glazed & Confused and he was going to pull something.

Further, there was little doubt there would be a number of customers at Glazed & Confused. Innocent bystanders who had no idea the perpetrators behind the firefight played out in Cherry Creek mall earlier that day were going to show and, very likely, obliterate their happy, donut good times.

And my life, and the lives of my friends, were in the hands of a bad guy who killed a cop who clearly really liked me.

He finished doing whatever he was doing on his phone and called, "Evan?"

I was noting the town car was slowing to a stop.

But we weren't at Glazed & Confused.

We were on Fifteenth Street close to Larimer Square.

Oh shit.

I looked to Cisco. "Why are we stopping?"

"This guy, your man, he's good to you?"

"Yes," I said swiftly. "Yes. Mag. My guy. My boyfriend. He...he's the best. The best boyfriend ever. Numero uno. I've never...he makes me really, *really* happy."

Cisco leaned deep and I sat solid and stared, feeling my eyes get big and my heart thump in my chest.

And a chill raced up my spine at the way he said his next.

"You tell him to stay good to you, Evan."

I didn't speak or move.

"Now get out, baby. That building," he tipped his chin. "Nightingale Investigations is in that building. Get you and your girls up there. They'll take care of you."

I couldn't believe what I was hearing.

"You...you're letting us go?"

His gaze slid down my torso then back up.

"Don't give me a chance to change my mind, because straight up, I got a strong urge to keep you."

I turned so fast, I opened the door and tried to get out without releasing my seatbelt.

I heard his chuckle, reached, released, and shot out of the car.

The girls were all out of their own cars, looking at me, each other, confused, but I reached my hand their way and shouted, "Come with me!"

They came with me, Hattie getting to me first.

She took my hand.

Pepper took Hattie's hand.

Ryn took Pepper's hand.

And we raced to the door of the office building.

I yanked it open and dashed in, only to slam into something solid, and I did it four times. The time I hit it. The time Hattie slammed into my back, Pepper into hers and Ryn into hers.

In a sandwich, I looked up at a tall, gorgeous, Hispanic guy who looked so much like Eddie Chavez, for a second I thought he *was* Eddie Chavez.

I didn't get to say hi or ask if he knew he looked just like this hot police officer I knew before he took my hand and dragged us all into the building.

He did not hit the elevators.

I was considering breaking my vow never to own workout clothes so I could take kickboxing classes by the time we raced up four flights of steps and we got to the floor where he pushed through the door.

Through my wheezing, I saw right away Shirleen standing in the hall outside a door.

She got a load of us and said, "Well, shit."

She then disappeared through the door that hadn't quite closed before the guy dragging our snake of strippers got to it.

He shoved it open, pulled us in and didn't stop pulling once we were inside.

I just had time to glance at Shirleen where she was standing behind an impressive, gleaming blond wood receptionist desk as he pulled us through and I saw she was on the phone, saying, "Our eyes weren't deceiving us. They're here. Hector's locking them down now."

This while I heard a buzz, and the guy, obviously named Hector, dragged us in another door, into a hall, down it, and then shuffled us into a small room that had a bed, a recliner, a bookshelf full of books and DVDs, a TV and that was it.

"You're safe," he declared. "And your men will get you after they deal with Cisco."

On that, he walked out the door and closed it behind him.

I stared at it.

And Pepper murmured a repeat of Shirleen's "Well, shit."

"Unh-hunh," Hattie mumbled.

Ryn stepped in front of all of us, put her hands on her hips, and remarked, "I'm pretty sure the Rock Chicks had a ton more drama. Am I crazy to think that was anticlimactic and be disappointed there wasn't more drama?"

This from the one of us who'd survived a gunfight in a mall parking lot that day.

In unison, we all answered...

"Yes."

The door to the room opened and Shirleen stood there.

We all looked to her.

I suspected we all also expected jubilation that we were alive and breathing. Congratulations we'd kept our shit together through another kidnapping. And news about what was going down.

We all had forgotten she'd lived through the Rock Chicks.

So we did not get any of that.

She asked, bizarrely, "Have all you all seen the movie *300*?"

"Greatest...movie...*ever*," Pepper decreed breathily.

"Right, I'll get the popcorn," Shirleen declared. "Be right back."

And then she was gone.

* * *

"Tex! Don't thump on it! It's already broken! It doesn't need to be wrecked beyond repair!" Indy shouted over Tex assaulting the cash register.

"I can't work under these conditions!" Tex boomed back, jabbing an irate finger at the till. "I'm on strike until that fucking thing is fucking *fixed*!"

"I'm sorry, I think I calculated that wrong. Hang on. Let me go again," Jet said to a customer, then she bent back over the calculator she was using.

"Fucking *fuck*! See! It's taking *years* just to get a goddamned order!" Tex bellowed.

"*For the last time*!" Indy screeched. "Stop saying *fuck* in front of the customers."

I was sitting on the couch in front of the window at Fortnum's, my fingers curled around the dregs of a Textual, my eyes aimed unseeing at the coffee table in front of me, listening to pandemonium at a used bookstore and coffee emporium.

Here's the catch-up:

I'd now met Vance Crowe and again witnessed all that was Luke Stark.

The latter had opened the door to the room right when King Leonidas bit into the apple.

We were all lying about the bed, piled on top of each other (though Shirleen was in the recliner), waiting for word (okay, maybe desperate for word), so we all jumped when the door opened.

And although I thought I might have heard Hattie sigh at the sight of the big, built, dark-haired man in the doorway, I just wanted to know how Mag was.

"It's all cool," Luke Stark announced. "Boys are at the cop shop, givin' a report. Time for coffee."

That was it.

He did not go into detail.

And he did not look like a dude you pressed for details.

Therefore, none of us pressed him for details.

Vance Crowe seemed slightly more approachable, but totally more impatient.

"One of his boys has the flu, he's hankerin' to get home," Shirleen told me.

"How many boys does he have?" I asked.

"A thousand," she answered.

That would require a large harem, and by the looks of that guy, he could not only amass that, he could also service it.

That said, I didn't think Jules would be down.

Without further ado, Stark and Crowe took us to Fortnum's.

When we arrived, a gaggle of the Rock Chicks were there. Shirleen had come with us. Gert was waiting fretfully for our return, then she got ornery when we showed and threatened to legally adopt me. Smithie was also there and declared after our latest scenario (even if it wasn't any of the guys' fault) he wasn't a big fan of any of his girls hooking up with a commando, so his vote was no across the board to all the matches. And Lottie was sitting with him, but she just ignored him and went to the coffee counter to get us Textuals.

And last, the cash register was broken so Tex was in a state.

"So... what? The bad guy has a crush on Evie?" Roxie, perched on the arm of a chair, was asking.

"Not surprised about that," Gert said.

Man, even if Cisco/Brett being into me still gave me the willies, I loved Gert.

"He's creepy, but at least it made him drop us off rather than keep us captive," Pepper remarked.

"I was kinda in the mood for a donut," Ryn put in.

"Then that's what we should do," Gert decreed. "Go get donuts. It's loud in here."

"We're not allowed to leave," Hattie whispered to Gert. "Luke Stark said we had to stay here until the guys got here."

"You don't have to say Luke Stark's full name every time you talk about him, Hatz," Pepper told her.

"That man is too much man for one name. Two syllables barely cover him," Hattie replied.

I had to admit, she was right about that.

"Okay," Jet was saying, "I know the latte is four dollars

and fifty-seven cents, with tax, and the cookie is a buck fifty. But no one just buys a cookie, so I'm just gonna have to guess on tax for that. So let's say six twenty-five and if you give me—"

Enough!

I couldn't hack it.

"Sales tax is eight point three one percent, which makes the cookie a dollar and sixty-two cents," I called, getting up and heading toward the barista counter. "Add the latte, it's six dollars and nineteen cents. She's giving you a twenty, that's thirteen dollars and eighty-one cents change."

Everyone had stopped talking (and shouting) and was staring at me.

I moved behind the counter and shoved through Indy and Tex, edged out Jet and stared at the cash register.

"I need a screwdriver and the key," I announced.

"On it," I heard Indy say.

"Key's right here," Jet said, reaching to the shelf under the register and pulling out a rectangular Tupperware filled with Sharpies, paper clips, baby binder clips, a couple bouncy balls and a pack of Bubblemint-flavored Orbit gum.

It also had a key, which she pulled out and handed to me.

I opened the top of the register and Indy showed with the screwdriver, so I also opened the plate at the base.

I pulled the top off, looked at the mess inside, made an immediate diagnosis and turned to Indy.

"From the looks of it, this has had approximately five hundred and twenty-seven coffees spilled on it. It's a miracle it worked at all. However, the latest spill means it's gasped its last breath. It's a wash. You need a new register."

"Shit," Indy muttered.

"You did all that math in your head?" Tex asked.

"I'm good with math. I'm usually good with this kind of stuff too." I waved a hand to the register. "But at a guess, that was made in 1982. It was probably time to say good-bye two decades ago." I turned my attention to Indy. "You should upgrade to a tablet-based POS system. Not only are they rad, they save tons of space, and have business, tech, data and environmental features you'll like. If you still want the feel of a register, or deal in a lot of cash, they've got tablet-based with a cash drawer. I can do some research for you and help you set it up if you want."

Indy, Tex, Jet (and I could feel it, everyone) were staring at me.

No one said anything.

And then Tex muttered (trying to make his lips not move, and failing) to Indy, "What does 'POS' mean?"

"Point of sale," Indy muttered back.

"Gotcha," he replied.

"Will you train us on it?" Indy asked me.

I shrugged my shoulders. "Sure."

"She charges one hundred and fifty dollars an hour," Gert called.

I shook my head at Indy trying to look like I wasn't shaking my head at Indy.

She grinned at me and said, "We'll work something out."

"Seven times forty-two," Tex threw out at me.

"Two hundred and ninety-four," I told him.

"Check that, Loopy Loo," Tex ordered Jet (he called her Loopy Loo, I had no idea why, but it was cute). Then to me, he shot, "Two hundred and ninety-four minus eighty-two plus one hundred and twenty."

"Three thirty-two."

"Three thirty-two times thirty-two."

That one, I had to give a second.

Then I answered, "Uh, ten thousand and um, six hundred and twenty-four."

"Holy crap," Jet breathed, looking up from her calculator. "She's right."

Tex grinned a maniacal grin (that was kinda cute too). "Fuckin' A, smarty-pants, I'm impressed."

I shrugged again but felt my cheeks heat, not with embarrassment, with pride.

That feeling was a first for me.

And it far from sucked.

"Got me a girl who's been hiding her light under a bushel, which can't be easy, since she's naked most the time she's in my joint," Smithie said.

Oh man.

I slowly turned my gaze to Smithie and caught myself from biting my lip, because soon, I would not be naked in his joint at all.

He looked at my face and then he screwed up his face and looked at mine harder.

Uh-oh.

"You're quitting," he accurately deduced.

"Smithie, it's just that I want to go to school and—" I began.

He lifted his hand my way and I stopped talking.

"You're quitting?" Hattie asked, sounding freaked.

"I knew she'd quit," Pepper said to Ryn.

"Mm-hmm," Ryn said to Pepper.

"Smithie—" Lottie started.

"No. Nope." He shook his head and dropped his hand, still scowling at me. He turned to Lottie. "I know men like this. All's said and done, I won't have any girls left. So I do not give *any* of these matches my blessing. Hear me?"

"Smithie," Lottie said softly.

"I like these ones," Smithie declared, throwing an arm out to encompass all of us girls. "If I have to get new ones, I might not like 'em."

"Smithie, you like everybody," Lottie reminded him.

"I don't like you right now," he retorted.

She smiled at him. "Big, softhearted liar. You want them all to be happy. You're just gonna miss her. Admit it."

"I'll come and visit," I called.

"You will?" Hattie asked hopefully.

"Totally," I told her. "And I'll arrange a...a game night at Danny and my place. We'll play Dungeons and Dragons."

Lottie, Ryn, Pepper, Hattie, nor Roxie, Shirleen, or Sadie (who was also hanging out in the seating area, another Rock Chick, this one married to Hector) looked fired up about D&D.

Smithie turned on me. "You movin' in with him?"

"We already live together, Smithie."

"Because you were in danger of being kidnapped," he returned. "That's how it goes. Bitch is in distress, man moves her in, covers her ass—"

"Then keeps her there, marries her and fills her with babies. You've been through this nine times, Smithie," Lottie told him. "It's time to get with the program."

"Eight," he fired back. "I wasn't around for Indy. And all but one of the other ones, that one being *you*, didn't dance for me," he shot back.

"Well, you know, it's next gen. Go with the flow," she advised.

The bell over the door rang at this juncture, and when it did, Gert said, "Oh Lord," and Shirleen said, "You got that right, sister."

I looked to the door.

And understood immediately what they were talking about.

Mag was standing there, all the guys fanned out behind him.

I didn't take in any of the boys.

Because Mag's eyes were on me.

Nope.

Scratch that.

His eyes shooting electric-blue gamma rays were pinning me to the spot, the heat from them so hot, it felt like the soles of my Chucks were on fire.

"We're leaving now," he announced, in a growly, hot, scary voice.

I didn't take this as an indication I'd get news about what went down at Glazed & Confused with him, the guys, my dad and Brett/Cisco.

I took this as Mag being pissed.

For some reason at *me*.

Oh boy.

CHAPTER TWENTY-THREE

Danny

EVIE

The first thing I noticed as Mag opened the passenger-side door of his truck was that my purse was sitting on the seat.

As was my Nordstrom bag.

I looked up at him.

"How did you—?"

"Get in the truck, Evan."

Okay, we were on uncertain ground here.

Frightening uncertain ground.

And in order not to escalate that feeling, wordlessly, I reached out, grabbed both bags and climbed into his truck.

By the time he angled in beside me, I had the Nordstrom bag on the floor at the side of my feet, my purse in my lap and my seatbelt on.

He said nothing as he engaged the ignition, scanned his mirrors and pulled out.

I also said nothing as he did this, for it was dawning on me I might have made a terrible mistake.

He had anger issues. He was very open about that. They were such, they concerned him.

But honest to God, until that moment, they didn't concern me.

I thought, even if I didn't have the tools to help him handle them, I'd have the patience where *I* could handle them.

Now, considering I didn't do anything for him to be angry about, but it was not only clear he was angry with me, it had been hours since we'd been set free and I had no idea what had happened at Glazed & Confused with my own *father*—something I felt *should* be reported to me with all due haste—but everyone was alive, well and safe, I didn't know *why* he was mad at me...or anybody.

And bottom line, I'd had a really bad day.

A *really* bad day.

My friends and I had been kidnapped, some of them shot at.

My dad was a big jerk.

Some bad guy was into me.

And maybe, I thought, with all of that, a little gentleness and understanding would not go amiss.

Thus, truth be told, I was a little hurt that I had Angry Mag and not my normal Sweet Affectionate Mag.

This was not cause to throw in the towel on our relationship.

It wasn't even cause to be angry myself.

What it was, was an indication that perhaps I'd been hasty in agreeing to fast-track a relationship with a man who had a life, a past, his own issues, and I did not have a lot of experience or understanding of any of that.

Truthfully, he seemed perfect.

And that was too much weight to put on anybody.

Even someone as strong as Mag.

He'd turned off Broadway to Lincoln and then onto Speer, heading north, when I began, "Danny—"

"You do not call me Mag."

I shut my mouth because that wasn't what I was expecting.

"You never call me Mag," he went on.

Okay, his voice was tight, a little rough, he was pissed, but not out of control.

I could work with this.

"But, I was trying to—"

"I know what you were trying to do," he bit out. "But you had my attention, Evan. You always have my attention. But after you're taken by Denver's most wanted lunatic, you absolutely fucking have my attention. So you do not *ever* call me Mag. I'm Danny to you."

One could say I was significantly confused as to why this had such great meaning to him, but I was sensing I should broach that subject at a later date.

And for now, say what I said.

"All right, Danny."

He let that settle for a beat before he spoke again.

"You should know, I was pissed. Out of my mind *pissed*. After it was all said and done, that's why it took so long to get to you. The boys saw it and they made me have a sit-down with them to talk it out. That was how pissed I was. I'm still pissed, but this is a discussion. I'm not gonna lose it."

"Okay," I whispered. "But can I, uh, ask, well...*why* you were so pissed?"

A very heavy vibe settled in the cab before he asked, "Why I was so pissed?"

I looked to him, saw how hard his jaw was, the tenseness around his eyes.

I nevertheless persevered.

"Yes, honey, I'm okay. The girls are okay. I'd like to know what's going on with Dad, but—"

"Evan, you do not *handle* a guy like Cisco. You do not *make deals* with him. You do not *work things out* with him. You do not do *shit* to circumvent what people who know what they're *fucking doing* are planning in order to get you and your friends safe. It doesn't matter. You're never gonna be in that position again. But, God fucking forbid, if you are, sit tight, shut up and wait for the people who know what they're goddamn doing to sort shit out for you."

Okay.

Now it was time for me to get pissed.

"All right, Danny, next time *you* get kidnapped, after you're safe, I'll weigh in on how you should have handled it. That work for you?" I asked sharply.

"Evan," he growled, "you are not hearing me."

"I heard every word you said," I snapped. "And really, as lame as this is, how fucking *dare you*."

He shut his mouth.

"He had that place wired to blow," I informed him. "The guys are my friends. I wasn't big on them being blown to pieces. *You* mean the world to me, so obviously, I didn't want that in your future. And by the by, if someone had perchance *talked* to me or *any* of the girls about what we saw and heard, we could not only tell you where that place is, we could tell you that Brett informed us there's a tailor on Evans who deals in explosives behind his shop."

"Brett?"

"Yes," I bit out. "*Brett.*"

"You know, baby," he said in a smooth, velvety voice that nevertheless gave me a chill, "I got a call, personally, from *Brett*, informing me where we could go to find your girls' bags."

Oh shit.

Mag must have felt my changing vibe because he purred, "Oh yeah. He was all about making sure he returned what he confiscated from you when he fucking abducted you."

Yikes.

"He also," Mag went on, "shared, if I didn't treat you right, he'd cut off my balls and shove them down my throat."

Eek!

"So," he continued, "you wanna talk to me again about how you should have handled that sitch?"

I was understanding now why he was pissed.

It wasn't jealousy, per se.

It also maybe kinda was.

"He's creepy," I said.

"*I know he's fucking creepy!*" Mag exploded. "Jesus Christ, Evan, could you not be *you* long enough you didn't give some crazy-ass felon the hots for you?"

It was highly inappropriate at that juncture, but I had the desperate desire to giggle.

I must have made a noise because Mag grunted, "Nothin' about this is fucking funny."

He was wrong.

I didn't share that.

"It's over, honey," I reminded him quietly.

"Yeah, you wanna know how over it is?" he asked, and the way he asked it, I knew I didn't want to know.

I still said, "Okay."

"It's very fucking over because *Brett* assured me not only that you no longer had to harbor any concerns that he might cause you or your friends any harm, you could rest in the knowledge that *no one* would cause you or your girls any harm or he'd intervene."

"Oh my God," I breathed, not wanting a cop killer at my back, and also wishing he weren't a cop killer because evidence was suggesting this guy could be redeemed, if he hadn't done something entirely irredeemable.

"Right," Mag clipped. "So, you got yourself a champion, baby. Though not sure how he'll keep his finger on that pulse, seeing as he's particles. Cops have that gun. He knows the cops got that gun. So, it's just a hunch, but I'd bet big money on the fact that Cisco is nowhere near Denver right now and has no plans of coming back."

That'd be my hunch too.

He was creepy, but he didn't give any indication he was stupid.

Mag continued speaking.

"They also have your dad. Eddie and Hank, Slim and Mitch want me to share the gratitude of the entire DPD that you sorted that for them. Though, as I mentioned, who they don't have is Cisco, seeing as he's got a sixth sense when it comes to the preservation of his own ass and he never showed at Glazed and Confused. My guess, he thinks your dad screwed him and is in the dark that it was you who tipped who had that gun, or he wouldn't throw down for you."

I homed in on one part of that.

"The cops have Dad?" I asked.

"Accomplice after the fact," Mag answered. "I put two and two together, and his fingerprints found at your pad and on your car that they previously put down to him being your dad, now he's being charged with vandalism and burglary. And a search of his home found that dope stash, which was too hot to move, but he was clearly willing to wait it out, so he kept it. This means they also got him on possession with intent to distribute. Considering he was found in possession of a weapon that killed a cop, even if it wasn't his, he didn't turn it in, the police are motivated to make something stick. So I'd brace, Evie, because he's going down, one way or another."

I looked to my lap and started to fiddle with the strap on my bag.

"Evie?" Mag called.

I stopped fiddling with the strap on my bag, faced front and said nothing.

But suddenly, I felt the mood in the cab lighten.

"Fuck, baby," Mag murmured, reaching out and taking hold of my hand. "I'm sorry. I was a dick in how I relayed that."

"It would hurt even if you were nice about it," I told him, my voice flat.

He heard my voice, which was probably why he forced his fingers through mine, and with them laced, held on tight, pulling my hand to his thigh.

"Yeah, it would hurt," he agreed. "But I should always be nice. I should never be a dick to you. It's no excuse, but when you called from the mall, flipped out, then were cut off, and then Axl called it in that Cisco got you, it tweaked me. It was a certain kind of hell, knowing he had you, tryin' to keep my head in the game as Hawk and the boys strategized a rescue mission. Then you called, and with how you did, I knew you were swinging your ass way out there, and that didn't tweak me, it freaked me."

Oh.

Well then.

One could say it didn't once occur to me to think how it would feel to be on Mag's side of this situation.

But now that he was sharing, I realized his day had been (almost) as bad as mine.

"Then my relief when the Nightingale team reported that you were safe didn't last long when Cisco made it clear you charmed his shit," he carried on. "I'm not a jealous guy, but I'm also not a guy who wants another guy openly into my woman. Definitely not throwing down for her. And *definitely* not someone like Cisco bein' her latest fan."

Hmm.

"I was kinda involved in what was happening to me and the girls," I admitted. "I didn't think about what you were going through."

"Babe, I didn't tell you that to get your sympathy. I told you that to explain why, since I saw you in Fortnum's, I was acting like a dick."

"Now that I know, it doesn't seem like you've been a dick. Just... venting."

"Right," he muttered, giving my fingers a squeeze.

I squeezed his back.

And there we were.

My uncertainty washed away, and I was back on the fast track with Mag.

Because Mag was ticked, he worked it out with the guys, he shared with me, we worked it out.

And we ended all that holding hands.

"I can get you in to see your dad if you want," he offered.

No.

I did not want.

"It could have been over for me. Easy," I declared. "I

had that bag to hand off to Snag and then I was out. Mick dragged me in, but Dad kept me in, and it's a miracle that things turned out the way they did. It wasn't fun, and you got hurt, but we can all move on, only by a miracle. Anything changed, like today, a stray bullet hit Ryn, or Axl took one, or Cisco didn't like me, or those calls I made to you or Dad didn't go as I'd hoped and that guy shot Pepper, and then Juno wouldn't have a mom. The alternate scenarios are too frightening to even contemplate. And my fucking *brother* and *father* put me and people I care about in those scenarios."

I looked to him.

And I then asked, "With all of that, what do you say to someone who did that to you? Who knowingly, for their own ends, put you in that spot? That someone, or those *someones* being your very own blood?"

"I don't know, honey," he whispered, his fingers tightening on my hand.

"Nothing," I said. "There's nothing to say." I turned forward again. "And the funny thing is, I also feel nothing. Not about that. But I'm pissed because what I *do* feel is like I'm mourning the death of someone I should care about. And I'm doing that even though they never gave me the people they were supposed to be for me. I've lost a brother and a father that I never really had in the first place."

I looked to him when I had to shift his way because he lifted my hand to press it against his heart.

And I watched when he lifted it again, to touch his lips to my fingers.

Then he set it back down on his thigh and spoke.

"Only thing I got to give you is, it's over."

For long moments, I stared at his long, strong fingers

threaded through mine, still feeling the soft touch of his lips, before I closed my eyes and again turned forward.

I opened them and muttered, "Yeah."

We fell silent.

We were close to his complex when I broke it to say, "Smithie knows I'm quitting."

"Well, shit," he said gently, "that means my girl *really* had a bad day."

That made me smile because he was right with what he was saying without actually saying it.

Everyone was okay.

But Smithie didn't want to lose me, he now knew he was losing me, it upset him, and Smithie mattered.

So upsetting him, even if we knew he'd get over it, even with all we'd been through that day, was what *really* made it a bad day.

"Do you like the movie *300*?" I asked.

"Fucking kickass," he said as answer.

And that made me smile, this time doing it big.

Because yet again, we agreed.

He pulled into his underground parking and we were parked, out, Mag had the Nordstrom bag, I had my purse hanging cross body, and we were holding hands and standing in front of the elevator after Mag tagged the button, when I broached it.

"Why is it so important to you that you're Danny to me?"

He looked down at me and did not hesitate to lay it out, and in doing so, lay *me* out.

But in a totally, freaking awesome way.

He started this by saying, "That guy was dead, until you."

I stared up at him. "What?"

"I used to be Danny. Danny the football stud. Danny the overprotective big brother. Danny the master at beer pong. Life was good with no indication it wouldn't always be that way. I had no idea how shit life could be for so many people. Entire countries filled with people living complete nightmares. And when I learned that, beer pong lost its meaning. Fun never seemed fun because in my throat, I could still feel the dust, and remember what others endured, continued to endure, and that tinged everything with a thick coat of shit."

"Danny," I whispered, all the distress and helplessness I felt weighing heavy on his name.

The elevator doors opened.

We both ignored them.

"Then you kept calling me Danny," he said. "And I didn't give it time to process it, I just knew I liked it. I knew how it made me feel. Today, I realized, I need to be Danny for you. I need to remember I can't make life okay for every being on this planet, and it sunk in that logically, that's impossible. But what I *can* do is make it okay for you. I can be the overprotective boyfriend. I can get off on making my girl breakfast, and eating pancakes with her that, for the first time in years, don't taste like sand, because I'm eating them at her side and life is good because I'm doing the only thing I have any control over doing. Playing my part in making it good for her, and for me."

Oh God.

I was going to cry.

No, I *was* crying.

I felt the tear slide down my cheek, followed by another one.

"Baby," he murmured, watching the wet fall.

"You wanted to rescue me today," I guessed.

His gaze came to mine.

"No. I *needed* to rescue you today."

Right, so maybe he was a little jealous of Brett.

And maybe he'd been tweaked, then freaked.

But mostly, he needed me to need him.

"I might have gotten the girls and me out of a jam today, honey," I began. "But I'm always gonna need you to be Danny for me. Do you understand that?"

He nodded once. "Yeah."

"And I'll never call you anything but Danny," I swore. "Not ever again."

He grinned at me, let my hand go and framed my face at one side, his thumb sweeping through the wet.

"And next time I'm kidnapped, I'll sit tight and let you rescue me." I promised that but quickly added, "Though I reserve the right to make alternate arrangements should there be certain peril for you, or, say, it's a group abduction, like today, and the majority vote is to try to escape. I wouldn't want to be a bad team player."

He frowned.

Again quickly, I continued, "And you can make breakfast for me every day until the end of time."

He stopped frowning.

"Deal," he said softly.

I swayed toward him.

His hand at my cheek slid into my hair, his other arm curled around me, the Nordstrom bag hit the back of my thigh, but I didn't notice because his head came down to mine, and we started necking in front of the elevator.

We did this like we'd never done it before.

In other words, it didn't get hot and heavy.

It was just about intimacy, sharing, closeness, and yes,

I was going to think it even if I wasn't ready to express it any other way.

Love.

We broke it when the elevator doors opened again, and a guy said, "Whoa. Sorry."

Danny shuffled me to the side, murmuring, "No, we're sorry."

The guy gave us an assessing look, lips quirking, and headed off to his car.

Danny pulled me into the elevator.

"Mentioning *300*, you wanna watch that tonight?" he asked when we were going up.

"Yeah. Maybe order Chinese?" I answered.

"You got it."

"We have ice cream, right?"

"Always."

Shit day.

But I was with Danny.

And we had ice cream and movies.

So it was going to be a good night.

The elevator stopped, the doors opened, Danny took my hand and pulled me out, but halted almost immediately.

I did it too, looked up at him and then in the direction of his stare.

Sidney and Rob were loitering outside his door.

Shit, damn, hell.

"Hey," I called.

"Hey?" Sidney asked irately. "You were kidnapped again today, and you say 'hey'?"

"Elvira," Danny murmured, my guess, as to the culprit of who spilled the beans to my family about today's adventures, not to mention gave them details about where Danny lived.

"I'm fine, it's all good, it's all over," I assured as I tugged on Danny's hand and took him their way.

"We know. Elvira reported in," Sidney shared.

Yep.

The elusive yet omnipresent Elvira.

"And Dad called me to see if I'd set up bail for him," she went on as Danny and I stopped close to them. "By the by, I'm pretty proud of myself that I didn't screech the word *no* in a pitch that was guaranteed to explode his eardrum, I just said it and then hung up on him."

Danny cut in at this point, letting my hand go to stick his out to Rob and say, "You're Rob, I'm Dan Magnusson."

Dan Magnusson?

I got a gooey, happy feeling because maybe today Danny didn't just realize why he needed to be Danny to me.

Maybe today he realized he could also give badass Mag a break, and let a cool, sweet, affectionate, handsome, amazing guy named Dan into his life.

And that was *awesome*.

"Dan, yeah, Rob," Rob greeted, taking his hand, studying his face, and when neither man moved for one beat, two, three, *four*, I dropped my eyes and noted how firm a grip they had on each other.

Right, so, he'd introduced himself as Dan.

But Mag was never going to be far away.

That made me happy too.

Because, not a shocker, I'd fallen head over heels in love with a commando called Mag.

"Before you two break all the bones in the other's hand," Sidney started, "maybe we can go in and get the rundown on Evan's latest abduction."

They broke off, Danny's mouth twitching, and he turned to the door.

"Again, I'm fine, everyone's fine. It wasn't a fun day, but at least it's all over," I assured, Danny having opened the door and claimed me again, so I spoke as he was tugging me inside.

My family, what was left of it, followed.

"I can see you're fine, but how is this all over?" Sidney asked.

Danny had dumped the Nordstrom bag on the island and was turning on lights.

I was turning to face off with my sister.

"Can I not have to do a blow by blow right now?" I requested.

"Anyone want a beer?" Danny asked.

I twisted to give him big eyes because I loved my sister, I loved Rob, but I was down for *300*, Chinese, an orgasm where I was sure Danny wouldn't mind doing all the work, and then sleep.

What I wasn't down with was having a beer with Sidney grilling me about my day, and Rob doing whatever he was going to do to ascertain he approved of my boyfriend.

But at my big eyes, he just allowed his face to go soft (nice, but that didn't cut it) and then he winked at me (shit, that worked) as Rob answered, "I'll have one."

"I don't drink beer. Do you have vodka?" Sidney asked.

I sighed.

Then I went stiff because two arms closed around me and they did this tight.

They were Rob's arms.

I relaxed and slid mine around him too.

"I'm okay," I whispered.

"Fuck, fuck, fuck me," he whispered back, these words thick and agonized and said into the top of my hair.

Right, so it wasn't only Danny who'd had a rough go of

the last few weeks while a woman he cared about was in danger.

And...

All right, yeah.

I still had family.

Also, a big fat *oh no*.

Because I was going to cry again.

I sniffled.

His arms got even tighter.

I lost it.

Damn.

Okay, so maybe it all came crashing down on me in that moment, but yeah, there I was, in Rob's arms, bawling.

And then I wasn't in Rob's arms. He shifted me so I was in Danny's arms.

Wow, that didn't take long.

A firm handshake, the offer of a beer, and comforting arms, and he had Rob Approval.

So, of course, this meant I started crying harder.

"She has to get it out," Danny said, obviously not to me.

"I'll do the drinks," Sidney offered quietly.

"And it really is over," Danny said, my guess, to Rob, specifically, but also to both of them.

"You sure about that?" Rob asked.

"Nothing's ever sure, man, and you don't know me, but I'm in love with your girl and you're important to her so I would never lie to you about something like that."

What?

Wait.

Whoa.

What?

Oh my God!

Holy shit!

Danny just told me he was in love with me by telling my stepdad he was in love with me.

I grabbed hold of his shirt and started wailing.

GAH!

"Don't let that freak you out, she's a crier," Sidney advised. "I had to turn off a video I thought was cool that had this fireman doing CPR on this cat, who he brought back to life through kitty chest compressions, because she completely lost it."

I tipped my head back.

Danny looked down at me.

"Y-you too," I said, meaning I was in love with him too.

He knew what I meant, and I knew he knew because I got his soft face again, but this time it was even softer, and it also was the most beautiful thing I'd ever seen.

"Good," he whispered, moving his hands to smooth my hair out of my face before he tucked my cheek to his chest and rounded me with his arms again, holding me warm and close.

I relaxed into him, held him the same way, and snuffled.

"We were gonna get Chinese," he announced. "You two in?"

Yeesh.

A beer was one thing.

Dinner?

But I knew what he was doing.

Today, I'd forever and always lost half of my family.

And I came home with the other half waiting outside the door to see if I was okay.

So he was making certain I knew I still had something of meaning.

Still, we could all go out for Chinese some other time.

Like, next week.

"I'm in," Sidney said.

"We're not intruding?" Rob asked.

Yes! I thought. *We just "told" each other we were in love!*

"Not at all," Danny said.

I let out a breath and relaxed further into him.

"Are you two gonna become one right there by the is-land? Or, Evie, are you gonna break off so you can give me and Rob a tour of this shit-hot pad?" Sidney asked.

I tipped my head back to look at Danny again.

He dipped in to touch his lips to my forehead.

Yikes, but I loved it when he did that.

"I'll order Chinese, you do the tour," he told me.

"Got it," I replied.

He gave me a squeeze before he let me go and asked the room at large, "Orders?"

Sidney was now at his windows that faced Denver.

I was swiping at my cheeks when she turned to me and declared, "Nighttime, just like this. Sister selfie. Denver at our back. Both of us in a tank top. Big hair. Red lips. I'll get, like, five thousand likes."

"I'm uncertain I want a social media presence," I told her.

She rolled her eyes. "How you can be a tech nerd and not have Snapchat is beyond me."

"The true tech nerds wrote the code that became the app that is Snapchat and you probably have no idea what they look like," I returned.

"Whatever," she muttered.

"Sidney likes spring rolls and moo shu chicken. Evie likes crab Rangoon and sesame chicken. I'll eat any of that," Rob ordered for Sidney and me, and the fact he could made me realize that I needed what Danny knew I needed when I didn't know I needed it.

Family.

And since he knew that, he gave it to me.

And that was how I would always and forever need Danny.

"Gotcha," Danny said, and when I looked to him, I saw his head bent to his phone, his thumbs moving on it.

I looked the other way when Sidney hooked her arm in mine.

We locked eyes.

"They're not a loss," she whispered.

"I know that now," I whispered back.

The relief in her face made my heart skip a beat.

How had I not noticed how worried my little sister had been about me?

"Good," she kept whispering. Then she prompted, "Tour." She pulled me along as she called, "Rob, you coming?"

Rob broke away from the island and came to us.

He then forced his way between us and slung his arms over our shoulders.

I took that as a yes.

I also looked over my shoulder when Rob had to angle us so we could walk in the door of Danny's room and not come unattached (guess Rob was kinda still tweaked).

But what I saw when I looked over my shoulder was that Danny was no longer informing Postmates of our dinner selections.

He was standing at the island, watching us.

And he was smiling.

And that, too, was what I always and forever would need from my Danny.

EPILOGUE
Super Fly

EVIE

I was really kinda into what I was doing.

So when Danny slid his hand along my cheek, cupping his other under my arm, tugging gently, and I got his message, I lifted my gaze up his glorious chest to his handsome face to share nonverbally I didn't want to stop.

When we locked eyes (and his were completely dilated), he growled.

Okay, I changed my mind.

I was *totally* onboard for whatever Danny decided was next.

I slid his cock out of my mouth.

He pulled me up his body then he put his hand between us to position me as he sat up.

And I took his cock inside when I went up with him.

At the feel of him filling me, my head fell back, and I glided up and down until he caught my hair in a loose fist, which meant I got his new message.

I tipped my head down, put my mouth to his, and we kissed.

God, I loved kissing this man.

Danny sadly broke the kiss, but fortunately, he did it to trail his lips down my neck, my chest. He curved a hand over my breast and lifted it, taking the nipple into his mouth.

He sucked.

Electricity shot from my nipple to between my legs, I stopped gliding, ground into him and clutched him everywhere I held him.

I heard as well as felt his groan, and all that was so fabulous, my head fell back again.

God, I loved loving Danny Magnusson.

Every way I could do it.

He released my nipple, ran his hand at my breast up my chest, the side of my neck and around to the back of it, and called a gruff, "Evie."

I looked down at him again, resuming my movements, riding up, floating down.

"Yeah?" I breathed.

"Love you," he whispered.

Oh yeah.

I loved loving Danny Magnusson.

"Love you too, Danny."

I felt my eyelids drift halfway down at the effort it took to witness his beautiful smile before I gasped when he whipped me to my back.

I rounded him with my legs to hold on.

Because one other thing I loved about Danny.

When he was on top.

*   *   *

"Serious?" I asked my sister, staring at the stuff that was littering her kitchen table.

This being face products. Cosmetics. Graphic tees. Housewares. Jeans.

"What do you think I do?" she asked in return.

"You're building a social media following."

"I'm building a social media following because I have a lifestyle blog. People send me shit to test and review on my blog, and if I dig it, we make a deal and they pay me to promote it."

She flipped open a rose-gold laptop, hit a few buttons and turned the screen to me.

On it was a highly stylized, and uber-cool website that was clean, bright, classy, modern, personality plus and just freaking awesome.

The top had a killer graphic flower surrounding a cool font spelling out THE SID SITUATION, and all of it looked like it was a neon sign.

"I do sponsored posts," she stated. "I'm an affiliate at a variety of sites, and I started my own shop where I sell my swag. I'm launching my podcast later this year with a video component for people who want to watch as well as listen."

I looked to her and asked, "To what?"

Her face pinched and she said, "Not that you'd notice, but I'm really good with makeup, hair, I got a dab hand with decorating, and I take great photos. The Pioneer Woman built a fucking empire with less than that and there wasn't even Snapchat and Insta back then."

"I wasn't saying anything mean," I noted softly.

"You weren't?" she retorted snidely.

"No, Sidney, I wasn't," I replied firmly.

"I know you and Rob think it's full of shit," she retorted.

"What me, and probably Rob, did not do is actually ask you about it. I didn't know what you were up to, which makes me not only the shittiest sister in the world, but just a plain bitch."

Her entire body relaxed, and she replied, "No you aren't. I wasn't exactly deep in your life either. I kept out of it because it took me a while to find my way, and you weren't a big fan of coming along for that ride. I get that. I did some stupid shit, some crazy shit, some shit I wasn't proud of until I found my niche. And then it was..." she shrugged, "safer. All that, you and Mom and Rob, Dad and Mick, it was messed up dysfunction and I didn't want any part of it. I knew you were getting buried under it, but I was so into my own thing, gung-ho to make it something, I let you get piled under their garbage. So who's the shittiest sister in the world and just a plain bitch?"

"Why don't we just leave it at the fact we both could have done better, we didn't, and now we will," I suggested.

"Yeah, I could do that," she muttered, gazing back down at her laptop.

"Sidney," I called.

She looked to me.

I flung out a hand. "This is really rad. I mean *really*. And if you need any help on the backend of your website and podcast or whatever," I touched my chest, "you call me."

"I hate the tech stuff," she said, her expression growing bright. "I took some online courses and went to seminars, but it still sucks."

"It's awesome."

"Because you're a freak."

"And I let my freak flag fly."

Her face split in a grin.

I returned it, then asked, "Are we going to lunch or what?"

"The last stand before you're back to school?"

I did two quick lifts of my shoulders. "Not really. I'm enrolled, but I don't start until the summer semester. But I'm going full-time Computer Raiders starting next week, so tonight's my last night at Smithie's."

She studied me closely. "You down with that?"

"Who would have thought I'd miss stripping," I mumbled.

"Babe, you know it's not the stripping you're gonna miss, right?"

I did another couple of quick shrugs.

Sidney got closer. "Those losers at school who didn't get you, they were losers. Everyone's a loser in school. Even the popular kids were losers, they just were better at pretend than the rest of us. The key to survival was to find your pack of losers. You never got that, so you never formed a posse. So allow me to share, if you have sisters, no matter what kind of sisters they are," she reached out and touched the back of my hand, "no matter where life leads you, you never lose them."

Man, I was glad I never lost my *actual* sister.

"You know the worst part about the Dad, Mom, Mick deal?" I asked.

"What?"

"I have them to thank for that. For making me realize what I had. For leading me to Danny." I reached out and didn't touch the back of hers. I took it in mine. "And getting me back to you."

She made a raspberry noise with her lips and returned, "You're a genius. You would have found your way to all of that, eventually."

"You're right. I'm super fly," I agreed.

"You are the definition of *not* super fly just calling your-self super fly, which is so dorky, it actually makes you super fly."

I burst out laughing.

My sister did it with me.

* * *

After lunch with Sidney, heading home, getting the mail, and finding what was in the mail, I made a few wardrobe adjustments, slicked on a heavy dose of some lip treatment, and was getting out of my car in the parking garage at Danny's offices.

And my phone rang.

I checked it and didn't know the number, so I didn't take the call.

It stopped ringing as I walked toward the elevators.

It started ringing again after I hit the button.

I looked to it.

Same number.

Statistically (my personal calculations were), it was a 92 percent chance it was a robocall.

But we'd had three whole weeks of no drama.

My landlord was kind of a dick about letting me out of my lease, even if I offered to pay April, let him keep my last month's rent, and I knew he had a waiting list so it wasn't like he couldn't turn it over immediately.

Then Danny paid him a visit, and he brought Mo along, and *poof!* I was released.

But that was all the hoopla we'd had.

I was moved in.

I gave official notice to Smithie I was quitting.

Charlie was ecstatic that I'd go full-time at Computer Raiders.

Gert demanded to go to the house showings Danny arranged in order to give her opinion on where we might end up next (but mostly, to get out of her house, also, because she liked to give Danny shit, and last, because he gave her shit right back and she had a hoot taking it—we'd only looked at two houses, both of which I liked, both of which Danny and Gert hated, so no offers had been made on a house).

And Rob had filed for divorce.

Oh, and none of the girls had caved to go out with the guys, which was upsetting me and ticking Lottie off.

To make matters worse, both Boone and Axl had started seeing other women.

And yes, even if it was so illogical, it was wrong, both Lottie and I (and I could tell, Ryn and Hattie) considered them *other women*.

But Danny told me it wasn't my life, even if it was semi my business because they were my friends.

Regardless, he advised that I needed to chill and let nature take its course.

"It'll happen how it happens. There are people more afraid of having it good than facing the bad," he'd said.

"And why do you think that is?" I'd asked.

"Because if you have it good after having it bad, the good would be harder to lose."

"I'm not gonna lose you," I pointed out.

"Babe, you told me that you were gonna end it with me just to protect me. They need to get past stupid shit like that."

We had then bickered about him calling it "stupid shit."

Danny had ended the bickering by kissing me then proceeding to go down on me on the couch.

And he'd been so good at ending the bickering, we hadn't bickered for a solid three days after that.

So, even though things seemed to be going great in the world of Evan Gardiner, I had lived my life as that life came, and a lot of it wasn't so great, so who knew what would come next?

I just knew I'd face it with more awareness and more support than I'd done before.

This all meant, two calls back to back from the same number, I took the call.

And I found immediately, as usual, I shouldn't have taken the call.

Because right after I said hello, my mom cried, "Evan, don't hang up!"

The elevator came, the doors sliding open, and I stared into it.

But I didn't get into it.

"Evan?" she called.

The elevator doors closed.

"Evan!" she snapped.

"I am not talking to you about Mick, Rob or Dad, and if you say ugly things to me, Mom, about anything, including me, or Rob, I'm hanging up and blocking this number too."

"Sweetheart, I'm not gonna say ugly things to you."

I made no reply.

"Your stepdad served me with divorce papers," she told me.

"I know. Danny and I see Rob a lot and I talk to him all the time."

She sounded hurt when she asked, "You do?"

"He never treated me like shit," I pointed out.

"Evie—"

"Mom, I'm doing something important. Is there something you need?"

"So Rob has met your man?"

"Yes," I said shortly.

"Your stepfather has met him, but your mother has not." Now she sounded pouty.

"I'll repeat, Rob never treated me like shit. Now, is there something you need?"

Silence.

"Mom," I prompted.

"Well . . ."

She said no more.

"Spit it out."

She spat something out.

The question, "When did you get so sassy?"

I wasn't going to answer that, with the answer being, "too late, but still, just in time."

"Mom," I said warningly.

"It's your brother," she said like she didn't want to say it.

"Don't," I again warned.

"Your stepfather left me high and dry. I got a job, but I've only been at it a week. I don't have the money to—"

And there it was.

Mick, with whatever Mick was up to now (though I noted he was alive and breathing to do it, unlike what he wanted me to think would be his state after all was said and done), needed money.

And Mom was now his only avenue to getting it, what with Dad copping a guilty plea for burglary, vandalism and possession with intent to distribute. He bought a nickel, and according to Jet, who asked Eddie, if he behaved himself, probably would be out in two, at most three years.

Not that Dad would ever front Mick money.

In fact, not that Dad ever had any money.

In the interim, after I heard Mick had survived a situation he tried to convince me he'd never survive, I had not kept track of Mick because I didn't want to know about Mick.

Not for the last two months.

Not now.

But clearly, he needed cash, and Mom needed someone—that someone being not her—to give it to him.

"Goodbye, Mom."

"Evie!"

I hung up.

I blocked her new number.

And I tagged the elevator button.

When I arrived outside the door to the suite, I hit yet another button and looked up at the camera above the door outside Danny's office.

I then waited for them to scope me out on their kickass system inside, heard the click and low buzz that meant I was in, opened the door and strolled into the command center with its theater-style rows of stations facing an array of television screens with glass-walled offices and conference rooms to the sides.

Seriously, and I didn't care how nerdy it meant I was, I wanted to dig into this setup. There were so many cable covers over stuff snaking on the floor and up to the workstations and into the walls, I almost salivated every time I walked in there.

I pushed thoughts aside of Hawk's system, and after spotting Danny standing on the third landing (along which was where his workstation was) with Hawk, a gorgeous blonde with a better ass than mine, and a little, insanely beautiful, dark-haired girl clinging to Hawk's leg, I looked to the ground floor office at the left, and found it empty.

Elvira was, again, proving elusive.

Her office was unoccupied.

Drat.

She'd been out the two other times I'd been to the offices as well.

Sidney had had cosmos with her three times and been vaguely invited over to Elvira's place for something called "boards."

Sidney said she was *spectacular* (that was the actual word she used).

And Danny and all the guys talked about her like she was their annoying, and ridiculously lovable, older sister.

As for me...

I'd never clapped eyes on the woman.

In other words, I was dying to meet her.

My heels clicked on the floor as I made my way to Danny, my attention moving to him, to see his gaze focused not on my jeans, not on my silky button-down top, but on my feet. And his lips were tipped up in a sexy way that made me wonder if my adjustments to my ensemble from lunch to now were for him, or for me.

I had to look away when I came abreast with Boone, who seemed to be leaving.

"I have words to say to you," I told him, stopping as my way to indicate he should stop so I could read him about spending time with some other woman who was not Ryn.

"Later, babe, I got an assignment," he probably lied (or maybe not), bent, kissed my cheek, then took off.

I turned to watch him go.

Or, more aptly, I turned to glare at his back as he left.

"You can't escape me forever, Boone Sadler!" I called.

He lifted a hand but didn't look back.

Fucking commandos.

When the door closed behind him, I pivoted smartly and walked (okay, maybe stomped) the rest of the way to Danny.

He greeted me by sliding an arm around my waist and murmuring, "Babe."

"Babe," I said back.

He silently chuckled. I knew this when his mouth curled, and his long torso shook.

I looked to Hawk. "Hey, Hawk."

"Evan, hey," Hawk greeted. "This is my wife, Gwen, and my girl," he put his hand on the dark head of the little one clinging to his thigh, "Vivi."

"Hey," I said to Gwen.

"Heya, Evan," she replied.

I looked down to Vivi.

"Hi there."

She was peeking under long dark lashes, cheek pressed to her father's thick thigh, and up close, I saw her cheeks were pink, her eyes looked tired, but they were riveted to my feet.

"I like your shoes," she mumbled.

"That's my girl," Gwen cooed.

"Someone kill me," Hawk muttered.

I smiled.

Danny's arm around me grew tighter.

"She's not feeling well. Maybe flu. It's going around," Gwen told me.

"Yeah, I've heard that," I replied.

"So, not being rude, I've been hoping to meet you, but we have to go. Though, before we do, I'm glad I have you, because Elvira's doing boards," she said.

I perked up.

"You don't want to miss them," she went on.

Oh my God!

Was this an invitation?

"I've heard about these boards," I shared, trying not to pant with excitement. "And what I heard is I definitely don't want to miss them."

"Well, you have to come around. Next Tuesday?" she asked.

"Totally," I answered, and okay, it came out breathily, but Gwen didn't seem to notice.

She just said, "Awesome," before she turned, leaned into her husband, put her hand on (the *wall* of) his chest, pushed up on her toes and touched her mouth to his. She then whispered a different kind of "Awesome" that made his eyes gleam, my toes curl and Danny silently chuckle again.

I looked down to Vivi. "I hope to see you again when you're feeling better."

"Me too. Maybe I can try on your shoes," she replied.

"You aren't wearing shoes like those until you're fifty," Hawk decreed.

She tipped her head back and pouted, "Daddy!"

He hefted her up into his arms and she immediately seemed a lot less sulky.

"Evan," he said to me, tipped his chin up to Mag, took his wife's hand in his free one, and started down the steps with his daughter's booty held in the curve of his arm, her little arms wrapped around his muscled neck.

"See you Tuesday, and cool to finally meet you," Gwen said to me while following them (or, more apropos, being dragged on her own pair of high heels by her husband).

"You too and can't wait."

They barely made the bottom floor when Danny had my hand in his and I was being dragged, this down the row to his workstation.

When he got us there, he twisted his mesh-seated rolling chair, sat in it and then drew me between his open knees.

"Seriously?" he asked.

"What?" I asked back.

"Babe, you walking in here in those shoes, this morning's blowjob seems like it happened a decade ago."

I tipped my head to the side and grinned at him, deciding the long-awaited maiden voyage of my red sandals was a success.

"You come here just to make me hard or is there some other purpose to this visit?" he asked. "Wait," he went on quickly. "Belated preface to that, you can show anytime you want, wearing hot sex shoes or your usual beat-up sneakers, I don't give a fuck."

God, this guy was easy to love.

"I picked up the mail when I got home from having lunch with Sidney," I shared. "And the present I ordered for you came. Since I got it for your workstation, and I had a free afternoon, I thought I'd bring it in."

His brows were up, and he asked, "Present?"

I dug in my bag, pulled it out and handed it to him.

When he saw what it was, he looked even more confused, until he took it and turned the writing around so he could read it.

Then he busted out laughing.

I pretended to be miffed even though I was *not*.

From the very beginning, I loved making him laugh.

"You think that title is funny?" I asked.

I barely got the last word out before he tugged sharply on my hand and I landed in his lap.

He held me in the curve of one arm even as he rotated us and leaned forward, taking me with him, doing this to set the old-fashioned, aluminum-framed plaque with its slide-in plate in faux wood with wording on it at the head of his workstation.

It said in white, #1 BOYFRIEND, and under that, DANIEL JAROD MAGNUSSON.

I watched as he adjusted it so it was centered perfectly, and I thought he was joking around until he titched it just a centimeter.

That was when I looked at his face to see he was genuinely concentrating on what he was doing like the perfect placement of that plaque was of the utmost importance.

"Danny," I whispered.

He lifted those crazy-gorgeous eyes with those fabulously amazing eyelashes to me.

"Won't move it, baby, until that title changes and you get me a new one."

Shit.

I was going to cry.

He saw it.

So he tipped his head further back, I got his message...

And kissed him.

I broke it with my hand cradling his jaw, but I didn't move very far away.

"Are we allowed to make out at your workstation?" I asked.

"No."

I gave him a small smile.

"Are you gonna get shit for your plaque?" I asked.

"Totally," he answered.

The smile on my lips died, but that didn't mean the happiness was gone.

"You don't care, do you?" I whispered.

"Not even a little bit," he whispered back.

"All my life, you know?"

"All your life what, baby?"

"Until you."

He curved both arms around me and his voice was growly when he asked, "Until me, what?"

"The people I loved made loving them hard. Until you."

I got just a growl for that as Danny slid a hand up my spine, into my hair, and then my mouth was on his again.

We made out and we kept doing it even when we heard the door open.

And we continued even as we heard boots on steps and Hawk muttering, "Yeah, Jesus, somebody kill me."

Only then did we break it off.

Because Danny was laughing.

I was giggling.

And all was right in the world.

Boone Sadler is the one man Ryn
Jansen wants—and the one man she
won't let herself have.

Don't miss their epic story in

DREAM CHASER

Available late 2020

Please turn the page for a preview.

CHAPTER ONE
Less and Less You

RYN

I was wiped.

Even so, I was still heading up the walk to my brother's ex's house at seven o'clock in the morning regardless if I drove away from Smithie's after dancing at his club only four hours before.

This was because Angelica called me, sharing she had another migraine, and she needed me to help her get the kids to school.

My brother's kids.

My niece and nephew.

And Angelica did not call on my brother Brian because she knew he was probably passed out so drunk, if she could wrangle miracles and was able to wake him, he'd come over and still be hammered.

So she called on me.

I made the door, knocked, but knew the drill.

It'd be open.

The knock was just a formality.

I pushed in and saw immediately that Angelica had not changed her ways in the two days since I'd been there to get the kids and take them to my place to hang because her back was spasming.

Although the house wasn't filthy, it also wasn't tidy.

There was kid stuff everywhere. Toys and markers and such. A basket of laundry was on the couch that I couldn't tell if it was clean, and needed to be folded and put away, or dirty and needed to be washed. A wasted chip bag that, considering nutrition wasn't high on her priority list for her or her children, it was a toss-up if it was left behind on that end table by Angelica, or one of the kids. Same with a can of Coke.

And...right.

Even not filthy, the carpet seriously needed to be vacuumed.

"Auntie Rynnie!" I heard a little boy's voice yell.

I turned my eyes to the opening of the kitchen and saw my six-year-old, dark-haired, blue-eyed nephew Jethro standing there.

I mean, serious.

From birth to now, that kid was *adorbs*.

And I loved him with everything that was me.

Or half of that.

I loved his sister with the other half.

I smiled at him even as I put my finger to my lips and whispered, "Shh."

His entire face ticked, the exuberance washing clean out of it, and my heart lurched seeing it.

Eggshells.

My two babies' lives were all about walking on eggshells.

With Daddy and his hangovers, if they ever spent time

with him, which was rare, but even so, he didn't stop drinking through it.

With Mommy and her migraines, her bad back, her bum knee, her creaky hips, if they ever spent any time with her, which wasn't as rare, but they were off to Auntie Ryn's place, or one of their grandmas, and they were this often, because Mommy needed peace and quiet and rest.

Sure, it takes a village.

And I was *so* down with being part of that village for Jethro and his older sister, Portia.

But bottom line, a kid needed to be able to count on their parents.

At least *one* of them.

I moved to him, asking quietly, "Have you had your bath, baby?"

"Last night," he whispered.

I put my hand on his thick hair, bent to kiss his upturned forehead, and as I straightened, I looked left.

My curly-blonde-haired, also blue-eyed Portia was at the table, eating a massive bowl of Cap'n Crunch.

I loved Cap'n Crunch.

I could make a pretty convincing argument that Cap'n Crunch was a major component of the meaning of life.

What I did not love was my seven-year-old niece horking down a huge bowl of sugary crunches that had no nutritional value, she'd burn it off in approximately fifteen minutes and then crash.

Another decimated bowl was beside Portia's, kibbles of cereal and smears of milk all around the bowl on the table.

Jethro's breakfast.

I said not a word because I knew Portia poured those bowls for her brother and herself. She "made" breakfast, seven-year-old-style, and did the best she could.

"Hey, honey," I called.

She had milk on her chin when she looked up at me and replied, 'Hey, Auntie Ryn."

I smiled at her and then looked down at Jethro.

"Right, want your face cleaned up, bucko. Anything you need to take to school today?"

He looked like he was concentrating, hard, to remember if he was supposed to take anything to school.

Then again, it wasn't his job to keep track of that. Not yet.

"I'll poke my head in and ask your mom," I told him.

"She needs quiet." Having been reminded of this fact by me, he was still whispering.

But at his words, Portia made a noise like a snort.

A disgusted one.

A lot like the sound I was making in my head.

Though I didn't want Portia having this reaction about her mom, I had to admit, my niece had been displaying signs of impatience that were about twenty years older than she was, and she'd been doing this for a while now.

I ignored her and said to Jethro, "I'll be real quiet when I ask her. Now go wash your face. And your hands."

He nodded and ran off, so I looked to Portia.

"After you're done, honey, you too with the washup. Do you need to take anything to school?"

She nodded. "Yeah. But my book bag is ready."

I hated to ask what I next had to ask because I had been that kind of sister to my brother when I was seven.

Keeping track of him.

Keeping track of me.

"Do you, uh . . . know about your brother?"

She shoved more cereal in her mouth and said in a garbled way I still could decipher before chewing it, "Show and tell day today. I put something in his bag. He'll figure it out."

"Chew and swallow, Portia," I urged carefully, not her mother, but needing to be motherly, which pissed me off because I wanted to be Fun Auntie Rynnie, not Fuddy Duddy Aunt Kathryn. "Don't talk with your mouth full."

She looked down at her bowl and her cheeks got pink.

Crap.

Fuddy Duddy Aunt Kathryn *sucked*.

I moved to the table and started to clean up Jethro's breakfast.

"You should make Mom do that, you know," Portia said.

"When she beats this headache, we'll just give her a little break," I replied.

"Yeah, another one," she mumbled, dropped her spoon in her still half-filled bowl and jumped off the chair she was using, having been sitting on her knees.

She took the bowl to the sink and dumped it in.

"I'll finish that. We need to get sorted and go," I told her.

"'Kay," she muttered, and didn't look at me when she walked by.

I stopped her retreat, asking, "Did your mom get lunches packed?"

She turned, looked me right in the eyes and asked, "You're kidding, right?"

Oh yeah.

Impatience.

And demonstrating a frustrated maturity that I was not a big fan of the fact that she was forced to be developing.

"We'll make lunches in a sec," I said.

She had no response to that. She just took off.

I rinsed the bowls, put them in the dishwasher, wiped

down the table, put away the cereal and milk and then moved out to find and check their book bags.

When it seemed all was set, I finished my inspection by zipping up Portia's bag and moved down the hall, hearing the kids talking low and quiet in the bathroom.

I knocked on Angelica's door softly then opened it to stick my head in, seeing complete dark and a lump on the bed under covers.

"Hey, I'm here, got the kids," I called.

The lump moved. "Heard. Um, can you come in a second?"

I slid in and closed the door behind me.

Angelica didn't turn on a light, but in the shadows, I saw her push up to an elbow.

"Listen, Jethro's got some end-of-year field trip he's going on and they need fifty bucks plus whatever money he'll need for lunch, which they say will cost fifteen to twenty dollars."

Fifteen to twenty dollars for lunch for a first grader?

I did not get those words out of my mouth before Angelica went on, "Brian's fucked me over for support again and things are tight this month. I'm already gonna hafta ask Mom to pay cable and electricity. But I don't wanna have to tell Jethro he can't go."

She didn't even hesitate anymore. Didn't lead into it.

No longer did I get a, "I hate to say this," or "This sucks I gotta ask."

Just, "I don't wanna have to tell Jethro he can't go."

Well, if you got a job and maybe cut the premium package on your cable, even if my brother is a deadbeat, you might be able to cover some of your bills and take care of your children, I did not say.

What I said was, "I'll leave some money on the table."

I said this a lot.

It was closing in on the end of May and I'd already given her three hundred and seventy-five dollars this month.

Last month, it had been over five hundred.

And next month, with the way the kids were growing, summer having already hit Denver, they'd need new clothes. And Angelica worried they'd be teased or bullied if they didn't have the good stuff, so I could plan on a plea to have a "Day with Auntie Ryn" which included taking them shopping. With the added asks that were sure to come, I'd probably be laying out at least a grand.

"Thanks," she muttered, the lump in bed shifted, and that was it.

I stood there a second, staring at her before I turned and left, clicking the door shut behind me.

My bad.

Conditioning.

I'd conditioned her.

Like I'd done with my brother.

When I started to get niggles of concern when there wasn't a get-together we had where he didn't get obnoxiously drunk, I should have said something.

And then it wasn't even get-togethers, just anytime I saw him, he'd be drinking, clearly on his way to being obnoxiously drunk, before he became that. Thinking he was funny. Or cute. Or waxing poetic about shit where he thought he was stunning all of us with his brilliance, when he barely made sense.

I should have said something then too.

I should have said, "Hey, Brian, go easy."

Or, "Hey, Brian, what in the hell-blazin' *fuck*? Honest to God, do you have to be fucked up *all the time*?"

I did not do this.

Like I did not tell Angelica maybe I didn't want to be a stripper for the rest of my life. Maybe I didn't want to need to have cash on hand to lay on her, or Brian when he came up short for the month, to help them take care of their own children. I didn't want to feel like I had to be careful with my time so I could be free—again, to help them take care of their own children.

I wanted to flip houses.

I wanted in on that from start to finish.

From finding a great pad, seeing the bones, dreaming what I could make it, negotiating a killer deal, then diving in from demo to design, and then negotiating another deal.

That's what I wanted.

I had a house.

A year ago, I'd driven by the perfect one, for sale by owner. Even in Denver's OTT real estate market, I couldn't let the opportunity pass. I'd been saving for my own place, so I went for it, and with the shape that house was in, I got it for a steal.

I started demo of the inside.

And now it had been sitting untouched for ten months because I didn't have the money—because I kept giving mine away—or the time—because I kept saying yes to Angelica when she needed me.

And my pride (yeah, I'll admit it) would not allow me to ask for help.

And my courage (yeah, I'll admit that too) wasn't up to the task of telling her, and Brian, to sort their shit out.

So now I was paying a mortgage on a house that was sitting there, rotting.

And I was still in a rental, helping my brother pay his mortgage, and his ex-partner pay his *old* mortgage.

It was my own damned fault.

All of it.

But when I walked down the hall to the kitchen and saw Portia helping Jethro make PB&Js for their lunch, all those curls, dark (like Angelica) and light (like Brian), it was hard to debate I'd made the wrong choice.

I looked and saw thin, little baggies filled to the brim with potato chips as accompaniment for the PB&Js and I fought back a wince because first, I agreed with my friend Evie that baggies should be outlawed, due to choking dolphins, or destroying the ozone layer, or some shit that I didn't really care what it was, none of it was good. And I kinda wanted my niece and nephew to inherit a decent world (not to mention, the kids I'd eventually have, maybe, one day, if I ever encountered a decent man). And second, the only thing that held merit in that lunch was kinda the peanut butter.

"How about we get you two some carrot sticks to go with that?" I suggested.

"Euw!" Jethro protested.

"Really?" Portia asked sarcastically over him. "We don't have carrot sticks. We don't have anything. This is the last of the bread and chips."

"Mom'll get us chips today, she sees we're out," Jethro declared.

No judge (okay, warning, there was about to be a judge), but I knew that was the truth.

Angelica put on twenty pounds with Portia, and I thought she looked cute, all new-mom curves.

Jethro was a surprise and came close on Portia's heels, definitely before Angelica had the time to lose her baby weight should she have wanted to do that. But with Jethro, she put on twenty more.

Now I'd guess she'd added another fifty.

It wasn't my bag, telling people what to do with their lives, what to put in their mouths, how to handle their bodies.

Be curvy and sassy, if that floated your boat.

Teaching your children that hanging in front of the TV was a major way to pass your time and having chips in the house was more important than getting them properly fueled and off to school, uh...

No.

Thus, there I was.

Three hours of sleep, mentioning carrot sticks and being sure to get the kids off to school, because someone had to make them understand there were people in their lives who gave a shit.

We stowed the lunches in their bags, hustled out into my car and took off.

I watched too many true crime programs to sit in my vehicle, let them out and watch them walk up to their school.

No way.

Predators were crafty.

I was one of those get-your-ass-out, walk-the-kid-in, make-eye-contact-with-an-adult, then-force-kisses-on-them before you let them go kind of school dropper.

And the teacher I made eye contact with smiled at me, probably because she'd seen me, or my mom, or Angelica's mom, more than she ever saw Angelica.

I didn't hang around, though.

I was dancing that night again, so I needed to get home and hit the sack, because stripping was a way to earn major cash. But strippers with shadows under their eyes who were too fatigued to pull off any good moves were just sad.

In other words, I needed to get home.

I had my phone out to text Angelica that the kids were

safe at school, something I'd do sitting in my car because people who walked and texted drove me batty, when I noticed a mom who was also a walk-her-kid-in kind of mom nearly run into a column.

She was not texting.

She had her head turned.

I looked where she was looking.

And saw Boone Sadler. He was my friend Lottie's boy, her man Mo's bud, and an uncomfortable acquaintance of mine.

He was leaning against the passenger side of his gleaming black Charger, arms crossed on his broad chest, long, sturdy legs crossed at the ankles.

What the hell?

He had shades on, aviators, the sun was glinting in his dark blond hair, his skin was tanned, his biceps were bulging, and where I was at in my head and in my exhaustion, the weakness nearly couldn't be beat.

I wanted to sink to my knees and beg him to make me his any way he wanted to do that.

Here's the deal:

My dad was deadbeat too.

And I was Portia, plus twenty-two years.

The big sister who (a change to Portia's plight) saw my mom busting her ass to take care of her kids. So I got to a point where I helped with dinner, and the dishes. Then I *made* dinner and did the dishes. I also did my own laundry starting at age eight, *and* my brother's.

Dusting.

Vacuuming.

Tidying.

Making grocery lists.

And when I could drive, going out and getting groceries.

Mom hated it that I did it, but she needed the help.

I didn't bitch, because I loved her, and I knew she needed it.

But I'd been on the ball, or learning how to be on it, since I was six.

Now, I did not research this stuff, maybe because I didn't want to know, maybe because it didn't really matter.

But if you asked me, if I wasn't just plain ole born this way, I'd reckon that I needed a man to take care of business *in that way* because I was so...*fucking*...*done* with having a handle on every aspect of my life, my brother's, and now Angelica's and the kids', I needed to give over.

Boiling this down, I was a sub, as in submissive, this being of the BDSM variety.

And Boone Sadler was a Dom, as in a Dominant, of that same variety.

He was also the guy my friend Lottie tried to fix me up with months ago.

Lottie had her shit together. Lottie had lived life and she knew how to read people.

Case in point, when she met her fiancé Mo, they knew each other maybe a few hours before she knew he was the one.

Second case in point, she set up Evie with Mo's bud Mag. They were living together within days of meeting (okay, so circumstances were such she had to move in with him, since her apartment had been torn apart, and that wasn't the beginning of the story, or the end). But they were now officially moved in together, Evie had been able to quit dancing at Smithie's, she'd gone full-time at her preferred job as a computer tech and was finally going back to college with an aim to finish it and earn her engineering degree.

Why I couldn't go there with Boone, I didn't know.

He was hot, like, mom-walking-into-column-at-the-sight-of-him hot.

He'd shared he was interested, this by asking me out to dinner three times, and also getting up in my shit after a lap dance I gave that he witnessed because he was a guy, a guy who'd asked me out, a guy who was into me, a guy who's job (not a joke) was being a commando.

And last, he was a guy who was a Dom.

As for me, I was into him. I was into him in a way I'd had so many fantasies about him—ranging from the many ways he could order me to take my knees and suck his cock to snuggling in front of the TV with him after a long day—that I'd lost count of the dizzying varieties these fantasies took on.

But I just couldn't go there.

Maybe it was that my dad was a deadbeat, but he was also other things, like mentally abusive, serially breaking women's hearts, when the spirit moved him (which was rare) demanding his fatherly rights (even though he was a deadbeat, which circled back to mentally abusive, and breaking women's hearts) and generally just an asshole.

And my brother was an alcoholic deadbeat who was either clueless, in denial, or both.

And I'd had two semi-long-term boyfriends, both who, after I shared, didn't "get" my "kink" and thought I was a loser who wanted to be abused, instead of a submissive, who needed to give over and allow someone to take care of me (or put in the work to try, and get their reward, I was kind of a brat).

Last, I'd had a really shitty Dom who took things too far and once completely ignored me saying my safe word (that had not been fun, in fact, it'd been terrifying when he shoved that scarf into my mouth after tying me up, so I was completely helpless, and not in a good way—exit said Bad Dom from my life).

So yeah.

Me: gun shy.

And Boone had given up, full stop. I knew this because he'd been seeing some other woman now for weeks.

I didn't blame him.

Though part of me did.

Because honestly, he didn't try that hard.

And sorry, not sorry, this girl wanted to be won.

Like I said, put in the effort...

Get your reward.

It sucked and for some reason it hurt (a lot, too much, especially when logically, I knew I had no claim on the guy).

But he'd moved on.

So why was he there?

I knew one thing with the way he was right then uncrossing his arms, his shades locked on me, his hand going up, and his finger crooking at me.

No, two things.

One, I was in imminent danger of a highly inappropriate orgasm while standing on the walk to an elementary school.

And two, he was not there playing bodyguard to some rich kid or because his new woman had kids he'd offered to drop off.

He was there for me.

Interesting.

I moved his way and felt a number of greedy eyes following me as I did.

When I got close, he pushed away from his badass car, straightened to his substantial height and tipped his chin down to look at me.

"Hey, what are you—?" I began.

"Your place," he growled. "Now."

And then I found myself standing there, blinking at him as he stalked around the hood of his car to the driver's side.

He'd opened the door, but didn't angle in, because I was still standing there.

"Now," he ordered.

Only then did he angle in.

All right, I was going home anyway.

But…

Again…

What the hell?

And, more.

Did he know where I lived?

Apparently, he did, because he made his point I needed to get my ass to my place by making his engine roar (and again, imminent orgasm, mine and probably a dozen other moms).

I hoofed it to my car, and once inside, glanced quickly at my reflection in the rearview mirror.

I'd pulled a brush through my hair because it wouldn't do to have semi-slept-on, teased out stripper hair when taking the kids to school.

But it was still a mass that was mostly a mess of honey-blonde flips and curls.

No makeup, and serious, I was such a makeup freak, even if I was living my dream of knocking down walls to create great rooms and grouting tile, I'd have makeup on.

I always had makeup on.

Gray oversized tee. Black skinny jeans with rips in the knees. Powder Valentino rockstud slides.

In that moment, I wasn't my normal edgy Ryn Jansen who (if I did say so myself, which I did) made Kendall Jenner look like a novice at putting together streetwear.

So I felt vulnerable.

But he'd already seen me.

And he was on some mission.

So I might feel vulnerable, but I also had no choice.

I hit my pad, which was the bottom quarter of a big house that had been broken up into four apartments in what loosely could still be considered Capitol Hill, on Pearl, a couple blocks south from Colfax.

There were parking spots out back, though I never bothered, because they were always taken by other tenants.

And even if street parking was always at a premium, Boone not only knew where my house was, he'd found a spot before I did, and I knew this because he was waiting at my front door.

"You wanna tell me what this is about?" I asked after I walked up to him.

"Inside," he grunted.

Oh shit.

With my morning and all that was Boone suddenly and unexpectedly invading it, I didn't even think.

"Is everything okay?" I asked.

"Inside," he repeated.

"Evie all right?"

"Inside."

"Lottie?"

"Ryn, get your ass inside."

Here's the second part of the deal:

If you weren't working me up to an orgasm.

And you were a boss.

And you bossed me.

My first reaction would be to fight the urge to knock your teeth down your throat.

Even wired, tired, worried about what this was with

Boone, and in a negative headspace, I successfully fought the urge to knock Boone's teeth down his throat (not that I'd achieve that, again, the dude was a commando, he'd probably ninja-move me, and it would end in humiliation).

I let us in.

So, my pad had character.

And not all of it was the good kind.

In fact, most of it wasn't.

The kitchen needed updating about two decades ago. It was small, cramped, had little counter space, a thin-piled carpet that had so many spills and smells and so much steam and grease soaked in, it was like a thin living stew (so I ignored it), but the rest...well, I was used to it.

We entered in the little vestibule/mudroom and I led him to the living room.

But down from the foyer was a narrow hall, where off to the left, first, was a tiny bedroom, down the way was a small bath, and at the back, was my bedroom, which was only slightly bigger than the tiny one.

Off my living room was a dining room (without a dining room table, or anything, it was a largish space in my small-ish pad that I'd only found a rug for and then stopped trying because I was going to flip houses, but ended up taking care of someone else's kids) which fed into my aforementioned scary kitchen.

Both living room and dining room had fireplaces.

They were rad.

Straight up, if I had the cash, and the time, I'd buy this house from my landlord and restore it to its former glory. The mantles, the tile, the wood floors, the high ceilings, the cornices, the ceiling roses.

Sublime.

As mentioned, I did not have the time or money.

Boone walked directly to the built-in hutch at the end of my dining room and stopped.

Beginning to seriously lose patience with this, whatever it was, I followed.

And stopped.

"Boone, what the hell?"

With my head where it was at, I didn't notice he had a folder with him.

He opened it and tossed an 8x10 full-color glossy on the counter of the hutch.

I looked down at it.

It was a picture of Angelica, looking pretty damned good, messy topknot in her hair, cute formfitting tank dress...

Valentino rockstud jelly thongs on her feet.

I stared.

Boone tapped the picture and I forced my attention from the $350 flip-flops she was wearing to the sign above the place she was walking out of.

It was a fucking *day spa.*

My head jerked when he tossed another photo down.

Angelica enjoying lunch *al fresco* with a friend. Another cute outfit. A sparkling glass of rosé wine in front of her.

My breathing went funny.

Another picture landed.

Angelica browsing in what appeared to be a Bath and Body Works, a Kate Spade shopping bag dangling from the crook in her arm.

"Worth those lap dances, baby?" Boone's deep, drawling, caustic voice broke into my brain, a brain that was paralyzed with shock and rage.

Oh no he did *not.*

My narrowed gaze went to him.

"Totally playin' you," he stated. "I bet you dropped money on her today, seein' as she's got a facial booked."

Oh my *fucking* God.

This couldn't be.

This...

This...

It just couldn't be.

"You're stalking my niece and nephew's mother?" I asked.

His chin shifted to the side.

"Ryn—"

"To what?" I swept an arm out over the pictures on the hutch. "Make some point?"

"Well, yeah," he replied. "And the point I'm makin' is, you're shoving your tits into horny assholes' faces so this bitch can have bi-monthly massages."

Bi-monthly?

I hadn't had a massage in...

I didn't remember the last time I had a massage.

And Angelica had two a month?

Off *my* back?

No, wait.

Her kids didn't have fucking *carrots* and were eating Cap'n *Crunch* and *she* was getting massages?

"She gets child benefit," Boone carried on. "She's conned her mom outta at least a couple hundred this month. Your mom outta a couple hundred more. And I don't know what she's telling you, but your brother ponied up, and he pretty much always ponies up, and if he doesn't, it's because he's a little short. Then you take up the slack. Even so, she went and reamed his ass, and after he handed over a check for fifteen hundred a week ago, he handed over another one for five hundred a coupla days ago, both of which, when she got them, she went directly to cash, *for cash*, and they cleared."

This was...

It was...

"So she's shaking you down," Boone continued, "and your brother's shaking you down so he can cover his own ass, and hers, even though he's gainfully employed, makes good cake, though I've no fuckin' clue how he manages to stay employed since what doesn't go to her that he earns or asks for from you goes right to Argonaut Liquor. And you're racing to her house to get the kids to school so she can sleep in. Because I can guaran-damn-tee you that woman does not have a headache."

Oh no.

He did *not*.

"How do you know she called about a migraine?" I asked quietly.

"Ryn," he bit down on my name impatiently. "I'm lookin' out for you."

"You've hacked my phone. You're stalking me too."

He drew in so much breath, his chest expanded with it.

It was a sight to see since his chest normally was pretty formidable.

But I could bite too.

And I did.

"You know, Boone, when I'm sucking your cock, you can invade my privacy."

His green eyes got wide (and I had to admit, with that hair, that tan, that bone structure, those mossy green eyes were insult to injury I actually *wasn't* sucking his cock).

"Are you outta your mind?" he asked.

"And since that's not gonna goddamn happen, especially now, you can butt right the fuck," I leaned his way, "*out.*"

"Kathryn," he growled, a stern set to his angled jaw.

No.

Hell no.

He was not gonna Dom me without earning the goddamned privilege.

"Don't you *even*," I hissed.

"I cannot believe you're fuckin' pissed . . . *at me*," it was him who swept his arm out to indicate what was on my hutch, "when your brother's ex is fucking you over . . ." and then he leaned *my* way, "*huge.*"

"Don't you have a girlfriend you can stalk, Boone?" I asked snidely.

"Just sayin', I'm not interested in her right now because she doesn't need a serious-as-fuck spanking, sweetheart."

My breath whistled between my teeth, I sucked so much of it in so fast.

This was because I was ticked at Boone, furious with Angelica, and incensed that his words caused my nipples to get hard and a surge of wet to saturate between my legs.

And I didn't need what happened next.

Boone proving what I'd spent countless hours wondering about since the first moment I clapped eyes on him knowing Lottie picked him for me.

That he was an intuitive Master.

I knew this when he didn't miss my reaction.

At least not the part that served his purpose.

Which meant he got closer, not super close, but close enough I could smell the residue of his shave cream.

Oh *God.*

Yeah, an intuitive Master.

And a skilled one.

"Should start small, tell you to open your mouth for me," he whispered. "Slide my fingers inside, let you taste who you belong to."

I stood still and stared into eyes that had lost almost all the green, they were so dilated.

He was turned on.

Fuckfuckfuckfuck*fuck*.

"But right now, I'd rather see you on your knees," he finished.

The words were trembling when I said, "Get out."

He ignored me. "Though you'd rather be across mine."

He was regrettably *very* right.

I fought back a shiver.

He dipped his face to mine.

And tore me apart.

"Your brother needs a fuckin' program. His ex needs the verbal shit kicked out of her. But you're so addicted to their dysfunction, set to be the enabler, you won't do dick. Not to help guide them to a path that's healthy for them, not to extricate yourself from a situation that is not healthy for you. You're one of those chicks who likes chaos. Drama. Needs to be needed even if it's dicked up how you gotta get your fix."

His words felt like ice water fell from my ceiling, drenching me, chilling me to the bone.

"You know what's good for them," he continued, "but you won't do dick about it. You know what's good for you, and you won't reach out and fuckin' *grab it*."

"Go fuck yourself, Boone."

"Think I've made it abundantly clear, I'd rather fuck you."

"That's not gonna happen in *twelve* lifetimes."

"Yeah, because you're so hot to get off on the bullshit, you won't grab hold of what's good for you."

"A macho asshole who thinks his shit doesn't stink and stalks me and comes on to me when he's got another woman in his bed?"

"We're not exclusive."

Seriously?

"Well, aren't you proving with all of this you're a keeper?"

His gaze moved over my face, down my body and back up. "Christ, you want it so bad, you're tearing yourself apart."

Of a sort, he was not wrong.

I was holding myself so still, if I moved an inch, it felt like my body would shatter.

"You've no idea what I want, Boone."

"One thing I know, whenever I spend time in your space, what I want becomes less and less *you.*"

With that supremely successful comeback, he prowled out of my apartment.

I ignored the nagging sensation that, even with that scene, the loss of his presence felt like a physical blow, something I felt from the first time we met.

Instead of thinking on that, I looked down at the photos on the hutch.

When I could trust myself to move, I separated them and took all they displayed in.

I didn't mind stripping. I'd embraced my sexuality a long time ago. Not to mention, I made buckets at Smithie's, even if, at first, I'd done it as a means to an end to my real estate dream.

And one thing my dad taught me, giving a shit what people thought about you was for the birds. I'd wanted his love, I'd wanted his attention, and I'd learned early wanting either of those things was straight-up stupid, because neither were worth shit.

That said, my desired life trajectory had never included slithering oiled-up in nothing but a G-string on a reflective stage for horny assholes.

I'd left a hundred dollars for Angelica that day, raced to her house to take care of the kids, and she was getting a facial.

In the beginning, I got it. Brian's descent was dramatic. Good Time Brian became Drunken Buffoon Brian so fast, it was terrifying.

So she'd kicked his ass out.

Portia had been two, Jethro one, Brian and Angelica had started early, moving in with each other right out of high school, whereupon Angelica got pregnant in a blink.

So both of them were young, and she was suddenly a single mom with the man she loved, spent six years with, lived with him for four, bought a house with him, made babies with him . . . gone.

So yeah.

I got it.

A woman lost all that, she'd need to lick her wounds.

Five years of that at the same time fucking over someone who looked out for her and her kids?

No.

I heard an engine roar in the distance, and I knew it was Boone's Charger.

I looked to the window at the front of the house and put my hand to my throat.

One thing I know, whenever I spend time in your space, what I want becomes less and less you.

Well, that pretty much said it all.

And it hurt like hell.

But I wasn't going to cry.

The last time I cried was a couple of months ago. After

I'd been in the midst of a firefight in the parking lot of a mall during a kidnapping (mine). But the waterworks only came because I thought a guy I knew and liked had been shot in said firefight.

So those were kind of stressy tears, and I didn't think they counted.

They weren't heartbreak tears.

The last time I'd cried before that?

When I was fifteen and in a frothy, tea-length gown, waiting on Mom's couch for Dad to show to take me to some father-daughter dance he had going on with whatever club that he belonged to.

Lions Club?

The Masons?

Whatever.

He didn't show.

I sat on that couch all dolled up for a date with my dad, while Mom looked on, appearing openly like she'd gladly murder somebody. And I sat there until ten thirty before Mom got me out of that gown, unearthed the ice cream, and I sat in her bed, snot-nosed and bawling, but still shoving that frozen goodness in my mouth.

That was the last and only time I cried over a man.

So now...

Fuck it.

I wasn't going to cry because Boone showed strong signs that he'd be a delicious Dom.

I wasn't going to cry because, even if it was vaguely fucked up, finding that shit out about Angelica was something he spent his time and resources doing what he said he was doing, looking out for me.

I also wasn't going to cry because Lottie had Mo, and her serenity and contentment at finding a good man to love who loved her floated like pearlescent clouds around her everywhere she went.

And Evie had Mag, and the adoration they shared for each other sparkled like glitter anytime one was near the other.

And I had no one.

And I wanted someone, someone special, someone who would look out for me, someone who would partner with me to navigate life, someone who was *mine*.

No, I wasn't going to cry for any of these reasons.

I wasn't going to cry at all.

So I didn't cry.

I gathered the pictures up, pivoted, and walked out my back door.

ABOUT THE AUTHOR

Kristen Ashley is the award-winning and *New York Times* bestselling author of nearly seventy romance novels, including the Rock Chick, Colorado Mountain, Dream Man, Chaos, and Fantasyland series. Her books have been translated into fifteen languages, with over three million copies sold.

Born in Gary and raised in Brownsburg, Indiana, Kristen is a fourth-generation graduate of Purdue University. Since then, she has lived in Denver and the West Country of England, and she now resides in Phoenix. She worked as a charity executive for eighteen years prior to beginning her independent publishing career. She now writes full time.

Because friendship, family, and a strong sisterhood are prevailing themes through all of Kristen's novels, Kristen has created the Rock Chick Nation, a series of programs designed to give back to her readers and promote a strong female community. Its programs include Rock Chick Rewards, which raises funds for reader-nominated, nonprofit women's organizations and has donated over $140,000.

You can learn more at:
KristenAshley.net
Twitter @KristenAshley68
Facebook.com/KristenAshleyBooks